DEEP WATER DESTINY

Captain Terrance Carver turned to the helmsman. "What's our situation, Jefferson?"

"We're at ninety-three fathoms, Captain. Speed, ten knots. Engine room answering all speeds available."

"Good," Carver said. "Greg, what's your status?"

"All nozzle rings deployed," Greg Burks answered from the Subscope panel. The panel showed a top-view silhouette of the *John Marshall,* striped with glowing, bright green bars. "Pumps ready. Polymer tanks full."

Carver nodded. "Activate the system."

As the pumps came on, the rings of tiny nozzles in the *John Marshall*'s hull sprayed a colorless, jelly-like substance. The water-soluble polymers quickly covered the four hundred and ten foot hull with an even coat, cutting its friction with the surrounding water to zero.

At the same moment, the helmsman called for flank speed. The effect was like kicking in the afterburner of an aircraft, causing anyone who had been standing to grab hold of something bolted down for support.

The sixty-mile-an-hour race across the North Atlantic had begun. . . .

THE SEVENTH CARRIER SERIES
By PETER ALBANO

THE SEVENTH CARRIER   (2056, $3.95/$5.50)
The original novel of this exciting, best-selling series. Imprisoned in a cave of ice since 1941, the great carrier *Yonaga* finally breaks free in 1983, her maddened crew of samurai determined to carry out their orders to destroy Pearl Harbor.

THE SECOND VOYAGE OF THE SEVENTH CARRIER   (2104, $3.95/$4.95)
The Red Chinese have launched a particle beam satellite system into space, knocking out every modern weapons system on earth. Not a jet or rocket can fly. Now the old carrier *Yonaga* is desperately needed because the Third World nations—with their armed forces made of old World War II ships and planes—have suddenly become superpowers. Terrorism runs rampant. Only the *Yonaga* can save America and the Free World.

RETURN OF THE SEVENTH CARRIER   (2093, $3.95/$4.95)
With the war technology of the former superpowers still crippled by Red China's orbital defense system, a terrorist beast runs rampant across the planet. Outarmed and outnumbered, the target of crack saboteurs and fanatical assassins, only the *Yonaga* and its brave samurai crew stand between a Libyan madman and his fiendish goal of global domination.

QUEST OF THE SEVENTH CARRIER   (2599, $3.95/$4.95)
Power bases have shifted drastically. Now a Libyan madman has the upper hand, planning to crush his western enemies with an army of millions of Arab fanatics. Only *Yonaga* and her indomitable samurai crew can save the besieged free world from the devastating iron fist of the terrorist maniac. Bravely, the behemoth leads a rag tag armada of rusty World War II warships against impossible odds on a fiery sea of blood and death!

ATTACK OF THE SEVENTH CARRIER   (2842, $3.95/$4.95)
The Libyan madman has seized bases in the Marianas and Western Caroline Islands. The free world seems doomed. Desperately, *Yonaga's* air groups fight bloody air battles over Saipan and Tinian. An old World War II submarine, *USS Blackfin*, is added to *Yonaga's* ancient fleet and the enemy's impregnable bases are attacked with suicidal fury.

TRIAL OF THE SEVENTH CARRIER   (3213, $3.95/$4.95)
The enemies of freedom are on the verge of dominating the world with oil blackmail and the threat of poison gas attack. *Yonaga's* officers lay desperate plans to strike back. Leading a ragtag fleet of revamped destroyers and a single antique World War II submarine, the great carrier must charge into a sea of blood and death in what becomes the greatest trial of the Seventh Carrier.

THE SIEGE OF OCEAN VALKYRIE

JOHN-ALLEN PRICE

ZEBRA BOOKS
KENSINGTON PUBLISHING CORP.

To my father, John Lee Price. My only regret is that he didn't live long enough to see me succeed at what he always wanted to become, a novelist.

ZEBRA BOOKS

are published by

Kensington Publishing Corp.
475 Park Avenue South
New York, NY 10016

First printing: February, 1992

Printed in the United States of America

Chapter One

THE WASHINGTON POST
TUESDAY, FEBRUARY 3, 1992.

Department: Congress.
Section: The Federal Page.
Headline: Revamped Sub to be Given New Test.
Byline: David Kurtz and Carol A. Burns,
Washington Post Staff Writers

One of the U.S. Navy's oldest nuclear submarines is finding itself in the middle of a growing controversy as it prepares for a new test of its capabilities.

The U.S.S. *John Marshall* (SSN 611) has had a troubled career ever since it was converted from its original role as a fleet ballistic missile submarine to a commando transport back in 1986.

Since that time the aging boat has been the victim of equipment failures, inexperienced crew and changing policies with regard to elite units, submarine warfare and covert operations in the Pentagon, State Department and White House. In the past eighteen months it has been revamped yet again with new weapons, advanced systems, a completely new crew and captain.

However, this has not stopped critics such as Democratic Senate Armed Services Committee Vice-Chairman Clifton Parker, who declared that the thirty year old submarine is hopelessly obsolete, despite its technological additions and personnel changes.

Other critics, both inside and outside the Pentagon question the need for a specialized submarine for commando operations. If such a vessel is needed, does it make sense to use a ship more than four hundred feet long on such sensitive missions?

Cecil Atwater, spokesman for Concerned Americans For A Sane Defense, condemned the very idea of a commando transport submarine. In a hastily organized news conference he called for it to be scrapped immediately. "The mere existence of a submarine with these capabilities is a dangerous escalation in the covert wars our nation is illegally involved in, and will lead inexorably to our active involvement in them," he stated.

Supporters of the *John Marshall* point out that the revamped sub is still viable despite its age, that its new systems have completely updated it, and that the *Marshall* is the most economical means of transporting commandoes in an era of tight defense budgets.

Tomorrow's test of the submarine will take place at Camp Lejeune in front of many official supporters and critics.

"Glenn, the charges are all set and ready to go," said Lieutenant Junior Grade Arthur Chen, when a trio of black camouflaged figures magically reappeared at his position. Though the dim light and dark face paint hid their features, Chen knew the middle one was his C.O., Commander Glenn Allard.

"Good, just give us thirty more seconds to make sure everyone's evacuated the site," Allard replied, checking his wristwatch as he dropped to a crouch. "Then set off some of your Chinese fireworks."

"Sure thing, just like my ancestors."

"Glenn, thirty seconds ain't a hell of a lot of time," said

6

one of the other men with Allard. "After all, this is just another exercise. And the Navy isn't showing us off, they're showing off the boat."

"This is supposed to simulate combat, and those Marines fought like it was real. I think the jar heads pulled a fast one on us—they used part of their battalion recon as the defending force. If this had been real, we would've lost almost a quarter of our men, including Martirri. It's just wonderful having another exec who's a fucking cowboy."

Allard glanced over his shoulder, at the "objective" his men had taken. Even from a slight distance, the radar tower and adjoining service building surrounded by barbed wire and sand bags looked impressive. In reality the tower was an old support frame to a water tank. The radar dish atop it was a fifties era museum piece, the service building a mere shell. The building had already been damaged in the initial assault by Allard's SEAL team, a few of whom were still running away from it when he turned back to Chen.

"Better put your fingers in your ears," Chen warned. "Here they go."

With the press of a plunger switch, the mock installation some fifty yards away was ripped apart by strobe-like flashes of light. The heavy, thunderclap explosions echoed across the scrub forest and dunes of the Camp Lejeune shore line. The men in Allard's group, and the few who were even closer to the target, felt the shock waves ripple through their bodies and the ground they stood on. Those farther away, standing in a observation and command platform, didn't feel the physical effects of the blasts but had their ears stung by the loud reports.

"Excellent," said the lone black woman on the platform. She turned to the ranking naval officer among the spectators and said, "Your men are doing well."

"My dear Claudia, that was just a pyrotechnic sideshow," Senator Parker cut in, stopping the Admiral before he could answer. "The real demonstration will be with the submarine. I trust we'll be able to see more of it this time than when it dropped off the SEALs?"

"Yes, the *Marshall* has acknowledged its new orders,"

said the Admiral. "If they're sticking to their timetable they should be coming around for the recovery. And if they're still on the timetable, the SEALs should be retiring to the beach."

As the Admiral raised his binoculars, so did most of the other observers on the platform. With him they scanned the narrow strip of forest and dunes between the fake radar site and the shore line. They searched for the naval commandoes; catching a swift glimpse of a unit or two as they sprinted from one patch of vegetation to another. To the untrained eye their maneuvers appeared random, like the mindless swarming of insects. However, there was purpose to their erratic behavior. The movement of the SEALs could not be predicted and no one ventured into open ground without being covered by the guns of another unit. In spite of the slowness of their advance, they were soon approaching the shore line, with Allard's three-man team in the lead.

"I hope you got the boats ready—I think we're running behind schedule," said Allard, gasping for air after he ended his run. "Sal, what the hell's going on here?"

It took him a moment to realize the inflated zodiacs had not been moved. They still had camouflage netting draped over them, and no one was checking their engines. Most of the work at the site concerned placing circles of stones around freshly dug holes in the sand.

"It's cookout time, Glenn," said Lieutenant Sal Martirri, digging into his backpack. "We gave the brass their blast, now it's time for ours. Take off your stopwatch and kick back."

"Are you out of your fucking mind, Lieutenant? We *are* behind schedule and the *Marshall* will be surfacing soon. Smith, Landham, drop the stones and get the zodiacs ready. Conners, Nichols, go help them."

"Relax, Commander. Our taxi won't go anywhere without us. This is just an exercise. It ain't the real thing and we can always say we were delayed. So kick back and roast a few franks with us."

Martirri pulled several packages of hot dogs out of his

8

backpack. He extended them to Allard, who immediately snapped them from his hand.

"The only thing that's going to get roasted around here is your dick!" Allard shouted, pitching the hot dogs far enough for them to land in the surf. "I see becoming exec hasn't cured your rogue attitude. Or do you wish to continue Capet's tradition of being a screw-up? This is a make-or-break exercise for the *Marshall* and Carver, and I'm not about to let Terry down. Get in that boat, cowboy, or I'll hog-tie you and leave you on the beach for the Marines."

"You sure know how to spoil a party, Commander," said Martirri. He zipped shut his backpack and skulked off to one of the boats.

As more units of the SEAL team returned to the rendez-vous point, work on the zodiacs increased dramatically. The camouflage nets were pulled off, then thrown into the boat wells along with the scuba gear and heavy equipment from the SEALs themselves. In spite of the fact they started out late, the team was less than three minutes behind schedule when the first of the zodiacs were carried into the surf.

When each boat reached knee-deep water, its six-man crew allowed it to float and jumped inside. They used paddles to muscle their way through the ceaselessly rolling breakers at the shore, later switching to outboard motors as they reached the less active chop a few hundred yards out. By then the radio man in Allard's boat had already made contact with the *John Marshall*.

"Glenn, the sub's going to meet us about a mile closer in than planned," said Conners, keeping his handset pressed to his ear. "They got a request from the observers to move in so the operation could be seen better."

"Acknowledge the change, then sign off," said Allard. "I hope Terry and his guys know what they're doing."

Allard used a flashlight to signal the other three zodiacs in his mini-flotilla to begin scanning for the submarine, then started to do so himself. Occasionally, at the tops of the higher swells, he could still see the retreating shoreline. In front of him was a grey-green seascape, flecked with

9

ridges of white. The growing, pre-dawn light made the individual waves discernible, as were the powered, inflatable life rafts bouncing over them.

If the exercise had been a real operation, the SEAL Team would not have waited until it was almost dawn before withdrawing. They would either have moved on to another objective, or would have pulled out hours earlier. Now they were making a noisy retreat across open waters; whatever protection darkness could have offered them was long gone. They were now vulnerable to an attack none of their weapons could stop, but at least it was a great show for the spectators.

Searching for a submarine's periscope while sliding through wave troughs proved difficult for even several pairs of eyes. It was a couple of minutes before one of the flotilla's other zodiacs flashed a signal to Allard.

"Concentrate on the port side," he advised, to the men in his boat. "That's where the *Marshall* will appear."

"Yeah, I got it," said Nichols. "Boy, that scope's riding high. The sub must be running shallow."

"It'll have to be, in this area. The shoals are constantly moving and the tide's dropping. Just up the coast is Cape Hatteras, and they don't call it the 'graveyard of the North Atlantic' for nothing."

Moments later the black slab of the *John Marshall*'s conning tower appeared. Squatter and longer than the sail on an attack boat, it immediately identified the *Marshall* as a missile boat, it's former occupation. When about a third of the tower was visible, the massive diving planes broke through the waves. Shaped like the wings of an aircraft, they were black like the conning tower and the wind whipped the water running off them into a spray. When the planes first breached the surface they made a deep tearing sound, as if they were ripping through fabric instead of water; it was audible even above the rattling of the outboard engines. The upper casing of the *Marshall*'s hull then appeared, water sheeting off it and rolling down her sides. But the submarine maintained its smooth ascent from the depths and its speed for only a few seconds more. As it started to slow perceptibly, its now-useless diving planes started to pitch up and down. The cruciform tail surfaces swung from side to side, causing the *John Marshall* to wallow as its speed continued to fall. In less than a minute, it had become apparent to the SEALs that their home had come to a complete stop.

"Jesus, they're reporting their blue-green laser system is down," said Conners, his handset back on his ear. "They're blind and they had to come to a halt or they'd run aground."

"Is the sub damaged?" Allard asked. "See if I can talk to Carver."

"*Marshall,* this is Wild Shot. *Marshall,* this is Wild Shot. Please advise on condition of boat. If possible Wild Shot Leader would like to hear from the Captain. Over."

"Signal the other zodiacs to slow down. Let's not go swarming over the *Marshall* until we find out what's happened." Until he got his answers, Allard elected to hold his men from rushing mindlessly to the submarine's rescue, if it needed rescuing at all. Without a plan, his force of two dozen commandoes and four inflatable boats would be of little use to their crippled home. "Conners, you getting anything yet?"

"Yes, sir. The sub's only damage is to its Three-D laser radar system. Either it's a computer glitch or damage to the exterior dome. They say you won't be able to talk to Carver for some time. He's on another channel to the brass ashore. Jake Hawkins says it's pretty heated."

"I can just guess what it's like," said Allard. "The brass is going to chew his ass off because of a technical failure, and because he did what they told him to do. Well, ask them if they would like us to help. Advise them we can suit up in our scuba gear and check the laser system dome for damage."

Except for the man operating the outboard motor, the rest of those in Allard's boat began pulling on their scuba tanks and regulators. In the other zodiacs, several men caught on to what they were doing and did the same. As the mini-flotilla circled the *Marshall,* the first divers rolled over

11

the side. She was a forlorn sight, a powerful engine of war, yet blind. She had ended up in water too shallow for her sonar to operate, and her advanced laser radar had gone down when she needed it the most. These problems were not apparent to those on shore; what they saw was a helpless giant.

"So much for your commando wonder weapon," remarked Parker, a hint of smugness in his voice. "It's now a four-hundred-foot-long sitting duck. A plane with a few rockets could sink it."

"It's not completely defenseless, Senator," said the black woman. "It does have two cannons and an anti-aircraft missile launcher in its remaining launch tubes."

"My dear Claudia, one of those Phalanx mounts has been crippled by a salt water leak." There was now a smug, arrogant smile on Parker's face; it mirrored the inflection in his voice. "It's quite defenseless."

"It still has the missile launcher and the other cannon. Plus there's the weapons the commandoes have."

"My dear Claudia . . ."

"That's Congresswoman Chalmers to you, Senator!" Claudia replied, her voice and anger rising. "I'm tired of your damn condescending attitude. I may not know the names of all the weapons, but I do know a cost-effective program when I see one. I also know a sabotage attempt when I see it. You were the one who demanded the *Marshall* come closer to shore. You knew it would have trouble in the shallows. You were hoping it would run aground. At least that didn't happen."

"You have an overactive imagination, my de . . . , Congresswoman Chalmers," said Parker, catching himself. "Are you certain you're seeing a cost-effective program? Or are you seeing the first black missile submarine captain?"

"The *Marshall* is an ex-ballistic missile submarine and Carver is a national hero. After taking command of that Russian sub during the last crisis, he deserves a ship like the *Marshall*."

"Yes, we all know how he single-handedly sailed the missile boat all the way to San Francisco. We also know how the navy kept him ashore for more than a year and that was unfair. But Carver isn't doing his career any good by trying to turn the white elephant out there into a fighting machine. Admiral, why can't the *Marshall* use its expensive sonar to maneuver through those shallows? And if it's really stuck, is the exercise over?"

"The *Marshall* has the BQQ-Five array, attack submarine sonar," explained the highest-ranking of the white-uniformed officers. "It's designed for deep water use. The physics of shallow, turbid water and shifting bottom topography 'confuse' it. Because the *Marshall* has surfaced, it can't use its thermal imagers. Its blue-green laser is its only reliable system. And until it's either repaired or the tide comes in, the sub is going to stay where it is. I'm afraid I'm going to have to call the exercise off. Colonel, stand down your men. I'll talk to Carver personally. I think he deserves it."

"Thanks, Everett. I appreciate this," said Carver, seated at the radio room's cramped console. "My electronic techs are still hunting the problem, but they're confident they can fix it. See you in Norfolk, Everett. *Marshall,* out."

Carver released the transmit key on the microphone stand and pushed his chair far enough away from the console to allow him to rise. As he got to his feet he advised the communications officer to keep him informed of any new messages, then entered the passageway.

Captain Terence Washington Carver had only to turn and walk a dozen feet before entering the *John Marshall*'s control center. As he walked he kept one hand on a passageway wall at all times, in order to steady himself against the rolling deck. In spite of his years at sea he wasn't use to it. Like all modern submariners, Carver had spent most of his time far below the surface and had little experience with heavy seas. However, so long as he found something solid to lean into, he could move.

Inside the control center the alarm klaxons and bells, which had started sounding as the *Marshall* surfaced, were now silent. Most of the shouting had died down. There were fewer men charging around the center; they were either back at their station or had been assigned to check on the equipment which had failed. In fact, the only one still raising his voice, still moving from station to station, was the submarine's executive officer, Commander Gregory Burks.

"Turn it down, Greg," said Carver. "The exercise has been called off and we're not going anywhere. At least until the ETs give us our eyes back or the tide rises. Has the situation changed any since I went to the radio room?"

"Glenn and part of his SEAL team have checked the exterior dome," Burks responded, bracing himself by grabbing hold of the periscope stand's guard rail. "They report no damage, or any evidence of leaks. Whatever the glitch is, it has to be internal. Seidel's got every ET in the crew hunting it down. He may yet prove he's the best sonar officer in the navy. Now that the exercise is cancelled, what's going to happen to us?"

"When we get out of these shallows, and I hope we don't run aground in the meantime, we're to return to Norfolk. No set arrival time, just whenever we can make it in. Between the lines, I read the thinking ashore as being 'don't rush a ship home when she's doomed to the scrap yard.' "

"And how do you feel, Terry?"

"Well, I have let my alma mater down," said Carver, glancing about the control center with a nostalgic longing. Then he realized most of the center crew had fallen silent and were listening to him. "When we put into Norfolk, I'm not going to let it happen a second time. I'm not going to let the politicians and the brass consign this Lady to a scrap yard because of some technical fault. They'll have to haul my black ass off her in chains before I'll let that happen. Don't apply for any transfers, gentlemen. If we have to fight the press, the politicians and the turf wars at the Pentagon we will, only I haven't thought of how we'll do it just yet . . . Greg, what's the word from the flying bridge?"

"We got a watch officer and a couple of observers topside," said Burks. "They're talking to the SEALs

14

and coordinating their work, but little else. They say it's cold and windswept, you'll need your heavy jacket."

"I see you already know what I'm thinking. I need some cold sea spray to think clearly about our problems. Who did you give watch duties to? Stackpole? Tell him to come down as soon as I return with my winter outfit. I'll take over as watch officer, for as long as I need to think about this disaster."

"Tower, this is Sikorsky Lima-November-Xray. We're still waiting for our final passengers but we request permission to start engines."

"This is Stavanger Tower to November-Xray, you're cleared to start engines. Please advise when you're ready to taxi."

"Roger, we'll advise," said the pilot, Captain Karl Abelord. "Lonnie, signal the ground crew to clear the wheel blocks. I'll finish the engine pre-start. Gunther, we'll leave the hatch open for your friends, but if they're not here in five minutes they'll have to swim out to your rig."

As his co-pilot ordered the blocks to be pulled away from the Sikorsky's main gear, Abelord ran his hands over the controls on his instrument panel and center pedestal. He activated the remaining systems, checked the gauges, and less than a minute later had the turboshaft engines whining loudly. The main rotor blades began to turn slowly, the centrifugal force they created rocking the helicopter slightly.

"Karl, there they are," said Gunther Fiske, tapping the pilot on his shoulder. "Always the last minute for journalists."

Fiske stood behind and between the two pilots, where the cockpit ended and the passenger compartment began. He pointed out the starboard cockpit window, at two men who were charging around the corner of a hangar. One was tall, blond-haired, obviously Norwegian; his companion had a darker complexion, and carried a heavy camera bag. He ended up several steps behind the Norwegian by the time they reached the helicopter.

15

"Hans, you finally made it. Good to see you!" Fiske shouted, with the noise of the turbines and rotor blades growing. "Someone close the hatch! Ah yes, Mohammad . . . Nice to see you made it, too."

"The name is Nazal! Abu Nazal," said the second man, pulling back the top zipper on his camera bag. He lowered his voice as the main hatch was rolled shut, cutting the decibel level in the compartment. "I've told you my name several times. If it's the last thing you do, you will remember it. Sivertsen, now!"

Nazal reached into the camera bag, then let it drop to the floor. His hand emerged wrapped around the pistol grip of an Ingram Mac-10. As he flipped the submachine gun upright, Hans Sivertsen pulled a Walther PK automatic from his jacket; and leveled it at an astonished Fiske.

"What are you doing? Have you gone crazy?" he said. "I know you're an environmentalist . . ."

"Hans, shut him up or kill him," Nasal ordered. "I want to speak with the pilots."

Nazal swept the crowd of oil rig workers in the passenger compartment while he spoke. They were transfixed by the sight of the weapons and, when Sivertsen clicked the hammer back on his automatic, even Fiske became silent and sat down with his crew.

"What is your name?" Nazal asked, stepping into the spot the rig official had abandoned.

"Abelord. Karl Abelord. What do you want from us? We only transport oil rig workers. We carry nothing valuable—"

"Shut up. Complete your takeoff as scheduled. We've listened to you in the past, so I know what to expect. Make no attempt to warn the tower. If you do, I'll start killing your passengers. Understand?"

"Yes, completely. Lonnie, check the engine gauges. We're ready to lift off, I must tell the tower about it."

Nazal grunted his approval and Abelord made a brief transmission to the tower at Stavanger's Sola Airport. After it was acknowledged, he twisted the throttle grip on his collective stick, increasing the speed of both main and tail

16

rotors. The helicopter rocked gently as it rose off its landing gear, and swung toward the main runway.

Staying no more than a dozen feet off the ground, the orange and blue S-61 Sikorsky followed the pattern of taxiways out to the runway's end. It clattered past the rows of civilian light planes and heavy-lift helicopters which dominated the flight line at Sola. There was only a handful of Norwegian Air Force rescue helicopters and civilian airliners at the airport. Most of its traffic turned west and flew out over the North Sea, to serve the forest of oil rigs and natural gas platforms. It was the direction the Sikorsky took after getting permission to depart.

"Stavanger Tower, this is November-Xray. We've reached flight level one thousand and our heading is two-five-zero," said Abelord, then, once departure control had acknowledged him. "Are you satisfied, Mr. Nazal?"

"Yes, quite. To the right, do you see those islands?"

Nazal pointed to a cluster of pine-covered rocks at the entrance to Boku Fjord. They were the Tungenes Islands and, though separated from the Norwegian mainland by only a few miles, winter effectively isolated them. They had few residents and intermittent ferry service. Despite their position in the mouth of a busy waterway, they were the perfect location.

"I know them very well. My family has a summer cottage on one of them."

"Good, land on the largest of the islands," said Nazal. "The one to the north."

"But we're being tracked by radar," Abelord reminded. "Stavanger traffic control and Air Force Search and Rescue will see us, and want to know why we're landing."

"Tell them you have an engine or mechanical problem and you're setting down to examine it. I don't care what you create, just so long as you do it now."

"All right. Lonnie, I'm going to need you help. Stavanger Tower, this is November-Xray. A gull has hit our tail rotor, I'm making a precautionary landing to check it over."

Departure Control told Abelord they would be watching him, and promised to get him help if he needed it. Together with his co-pilot, he spiralled the helicopter down to the islands off their starboard side. Nazal gave more instructions as they approached the largest of the islands. He ordered them to land in a level, snow-covered clearing, one of the few on an irregular landscape covered with a thick pine forest.

When the heavy transport helicopter clattered over the site, someone stepped out of the forest and ignited a smoke marker. The dark-colored plume indicated in which direction it should approach from, and as it came in, was directed to a patch of hard-packed snow. The S-61 kicked up only a slight veil of ice crystals as it settled down. The moment the engines were killed, it was surrounded by heavily armed men and women.

"Success, my friend!" shouted one of the men who rushed up to embrace Nazal as he jumped from the main hatch. "Our operation is successful!"

"No, Jassem," said Nazal. "Only Phase Two is complete. We'll not be successful until we're returning to Libya. Sivertsen, order the rig crew to disembark, and to bring with them their belongings."

The next person to emerge from the Sikorsky was Fiske, leading his crew of two dozen rig workers into the clearing. They carried their bulky personnel bags with them, and had their winter jackets zipped up against the deep cold. Several of Nazal's men escorted the workers, while others rushed to the helicopter. The last man to emerge from the giant aircraft was Hans Sivertsen. He was embraced by one of the women in the landing site group, one of the few Norwegians in it.

"My love, I was so worried for you," she said, kissing Sivertsen; holding onto him. "I was afraid you would be caught and arrested. I wish all this would be over."

"It soon will be, Edda," he replied. "And for a clean land, a purified land, it will be worth it. I hope you're already composing songs about what we're going to do. They'll be our one link with each other once I'm in jail, or in hiding."

"Please, don't say these things. I can't stand being without you. How I wish I could go with you and our friends."

"Hans, better say good-bye to her now," said Nazal, returning to the helicopter. "We're starting to load our equipment. We can't stay down for long. The officials are already suspicious of us."

As soon as the Sikorsky had been emptied, it was rapidly filled once again with people and equipment. This time those who came aboard didn't carry clothing with them or personal items, but weapons and other combat gear. Among the first things to be loaded were two heavy steel boxes, prominently marked with three stylized, interlocking rings—the bio-hazard symbol. In a little over a minute the oil rig workers had been replaced on a one for one basis by the people in the clearing.

"Hans, if you and Tunheim don't board now, we'll leave you behind," said Jassem, appearing at the main hatch; already the whine of turboshaft engines was filling the air. "After the help you gave us, your group deserves to be represented."

"I know. Jan, get in there," Sivertsen ordered, and one of the other Norwegians who met him climbed inside. "Edda, whenever you sing about us, we'll be together. Our journeys begin, and one day we'll be reunited."

Sivertsen and Edda embraced and kissed one final time then separated; Sivertsen was helped inside the passenger compartment and Edda was led away by the Norwegians who remained behind. Rotor blades began to fill the air shortly after the engine whine was heard. The anti-collision and navigation lights started flashing again; the Sikorsky was ready for flight.

"Mr. Nazal, I feel the aircraft may be overloaded," said Abelord. "I don't think we can—"

"We are not fools," said Nazal, cutting him off. "We know the performance of this S-61 model. It will lift what we've brought with us. Do it now, or your co-pilot will do it alone."

To reinforce his threat, Nazal allowed the muzzle of his submachine gun to brush against Abelord's ear. The whisper of metal and the smell of gun oil had their effect. Abelord stiffened up, gripped the joystick and collective stick tighter, and pulled his fully-loaded aircraft off the hard-packed snow.

The Sikorsky raised a heavier curtain of ice crystals on its departure than on its arrival. To those left on the ground it was almost impossible to see the helicopter until it was above the surrounding trees and already swinging out to the west. Edda Anders waited near the landing site to catch one last glimpse of her lover, but she saw no recognizable faces in the fuselage windows. By the time the Sikorsky was an angrily buzzing insect against an overcast sky, she realized she had fallen far behind the rest of her group.

"We'll deal with her in a minute," said the Libyan Nazal had left in charge. He turned away from the lone figure still in the clearing and faced the oil rig workers, now held in a tight cluster at the edge of the forest. "Hakeem . . . Ezir . . . It's time to do them."

"What do you mean?" asked one of the Norwegian environmentalists, speaking as the remaining Arabs pulled back the bolts on their weapons.

Fiske and one of his companions stood up, they were never allowed to speak. The first bursts of gun fire caught them in their upper bodies, hitting them from several angles. Their heavy winter coats hid the damage the slugs did to them, even when they re-emerged little blood was seen; mostly it was spurts of insulating material from the coats themselves.

Their first victims were still falling as the Arabs spread their fire to the rest of the group. Most of the workers tried to hide, or begged to be spared; only a few tried to escape. Most of those attempted to crawl into the forest, anyone who stood became an immediate target.

"Stop, no killing!" shouted one of the environmentalists, trying to grab one Arab's AKM rifle. "You promised no killing!"

The brief struggle caused a few shots to go wild, until the Arab struck the Norwegian in the chest with the AKM's

20

wire stock. The blow caused him to stagger backwards, far enough to allow the Arab guard to spin around and train his rifle on him. A burst of fire hit the Norwegian in the stomach and exploded out his back. The multiple impacts lifted the six-foot-tall man off his feet; by the time he came crashing to the ground he was dead.

At first Edda didn't realize the chattering she heard was automatic weapons fire. Only when she saw the first bodies jerk and fall did she realize a massacre was under way. She stumbled for a moment, unsure of whether to flee or stop the murders, then broke into a run. Waving her arms wildly and shouting Arabic and Norwegian names. Shouting for them to stop.

Edda's shock turned to horror as she closed on the massacre site. She watched people die with parts of their heads blown away, or attempt to crawl and spasm when lines of bullet holes stitched across their backs. She watched her friends in her environmental group get shot as well as the prisoners they had just taken. The Arabs who claimed to be their allies committed one murder, one betrayal, after another.

"You're insane! You're butchers!" Edda screamed, her horror turning to reckless anger. "You're destroying everything we could gain. We're environmental liberationists, not murderers!"

"No. We are whatever will meet our goals," said the leader. "And your goals were never ours."

He turned to face the woman charging at him and raised his submachinegun. When he squeezed the trigger his weapon barked only twice, then was empty. But it was enough. One of the slugs tore through Edda's throat and lodged in the spinal column; severing the spinal cord. Her last action was to clamp her left hand over the wound. Her last sound wasn't the silken rendition of a folk song's lyrics, but a cry drowned out by the blood filling her esophagus and spurting between her fingers.

Edda collapsed backwards, landing face up in the snow. She felt nothing from her neck down, was unable to make any part of her body move; couldn't even feel the blood flowing into her lungs. However, she could feel the blood trickling out of her mouth, every time she coughed more of it came up. Her last sight was of the Arab leader standing over her, changing the clips on his weapon. He pointed it down at her. Then, blackness.

"No, you're not worth wasting more ammunition on," the leader remarked, watching the blood continue to spurt between Edda's fingers. There was so much of it, it began to pool around her head and, because of its temperature, thin wisps of steam rose off it. "You'll die soon enough. Join your friends in Valhalla, or whatever you call paradise." He turned to face a young man who came up behind him. "Yes, what is it?"

"Sir, we've finished off the rest," said Ezir, walking up to the leader. "What are your orders?"

"Check them, shoot any who are still breathing. In this weather that should be easy to spot. Do it quickly. I want to reach the boat and be off this island as fast as possible. If we fail in our escape, we could still endanger the operation. So hurry—time is important."

Chapter Two

"Naser, my old friend. Thank you for finally arriving," said one of the few military officers in the conference room as he greeted the latest arrivals. "What delayed you?"

"We suspected we were being followed by Israeli aircraft," Naser Al-Mouk answered, leading his delegation into the room. "Even at this stage in our operation, we can't afford to have the Israelis become suspicious of us."

The delegation took a section of chairs at the massive table, the ones marked by the red, black and white flags of Syria beside each name plate. With their arrival, everyone who had been expected to attend was in, despite the fact that there were several empty groups of chairs.

"Those flags over there are Saudi Arabian," said one of the other Syrian delegates, motioning toward some empty chairs on the table's opposite side. "Will the Saudis actually come here?"

"That's merely Colonel Nazih's idea of a joke," said Al-Mouk. "As are the Venezuelan flags farther down this side. Neither country endorses, or has ever sent a delegation to, this operation. Even though it will benefit all members of OPEC."

"On the other hand, both of those countries know of our operation and have said nothing about it," added Nazih, taking a seat at the head of the table. "I think we can regard their silence as tacit approval. Since all parties are here, this briefing can begin. Lights please."

In response to Nazih's order, the room lights dimmed until

all those at the table became shadows; a translucent screen on the wall facing Nazih started to glow brightly. At the press of a button he brought up a map of the North Sea, then continued with the briefing.

"I'm pleased to announce that, thirty-five minutes ago, we received a message from the Libyan People's Embassy in Oslo. Our strike force has successfully captured a transport helicopter and is enroute to *Ocean Valkyrie*. The support units are withdrawing. Our operation is under way."

A smattering of applause and subdued gasps rippled through the delegates at the table. Though they could not see him, Nazih smiled at the response; he paused long enough for a question to be raised.

"What's the weather in the North Sea like?" asked an Iranian. "You said it would be key to our success."

"Perfect — we couldn't hope for better conditions," said Nazih. "An extreme low-pressure front is moving into the area. In six hours there will be gale-force winds and twenty to thirty-foot seas. Even for a semi-submersible rig the size of *Ocean Valkyrie,* a helicopter landing will be impossible for the next several days."

"Will the strike force stay with the plan we agreed on?" a Nigerian representative asked, his British accent instantly identifying him. "And is any police or intelligence service suspicious of them?"

"So far, Abu Nazal has adhered to the plans we voted for. When the strike force seizes the oil rig, they'll notify us of their success, then announce to the world Norway's 'Purify the Environment' group has taken *Valkyrie.* No European police or intelligence service is aware of our strike force and support units. If the operation goes according to plan, by the time the announcement is made the support units will be out of Norway."

"The new members of my delegation would like to know when the bio-capsules will be injected," said Al-Mouk, after he felt one of them tug at his jacket sleeve.

"The actual mission won't begin until the storm weakens," said Nazih. "Though once under way it'll only be a few hours before it's completed. Even if the injection process has to

24

be cut short it will still succeed. It will only take longer."

"Yes, a year or two instead of several months," noted one of the men sitting beside Al-Mouk. He opened a report folder and snapped on the tiny work light at his seat. His face was the only one in the room to be illuminated; it was one Nazih did not recognize.

"Naser, who is this man?" he asked. "I don't think he's ever been here before."

"You're right, he has not," said Al-Mouk. "Nageeb Assad is chairman of the geology department at Damascus University. Because he's also a Colonel in state security, he has the clearances to review our operation. Nageeb, if you're ready, I think our friends will be interested in your conclusions."

"Could we not hold this for another time?" protested another member of Nazih's Libyan delegation. "We've waited years for this moment. What he has to say can wait."

"No. Assad's studies is one aspect of our operation we've overlooked. One which can have serious consequences."

"Yaseed, let them speak," said Nazih, cutting off the argument. "We'll be here for some time. At least until we receive the expected message from *Valkyrie*."

"Thank you, Colonel," said Assad, nodding in his direction and flipping through the report to its end pages. "Basically, I found your operation to be original and ingenious. The world's first case of genetically engineered warfare. I fully believe it's possible to destroy the entire North Sea oil field from a single injection point. The region's major oil-bearing formations are all connected to the same reservoir of saline water; this would be the common infection source. The selection of the *Ocean Valkyrie* rig is nearly perfect. The deposits it's tapped are among the deepest in the field, and close to the center of the reservoir. However, there's a critical aspect of the North Sea geology you have either ignored or overlooked."

Assad turned his report around and tilted it up for everyone to see. He unfolded its last page, revealing a map of the sea bed strata. In the work lamp's harsh light, many of the fine details were washed out; but a series of heavily darkened, undulating lines was easily discerned.

"The strata I've marked are layers of impermeable shale. They run all the way across the North Sea. They provide an effective barrier to any natural gas leaking out of the fields. The bacteria you're using will convert the oil into a gas, which will become trapped under these layers until the pressure build-up causes them to crack. The results will be sea quakes, they'll be powerful enough to create tsunamis, tidal waves, that will inundate the coastal regions surrounding the North Sea."

Whispers and hushed words started around the conference table though Assad was only part way through his conclusion. By the time he made his last remark they had grown to demands of proof, and accusations that he was a liar.

"Quiet, please. Quiet!" shouted Nazih, raising his voice for one of the first times at the meetings. "When we formulated this operation, we were not unaware of the possible consequences you outlined, Professor. As you said, we ignored them. They're not the consequences we're concerned about."

"Not concerned about," repeated the Nigerian. "Are you aware of how densely populated the coastline of Europe is? Are you aware most of Holland is below sea level? What Professor Assad said could mean the deaths of thousands, maybe more. My country endorsed and financed this operation to increase our revenues, and the influence of OPEC — not to be a party to genocide. Perhaps the Saudis were right to stay out."

"What the West is doing to us is economic genocide," said Nazih. "They have no conscience or regret over our conditions. The collapse of our economies, our mounting debt to their banks, the shortages — or have you forgotten the food riots in your own country? What do you and my friend Naser wish to do? Withdraw from this unit and expose our operation to the West?"

"Nothing so drastic, Ahmad," said Al-Mouk. "But we need to consider the problems Nageeb outlined. If they come to pass, and should the West learn of our involvement, their retaliation will be harsh. There could even be an attack by combined NATO forces. And I'll warn you, in spite of our many treaties with the Russians, they won't be so eager to act as our protector."

"No one will ever discover our hand in this operation. All of you know the plan. Once our strike force is finished with the oil rig they'll mine it and leave. The *Sword of the Revolution* is moving in place to retrieve them. There will be no survivors, no physical trace of our involvement. All outsiders connected to the operation either have been or will be eliminated."

"Will this include the Dutch scientist you brought in to work on the organism?"

"In light of what our brother from Lagos said, it will be imperative to kill Stanmeer," Nazih promised. "Both him and the French whore he insisted on bringing with him. They're the only ones at this base I don't know everything about and don't completely trust. Their deaths have already been planned. My friends, we are so close to success, let's not waste our time arguing over abstract disasters which may never happen. Let us enjoy our revenge against the West. Nothing is going wrong. At this point, only we can spoil it for ourselves."

"This is Sikorsky November-Xray to *Valkyrie* Traffic Control, we're descending from two thousand meters to one hundred," said Abelord, watching the altimeter unwind on his instrument panel. "We will circle the rig before we land on."

"Roger, November-Xray, we copy. What's the reason for breaking procedure and orbiting us?"

"We . . . we have a request from the journalists Fiske brought along. They wish to see the rig before landing. This is November-Xray, out."

"Good, Captain," said Nazal, back in his position between the pilot and co-pilot seats. "Do what I say and remember, the lives of the hostages we left behind depend on your actions."

From more than a mile above the North Sea the orange and blue Sikorsky spiraled down until it had reached three hundred feet and was circling the steel spires of *Ocean Valkyrie*.

Apart from photographs, it was the first time any of the terrorists had actually seen their target.

The oil rig was a rectangular, multi-story slab of steel with the area of a football field. Its central "spire" was its drilling derrick, flanked by service cranes and injection wells. The massive work platform stood on four columns, or base legs. Some sixty feet below them were the huge, submerged, pontoons giving the rig its buoyancy and stability; *Ocean Valkyrie* would need it in the coming storm.

As the transport helicopter swung around the rig, the terrorists crowded its windows and ran down the objectives they were to take, at least the ones they could see. The Sikorsky only made one complete orbit; when it was finished it aligned itself on *Ocean Valkyrie*'s helipad.

"What's going on? Normally the helicopter makes a straight-in approach and would be down by now," said Erica Johensen, standing at the head of a line of rig workers. "Ned, what did you hear?"

"Operations told me there's a couple of journalists on this flight," answered Ned Jansen, walking to the front of the line. "I find that odd."

"How so? For the last eight months, ever since we made *Valkyrie* operational, we've had a constant stream of journalists coming out here."

"I know, but journalists are fair-weather birds." Jansen turned his face into the wind and watched as the Sikorsky came around and dropped in toward the rig's helipad. "They've only come out when conditions are good. We're only a few hours away from a gale-force storm. Unless these journalists enjoy being seasick, I can't understand why they're coming out."

What had been a dark, humming insect was now an angrily buzzing and garishly colored machine only a few hundred yards away. It hovered in front of a darkening sky of forbidding greys and blues; appearing to race the storm to *Ocean Valkyrie*.

* * *

"They're the crew waiting to be taken off," Abelord replied. "Their leave begins now."

"Correction, their leave was to have begun," said Nazal, watching a line of people in winter coats move closer to the helipad perimeter fence. "Jassem, Yussuf, if they give you any resistance, kill them. This is the most critical part of our operation. We can tolerate no interference if we're to be successful. Prepare to land."

The Sikorsky was less than a hundred feet above the red and white helipad. It had lost almost all its forward velocity, making it subject to the winds swirling around the rig structure. The transport helicopter rocked in the unsteady air, so much so Nazal took hold of the pilot seat headrests until the machine had settled firmly onto the pad. Outside, the plane director signaled Abelord to cut his engines while the rest of the crew swarmed around the machine, setting the wheel blocks in place and tying it down to the windswept deck.

"Abu, shall I open the main hatch?" Jassem asked, grabbing its locking lever.

"No, let the handlers do it," said Nazal. "Whoever the unfortunate ones may be. Everyone, arm your weapons and remember your objectives. Sivertsen, stay with the helicopter."

As he stepped away from the cockpit, Nazal could hear the soft, metallic clicking of bolts being pulled back and safeties released. The dying whine of the turbines partially hid the noises, as did the heavy clunking of the starboard hatch being unlocked. By the time it opened, Nazal was standing in front of the hatch. The moment the man in the yellow slicker finished rolling it back, Nazal squeezed the trigger on his Mac-10.

"Look, he slipped," Erica remarked. "Ned, I warned the pad is dangerous when wet. Captain Reitan should have a safety rope for us. I don't want to greet my daughter with a broken leg."

"You worry too much about things," said Jansen. "No one's ever been seriously injured on this rig's helipad. As safety officer I'd have it shut down if I thought it were dangerous. The pad crew slips all the time. Still . . . I'm going out there. He's not getting up."

Nazal opened fire from well inside the helicopter cabin, so most of the noise and muzzle flash were hidden from those outside. He only saw the face of the man he killed for a moment, then the worker was sprawling over the deck. Half a dozen spent shells tumbled from the Mac-10 and bounced across the cabin floor; before they had finished rolling, Nazal and the other terrorists were leaving the helicopter.

The next worker they met was someone who had rushed over to discover why the first had fallen. Both Samad Jassem and the terrorist behind him opened fire; multiple hits lifted the man off his feet and sent him crashing to the deck. The constant wind picked up the shells the weapons ejected and pelted the terrorists still coming off the Sikorsky with them. What the wind couldn't carry away were the muzzle flashes and staccato barking; they were the first real signs the *Ocean Valkyrie* crew had that they were under attack.

"Who the hell are you? Why the hell are you here?" shouted the plane director, when he turned to face Nazal. For his challenge Nazal shot him in the legs and groin and he fell to the deck screaming.

"Why did you do it? He wasn't resisting!" said Jassem. "I thought we were only to shoot those who resisted?"

"Shut up and take your objective!" said Nazal. "He interfered! I'll not tolerate that."

Nazal then spun around and trained his submachinegun on Ned Jansen, who raised his hands and started shouting in Norwegian, English and German not to shoot. Most of the others waiting beyond the helipad's perimeter fence did the same thing, a few even dropped to their knees. However, two workers at the end of the line dropped their luggage and turned to run.

"Kill them!" ordered Yussuf Gunni, sprinting to the fence with his team. "They'll alert the rest of the oil rig."

The workers, a man and a woman, were caught in a barrage of automatic weapons fire while on a flight of stairs leading from the helipad. The impacts threw them from one guard rail to the other. Sparks and shrapnel filled the air as bullets ricocheted off metal; there were occasional spurts of insulating material as other slugs ripped through the tumbling bodies and exploded from the winter jackets. By the time they reached the foot of the stairs, they were dead.

"Shut up! We've only just started!" said Nazal, quelling a cheer among his men. "Azali, watch the prisoners. The rest of you, take your objectives. Let no one interfere with you."

As the rest of the terrorists finished spilling out of the helicopter, they split into groups ranging from three to six people and fanned out to the various stairways leading from the helipad. In less than a minute they were gone, except for those ordered to stay behind. After the storm of gunfire, all that was heard on the pad were the cries of the wounded and the whimpering of the terrified.

"Ned, are you hurt?" Erica asked, raising her voice just enough to be heard above the wind and the distant chatter of small arms fire.

"Shut up whore!" screamed Azali Eshqi, training his Mac-10 on her. "Shut up or I'll kill the rest of your friends!"

To reinforce his threat, Eshqi swept the prisoners with his submachinegun, causing the level of whimpering to rise. It forced Erica to duck her head under her hands, but not before Jansen gave her a thumbs-up signal he was all right.

"What the hell? I've been cut off," said Tryggve Nordsen, *Ocean Valkyrie*'s executive officer. "I was just talking to the floormen boss at the wellbore."

Nordsen kept the handset to his ear while he tapped the cradle buttons. After failing to re-establish contact, he started to punch in the number for the oil rig's switchboard.

"Trig, look— Who are those people?" asked one of the other workers in the rig operations center. He pointed out the observation windows at a group of people charging toward the center. It was a few moments before anyone spotted the diminutive submachineguns the mystery visitors were carrying.

"Alert the Captain," said Nordsen. "I'll seal us in here. Then we alert the crew."

Nordsen's calm response belied the urgency of his orders and the way he dropped the telephone and bolted for the center's exterior entrance. Unlike the ship-style hatchways found through most of the rig, the operations center had conventional doors; it was less like the bridge of a ship and more like a production control room at an oil refinery. Nordsen had scarcely reached the door and locked it when he felt a weight slam against it.

"Damn it, they know about us!" Nazal shouted, stepping back from the door. "No, don't shoot through the windows! We need this center."

"We have plastic explosives," said a member of his team. "Should I wire a charge to the door?"

"No, I can do it quicker. Stand away, Kaniel."

Nordsen had just turned from the door when a concentrated burst of automatic weapons fire ripped through it. The nine millimeter slugs virtually exploded the doorknob and, as they spun off on wild trajectories, several hit Nordsen. His right leg gave way as if someone had hit it with a sledgehammer. He fell against the injection well monitoring console and was on the floor by the time Nasal kicked open what remained of the door.

"No one move!" said Nazal, but from the corner of his eye he caught some movement.

He swung to the right and found a woman backing up; her outstretched hand reaching for the collision alarm button. Nazal didn't aim his weapon, at this range he didn't need to, he just sprayed her with a four-round burst. The first bullet missed the woman, the next two hit her in the upper abdomen, spinning her away; and the fourth struck her in the side, under her left breast. It pierced her heart, by the time the diminutive brunette finished slumping against the wall she was dead.

"You bastard! I was to marry her!"

The third worker in the operations center, the one who had first spotted the terrorists, flew at Nazal in a blind rage. Nazal trained his Mac-10 on him and pulled the trigger. Beyond a hard click nothing happened; the submachinegun's clip was empty. The charging man almost got his hands on Nazal's neck when a series of explosions threw him over a console.

"Good, you can now join her in paradise," said Nazal, before he turned to the man coming up beside him. "Thank you, you showed good teamwork."

"And you should count the rounds you fire," replied Kaniel Akkad. "We have Operations, what next?"

"Find out from this prisoner where the Captain is and bring him here. Or perhaps we can use the prisoner to make the Captain come to us. Either way, we hold this center. All teams have orders to report here when they take their objectives."

"Something *is* going wrong with this system. I just lost touch with ballast control," said the watch officer for the communications center.

"How could that be? It's brand new," said a technician, swivelling his chair around to face his boss. "We're brand new, and we haven't had a problem for months."

"Haven't you ever heard of 'bugs'? Or perhaps with computerized equipment I should say, 'viruses'? Whatever they are, we got a few causing us problems. Run a diagnostic check on the entire voice com system."

The technician groaned as he swung back to his console and aligned his chair with its computer display screen. With a tap of a few keys, he found a diagnostic program for the telephone system aboard *Ocean Valkyrie*. With the tap of another key the program commenced its run, seeking out faults in the miles of wiring, junction boxes and other equipment.

"This will take a little time," said the technician, when the watch officer came over to his position. "Remember, this system is as large as a town's. What should we do if we can't locate the problems? Have the rig go over to portable radios?"

"God, I hope not. In all this steel we'd have a hell of a time with weak signals, scattered signals and attenuation. Yes? Who's there? What do you want?"

The watch officer looked over his shoulder at the one entrance to the communications center. Located in one of *Valkyrie*'s base legs, the center had a single, ship's-style hatchway. The locking gear on the hatch clicked and rotated swiftly; someone on the other side was in a hurry to get in. Still, in spite of the rush, the watch officer had walked to the hatch by the time it opened.

What he saw was an assault rifle being swung at him by a huge pair of hands. When the AK-47's wooden stock made contact with his jaw, there was a snapping sound of bone being broken. The watch officer whirled away from the impact; by the time he collapsed to the floor, he was unconscious.

"God in heave . . ." said the technician, his voice trailing off as men and women in combat fatigues filled the center.

"Shut up or you will join God!" shouted the leader, the one who had knocked out the watch officer. He charged across the room and pressed the muzzle of his AK-47 against the technician's chest. "You will cut all links with the outside. Video, voice and data transmission. Do it now, and don't send anything until we hear from your operations control."

"Michael? What are you doing in here?" asked the rig's medical officer, when a worker burst through the entrance to the examination room. "Are you ill?"

Though he was gasping for air and had a terrified look on his face, the young man shook his head "no." Once the door closed behind him he put his back against it, as if to brace it, then he looked at the other occupants of the room.

"Dr. Lunde, there's people in the hallways," said Michael, still catching his breath. "Arab people . . . with guns, machineguns! I think they're taking us over!"

"It's someone's sick joke," said Lunde. "And you were taken in by it. Years ago, the Turkish crew of a supply boat ran around a British platform with toy guns. We were scheduled for a transfer today. It's the same joke."

"Doctor, we're scheduled to receive a helicopter," said Lunde's patient, drawing her examination gown close around her. "Not a boat. I should know, my sister works in Operations."

Lunde's expression changed from bemusement to concern; then came the avalanche of noise and voices from the outer rooms. Shouts for people to raise their hands, to shut up, and the stamp of boots; and the crash of a body against the examination room door. It moved in an inch or two, but Michael flattened himself against it and managed to push the door back.

"Get away from there!" Lunde ordered. "Don't be irrational. We can't keep them out."

"But we must. We're safe here," said Michael, before his body spasmed in reaction to an explosion behind him. An instant later a bullet punched through his chest and shattered the window of a medicine cabinet in front of him. Instead of clutching his wound, Michael tried to wipe the blood off his shirt. When he looked up, his expression was less one of pain than fear. "Karl . . . make it stop . . ."

The woman Lunde had been examining got sprayed with Michael's blood. In spite of her hysterical screaming, and attempts to grab him, Lunde managed to catch Michael as he collapsed. He went into convulsions as the door he'd been guarding burst open.

"I should kill all of you for resisting!" said the woman standing before Lunde, a smoking AKM assault rifle in her hands. "But you're the rig's doctor, aren't you?"

"Yes, I'm Karl Lunde. Please, this man is dying."

"If he's dying forget him. There are other wounded for you to care for. Shut the whore up or I'll kill her too!"

When the young rig worker stopped convulsing, Lunde knew he was dead. Carefully, he laid him aside; then rose to comfort his original patient. When he looked back at the door, Lunde found the darkly beautiful woman had been replaced by a man; she was moving through the rest of *Ocean Valkyrie's* hospital, snapping out more orders.

"What's going on? What's the commotion by the doors?" asked Arne Landstrom, after he laid his lunch tray on the table.

"I think the rest of the crew has learned these are our last steaks," said his co-worker, plunging his fork into the sizzling piece of beef on his plate. "We better hurry and eat these before there's a food fight."

A rapid series of explosions cut through the din of conversation in the cafeteria. The deafening reports caused people to spasm as if they had been hit by electric shocks. Some dove under the tables, others froze in their place; and a few stood up to find out what was creating the noise.

"Dan, get down!" said Landstrom, tugging at his friend's shirt sleeve. "And drop the knife!"

From the corner of his eye, he caught a glimpse of figures advancing from the cafeteria's main doors. It didn't register on Landstrom who they were or what they were shouting; what did register were their weapons.

"Who the hell are you?" said Dan, pointing his steak knife at the figures.

Only one of the terrorists turned to face him, as they had been trained to do. A short burst of submachinegun fire caught Dan in the chest and neck. The knife flew from his hand and was still clattering on the table behind him when he crashed next to Landstrom, bleeding profusely. In minutes he would be dead; the last worker to be killed in the taking of *Ocean Valkyrie.*

"Azali! Azali, bring your prisoners down!" shouted a terrorist who appeared at the helipad's main stairs. "Take them to the Activities Lounge! Prisoners are to be held there, the cafeteria or the hospital."

"What of our Norwegian friends!" asked Eshqi.

"Tell Mr. Sivertsen to follow you! Mr. Tunheim is to stay

with the helicopter!"

"I understand! You, go to the helicopter and bring me the man named Hans Sivertsen."

Eshqi aimed his submachinegun at Erica and motioned with it for her to go over to the Sikorsky. Trembling, she rose from her knees and walked across the helipad to the silent aircraft. Erica briefly ducked her head inside its main hatch, then stepped back as Sivertsen emerged. Together, they returned to where Eshqi was holding most of the prisoners; Sivertsen paused briefly as they passed the bodies of those killed in the opening moments of the assault.

"The oil rig is ours, Mr. Sivertsen," said Eshqi. "We're to take the prisoners below. You, whore, and your friend out there. I want you to carry the wounded man to the hospital."

"Why must you call me a whore? My name is—"

The rest of Erica's words froze in her mouth as Eshqi swung his Mac-10 over his head, and prepared to strike her with its wire stock. Only Sivertsen prevented her jaw from being broken.

"No, Azali!" he shouted, grabbing Eshqi's hands. "She's no threat! Can't you see we've frightened her?"

"I will do more than scare her," said Eshqi. "She will obey or die! She's decadence, Western poison! In my country, women obey men or die. Go, whore. Go and bring him back."

Almost convulsing with fear, Erica went over to Jansen and together they lifted the plane director off the helipad's deck. It was a struggle carrying him, until they got him past the fence and more rig workers lent a hand.

With Eshqi leading, and Sivertsen guarding the rear, the group filed down the stairs from the helipad. They passed the operations center, where Nazal was already conferring with the other terrorist leaders, then entered the oil rig itself. What had been until a few minutes ago their home and work place would now be their prison.

"*Shalom,* Haskel. Thank you for seeing me on such short notice," said the man entering Director Haskel Gazit's of-

37

fice. He immediately shut the heavy door behind him, closing out the din of noise from the rest of the center. In a few strides he was at Gazit's desk and laid a slim folder on it.

"Yes, five minutes is rather short notice," said Gazit. "Usually I make you wait at least ten minutes, Ben Adir. But then you did say this was extremely urgent."

Gazit pulled the folder toward him and opened it. While he examined its single sheet of paper, Avrom Ben Adir started checking his watch again. With each movement of its second hand another bead of sweat formed on Adir's forehead.

"Patience, my friend. It doesn't take long to read a single line of words. Are you certain this is what she transmitted?"

"No errors, Haskel. I had the operators recheck everything," said Adir. "Gavi feels her life is in grave danger and needs an immediate extraction. Given the sensitivity of her assignment, we should treat this very seriously."

"I note she hasn't used the codeword which indicates her cover has been blown," said Gazit, laying the transmission down. "What do you think is going on over there?"

"Difficult to say. Libya has always been a hard country for us to penetrate and Gavrilla's in a very remote location. Her written reports are sporadic but . . . this 'Blood Revenge' terrorist unit could be starting its first operation. We know several of its teams are already in Western Europe."

"Blood Revenge . . . yes, they're the intelligence unit doing the bio-engineering experiments. Have they succeeded?"

"We can't say for sure," Adir replied. "The codes Gavi was trained on don't work well with highly technical or scientific data. One of the little mistakes we made, but it couldn't be helped. We know they're producing an organism of some kind; perhaps they have succeeded."

"Then perhaps the Libyans no longer need this geneticist they recruited. We know Libyan intelligence to be ruthless — it wouldn't be below them to kill him. Perhaps our Gavi realizes this, and understands she is even more expendable than he is. How do you wish to extract her?"

"The fastest means possible, Sirat Hatzalah. We know very little about what 'Blood Revenge' has planned. Gavrilla is our best, our only, source of information on them."

"Sirat hatzalah," Gazit repeated, glancing back at the transmission. "Retriever boat. You certainly believe in pulling out all the stops. If I approve it, it'll be the second time this year we've gone to the Americans for a Combat Talon."

"Given her location deep in the country, and the urgency of her request," said Adir. "The American Combat Talon is the only way to get her out. How long will it take for it to arrive?"

"Well, first I have to kick the 'request' upstairs. Remember, I'm just the head of the Foreign Operations Directorate and we're not in the position to order the Americans around. Their Air Force crews already call the Combat Talon fleet 'Mossad Airlines.' After my superiors have evaluated the request it must go to the American embassy, then onto the Pentagon and finally to the air base where a Combat Talon is currently stationed."

"Haskel, please. How long?"

"From request to arrival took three hours the last time," said Gazit, at first irritated until he saw the concern on Adir's face. "You can base your operation's time table on this. The only problem could come from Egypt granting us permission to overfly its territory. I take it you would like to accompany the aircraft?"

"Whether it's the Army or Intelligence, I wouldn't ask my men to do something I would not be prepared to do myself. Besides, I am Gavi's control officer."

His last remark caused Adir to look yet again at his wristwatch; then he glanced involuntarily over his shoulder at the office door. When he turned back, he found Gazit with the folder in his hand and a knowing smile on his face.

"Yes, my friend, it's time to go and transmit her extraction time and removal point to Gavrilla," said Gazit, handing back the folder. "After you finish contacting her and making your plans you should catch some sleep. Trust me, Ben Adir, you'll get very little of it in the next few days."

"Greetings from the rest of the world, Terry. Burks told me I'd find you down here," Allard remarked, descending the stairs from the *Marshall*'s control center to what had once been its missile launch room.

In place of his wet suit, Allard was now wearing a freshly pressed naval officer's uniform, identical to Carver's except for the rank insignia and the absence of dolphins over the left breast pocket. When he got to the foot of the stairs he only had to take a few strides to reach Carver and drop into the seat next to him at the main console in the Tactical Attack and Situation Control (TASCO) room.

"It's good to feel the old girl under way again," said Carver. "I'm glad we didn't run her aground, or that would've ended her days and my days at sea beyond a doubt. As it is, this could well be my Lady's last cruise."

"Let's see, where are we?" said Allard, checking the room's main display screen. It showed the southeastern seaboard of the United States, from Georgia to Maryland, yet Allard was unable to spot the marker for the *John Marshall;* until Carver pressed a button on his keyboard, and a triangle near Cape Hatteras began flashing.

"Sorry, I should've remembered you web-foots have trouble with tacticals, especially here in the TASCO room," Carver observed, a sly grin on his face.

"Very funny, Terry. My family probably built this system. Allard Technologies won the contracts away from Raytheon a couple of years ago. How long before we put into Norfolk?"

"About six hours. I say 'about' because there's a carrier ahead of us, and a ship doomed to the scrap yard doesn't have to be rushed home."

"You certain that will happen?" asked Allard. "Greg seems to think so; he's pretty despondent about the old girl's fate. It would be a shame to scrap her. We got most of the bugs worked out, the right equipment on board. This sub is operational."

"I'm afraid it had one bug too many," said Carver, his voice dropping, the smile disappearing from his face. "This glitch with the laser radar was the final straw, and my alma mater has a lot of powerful enemies in Washington. Who loves this Lady? Only those who've served aboard her."

40

"Like you and Greg. Well, there's a few more of us who'll support you. I wish I could get my family to help you but hell, I bet they got deals with General Dynamics and Newport News to supply the electronics for the *Marshall's* replacement boat. I bet they'd work to get the *Marshall* scrapped just to bring me out of the Navy and back into the fold."

"They still trying to get you to return to Allard Tech?"

"Yes, they want me to replace Ben Warde as head of the Tiger security force," said Allard. "If they really want someone they could take Martirri out of my hair. Fucking cowboy."

"I heard about your problems today." The smile reappeared briefly on Carver's face, only to vanish as he turned serious. "At least this exec didn't stick a rattlesnake down his mouth like the last one. Inspite of your efforts you still have a discipline problem, with your officers as much as your enlisted men."

"Yes, it's a never-ending problem. I don't know a single elite unit commander who doesn't have discipline troubles. Though it's apparent to me the SEAL Teams have it worse, a fact Navy brass is trying to keep under wraps."

"Are you going to remove Martirri from your unit when we reach Norfolk?"

"I don't know. I've already relieved one exec, and Philip Capet was popular with the men," Allard replied. "But Sal Martirri has certainly displayed enough insubordination to be court martialed, even from a SEAL unit. Looks like we're both going to face a lot of fighting and hard choices when we return."

"I think so. You with your men, me with the rest of the Navy. And I meant it when I said they'll have to drag my black ass off this sub in chains before I'll let them tow her to a scrap yard."

Chapter Three

"Captain, thank God," said Dr. Lunde, almost shouting when he recognized the latest individual to enter *Ocean Valkyrie's* hospital section. "Thank God you finally came. Who are these people? Why have they taken us?"

"They're Middle East terrorists," answered the man with gray-flecked, sandy brown hair. Captain Erik Reitan waited until the main doors had been shut behind him, putting the men guarding the hospital out of earshot, before completing his answer. "Libyan terrorists, Iranian terrorists, Arabian terrorists—I don't know, and I don't care who they are. I only care about what they did to my crew, and what they plan to do. What are the casualties like, Karl? The leaders wouldn't tell me anything but I've seen bodies, and in the activities lounge Erica is pleading for the wounded to be flown off."

"They've killed eighteen and wounded or injured twenty-one more. I don't know the names off all the dead, I only know their number from what the wounded and their bearers have told me. Have you seen my wife, Erik? I have to know if she's alive."

"Adele's alive, Karl, don't worry about her. She's in the Activities Lounge with Erica. Show me who the wounded are. I don't have much time before the leaders come for me."

Lunde turned and led Reitan down the corridor to one of the hospital's two twelve-bed wards. Every bed in it was filled, with most of the patients running IV lines. Most of them were also conscious, and looked up when Reitan and Lunde entered the cramped, windowless room.

"Trig, I'm so relieved to see you alive," said Reitan, moving over to one of the beds; and shaking its occupant's hand. "The bastards told me they shot you, but they didn't say how badly. Only that you were brought here. Doctor, how serious is he?"

"Superficial wounds to both legs and the right hip," said Lunde. "He also has a bruise on the left side and possible broken ribs."

"Would you say his wounds are life threatening?"

"Only if they're untreated. We can care for him well enough here. Why do you ask? I have more seriously wounded in the private rooms, people I can only barely stabilize. Without more help they'll die. Altogether I have thirty-one wounded, five of them serious. Why are you asking about Trig?"

"Yes, Captain. Why me?" asked Nordsen. "There are other people in this room alone who are more seriously injured."

"Because, if Erica Johensen is successful, the more seriously wounded may be evacuated in the transport helicopter," said Reitan. For the first time in more than an hour he didn't have heavily armed men pushing guns in his face and screaming at him. He wasn't being dragged around by guards or kept under constant surveillance. For the first time in more than an hour he was alone and, instead of being told what to do, was thinking for himself. "Those who'll go won't be in much condition to tell authorities about our situation and those who've taken us. Trig has seen the terrorist leaders when they met in Operations, he can identify them. Can you make him look more serious than he is?"

"Easily. A few injections and he'll appear ready to die," said Lunde. "If he's willing to do it."

"I'm not a hero," Nordsen admitted. "But I saw two people killed, Anna and Norland. They didn't deserve to die that way. I'll do it, Erik. When do we begin?"

"Immediately," said Reitan. "Doctor, get him ready. Thanks, Trig, I hope we'll be able to meet again after this nightmare is over. I know you'll be busy, so I'll show myself around. And I'll delay the terrorists if they come for us."

While Lunde and some of his medical technicians carried Nordsen to a private ward, Reitan moved through the rest of the hospital complex. Almost every bed he found was filled and the examination rooms were still busy with the less severely wounded. He returned to the complex's main entrance in time to hear a rush of voices and the stamp of boots in the passageway outside.

The guards swung the doors open, allowing Nazal and the other terrorist leaders to enter unhindered. Beyond them, and the guards at the hospital entrance, the only other members in the entourage were Erica and Adele.

"If it isn't Commander Shut Up," Reitan whispered to a nurse, before he turned to the leaders. "Mr. Nazal, have you reached a decision about my wounded?"

"I have, your women have made many tearful demands," said Nazal. "Especially these two. And we've decided to allow the most seriously injured to be evacuated by the helicopter."

An audible sigh, and even some cheering, rippled through the assembled audience of nurses, medical technicians and patients. In spite of the worried looks on their faces, Erica and Adele managed to smile when the announcement was made. A moment later Adele Lunde's expression changed to genuine happiness when she caught sight of her husband.

"My dear, I was so worried," said Lunde, wrapping his arms around his wife when she rushed to him. "I was afraid for you, until Erik told me you were safe."

"If I may be allowed to continue," Nazal demanded. "As a further show of our humanitarian concern, we'll allow a number of your women workers to leave the rig. Among them can be these two, Erica Johensen and Adele Lunde."

"No, I won't leave my husband," said Adele, continuing to hold onto Karl. "If he stays, I stay. We made a promise when we married, never to leave each other."

"I will not decide, your Captain will decide the women and your doctor, the wounded. Whoever you decide, you had better make it fast. The weather's growing worse, and soon the helicopter crew may not risk a takeoff. Let us know when you're ready to be escorted to the helipad, and my offer for these two women still stands."

As Nazal wheeled around, so did Jassem and Gunni. When the guards closed the doors behind them, the Norwegians in the hospital were once again alone.

"Erik, I'm going to check on the seriously wounded," said Lunde, finally releasing his wife. "I'll prepare them for transport. I'll need stretcher bearers, Erik, a lot of them."

"Yes. Yes, I'll get on it," said Reitan, absently. He was lost in thought, so much so he didn't realize Erica had approached him until several moments had passed. "Erica, thank you for your help. It was very courageous of you. Is there something you wish?"

"I'm . . . I'm not a hero, Captain," Erica admitted. "My daughter is waiting for me ashore. If the terrorists said I could leave I would like to. Would you object?"

"No, not at all. You've already done more than most of us, even me. It's just . . . they've left us alone, they aren't checking the wounded we wish to evacuate, and they requested that you and Adele leave. You two have had more contact with the terrorist leaders than most of us. I guess I shouldn't worry, I'm not a terrorism expert, but none of this makes sense."

"Of course, none of it makes sense. It's all a nightmare, Captain. It's madness."

"But there's method to the madness of terrorists," said Reitan, before the activity in the hospital's entrance room started to distract him. "They should be watching us. They don't seem to care who we put on the helicopter. This is a serious mistake on their part, a lapse in their thinking. And we had better work quickly to take advantage of it."

"This is Nesher Tower to Falcon Zero-Four. You are cleared to land, and welcome to Israel. You'll be met at the end of the runway by your friends."

Apart from its anti-collision and landing lights, the C-130 making its approach was all but invisible. Her matte black paint scheme was devoid of national markings, did not reflect the airfield's ground lights and allowed her to be swallowed by the early morning darkness. And, other than the runway threshold and perimeter lights it had just activated, the Israeli airfield was equally invisible. None of its hangars, service or administrative buildings were above ground, just a diminutive control tower.

As the Hercules touched down the bulges in her nose and along her fuselage sides were visible in the glow from the runway lights. Above her cockpit was a small, wave-shaped bump with white grid marks around it, virtually the only markings on the transport's surface. Farther down her spine a canoe-like fairing ran to the base of the tail fin, and atop the fin was still another pod. Only these electronic arrays and the STAR system yoke betrayed the C-130 as an MC-130E, a Combat Talon.

"Welcome to Mossad Airlines, gentlemen!" shouted the airman who opened the side hatch. He admitted in the Israeli team waiting for the aircraft.

"Haskel was right! We're becoming too familiar," said Adir. "I'm Avrom Ben Adir and these are my companions, Captain Yehuda Eshel and Major Shlomo Ben Shoham. They're from Air Force security."

"Loadmaster Marty Hitter. Welcome aboard. I'll introduce you to our Elint Team; they're already in the box." Ritter waved at the padded cubicle anchored to the cargo deck of the Hercules. "We better hurry. It feels like Phil and Herb are swinging us around."

The C-130 had resumed moving almost from the moment its side hatch was locked. As the jeep which delivered the Israelis drove back to its underground garage, the Lockheed giant gunned its engines and rolled forward. It edged over to the left side of the runway, then swung to the right and executed a swift one-hundred-and-eighty-degree turn.

For a few moments it slowed again, as flaps were lowered and final checks made, then the throttles were pushed to their gate stops. The Combat Talon accelerated down a runway where dust was still settling from its arrival. Apart from the passengers it collected, and what they brought with them, the aircraft received nothing else during its brief stay on Israeli soil. Refueling, crew briefing and other matters would be handled en route to its target. The operation had already begun, and the clock was ticking away.

"All stretcher bearers, may I have your attention," Lunde announced, stopping the procession of wounded and other

46

evacuees at a set of double doors. "We're about to leave the first level and the weather outside is terrible. Keep your patients covered and under no circumstances are you to let them fall. Anything like that would kill them. Please, be safe."

At Lunde's signal the doors were pushed open, and a blast of cold arctic wind swept into the passageway. The blankets were pulled tighter around the patients before being carried onto the drill platform. A light, freezing rain was dropping and the strong winds and growing darkness made everything slippery, dangerous.

The procession moved cautiously across *Ocean Valkyrie's* top deck, except for Nazal and his escorts. They reached the helipad several minutes ahead of the others and had the Sikorsky crew doing their pre-flight checks.

"I thought you'd forgotten about us," said Jan Tunheim, emerging from the helicopter. "It's been over an hour. Have you made the broadcast that we've seized the rig?"

"Not yet. You and Hans will have the honor," said Nazal. "Hans, take him to the cafeteria. First you have some coffee, then we'll make the broadcast."

Sivertsen and Tunheim had to wait for the procession of wounded to thread its way up the stairs to the helipad. They averted their gaze from their countrymen; what they saw was not something they were especially proud of. Once the stairs had been cleared they descended and made their way to the drill platform's main entrance.

"Fold down the seat backs and tie the stretchers to them," Lunde instructed the bearers. "Attach the IV bags to the hooks in the cabin roof. Work fast, but be careful."

"I'll try to lift off as smoothly as I can," said Karl Abelord, after he completed the walk-around inspection of his aircraft. "But the weather is growing fierce. I can't guarantee anything."

"Neither can we," Reitan added, waiting until Nazal and his men had moved away. "I still don't understand why they're allowing you to leave at all. Either they're very confident of themselves, or they just aren't thinking right."

"But, as you stated yourself, 'whatever it is we'd better take advantage of it,' " said Lunde. "These people need more medical attention than I can give them. Let's just get them away before these animals change their minds."

The Sikorsky's passenger cabin rapidly filled with the stretchers containing the seriously wounded. Most of the cabin seats were folded down with stretchers tied to them. Among the last to be secured, and the closest to the hatch, was Tryggve Nordsen. Even through his drug-induced haze he could see and recognize Reitan. He waved to him briefly, then his head began to swim and he dropped back into a twilight sleep.

"Good luck, Erica. I wish we could keep you here. In a storm like this we need your expertise to keep *Valkyrie* stable," said Reitan, then, under his breath. "Remember everything you've seen and tell it all."

"I will, Captain, I promise," Erica replied, hugging Reitan. "I'll tell your family you send them your love."

"Yes, do that. Please!" he added, as Erica climbed into the Sikorsky and its main hatch was rolled shut by the terrorists outside. He and Lunde were led off the pad and stood behind the same perimeter fence where Erica had stood less than two hours before.

"I see the bastards have given us an all-girl passenger list," said Abelord, looking over his shoulder to watch Erica take one of the last seats on his aircraft. "Are you going to be our nurses?"

"Please, please! This isn't a time for your damn humor," said one of the women passengers.

"I know . . . Lonnie, finish the systems check and start the engines. Do you see the lockers on this wall?"

Abelord pointed to the small cases on the port cabin wall; they were mounted above the windows and displayed prominent red crosses. Erica jumped out of her seat and reached for the nearest case.

"Do you mean these?" she asked.

"Yes. They contain rescue gear," said Abelord. "The middle one has lightweight exposure suits, enough for all of you. Put them on now. Something your captain told me is giving me a sense of foreboding. I think we can escape, but we better prepare for the worse. Please, just put the suits on. We'll breakout the other things after we're airborne."

"I don't think all these people need to stay out here," said Nazal, glancing down the line of stretcher bearers. "Sherina, take them below. Take the doctor, he has other patients to care for. Leave the captain with us."

The woman beside Nazal motioned toward the stairs with her AKM rifle; most of the Norwegians lining the perimeter fence started moving toward them. In less than a minute the only people still at the helipad were Nazal, his men and Reitan.

"Why am I kept here?" Reitan asked, as the Sikorsky's turboshafts rumbled to life and the rotor blades began to turn. "Is it you want me to witness their departure?"

"A departure? Yes, and a demonstration," said Nazal. "A demonstration of what we are."

"Final check's complete," said Abelord. "I'll take her over, Lonnie."

Abelord grabbed his control and collective sticks as his co-pilot released his own set. A slight twist on the collective's grip increased the speed of the main and tail rotors; causing the S-61 to rock harder; trembling as if it were ready to fly.

"Captain, we're dressed," Erica advised. She now wore a bright yellow, one-piece jumpsuit, as did the other women in the main cabin. She pulled her winter coat back over her jumpsuit, then slipped on the yellow thermal gloves.

"Good, take your seats," said Abelord, sparing a moment to look over his shoulder. "But be ready to evacuate at any moment. Shout if you see anything dangerous. Anything. Here we go."

Watching the rpm, temperature and pressure readings climb; Abelord increased power again and pulled back on the control stick. The Sikorsky swayed heavily as it rose off the pad; in the heavy wind it needed both her pilots to maintain stability. As it climbed the helicopter backed away, until it was sufficiently clear of the rig superstructure to swing around.

Erica strained to catch one last look at the people still on the helipad, but couldn't quite recognize Reitan among the Arabs at the perimeter fence. Then the S-61 swung to the right; when it completed its one hundred and eighty degree turn Erica was almost at eye level with someone she did recognize.

It was the terrorist who held her group when the oil rig was being seized; she immediately identified his burning, hateful eyes. Azali Eshqi stood on the top platform to one of *Ocean Valkyrie's* saline water injection wells. He was leaning against the platform's guard rail, to prevent the wind from blowing him away. As the helicopter started to surge forward, Erica realized her tormentor wasn't cradling a diminutive submachinegun in his arms, but a long tube.

"Now for the demonstration!" Nazal shouted, the thunder of the Sikorsky's liftoff temporarily drowning out the noises created by the wind. "Remember it, Reitan. Remember it well."

Nazal turned and waved to Eshqi, who nodded an acknowledgement before shouldering the orange tube he carried. He had already removed the fore and aft protective caps from the SAM-7 launcher; all he had to do was align its simple optical sights on the fleeing helicopter and wait for the acquisition light to indicate a target lock had been made.

"He doesn't need a machinegun to shoot us down!" said Abelord, after Erica warned him. "That tube he's got is a missile launcher! Lonnie, do exactly what I say."

The Sikorsky already had its nose tilted down to increase its forward speed, all it took was a little extra stick pressure to push the helicopter into a dive as it cleared the rig's massive platform. In seconds it dropped to wave-top height and Abelord was shouting for his co-pilot to help him swing the aircraft to the right while they were still levelling it out.

"Erica, are we going to die?" asked the woman sitting next to Johensen.

"I don't know," she said, clutching her seat's arm rests. "Just be ready to evacuate if we have to."

* * *

"Bastards! You will not cheat me!" Eshqi screamed, after the helicopter disappeared from his launcher's optical sights. The acquisition light briefly flickered on, then went out, indicating the lock had been lost.

Eshqi lowered the SAM-7 and moved along the platform's guard rail, scanning for any sign of the escaping Sikorsky. For a few seconds the only activity he saw were his leaders racing across the helipad beside and below him. Eshqi could only hear the wind swirling around him; he had to wait until he caught sight of a blur of rotor blades emerging from under the top deck's overhang before he could reshoulder his missile launcher.

"Another two or three meters and we would've hit the water," said Lonnie.

"I know, I know. Now start zig-zagging the aircraft on my count," said Abelord. "Their missiles are heat-seeking—we have to fool them!"

As close as the helicopter's fuselage had come to the wave tops, its main rotor blades had swept even closer to the oil rig's base legs. Abelord had wanted to continue hugging *Ocean Valkyrie,* using the deck's overhang to block any missile fire. But the risk of collision with the dauntingly huge structure was more real to him than being shot down. A civilian pilot, Abelord had never been trained to deal with military threats and could only guess at how to handle them. The moment the Sikorsky passed the northeastern base leg he ordered it swung to the left, beginning a series of sharp, erratic S-turns low over the North Sea.

This time the acquisition light snapped on and stayed on. Keeping the S-61 in his sight, Eshqi stroked the trigger on his launcher. The tube spasmed, kicking hard into his right shoulder as it ejected a slender missile. The SAM-7's booster engine momentarily bathed Eshqi and the injection well's upper platform, in exhaust gases. Eshqi felt the heat through his heavy jacket and pants. He closed his eyes and held his breath for several moments; when he again looked around him he found the SAM-7 glowing like a tracer round and snaking after the retreating helicopter.

"I think I saw a flash! They've fired a missile after us," warned Abelord. "Erica, get ready. Lonnie, hard starboard!"

With both pilot and co-pilot muscling it, the transport helicopter turned sharply to the right. The missile overtaking it immediately altered course to follow the maneuver. Against the cold backdrop of the ocean's surface the exhaust pipes of the turboshaft engines practically glowed to the infrared seeker head in the SAM-7. Travelling at more than five times its target's speed, it reached proximity distance just as the Sikorsky turned again.

The tail swung into a direct line with the missile, which the proximity fuse read as being much closer than the main body of the aircraft and instantly detonated the warhead. The explosion ripped the blades off the tail rotor and the stabilizer from the tail boom. With no way to counteract the torque created by the main rotor, the helicopter's fuselage began spinning in the same direction as the rotor.

"Get out! Get out, pull the hatch!" Abelord shouted. "Jump now! Don't wait for the crash!"

Erica kicked the rescue package at her feet over to the woman next to her and unlocked her seat belt. In spite of the increasing centrifugal force she managed to stand and reached out for the side hatch. She took hold of its red lever, tugging it with both hands.

With a sharp crack, the starboard hatch was released from its frame. The moment it was free, it sailed away from the spinning helicopter like a discus being launched by an athlete. Still holding onto its emergency lever, Erica let out a surprised cry and disappeared with the hatch. The woman who had been sitting beside her was ejected through the opening next, clutching the package she had just picked up. Then the doomed aircraft hit the water.

The remnants of the tail boom dug into the waves first, snapping it off from the rest of the fuselage like a dry branch and flipping the helicopter on its side. The main rotor blades struck next, each disintegrating on impact and creating hundreds of shards moving at nearly the speed of sound. Most skittered across the ocean's surface, others sliced through the Sikorsky's fuselage; killing or maiming anyone unfortunate enough to be in their path. Abelord was decapitated by a rotor blade shard the length of his arm. He died before his machine completed its destruction. Next to him, Lonnie was already unconscious. He would never feel the water filling his lungs.

When the fuselage itself hit the water, the force of the impact tore it open and wrenched seats out of their floor mounts. The Sikorsky disappeared in a fountain of sea spray. After the missile hit there were no fires, no explosions. A few seconds later nothing more could be seen of the helicopter by the people on *Ocean Valkyrie*.

"You animal! You bastard! Why did you order this?" Reitan demanded. "Why did you force me to witness it?"

"To demonstrate how we'll deal with any interference," said Nazal, his voice as cold as the wind swirling around him. "We'll not tolerate, I'll not tolerate, any resistance by you or your crew. Control them, Captain. For your sake, for their sake, I hope they listen to you. Take him below, Kaniel."

It took a little prodding from the muzzle of an AKM rifle to get Reitan to move off the helipad. After he left, only Nazal and the other leaders remained.

"This demonstration can cause us problems, Abu," said Yussuf Gunni. "It could make these people eager for revenge. Probably there are already rumors circulating about it. What will we do?"

"Let them spread, my friend," Nazal replied. "The way we'll control these people is by fear. If they know how ruthless we are, no matter how they hate us, they'll be reluctant to resist us. How else can we control them? We're only two dozen—they are several hundred. Don't worry, Yussuf, it will work."

* * *

At first Nordsen thought the screaming and wild gyrations were part of a carnival ride. He wondered what had happened to the helicopter and why they would do this to a wounded man? It wasn't until the Sikorsky crashed into the North Sea did it break through his drug-induced dream that he was still on the aircraft.

The impact tore his stretcher off the seats it had been tied to; then the cold sea water hit Nordsen like an electric shock. It washed away the haze created by the drugs, and for the first time in an hour, he was thinking clearly. He realized there had been a crash and his only thought was to survive.

Nordsen was still bound to the stretcher by one of its straps. As the helicopter's fuselage sank below the waves he dug at the strap's buckle until it loosened, allowing Nordsen to kick himself free of the stretcher and the blanket covering him.

He rose through murky water thick with debris. Jagged scraps of metal cut him and tore at his clothing; he had a constant fear of being caught and trapped in a larger piece of wreckage. He had the sickening feeling some of the things he pushed out of his way were the bodies of his crewmates. He broke through the surface, gasping for air, and getting a mouthful of spray.

For a time, Nordsen didn't know how long, he foundered in the storm-swept sea. The numbness induced by drugs was quickly replaced by numbness created by exposure. He felt reality slipping from his grasp again when gentle hands took hold of him and pulled him into a life raft.

"This is Falcon Zero-Four to Rest Stop One, our tanks read eighty-five percent. Ready to disengage, over."

"Roger, Zero-Four. Terminating fuel flow. Good luck, you guys. Rest Stop, out."

A brief trail of white mist spurted from the wave-shaped bump above the C-130's cockpit. The door to the refueling receptacle snapped shut as the probe withdrew, then the massive, winged boom swung back into its stowed position. The KC-135 surged ahead of the Hercules before it had finished the clean-up of its refueling gear. Its pilots had been hanging the tanker too close to its stall speed for too long and wanted a more comfortable flight regime. By the time its boom was tucked safely under its tail, the KC-135 was several miles ahead of the Combat Talon and several thousand feet above it.

"Cutting back to cruise speed," said the transport's pilot, Major Philip Ratz, as he retarded the throttles on the center control pedestal. "Pilot to tactical. Fuel transfer complete. Have you made contact with our escorts?"

"Roger, Phil. Contact established and they've raised us visually. With the tanker departing we'll advise the escorts to make their rendezvous. Mr. Adir, if you'll do us the honors?"

Captain Nathan Hynek, commander of the Combat Talon's Electronic Intelligence and Electronic Countermeasures teams, offered a headset and microphone to the civilian seated next to him, the only civilian in the cramped, dimly lit box on the C-130's cargo deck.

"I would be honored," said Adir, accepting the headset but not slipping it over his ears. "However, I'm just intelligence, Major Shoham and Captain Eshel are air force. They know better than I how to talk to the fighters. So, if you'll please . . ."

Adir finally slid the headset on in time to hear Captain Yehuda Eshel make contact with the approaching flight of Israeli Air Force F-15s.

"Gidi Lead, Gidi Lead. This is Falcon Zero-Four," said Eshel. "Refueling completed, Gideon. You may bring your avirons in."

"Roger, Zero-Four," replied a voice on the compartment loudspeakers. "We'll join your party once we separate from our friends."

Approaching the lone Hercules was a massed, ungainly formation of Russian and American fighters. Ever since crossing into Egyptian airspace the Israeli F-15s had had an escort of their own. On each side of the four massive, angular fighters was a flight of much smaller Egyptian Air Force Mig-21s. With the limited visibility even a clear night provided, the Migs did not maintain the same tight formations as the Eagles did.

Once they got the advisement to break off, the Egyptians dipped their wings to the Israelis then fanned out, splitting their formations and diving away to regroup at a lower altitude. In a few moments there were only the four F-15s still closing on the C-130.

"Falcon, this is Gidi Lead," said the commander of the F-15s, Lieutenant Colonel Caleb Ben Zion. "We'll complete the rendezvous in twenty seconds. Gidi Three, on my mark. Break."

As the Eagles swung in behind the Hercules, they divided into two pairs. Ben Zion and his wing man closed on the transport's left wing while the second set of jets, commanded by Gideon Three, closed on the right. They rapidly overtook their target, even though they were constantly retarding their throttles during the approach. But, almost exactly on their leader's time estimate the F-15s slid into their positions on the Combat Talons wing tips.

For a few minutes the formation maintained their altitude and direction. Then, on command from the Hercules, they dropped their left wings, changing their course by ninety degrees and diving until they were less than a thousand feet above the desert landscape. Even though they were still several hundred miles from the Libyan-Egyptian border, they were already preparing to penetrate it.

"Jake, where's Terry? The bitchbox told me to report forward," said Allard, magically appearing at the hatch to the radio room. "He got a priority message?"

Jake Hawkins jumped out of his chair and spun around with a start until he realized who his visitor was.

"Commander! Yes, yes he did," responded the black officer manning the console.

"It's a COMSUBLANT bulletin. The Captain said he was going to his quarters, and he called for Burks. Jesus, Commander, how'd you manage to sneak up on me?"

"Easy. You don't wear shoes or boots when you sleep. If I ever have to take over a sub, I'll do it in my socks. Thanks,

Jake."

Clad only in briefs, a T-shirt and heavy wool socks, Allard took a few more silent steps down the passageway and entered the *John Marshall*'s control center. Again, it was a moment or two before people became aware of him; there were a few who didn't notice Allard until he stepped through the hatch at the forward end of the center. Just beyond it he turned left and opened the door to the captain's cabin.

"Mister, where's your uniform?" Carver demanded, half seriously.

"My men ate it," said Allard. "Might take them awhile to realize I'm not in it. What's up, Terry? Jake says this message you got is a COMSUBLANT bulletin?"

"Greg, could you close the door? You can read it, but I can tell you what it says faster."

While Allard stepped forward to give Burks enough room to close the door, Carver handed him the priority-stamped tearsheet. He went on to explain its contents.

"A Norwegian terrorist group has hijacked an oil rig in the North Sea. They've issued a list of demands for cleaning the environment in Norway and they'll sink the rig if those aren't met, or if anyone tries to attack them."

"It's a semi-submersible rig," Allard noted, reading further into the bulletin. It's one of those big ones, half-football field and half-submarine. Looks like the British will do the negotiating instead of the Norwegians. The last line is a rather broad order. 'All special forces commands are to take whatever steps they deem necessary at this point, including the recall of personnel and prepositioning of resources,' "

"Yes, and I'm going to give it the broadest possible interpretation I can," said Carver. "I hope you're seeing what this means for us."

"I think I do . . . but I'd like to hear it straight from the horse's mouth."

"Fair enough. What we got here is one last gift for an old sailor. One last chance for a grand old Lady to have a new life. I also happen to have another transmission, from NATO." Carver held up a second tearsheet; its message wasn't as long as the first and it didn't have priority or classified stamped on it. "This is a weather report on the North Sea. A gale-force winter storm is settling over it, ruling out helicopters and surface ships to ferry in a commando team. The bulletin says a Royal Navy attack sub is speeding to the vicinity of *Ocean Valkyrie*. But it can't possibly have an elite force on it."

"However, we have," said Allard, handing back the bulletin. "But we're on the wrong side of the Atlantic and I only have half my force with me. I can guarantee you that's not enough to take an oil rig."

"We'll get more—our planning has only started. We have a lot to do in the next few hours. One factor working for us is we have no 'official' arrival time for Norfolk. We'll start contacting people on the other side of the Atlantic, a few friends of mine, and we'll get updates on the situation. We'll be nearing the surface soon. Hawkins is going to be very busy."

"Would one of your friends happen to be the captain of this British SSN? HMS *Spartan*."

"I'm not that lucky," said Carver. "Though I do have others. Of course you know I made a few a couple of years ago. They'll pull for us, but now we have to pull for ourselves. Greg, who have you talked to?"

"Doran, Patino and Seidel," said Burks, still standing behind Allard. "Faith, Hope and Charity. Weapons, propulsion and sonar. They should be ready for you in the TASCO room."

"Then let's go." Carver searched his tiny desk for an empty folder; when he found one he dropped the messages into it. "Glenn, see if you can get your uniform from your men, and report to the TASCO room in ten minutes. Let's make this last gift work."

"Frieda, how is he?" Erica asked, swimming back to the tiny, crowded raft. In spite of the fact that it was bright yellow, it proved nearly impossible for her to see it.

"Trig's not wearing a survival suit like we are!" said Frieda Gran, huddling closer to the raft's one other occupant. Because of the wind and the noise of sleet hitting the water she had to shout even though Erica was less than a foot away from her. "And he's bleeding! I think all his wounds were re-opened!"

"What equipment do you have?"

"Some flares, a signal light and a radio that doesn't work! We have no rations, no medicine supplies!"

"I'll get us some. I know where they are."

Erica looked past Frieda to the one collection of light in a world of blackness, noise and cold. *Ocean Valkyrie*. It stood ablaze in work lights, safety lights and anti-collision beacons. It was several seconds before Frieda Gran realized what her friend was really looking at.

"No, you can't go back!" she shouted. "It's too far, and those people control it!"

"It's not that far!" said Erica. "And there are rooms full of survival gear in each base leg! There were only a few terrorists and they can't guard everything!"

"Please, no! Climb in here and stay with us!"

"Frieda, this is too small for three of us! If we're to survive we need something bigger and more supplies! Take care of Trig and don't worry, I'll return! I promise!"

Erica waited until a wave pushed the raft up higher than normal before kicking away. She aimed for *Valkyrie* and dove across the wave's slope; hitting its trough before being picked up again by another wave in the increasingly chaotic sea. Almost at once Erica lost sight of the raft and her friends. Soon she was alone, battling numbness and a winter storm to reach the one oasis of humanity for dozens of miles. One controlled by people who wanted her dead.

Chapter Four

"Bring us up to periscope depth, Mr. Bryan. Reduce speed to five knots."

"Aye, Captain. Five knots it is. Fifteen degree up-angle on bow planes. We'll be at periscope depth in two minutes."

The senior helmsman pulled back his control yoke gently and watched the numbers change on his displays. Seated beside James Bryan, the second helmsman operated the propulsion controls. Behind them Captain Stanford Leigh Taylor watched them and the helm displays until HMS *Spartan* had trimmed out at sixty feet.

"Periscope depth, Captain," Bryan reported. "Bow planes, neutral. Buoyancy, neutral. Our heading is nine-four degrees and our speed is five knots."

"Thank you, Mr. Bryan. Sound room, report on any contacts. Mr. Holbrook, prepare the search 'scope."

Stepping back from the helm station, Taylor mounted the periscope stand where his executive officer, Jonathan Holbrook, was busy checking the controls to one of the attack submarine's two periscopes. As he waited, Taylor received an update from the sonar officer.

"Sound room here. We show no contacts on either active or passive arrays — save for the stadium-sized chunk of metal floating next to us."

"Understood, Mr. Greenway," said Taylor, returning the hand mike to its cradle. "Raise the 'scope, Johnnie."

"Shouldn't we go with the attack periscope first?" Holbrook asked. "It's smaller, and won't be spotted by

60

any lookouts."

"In this weather I doubt they've posted lookouts on the oil rig, and the night makes for an excellent cloak."

The whirr of motors resonated from the conning tower above the attack center. A slender tube rose out of the tower's roof and broached the roiling surface a few seconds later. Taylor swung down the periscope's handles and adjusted the eyepieces. Then he walked the 'scope, moving it slowly a full three hundred and sixty degree circle to visually check the surface.

"It's impossible to see anything," Taylor said finally. "Save for bloody *Valkyrie*—it's awash in light. I'm switching over to image enhancement and activating the monitor. I want you to help me, Johnnie."

On either side of the Barr and Stroud periscope, set above and below its handles, were panels of buttons for the systems tied into it. Taylor pressed the buttons for the low-light level TV camera and the television monitor on the periscope stand. When the image enhancement system came on line, the world he was trying to view changed from varying concentrations of black to shades to luminescent green. Taylor walked the periscope again, with his exec watching the same scene in a more expanded form on the monitor.

"Wait, Stan, wait!" Holbrook warned. "Back it up ten degrees. I saw something . . . like a raft."

"All right, let's see . . ." Taylor reversed his walk, then froze as he studied the area for several seconds. "You're right, it does look like a life raft. Switching to infrared."

The scene on the monitor, and in the periscope's eyepieces, changed again. Back to black but this time, near the middle of it, floated an amoeba-like mass of yellow and green. Something on the surface was giving off heat.

"It is a raft, and someone's in it," said Holbrook.

"Yes, and we better act immediately," said Taylor, picking up the hand mike. "Captain to wireless office. Priority signal to Admiralty. 'Have reached *Ocean Valkyrie,* have spotted survivors in water. Will effect rescue.' After you've sent that, contact the Nimrod again. Let's see if they have anything new."

* * *

For the last hour Gavrilla Eitan had been driving as fast as her car and the road conditions would allow; for the last half-hour she had been driving without headlights or running lights. She was deep in the Libyan desert, in an area called the Rebiano Sand Sea. To the south were the Tibesti Massif mountains, to the west lay the installation she was fleeing, while north and east was only more sand, more mountains.

Though the moon had yet to rise the night was clear, providing just enough light to allow Gavrilla to keep the car on the sand-swept strip of asphalt. Occasionally she would snap on a flashlight to check her odometer. When it reached a hundred and twenty kilometers over its original figure, she brought the car to a stop.

After shutting it down she climbed out, taking with her a backpack which had been sitting on the front passenger seat. Gavrilla dropped the flashlight into it and pulled out a compass and the Skoda automatic she had stolen earlier. She checked the weapon to make sure its clip was full, and used the compass to find the direction she had been ordered to take.

Her last actions before she abandoned the sedan were to lock all its doors and throw its keys as far into the night as she could. Gavrilla took one last look to the west, checking if any security or military forces were pursuing her, then charged into the desert on a south by southeast heading.

Not a light burned on that or any other horizon she scanned. Gavrilla was as alone as the stars glowing above her, yet her heart was pounding. Somewhere out in the silence and blackness, someone was indeed pursuing her. She prayed for her luck to hold. If it did, she would be rescued within the hour.

By the time she reached *Ocean Valkyrie*, Erica was exhausted and growing sick. She had swallowed too much salt water, and though a strong swimmer, had never done what she was doing now: crossing over a thousand yards of storm-lashed sea. And once she arrived, Erica found the rig in the midst of a storm heave.

The massive structure, with the displacement of an aircraft carrier, was a victim of the rhythmic rise and fall of storm generated waves. Though its vertical movement was only three feet, it proved almost impossible for Erica to surmount. As she neared the closest base leg she could feel a current pull her forward, then push her away.

If she wasn't careful the suction could easily pull her under the rig. Erica waited until *Valkyrie* had started to rise before swimming against the outrushing current. Swallowing more water, she grabbed the rungs of an exterior service ladder and hung on while the inrush swirled around her. It felt like being taken on a ride through an undertow, but when it stopped Erica began her next move.

She climbed the ladder as fast as her worn muscles and water-soaked clothes would allow her. She reached the exterior hatch on the base leg before the rig started to fall. The locking levers only gave when Erica put her weight on them; she nearly slipped off the ladder as the last one rotated and the hatch swung open.

Erica threw herself into the compartment, crying loudly as she landed hard on the steel floor. The jarring collision set off her stomach; she could feel its contents rise into her throat, and after a series of deep gasps she began to vomit.

A storm swell washed through the open entrance, temporarily flooding the compartment with a foot of water. Although the wave had spent most of its energy crashing against the rig, it had enough force to lift Erica and push her into the compartment's opposite wall. The impact stunned her, until she got the distinct sensation that her lungs were filling with fluid.

Erica was drowning, whether from the water and stomach contents she was throwing up or the water flooding the room; she didn't know or care. With great effort she raised her head above it and leaned against the wall. Then, suddenly, it was gone. The water drained back out the hatch, as if it had been sucked out by a vacuum. Erica stopped vomiting.

On unsteady legs she stood up, feeling along the wall until

she located an electric switch. When Erica hit the toggle a dazzling light blinded her. Having been in darkness for so long, even the modest illumination of the compartment work lights was painful. After her eyes became adjusted to the glare, she searched the compartment and quickly found its emergency equipment locker.

Its entrance wasn't a ship's-style hatchway, like the exterior hatch, but a simple door. When it swung open, Erica found all the gear and supplies she would need. Life rafts, exposure suits, medical kits, rations, drinking water. Most of it strewn on the floor. The shelves were never secured for the storm, so only a few of the heavier items remained on them.

"God, help me!" Erica cried, as she staggered into the tiny cubicle and stumbled over the boxes in the doorway.

She landed on top of the mess, a softer impact than before, and began sobbing. She tried to think of her friends; tried to think of the supplies they would need. But they seemed so distant and the task too insurmountable to contemplate. Everything seemed distant. A distant wave surged into the compartment and crashed against the locker door, slamming it shut.

Darkness overtook Erica Johensen. With her last reserves of strength sapped away by exhaustion and frustration, she lapsed in moments into a deep, coma-like sleep.

"Frieda, it doesn't hurt anymore," said Nordsen, his voice barely above a whisper, yet Frieda had pressed close enough to him to hear it.

"Trig, what doesn't hurt anymore?" Frieda asked, raising her voice and placing her hand on his face. "What, Trig? Tell me, is it your wounds?"

"No, the cold. I don't feel the cold anymore. Sorry to complain about it."

What she felt only confirmed Nordsen's answer. His face was ice cold. None of the sleet hitting it now was melting, and it had lost all of its color. Frieda realized he had reached an advanced stage of hypothermia. He wasn't shivering, he no longer felt the cold, yet was himself cold to the touch. Soon he would drop into a coma, and by morning would likely be dead. Frieda knew there was nothing she could do about it.

Even with her exposure suit, she could feel the disorienting effects of hypothermia. No longer certain of direction, she thought the storm was blowing the life raft in a circle. She saw lights where she knew there weren't any. And why was that one wave out of all the others following them?

"Rescue party, man the sail," ordered Taylor. "Captain to crew, rig for surface running. Johnnie, you have the con. Tell Radar and ECM I want to hear from them once I'm on the bridge."

Wearing a heavy winter jacket and carrying a Starlight scope, Taylor started up the access ladder after the team of seamen dressed in wet suits. They left the warm, comfortable world of the *Spartan's* attack center and entered the cold dark one of its conning tower.

Condensed moisture ran down the sides of the tower's compartments. Voices, the clinking of equipment and the stamp of Taylor's shoes on the ladder rungs echoed in the structure. That, plus the increased wallowing, were sure signs of the submarine having broached the surface.

The first compartment in the tower was the largest and here the rescue detail gathered; Taylor ascended through the increasingly smaller ones above it until he was unlocking the roof hatch to the flying bridge. The moment it opened, sleet and sea water sprayed him, causing Taylor to zip up his jacket and discard his wheel cap before climbing onto the bridge.

"Captain to rescue party, I've spotted the raft," said Taylor, using the telephone handset at the bridge's com station. "It's on the port side, deploy immediately and begin retrieval. I'm raising the safety lines, activating exterior lights."

From their recessed wells in the attack sub's upper casing, twin sets of guard rails popped into view in front of and behind the squat conning tower. On the tower itself fore and aft emergency floods snapped on and bathed the upper hull in a subdued red light. Apart from *Ocean Valkyrie,* HMS *Spartan* was the only island of illumination on the North Sea.

"Spread out and attach your lifelines to the cleats, gentlemen!" shouted the rescue detail commander. "No one enters the water until your line is secured!"

The first man to emerge from the hatch on the conning tower's port side, the commander, moved forward and grabbed hold of the nearest guard rail. Just ahead of the tower he stooped and pushed open a hinged panel in the hull. Beneath it was a ship's cleat, which he pulled up until it locked in place. He hooked his line to it. The other men coming out of the tower did the same thing, or moved aft and deployed more cleats. After half a minute the detail was ready to start their rescue.

"Jones, Slater, time to go in!" said the commander. "Grab the raft and we'll try to pull all of you back!"

Sliding over the guard rails, the tethered divers plunged immediately into the wind-whipped seas. The moment they went in, Taylor pulled out a stopwatch and clicked it. He looked up at *Ocean Valkyrie,* and scanned it with the Starlight scope. To the naked eye the rig appeared as little more than a geometric array of lights. In the scope, the night was stripped away and the massive structure loomed ominously close to the submarine.

Unfortunately, the scope lacked the magnification capability to allow Taylor to see the detail he wanted. None of its personnel were visible and no movement could be seen. Taylor hoped it meant the storm had already grown too severe for the terrorists to mount a watch. When he switched to the life raft, the divers had almost reached it.

"I can't believe — are you real?" Frieda asked, when two dark shapes moved close enough for her to identify them as men.

"Quite real, madam!" said the diver closest to her. "We're Royal Navy! Are either of you wounded?"

"I'm not, but Trig is. And I can't wake him."

"All right, we'll take everything in. Jones, go to the other side and give your line a snap. We'll steer. Let the others do the bull work."

* * *

"Captain, they've signalled to be hauled in!" said the commander, using a megaphone so his words would carry to the flying bridge.

"Retrieve them as fast as you can," Taylor replied, switching his communications station to external speakers. "We've been almost five minutes on the surface already."

The balance of the rescue detail took hold of the divers' safety lines and, on command, began reeling in the nylon ropes. At first the retrieval went smoothly. The raft and divers slid down the back slope of a retreating wave; causing the lines to go slack and making work easy for those on the submarine.

Then, a wave paralleling *Spartan's* course picked up the raft, raising it more than a dozen feet. The lines snapped taught, threatening to wrench the divers away from the raft and actually pulling one of the retrieval men over the guard rail. For a time, helping him back onto the upper casing took precedence over the rescue operation.

"Captain, the men need more light!" the commander advised. "Request permission to fire star shells!"

"Request denied. No more illumination than what we have now!" said Taylor. "We're taking too great a risk as it is. A half-blind destroyer captain could see us in this weather!"

A moment later the chaotic sea created another wave which pushed the raft, virtually throwing it at the *Spartan*. It closed to within fifty feet before an opposing wave crashed over the submarine and nullified the first with an audible clap. For a second the raft was almost at the same height as the bridge on the conning tower; Frieda even caught a fleeting glimpse of Taylor. Then it dropped back to nominal sea level.

There the raft and the divers guiding it remained for several moments, unable to move forward effectively until the men on *Spartan* had collected the slack in the lines. Suddenly, it started to drop below the *Spartan's* upper casing. The raft was caught in the trough of an approaching wave, a wall of water discernible in even the conning tower's weak light.

"Frieda, hold onto your friend!" warned one of the divers. "This will be dicey!"

The life raft picked up momentum as the wave overtook it, slamming it into the attack sub's cylindrical hull. The velocity wasn't great but the force of the impact was enough to eject both Frieda and Nordsen from the raft. She tried to hold onto him and swim for the surface at the same time. But he was unconscious and his waterlogged clothes made him much heavier. The thought of drowning with Nordsen panicked Frieda, until strong hands took him from her and carried him to the surface. A hand took hold and guided her as well; after swimming upward a few feet she broke through the surface where more hands waited for her.

"Rescue party, over the side," said Taylor, his free hand on the com station's control buttons. He pressed one for the internal public address system. "Medical Team, to the sail. Survivors coming aboard. Attack center, standby to submerge."

Despite the fact that most of the men were busy with Nordsen, Frieda was the first to make it onto the submarine. She could barely stand upright, and really didn't have time to. While someone guided her, a hatch opened in front of her and immediately she was pulled inside.

In the conning tower's lower compartment the medical team wrapped Frieda in a blanket and helped her down the ladder. By now the effects of exhaustion and exposure to the storm were taking their toll. To Frieda, her descent to the *Spartan's* attack center felt like a freefall. By the time she reached it, she collapsed unconscious into awaiting arms.

"Attack center to bridge. Both survivors are aboard, Captain," Holbrook reported. "Rescue party and medical team are secured. The sail is secured and we're awaiting orders."

"Exterior lights, off. Guard rails, retracted," said Taylor, running down the control panels at the bridge. "And the anchoring cleats are stowed . . . crash dive, Johnnie. We've been ten minutes on the surface and that's too long for us."

Taylor dropped the receiver back on the com station's cradle and sealed its cover. He felt a familiar rumble shake his boat. The ballast tanks were being opened and the air vented out. In minutes it would return to its true home, which gave Taylor just enough time for one last look at *Ocean Valkyrie*.

In darkness, and without the Starlight scope to help his vision, the oil rig was a phantom-like collection of light. Threatening, ominous, surrealistic in the way it stood motionless on a storm-tossed sea while the submarine pitched and rolled. It was enemy territory, and would be a mystery to him until the people his crew had rescued could speak.

"Terry, latest messages from *Gato* and *Courageous*," Burks announced, handing Carver a pair of tearsheets.

"Excellent, we're clear at least as far as *Courageous* for a Sub-scape run," said Carver, as he read what he was given. "Helm, standby to take us down. Let's see if David's got anything new. Sonar room, what's your report?"

"Captain, this is sonar. The way ahead is clear."

"Roger, keep pinging until we commence our run. Clarence, take us down, five hundred feet and steer zero-four-zero degrees, true. Captain to crew, standby for Sub-scape run."

"Helm is answering, Captain. Steering zero-four-zero degrees," replied Clarence Jefferson, the *John Marshall's* senior helmsman. "Flooding forward trim tanks. Speed, ten knots."

The massive submarine, more than four hundred feet long, turned and maneuvered like an aircraft. As it swung onto its final north-northeast heading, its bow dropped several degrees. It descended from a standard periscope depth of sixty feet to almost six hundred. At ten knots, just under twelve miles an hour, it took the *John Marshall* several minutes to reach its new depth — time in which her crew made the final preparations for the Sub-scape run.

"Terry, I've taken an account of my unit," said Allard, joining the officers around Carver. "And the news isn't good. I have at best only half the number of men needed to take the rig, and almost none of the equipment to do it. I hope your friend in England can supply us with what we need."

"You mean Robert Boyd? Yes, his SBS unit will have

69

everything you'll need," said Carver. "I sent *Courageous* a message to relay to him. By the time we reach them, they should have an answer for us."

"Have you received a reply on your message to Norfolk?"

"No, Hawkins just sent it out. It was the last transmission he made before retracting the aerials. In addition to decoding it, it'll probably take the brass ashore a little while to decipher what I meant by 'responding to COMSUBLANT request to preposition special forces resources.' By the time they understand it, I hope the British will have requested us. Clarence, what's our situation?"

"We're at ninety-three fathoms," said Jefferson, scanning the readouts at the helm station. "Five hundred and sixty feet. Our heading is zero-four-zero degrees, true. Our speed is ten knots. We have neutral buoyancy. Engine room is answering, all speeds are available. Including Sub-scape setting."

"Good. Greg, man the Sub-scape panel," Carver ordered, as he picked the hand mike off the periscope stand again. "Captain to sonar room. What's your report, Dave?"

"We have no contacts, either fore or aft," said Seidel. "We're clear to begin our run."

"Activate laser radar and thermal imagers. Keep pinging until you lose efficiency. Dominic, what's reactor status?"

"Our 'museum piece' is ticking like a fine old watch," said Dominic Patino, the *Marshall*'s propulsion officer. "Full power is available at your command."

"Good, head back to nucleonics and keep an eye on it," said Carver. "Greg, what's your status?"

"All nozzle rings have been deployed. Primary and secondary pumps are ready," said Burks, standing at the control center's safety station. On the open panel was a top-view silhouette of the *John Marshall*, striped with glowing, bright green bars. The Submarine Escape System (SES) had been activated. "All polymer tanks are full."

"Captain, laser scanning and thermal imagers are on line," Jefferson advised. Additional screens at the helm station had come to life. "We're clear fore and aft."

"Terry, doesn't the navy frown on the use of Sub-scape in

anything less than an emergency situation?" said Allard.

"But it's captain's discretion as to what constitutes an emergency," Carver replied, grinning slyly. "And I say this situation is an emergency. Using Sub-scape will cut our transit time across the Atlantic in half. Anything which gets us there faster is better for everyone. If it all works out, the navy won't care what toy I used. If it doesn't, they'll have worse charges than this to hang my black ass over—and likely everyone else here. If I haven't said it before, thank you for your loyalty. Mr. Burks, activate the system and give the call."

"Thanks, Terry. Tank valves, open. Primary pumps, on," said Burks, flipping toggle switches on the panel. Then, turning to the helmsmen. "Mr. Sulu, warp factor one."

As the pumps came on, the rings of tiny nozzles in the *John Marshall*'s hull sprayed a colorless, jelly-like substance. The water-soluble polymers quickly covered its massive hull with an even coat, cutting friction with the surrounding water to zero.

At the same time, Jefferson and the second helmsman called for flank speed from the engine room. Already moving at ten knots, the ancient missile sub had almost reached twenty before the polymer film achieved peak coverage, and peak efficiency. If the *Marshall* had been an aircraft, the effect was like kicking in afterburners.

Speed immediately jumped to thirty-five knots, causing anyone who had been standing to grab hold of something bolted down for support. Yet there was no increase in engine noise and, as velocity increased, the ride smoothed out. Past forty knots the submarine was moving as if it were on a sheet of glass.

By then even the passive sonar arrays were no longer effective and had been shut down. For now the *John Marshall* would have to rely on its three-dimensional laser radar and infrared thermal imagers, short-range systems only. She was also deaf, and would not be able to communicate with the outside world until it reached HMS *Courageous* and slowed down. Even at its final cruising speed of more than sixty miles an hour, that was several hours away.

71

"Samad, why isn't Yussuf here?" asked Nazal the moment he entered *Ocean Valkyrie*'s operations center. "I called this meeting for all strike force leaders."

"He knows, but Hans Sivertsen and the other Norwegian demanded to meet with us," said Jassem. "Mr. Sivertsen appears to think we really do consider him a leader of our unit. He abandoned his post at communications and is coming here, leaving Yussuf to talk with the Norwegians and the British."

"Which means they now know there are Arabs in this supposedly 'Norwegian' environmental group. Sivertsen is ruining things for us. He's destroying our cover! Why is he coming here? Do you know?"

"Yes, it's the downing of the helicopter. Apparently our Norwegian friends have consciences. I think the killings have made them realize our goals aren't their goals."

"Then they have ceased being useful to us." Nazal pulled a Baretta automatic from his shoulder holster and flipped the safety off. "They're surplus to our operation."

He admired the weapon for a moment, then returned it to his holster as Hans Sivertsen and Jan Tunheim entered the operations center through the interior service entrance. Like most everyone else, they had since stripped off their winter coats and appeared even taller than their Arab cohorts. They ignored the greetings from the center's guards and went directly to Nazal and Jassem.

"I take it you've been talking with your country's authorities?" Nazal asked.

"Yes, and the British too," said Sivertsen, trying to hide his anger with a courteous answer. He didn't succeed for long. "They've all asked me about *Valkyrie*'s rig crew, are there any wounded and about the helicopter. What should I tell them? How you killed the wounded by shooting down the helicopter? We're environmental liberationists, not murderers! You've killed nearly forty people! How do you expect us to have a purified land with so much blood on our hands!"

"Why did you find it necessary to kill the wounded?"

Tunheim added. "What purpose was served in doing so?"

"To borrow a western phrase, we killed two birds with a single stone," said Nazal. "And your goals were never ours. You should've stayed where I told you to stay. I wanted the authorities to believe this was purely a Norwegian action for as long as possible. You ruined that! You've ceased being important to this operation."

Deliberately, Nazal pulled his automatic again and levelled it at Sivertsen. Both he and Tunheim reacted as if they had been hit by electric shocks; their bodies spasmed as they jumped away from Nazal. Only Sivertsen had the presence of mind to draw the gun he had in his belt holster.

"Hans, we gave you those weapons," said Nazal, a hint of laughter in his voice. "Do you think we'd give either of you a loaded one? The bullets in your clips are imitations. Still, this almost makes it a challenge."

Sivertsen jerked back the slide on his Walther automatic, cocking it. When he pulled the trigger there was a metallic snap, nothing else. He had to work the slide again to recock the weapon, an action he never completed before Nazal's Baretta emitted a flat, deafening bark. The Walther PK flew out of Sivertsen's hands, almost as if he had tossed it away, and he was blown against the center's dehydration control console.

Jan Tunheim made marginally better use of the pistol he had been given; he threw it at Nazal before turning to flee.

"Abu, he's getting away!" Jassem shouted.

"Asir, Moussa. Hunt him down and kill him," said Nazal. "I'll deal with this one."

The nine millimeter slug had hit Sivertsen in the chest and torn through his left lung. While his wound didn't bleed heavily, his breathing was labored and painful. Sivertsen barely had the strength to pull himself off the console, let alone make an attempt to run. When he raised his head he found Nazal standing only a few feet away from him.

"Edda. Edda . . ." Sivertsen gasped, blood starting to trickle over his lips.

"You will join her, Hans. I can assure you," said Nazal. "She was dead the moment we left the island. So are the rest of your friends."

The Baretta exploded again, and a second bullet struck Sivertsen in the chest. This time it punctured his heart, causing a brief geyser of blood to spurt from the wound. He gave a strangled cry, and grabbed the edge of the console to maintain his balance. Sivertsen tried for as long as he could to stand, to meet Nazal's gaze with his eyes, but he quickly sagged to the floor. After a final series of spasms he died, his blood spreading out to meet the dried patches of what had already been spilled in the operations center. A few moments later Nazal and Jassem heard the reassuring chatter of automatic weapons fire.

"It is done," said Nazal, a grim smile on his face. "We're rid of our wild cannons."

"I think the term is 'loose cannons,' my friend," Jassem replied. "We've also lost our cover. It will not take the authorities long to realize they're not dealing with a Norwegian environmental group. What will we do then?"

"Nothing, Samad. It's already too late for the British or Norwegians to do anything." Nazal turned and swept his hand past the center's observation windows. "Do you not see it? Do you not feel it under our feet? The storm is at its full force. Even if the elite forces could mount an operation, they wouldn't. And even though we haven't heard from any military officials, I know NATO elite forces are on alert. But they cannot try anything until the storm dies down. We can do the injection of the bio-weapon in a matter of hours. If we keep to our plan, we'll do it at the tail end of this storm and be off *Valkyrie* by the time the military arrives."

"How long will the storm last?"

"This is the latest weather report from England's Royal Meteorological Office." Nazal walked over to the printer station and picked a sheet of paper out of its arrivals tray. He held it out to Jassem, who immediately accepted it. "The forecast says this storm will remain at gale strength for the next forty-eight hours. For that time we'll have little to worry about. Conditions are too severe for a helicopter landing or a surface ship assault. And no single submarine can transport enough commandoes to take this rig from us."

"Then what are we to do until the storm has weakened enough for us to inject the bio-weapon?" Jassem asked. "Just sit?"

"Valkyrie has been secured for rough weather and severe sea state conditions. We're in no danger there. We must select the rig workers we'll use on the operation, and lay the scuttling charges. Abdelgalil and Kaniel Akkad are taking inventory of this rig's demolition explosives. We know there's a large stock, but it will have to be carefully placed and wired to ensure *Valkyrie* will sink, and sink quickly. We must ensure there are no survivors, and no trace of us for anyone to find. When Yussuf arrives, we'll decide how best to do it."

She was near exhaustion, and when she stopped to check the time again, Gavrilla dropped to her knees. Her watch indicated she had been running for almost forty minutes. Whether she had run three miles or thirty she didn't know or care. What Gavrilla did know is that when she straightened up and looked back over her shoulder, she no longer saw her car or the road she left it on. It was time to signal her rescuers.

Gavrilla loosened her backpack and let it fall from her shoulders. She unzipped its top flap and pulled from it a transistor radio. With its antenna deployed, all she had to do was press in the tuning dial to transmit an omni-directional signal on alternating frequencies—a signal only specially adapted receivers would be able to detect and interpret.

"Sirat Hatzalah," said Gavrilla, in between gasps for air. "Let's see what they've sent for me."

"Tactical to pilot, we got a pickup signal," advised Nathan Hynek. "Tyrone, you got a range and bearing yet?"

"Affirmative," said the black Lieutenant sitting two seats down from Hynek. Tyrone Walker had the numbers glowing on readouts in front of him but he turned to one of the Israelis instead of immediately giving them. "C'mon, Slow-Mo, is this your guy or not?"

"It should be—the encryption coding is for the agent we're

to retrieve," said Major Shoham, watching his own display. "It's her transmitter we've detected."

"Range, thirty-five point three miles. Bearing is Two-Nine-One degrees. Nate, at our current speed we'll be there in just over seven minutes."

"Thanks, Ty," said Hynek. "Tactical to pilot, we got a new course for you. Captain Eshel, contact our escorts."

"Lieutenant, why do you insist on calling me 'Slow-Mo'?" asked Shoham. "My name is *Shlomo* Ben Shoham. What is this Slow-Mo? Is this what is meant by Comment Officer? I thought you were just to warn us of enemy threats?"

"Hey. Be cool, man," said Walker, raising his hands. "Sooner or later we all get nicknames here."

"Major . . . it's just an American custom," Adir added. "They mean nothing by it. It's just their version of informality. But I must admit it is appropriate for you, Shlomo. You have been a little slow on responding. Pay his prickliness no mind, Lieutenant. We sabras tend to act this way with outsiders."

"Pilot to tactical, changing course to Two-Nine-One degrees. I want an update on Libyan defenses and order two of our escorts to precede us to the recovery area and check it visually. Pilot to loadmaster, prepare for STAR drop."

The Combat Talon banked gently to the right, changing to a more northerly heading. The F-15s still hanging on its wing tips repeated the maneuver perfectly, not moving from their positions until after they had leveled out. Then, the fighters on the C-130's left wing opened their throttles and surged ahead.

"Gidi Lead to Zero-Four," said Ben Zion. "Increasing speed to five hundred miles an hour. Our ETA is four minutes, twenty seconds."

Freed at last from several hours of tight, slow formation flying, Ben Zion and his wing man separated and opened up the distance between them by several hundred feet. As they flew ahead to survey the recovery site, the remaining pair of F-15s also separated. Gideon Three left his wing man on the right side of the MC-130E and slid across its top, eventually taking the position vacated by the lead fighters.

76

"Gidi Lead to Zero-Four, we have a bogey. Distance, thirty miles from our position. It's at low altitude and moving slowly. It does not appear to be aware of us."

"Colonel, the helicopter reports it has found a car ahead of us," said the scout car's radio operator. "The crew would like to know if you want them to land?"

"Negative, no landing," said Nazih. "Tell them not to even get near the ground. I don't want their rotorwash to obliterate any details. Advise the rest of the column."

Sitting in the scout car's gunnery chair, Nazih easily reached up and opened the turret's roof hatch. Poking his upper body into the night air, he spotted the Alouette III a mile ahead of his vehicle, orbiting slowly, its spotlight beam playing on a dark-colored sedan. Behind him, Nazih checked on the rest of his convoy: a collection of Soviet trucks, Italian panel vans and another Brazilian Cascavel scout car like his own.

"We've found what we're after," he continued. "Hadami, tell the column to establish a standard perimeter and search pattern when we stop."

The helicopter continued to circle the abandoned car, never dropping below three hundred feet. As he approached it, Nazih activated the Cascavel's turret and aimed the twenty millimeter cannon at the sedan. Since their turnover to internal security forces, the EE-9 scout cars had been 'down-gunned' from their original ninety millimeter weapons.

Nazih kept the gun trained on its target even after it was apparent the car was empty. His vehicle came to a stop some fifty feet from it. The moment the trucks and vans behind him stopped, troops poured from them to surround the area. The Alouette backed off to a higher altitude, to lessen the noise level and increase the ground covered by its searchlight.

"Colonel, the car is locked," said an officer walking back to the lead Cascavel. "We see no keys and cannot get inside."

"Zionist bitch, she knows how to anger me," said Nazih, climbing down from the scout car's turret. "Smash one of its windows, Captain. Lieutenant, bring the prisoner forward."

As Nazih walked up to the sedan, one of the officers he talked to ran back to the convoy. He stopped at a van and waited until a man in handcuffs had been dragged from it by security guards. By the time they returned, Nazih was personally leading the inspection of the sedan.

"No, idiots! Smash a side window, not the rear one!" he shouted. "Before opening the door, check it for wires or anything suspicious near it. The whore may have boobytrapped it. Stanmeer, have you keys for this?"

"No, Gabrielle had the only ones," said the geneticist, staggering, trying to shield his eyes from the glaring spotlight. "Ahmad, why have I been arrested? What have I done? What has Gabrielle done? Your men told me nothing. They've hit me!"

"Worse will happen to you. Your French whore is a Zionist spy! You've betrayed and endangered this operation!"

"Betrayed? I've created the organism for you. I did everything I promised. How can Gabrielle be an Israeli? She's French! You cleared her to come with me. You're paranoid about the Israelis, always have been."

"We had to allow the whore in, if we were to get you," said Nazih, stepping away from the abandoned sedan as a side window was smashed and soldiers opened the doors. "Since we have the bacteria culture, our own scientists can care for it. You're no longer needed."

Deliberately, he drew a Skoda automatic and pulled back its slide. The guards on either side of Stanmeer withdrew, causing him to glance nervously at the men around him. Then his eyes returned to Nazih; the look on his face was like that of a trapped animal.

"Ahmad? Colonel, please!" Stanmeer cried, his gaze dancing between Nazih's stern face and the gun in his hand. "Don't! I can't understand, we share the same goals. We want a clean environment, you told me so! I believed you!"

"Yes, and how easy it is to seduce you environmentalists," said Nazih. "Say the right words, the right phrases, and you do anything that's asked. I wonder if American environmentalists will be as easy as you?"

Stanmeer gave a whimpering cry and turned to run. Because his arms were handcuffed behind him, he stumbled off-balance in his turn and nearly fell before picking up his stride. Nazih kept the gun levelled on him but waited until Stanmeer broke successfully into a run before pulling the trigger.

The flat barks of the automatic caused all conversations and activity around the car to stop. The first bullet punched Stanmeer in the back, striking the right shoulder blade and deflecting down into his liver. The second struck him lower in the back, where his kidneys were located. The third missed him entirely, kicking up a spurt of sand in the desert beyond the road.

Stanmeer was falling, and crying, after the first bullet hit him. The impact of the second sent him tumbling hard to the road surface. He landed on his face and right shoulder, causing his nose and lower lip to bleed. His legs jerked spasmodically, but it was obvious Stanmeer was trying to get back on his feet.

Nazih took more careful aim and emptied the rest of his Skoda's clip at the dying scientist. But the rapid succession of muzzle flashes blinded him and only two of his shots hit Stanmeer; when Nazih was through, he still cried weakly.

"Finish him!" he said, turning angrily to the Captain who waited at his side. "Yes, what is it?"

"Colonel, we found a single track of foot prints leaving the area," said the Captain. "Heading to the south."

"Take a squad with you and capture her. Alive, Captain, alive! Order the helicopter to follow the track, and to arm its weapons. We're within helicopter range of Egypt, Sudan and Chad. Our machine can deal with whoever's out there to rescue her."

After being in silence for so long, the sudden burst of distant noises startled Gavrilla. First there was a soft popping, which she immediately recognized as helicopter rotor blades; then came the gun shots. Single, echoing, cracks with a brief chatter of automatic weapons fire. Less than a minute later came a deep rumble like a far away thunder storm. But it was sustained, and came from a different direction than the earlier noises. Not being able to see what was causing them raised Gavrilla's anxiety. She wished she could see something, anything, until she noticed two shadows rapidly approaching her.

They moved so fast it was all Gavrilla could do to keep track of the movement and not lose the aircraft in the shadows. Instead of trying to hide, she froze, and suddenly they were on top of her, climbing steeply and producing a shock wave of thunder. Immediately after them came a ripple-like tearing as the air superheated by turbofan engines cooled and condensed.

The shock wave knocked Gavrilla on her back. It had stunned her, and by the time she recovered the fighters were high above her and looping onto their own backs. She watched them, still frozen by the terror until her aircraft recognition training kicked in and she identified the twin tail fins, the broad, angular wings and needle-like nose. The Eagles had arrived.

"This is Gidi Lead to Zero-Four," said Ben Zion. "We're at the recovery area and we can see only one person. As you Americans would say, 'everything looks kosher.' "

"Roger, we are go for retrieval. Watch it, Gidi Lead. Passive jamming doesn't work too well when you climb and give them an obvious radar target."

"Roger, Zero-Four. We're still tracking the bogey. We'd like an update."

"Your unknown is an Alouette Three. Radar shows it has possible external weapons and ESM confirms it is in contact with ground forces. You're cleared to neutralize it."

"Roger, Zero-Four. Gidi Two, it's mine. Weapons, armed."

As his F-15 bottomed out of its loop, Ben Zion tapped the master arming switches on his weapons' panel. The armament schematic immediately changed its status lights from green to red. With the touch of a button on his control stick, he selected his quartet of AIM-9M Sidewinders. The moment he did so, Ben Zion got a target lock growl on his headphones. All he had to do was check his HUD, or head-up display, to confirm the lock was on the distant group of lights, before he launched a Sidewinder.

The huge fighter slowed perceptibly as the missile burned away from its starboard pylon. Ben Zion rolled and turned sharply to the right as his wing man swung to the left. They did so as much to avoid being blinded by the Sidewinder's tail fire, as not to overrun the target, which was advancing toward them.

"Ground Control, this is One-Seven. We just saw a flash of light ahead of us," advised the Alouette's pilot. "I estimate five hundred to a thousand feet in altitude. We think the Zionist has put up a flare to signal the rescue plane. All weapons are armed."

The pilot reached forward and activated his gun sight. On a panel below it, lights confirmed the helicopter's rocket pods and machine guns were ready to be fired. Behind him and his co-pilot, door gunners manned an additional pair of light machineguns. When he turned to look at them, they signalled thumbs-up; then their world exploded.

The Sidewinder ran headlong into the Alouette, exploding less than ten feet in front of it. The warhead, more than twenty pounds of explosives and shrapnel, enveloped the helicopter in a globe of white light and ripped it apart. Its fuel tanks and ammunition detonated next, sustaining the fireball which could be seen for miles.

"What in heaven!" shouted Hadami, standing a little higher in the Cascavel's open hatch. "Colonel, I'm no longer receiving the helicopter."

"Zionist butchers. Give me a microphone!" said Nazih, reaching into the scout car himself to get the hand mike he wanted. "Captain—Captain Nader, the Israeli rescue force has landed and is obviously armed with heavy weapons. Advance and destroy them before they can escape! I'm sending one of the armored cars to help you."

* * *

Gavrilla was amazed by the aerobatics being performed around her. She watched one of the F-15s fire a missile then wheel away while its wing man broke in the opposite direction. The Sidewinder burned through the night sky like a comet and, once the screech of the jets had subsided, Gavrilla could hear it hiss like the snake it was named after.

The approaching helicopter vanished in a blossom of fire, though it was several seconds before the thunderclap of the explosion echoed across the desert. It had barely died out when it was overwhelmed by a deeper rumble, spreading over the desert from the opposite direction.

Gavrilla turned and caught sight of a C-130 with another pair of Eagles riding on its wing tips. They overflew her position at five hundred feet, low enough for her to see some detail on the aircraft even though they were not using exterior lights. The only lights Gavrilla saw was when the formation had passed overhead and she could see into the transport's fuselage; the loadmasters had left the cargo deck lights on.

A moment later a black container rolled off the tail ramp and a canopy of silk opened above it. In seconds it had landed in the sand behind her with a soft crunch; Gavrilla reached the package before the parachute had finished settling over it.

"Loadmaster to tactical, the STAR package is down!" said Ritter, standing in the open tail of the Hercules. "And our future passenger is opening it up!"

"Thanks, Marty. Secure from drop and prepare for aerial retrieval," said Hynek. "Tactical to pilot, reduce speed to two hundred knots and execute a right turn. Make it wide and slow. Maintain this altitude until we go in for the pickup."

"Nathan, you better check what I got on the low-lights," Ratz warned, as he chopped the throttles back, causing an audible drop in the buzzing of the C-130's four turboprops. "They also register on the FLIR."

Hynek immediately punched in the Low-Light-Level TV cameras and the forward-looking infrared sensors on console monitors. The image on each screen was identical, except one was black and white; tinted with green, and the other was a mixture of black, reds, yellows and blue. They both revealed the Libyan military convoy strung out on the distant road.

"Can anyone identify these vehicles?" asked Hynek. "They look like mostly trucks and vans."

"Except for those two," said Shoham, pointing at the vehicles at the front and back of the convoy. "They're armored cars, I think Brazilian Cascavels."

"That's enough of a threat for me. Major, order Gideon Lead to neutralize the convoy, especially the armored cars."

Shoham had just raised Ben Zion and his wing man when the cabin rocked gently to the right. The C-130 banked into its turn, barely dipping its wings out of line with the horizon. The F-15s escorting it easily repeated the maneuver while the first pair of Eagles reformed above and behind them.

Gavrilla unlocked the latches on the container's sides and, with a little effort, it split open along its raised seam lines. Inside she found a helium gas cylinder, a coil of nylon rope, a harness, air tubing, a helmet and underneath it all a large, neatly folded plastic bag. There was no instruction manual among the equipment and for a moment Gavrilla was confused until she noticed the stenciling on the helium cylinder: SHORT TAKEOFF AERIAL RETRIEVAL SYSTEM.

As memories of her training on the system washed over her, she grabbed the harness out of the container and slid it over her shoulders. She glanced up when the deep scream of turbofans heralded the return of the first jets to overfly her. The grey and black shadows roared past Gavrilla, a little lower and slower than they had the first time.

She watched them long enough to deduce they were heading in to attack the convoy. Then she sprinted out to where she left her backpack and scooped it up before continuing to deploy the STAR package.

"Gidi Lead to Gidi Two, take the lead armored car," said

Ben Zion, selecting the air-to-ground gunnery mode on his HUD. "I'll hit the other one. Right turn, zero-six-zero degrees."

The Eagles were almost on top of the road when they dipped their wings and swung sharply until they were in line with it. Ben Zion watched the glowing numbers on his HUD change as he swung his fighter through its tight maneuver. The gunnery circle below the numbers drifted, then corrected and centered on the vehicle moving away from the road and across the desert.

From the corner of his eye he caught sight of a bright yellow flare on his wing man's aircraft; he was opening fire ahead of his leader. An instant later Ben Zion stroked the trigger on his control stick. The Vulcan cannon buried in the F-15's right wing root erupted with a similar spurt of flame. The aircraft slowed and kicked to the right, but Ben Zion held it steady, watching the line of tracers arc out toward their target.

Nazih had just started walking back to the abandoned car when he saw the muzzle flashes appear in the night sky. He froze until the tracers streaked over his head and slammed into the Cascavel some fifty feet behind him. A storm of armor-piercing discarding sabot and high explosive incendiary shells lashed the scout vehicle as Nazih dove off the road.

Though they were just twenty millimeters, less than an inch in diameter, the cannon shells easily punched through the vehicle's thin armor plate. They found and ignited its ammunition supply and fuel tank. Anyone in or standing near the Cascavel was consumed by the resulting explosions. The shells continued to walk down the rest of the convoy, touching off more explosions in the vehicles they hit.

A hundred yards to the left, the second armored car lasted a few seconds longer than the first. Its turret was bringing its main gun to bear as another line of tracers stabbed out of the darkness. The concentrated burst of more than a hundred shells virtually shredded the remaining Cascavel. It disappeared in a fireball that could be seen for miles, and illuminated the Israeli fighters when they shot overhead. The largest remnants were the tires, burning furiously, and the turret, which crashed back to earth while the fireball was still boiling into the sky.

"Captain, what — what are we to do?" asked a member of the squad sent out earlier. "The Israelis have sent more than helicopters. They've sent jets!"

"Zionist butchers, they know what their agent has is valuable," said the Captain. "They haven't spotted us, or we would've been attacked by now. Corporal, are you receiving anything from the convoy?"

"No, sir. Only static," said the radio man. "What should we do?"

The squad was halfway between the wreckage of the convoy and the still burning remains of the helicopter. For a time they saw the attacking jets until the night sky swallowed up the grey shadows again. Below the roar of the turbofans the squad members could hear a deeper rumble: the noise of the C-130's turboprops. They were isolated, apparently surrounded by enemy forces, but their commander knew their quarry was within striking range.

"Continue. If we're lucky, we can still stop their agent," the Captain said in a level voice, until he realized his troops were reluctant to stir. "Move! You're part of Blood Revenge! The blood the Jews have spilled must be paid with their own!"

When she returned to the STAR container, Gavrilla strapped on her backpack and grabbed one end of the coiled rope. She hooked it through the eye on the back of the harness; then attached the opposite end to a web of lines connected to the plastic bag.

The helium cylinder was heavy and difficult for her to move; but she managed to drag it out of the container and attached the air tube to it. With a loud hiss, Gavrilla opened the cylinder's valve. The tubing became rigid and the bag into which the other end had been inserted began to expand.

The last thing she pulled from the container was the helmet, before the bag pinned it against the container's side. The noise of aircraft was omnipresent, though it took Gavrilla several moments to relocate the C-130 and its escorts. They were in the distance and had again become barely discernible shadows. But this time she knew they were out there and found them almost due south of her position.

"Roger, Gidi Lead. Break off attack and orbit at one thousand feet," Hynek ordered. "Tactical to pilot, deploy STAR system. Are you still monitoring the recovery area?"

"Yes, and our future passenger appears to be inflating the balloon," said Ratz. "She'll be ready in a couple of minutes. Reducing airspeed, deploying STAR system. Advise our escorts we'll be dropping close to their stall speed."

Ratz cut the throttles again, and watched the Israeli F-15s slide off his transport's wing tips and surge ahead. He reached for a side panel in the spacious cockpit, where he lifted the guard plates off a set of buttons. Pressing the first one enabled the aerial retrieval system. The second one started the motors which extended the STAR capture arms from their nose housings.

The Hercules rocked slightly as the arms protruded into the slipstream; partway through the deployment there was a loud clank when a housing in front of the cockpit opened and released the snare wires and cutting cord. In just over a minute the thirty-foot-long STAR arms were fully extended with a web-like array of wires stretched between them.

"It looks like our passenger's got the inflation process well under way," said Ratz's co-pilot, Captain Herb Goldberg. He was wearing night vision goggles and glancing repeatedly out the cockpit's right side. For the moment, Ratz was flying the Combat Talon alone. "I'm glad those fighters aren't on our wings anymore. Doing one of these grabs is always tricky and we need room to maneuver."

"Right, Herb. Let's hope the Israelis have neutralized all the threats in the area," said Ratz. "Flying low and slow isn't what I like doing in a combat zone."

As the bag filled with helium, it took on the form of a miniature barrage balloon. When it gained enough buoyancy the balloon popped out of the container half it had nestled in. Not fully inflated, it sagged and drifted with the desert wind until Gavrilla caught one of the tail fins and held it steady.

Half a minute later the balloon's skin was rigid to her touch. It tugged at the hose linking it to the helium tank, the only anchor keeping it on the ground. Gavrilla closed the tank valve and disconnected the hose; the moment the balloon was free it shot skyward. The hiss of its inflation was replaced with the whipping noise of the rope uncoiling.

Even though she watched the line play itself out, Gavrilla was still surprised by the sharp jerk it gave her when the balloon reached its full height. She stood at the base of a five-hundred-foot line with a glistening white teardrop floating above her. Both the balloon and the nylon rope were an almost luminescent white; even in dim light they practically glowed.

"Captain, look! It must be the Jew!" shouted the squad's point man; waving his hand at the balloon. He then wrapped both hands around his AK-47 and squeezed a long burst at the new target until he was pushed to his knees.

"Idiot! We're out of range," said the Captain, standing over the soldier. "No one else fire! It will only give us away to the agent. I've heard of this—it's some kind of American pickup device. The agent is attached to the line, she can't go anywhere. Keep running, we still have time."

"Pilot to tactical, the balloon is up," said Ratz. "We're heading in. Advise the fighters and tell Marty to prepare for a new passenger. C'mon, Herb, get the goggles off. I need a second pair of hands here."

Goldberg quickly removed the night vision equipment he'd been wearing, but had some difficulty sticking them back in their storage case. When he finally grabbed his control yoke, Ratz banked the Combat Talon into a moderate right turn and aligned it on the silver thread and white teardrop hovering in the distance; the fragility of the STAR system prevented Ratz from executing more strenuous maneuvers.

"Zero-Four to Gidi Three, we're heading into the recovery area," said Shoham. "We want you to make a final overflight of the area before we arrive."

Moments later the radio crackled with a reply and the two F-15s far ahead of the C-130 broke sharply to the right. Though they started several seconds behind the transport, their higher speed would allow them to reach the area ahead of it.

The chatter of automatic weapons fire reached Gavrilla as she was slipping on her helmet. She finished snapping the chin strap in place before reaching into one of her pockets. She produced her Skoda automatic, pulling its slide back and flicking its safety off.

Even with the pistol Gavrilla stood little chance of defending herself against a larger force of armed men. She looked toward the C-130; which suddenly appeared to be flying too slowly. Her apprehension and fear over the way she would be rescued quickly escalated. So close to being saved, Gavrilla felt more pursued than ever before.

"Phil, look. We got a problem," said Goldberg, shifting his gaze to the monitor for the low-light-level cameras. "We got visitors."

"Shit! It looks like a column of men," Ratz observed, the TV screen clearly showed a line of dark objects moving in the distance. Far away from the lone figure awaiting recovery, but clearly moving toward it. "Pilot to tactical, take a look at the low lights. Our passenger's going to have company."

"We see it, Phil. Continue the pickup," said Hynek. "Major, alert the fighters . . ."

"Phil, what should we do?" asked Goldberg, his question overriding the conversation from the tactical team. "As aircraft commander you can call this off if you think it's too dangerous."

"Continue. That girl's got only one chance to live." Ratz put a hand on the center pedestal's throttle levers and pulled them back another notch. "Airspeed, one hundred knots. Flaps, ten degrees. Arm flare dispensers."

"Captain, I can see her. And the plane rescuing her!" shouted the point man, standing on the crest of a dune. "It's flying slowly. We can shoot it down!"

"No, idiot! We're still out of range," said the Captain. "Nobody fires until we're closer and in position. Keep moving, we'll have to rely on massed fire to bring the plane down."

The soldiers following the point man all stopped at the crest to get a view of the woman they were after and the approaching C-130. The buzz-like rumble of its turboprops was omnipresent now, masking out all other noises except for shouted commands. They never heard the other approaching aircraft. By the time they saw the bright yellow flares in the night sky it was too late.

Twin streams of tracers cut diagonally through the squad's line of march. The cannon shells turned one man into a cloud of blood, severed limbs and torn fragments of clothing. But beyond him, no one else died or was seriously injured. For all their potential destructiveness, most of the shells merely raised giant fountains of sand.

The ground heaved as Gideon Three and Four overflew their target. They were barely a hundred feet above the dunes. Their ear-splitting roar hit the survivors like a shockwave and the heat of their exhaust melted away the chill of the desert night. As a parting shot the F-15s ignited their afterburners. The sound of raw fuel exploding in the twin chambers on each aircraft was like artillery fire. It would take several precious moments for the rest of the squad to recover their senses.

* * *

"Forget the jets, Herb, we see plenty of those," said Ratz, when he noticed his co-pilot following the Eagles as they shot across their path. "Concentrate, concentrate . . . airspeed, ninety. Flaps, twenty. Ready to capture."

On the ground Gavrilla could see the Lockheed giant bob and weave on its approach. She could hear the changes in propeller pitch and power settings. She was certain it would miss, then the line slid between the capture arms and the snare wires wrapped around it.

The nylon line began to stretch, giving her a moment to realize she was being rescued before getting yanked off the ground. Gavrilla's shoes were torn from her feet and her finger slammed against the Skoda's trigger; causing the gun to fire as it slipped from her hand.

By the time it hit the ground she was more than a hundred feet in the air and travelling over a hundred miles an hour. By the time the squad pursuing her had regrouped, she was half a mile away and almost a thousand feet in altitude. The cutting cord freed the STAR balloon, and the rest of the retrieval gear reeled in the Combat Talon's latest passenger.

Looking over her shoulder, Gavrilla saw the open beckoning, tail ramp of the C-130. Soon her mission would be over, yet would only be beginning.

Chapter Five

"Inertial navigation shows our position to be seventy-one degrees, forty-three minutes west. And thirty-five degrees, nineteen minutes north," said Burks, standing at the control center's INS station. "We're in position, Terry."

"Deactivating Sub-scape system," Carver replied. "Pumps, off. Valves, closed. Helm, speed reduced by one-third. Greg, tell nucleonics they can cut reactor power accordingly. I'll advise sonar and see if the radio room has anything."

When Carver finished hitting the rows of toggle switches on the Sub-scape panel, he came forward and picked a hand mike off the periscope stand. He stood behind the helmsmen, where he could see they were already cutting back the submarine's abnormally high speed. He could also see the screens for the infrared imagers and 3-D laser radar. For as far as their limited range would allow, there was nothing in front of or behind the *John Marshall*.

"Exec to nucleonics, we are secure from our Sub-scape run for the time being," said Burks. "Reduce power by fifty percent, but be prepared to resume the run in ten minutes."

"Roger, control center. We'll give the museum piece a rest," Patino advised. "We're switching to low-pressure pumps."

"Captain to sonar, start pinging when you get five percent efficiency," said Carver, keying the hand mike, then he hit another station switch on its control box. "Captain to radio room, you can start broadcasting a hailing message. The *Courageous* should be in the area."

"Captain, I got something on the bow imagers," said Jefferson. "At extreme range. Can't tell for sure but it looks more like a submarine than a whale."

Carver shifted his attention to the helm station, where he easily found the one monitor screen with any sign of activity on it. Floating in its upper left corner was a small lozenge of blue and green. As minimal as it was, to the practiced eye it had the shape and coloration of a submarine. In spite of the *John Marshall*'s decreasing speed it steadily grew larger and became centered in the screen, the result of Jefferson maneuvering toward it.

"Radio room to captain, I have a response from HMS *Courageous*," informed the center's loudspeakers. "They have updates and are ready to squirt them over."

"Tell them to begin. I'll be right there," said Carver, speaking into his hand mike. "Captain to Commander Allard, report to the radio room. Greg, you have the con. Slow the Lady to station keeping."

Carver walked to the back of the control center and stepped into the aft passageway. A few long strides took him to the communications room, where he was joined moments later by Glenn Allard.

"I got *Courageous* on short-wave, high-frequency radio," said Hawkins, glancing over his shoulder. "Right now it's tied up with data transmission, Captain. The updates are coming in on the teletype."

"Here, Glenn, you take this one. I'll read the other as the printer finishes it," said Carver, standing over the softly clacking machine. He tore the sheet feeding through it along a perforation line, and handed the first completed report to Allard while he concentrated on the second.

"This is from HMS *Spartan*," Allard remarked, after finishing the report. "They rescued survivors from a helicopter off *Ocean Valkyrie*. The survivors say they were shot down by a missile the terrorists fired at them. Sounds like a SAM-7 or 14. Almost twenty people were killed in the helicopter downing, another eighteen when the oil rig was seized. These terrorists sound pretty ruthless. I thought we were just dealing with some crazy environmentalists. And I thought they were just Norwegians, but the survivors say the terrorists are mostly Arabs."

"Something odd is going on here, Glenn . . ." said Carver, deep in thought as he studied the next report. "This is from the Royal Norwegian Air Force. Your helicopter landed on an island off Norway before going to the rig. When the air force got a police squad out to it, they found thirty-one bodies. Some of the dead have been identified as members of this Purify the Environment group. What the hell is going on?"

"I think we got a wolf in sheep's clothing — something a lot more sinister than what we first thought we had. People other than environmentalists are running this operation. I hope the officials are keeping these revelations from the press, it would only make things worse. Terry, this cable's from NATO. It says the SAS and SBS have been put on alert, I think it's the answer to your message."

The teletype was still clacking away, finishing another update while Carver and Allard had been reading the earlier ones.

"Yes, I think it is," said Carver. "The cable originates from Poole in Dorset. That's where the Royal Marines base their SBS units. Team commanders will be meeting soon at Special Air Services headquarters in Bradbury Lines. All we can do now is hope. If they don't request us, my career is over and this Lady's doomed to be scrapped. It all hangs on one old friend."

"You're new to elite forces, Terry," said Allard. "You took this command because it was your alma mater, and the Navy refused to give you a Trident boat. This isn't the regular military. Sometimes the *only* thing you need is one old friend."

"I guess I'll have to trust you, you're the expert in this area. Jake, has the *Courageous* finished its transmission?"

"Yes, Captain," Hawkins answered, hitting a series of switches on his tiny console. "Data transmission has ended and we're back to voice. The teletype will keep printing for a few minutes, though. What the *Courageous* squirted over has been stored in its memory. Is there anything you wish to tell them?"

"Yes, I'd like to do it myself." Carver reached for the microphone stand and lifted it off the console. He waited for Hawkins to give him a "go" signal before pressing the transmit key. "This is Captain Terence Carver, commanding USS *John Marshall* to HMS *Courageous*. Thank you for your help. Before we depart we'd like to make one final request of you."

"This is Commander Harden, Captain of Her Majesty's Submarine *Courageous*," replied a voice on the compartment's loudspeakers. "We're glad to be of assistance. How else may we help you?"

"I'd like you to transmit a message to both COMSUBLANT and headquarters, NATO Atlantic Naval Forces. Advise them the *John Marshall* is continuing the prepositioning of its resources to the vicinity of the *Ocean Valkyrie* crisis. Thank you again. I hope this doesn't land you in trouble."

"We may get yelled at, Captain. But our headquarters is Whitehall, not the Pentagon. We'll relay your message. Good luck, *Marshall*. *Courageous*, out."

Several minutes later, the submarines parted company. After hovering in place for most of the encounter, the *John Marshall* surged ahead, its hull acquiring a new coat of polymers, while the *Courageous* emptied its ballast tanks. It rose toward the surface. When it got within sixty feet it would unreel its trailing wire antenna and begin coded transmissions. By then the *Marshall* would have resumed its Subscape run and would be miles away.

The first sensation Erica felt was cold. It wasn't until a little later, when she tried to move, that she felt pain. Every muscle either ached or felt stiff. With great effort she rolled onto her back, and slowly realized she was still in the emergency equipment locker.

She opened her eyes to more darkness—the only light she could see was an outline around the door, and she could hear the storm raging outside. The external hatch banged repeatedly; it had not been locked, she remembered. Waves flooded the outer compartment, a brief spray of sea water erupting around the door frame with each one. Erica had begun to think of going out to close the hatch when she heard voices.

A loud clanking accompanied them, and initially it sounded like they were coming from the ceiling. The ring of boots on ladder rungs indicated they were climbing down from the upper compartments in the base leg. As they reached the floor, the voices became more distinct and Erica recognized the heavy accents. They were Arabic.

"What a mess!" shouted the first voice. "Azali, stay on the ladder until I get the door."

"Will this water cause problems with the explosives?" asked the second.

"Only if it washes them away." There was a creaking and another loud clank, then the noise of the storm fell off dramatically, and both voices were more clearly heard. "After all, these are marine demolition charges from the rig's own stores. Here, let me help."

Erica recoiled in terror from the locker door and looked around desperately for a place to hide, but the equipment locker was just a steel box. The shelves lining either wall were too narrow and flimsy for her to use. There was no place at all, she thought in panic, until Erica realized she had been lying on top of it.

She moved off the pile and, in the darkness, tried to find its edge. When she touched cold metal, Erica knew she had the floor and started to root her way through the pile. She pushed aside the smaller objects and found enough larger ones, life rafts and exposure suit packs, to crawl under. Though she tried to make as little noise as possible, Erica knew she was creating it and prayed it would not be noticed.

"Did you hear? There were noises," said the second voice.

"They're all around, Azali," said the first. "We're in the middle of a storm."

"No, something moved behind this door. Haven't you wondered why we found the hatch opened? I think someone escaped, or tried to escape, from this room."

"We know what happened to all rig personnel. They were accounted for. Tie down the charges tighter, we can't let them roll around. We must make sure the rig will sink when we're finished with it."

"We didn't count the crew, the Norwegians did. They could've purposely overlooked someone."

"Azali, you're paranoid. I'll prove it to you."

Erica's pounding heart skipped a beat when she heard tools being dropped and footsteps approach her hiding place. She covered her face and put her hands over her mouth, to strangle any cry she might involuntarily utter. The locker door opened with a explosive crack, and for an eternity there was silence. Erica laid as still as she could, didn't even breathe until the first voice spoke again.

"And you thought what we're in is a mess. You see this one? Perhaps you're right, maybe someone did try to escape. Whoever it was is probably dead by now. Everything's been thrown off the shelves, it's all in a pile."

"You see, I told you someone tried to escape. Should we put everything back, Kaniel?"

With the door open Erica heard the voices distinctly, and finally recognized the second voice as the terrorist who guarded her, threatened her, and shot her down. For a moment anger flared in her, until she heard Eshqi suggest that the pile of equipment she was hiding under be cleaned up. The fear surged back, paralyzing her, and there was another eternity of silence.

"No, we have other duties," said the first voice, finally. "We should keep to our schedule. We have another of these base legs to plant charges in and besides, I doubt we'll use what's in here. By the time *Valkyrie* sinks, we'll be far away."

The door slammed shut, echoing slightly, and a metallic clicking followed. Erica was now locked inside the tiny room. She knew it, yet did not move. The terrorists could still be heard, and fear now consumed her. In fact she refused to do anything at all until she could no longer hear the familiar, terrifying voices outside.

"I'm placing the detonators in the charges," said the first voice, and for a few more moments there was silence. "There . . . and make sure you don't step on the wires on the way up."

"I know, it's almost the only thing you say to me," Eshqi replied sharply. "I've done more than most on this operation, so why am I here? Others in our unit have had nothing but easy duties. When we return, Nazal and Jassem will hear of this."

"Frieda, you should have something a little stronger in your coffee," said Taylor, approaching Frieda Gran with a small, rectangular bottle of dark liquid. "Though it's been nearly two decades since we dispensed with grog, small supplies of rum are still carried on Her Majesty's Ships. This will calm you."

A section of *Spartan*'s officers' quarters had been turned into a makeshift sick bay. The beds were larger and more comfortable, there was more room to work, and they were only one level down from the submarine's attack center, where the survivors had first been brought on board. The section had been partitioned off by heavy blankets used as curtains. They not only kept out the rest of the crew, they kept the heat in. Electric heaters had raised the ambient air temperature to ninety-five degrees. While the patients had yet to feel it, Taylor and the medical orderlies were in short sleeves and sweating heavily.

"Thank you," Captain," said Frieda, after a shot of rum had been added to her coffee. She sipped it through teeth which still chattered constantly. "I wish I could have one of those blankets to wear, instead of a seaman's uniform."

"Our senior Med Tech says they're not necessary or even wise," Taylor replied. "Best treatment for hypothermia is passive warming in light bed clothes. Mr. Nordsen, however, had a lower core temperature than you. The addition of his wounds makes his condition even more serious, which is why we have him on plasma and epinephrine."

"If he's serious, shouldn't we take him to a port or navy base? Where they have a real hospital? We haven't moved from the vicinity of *Valkyrie* since you rescued us."

"We have enough facilities here to care for both of you. Isn't that right, Mr. Newcane?" The Captain's voice was firm, but not unkind.

"Yes. Your friend will be quite all right here, miss," said the medical orderly with petty officer badges on his sleeves. "This is a nuclear submarine and we're designed to be self-sufficient. We have enough medical equipment and knowledge to handle your friend. I just checked Mr. Nordsen. His pulse rate, core temperature and venous pressure are all improving and we have him on an ECG monitor."

"Thank you, Mr. Newcane, I'm sorry I doubted you," said Frieda, staring into her coffee. Her teeth were chattering less, the rum was taking effect. "Did you tell London about what happened on the rig?"

"I just came from the wireless office. They have the full report," Taylor answered. "I didn't know how prophetic I'd be when I said 'bloody *Valkyrie*.' They also had some questions for me. They need more information. Are you up to answering them?"

"Yes, I think I can. What do they wish to know?"

"You said most of the terrorists who took your oil rig were Arabs and they were clearly in charge. Did you hear the names of the leaders?"

"One of them was called Nazal," said Frieda, responding slowly, as she thought back to what she'd been through. "I think Abu Nazal. And another was named Gunni, he argued a lot with Nazal. The only Norwegian whose name I heard was Hans Sivertsen. He's an environmentalist, I'd heard of him before. He lives with Edda Anders, the singer."

"Ken, could you loan me your notepad?" Taylor asked, reaching to accept the pad Newcane had in his hand. The moment he got it, he was scribbling down the information Frieda was giving him. "Anders. That's a familiar name, unfortunately. We also received a report from the Norwegian Police. On an island in one of your fjords, they found a massacre site. More than thirty dead, most are identified as the original passengers of your helicopter. But there were others, and one of them was this Edda Anders. Now, did these Arabs even mention their organization, or the name of the country they're working for?"

"What's this world coming to? Why did they kill her?

98

Edda Anders was a popular singer in my country, and Sweden. She was called the Joan Baez of Norway — I once saw one of her concerts."

The Captain's face was grim. "This isn't the time for moralizing or existential questions, Frieda. We're dealing with a ruthless, well-armed terrorist group. For all we know it could be some military unit from a Middle East country. Did they mention any country's name?"

"No. Apart from insulting ours, they did not," said Frieda, wearily passing a hand over her eyes. "I'm very tired, Captain."

"Please, we need the information. Did any of the terrorists tell you why they took the oil rig?"

"The two Norwegians talked about pollution, but the Arabs said nothing. I did see them bring in two steel cases, with a lot of guards. The only marking on the cases was something like the rings on the Olympic flag."

"Olympic flag? Could you draw it for me?" Taylor handed over the pad and pen to Frieda, who quickly drew three stylized, interlocking rings. When she returned the pad, Taylor immediately recognized the design; though the look on his face was a mixture of both apprehension and confusion. "Good God, this is the bio-hazard symbol . . . what could they have aboard bloody *Valkyrie?* What type of biologically dangerous material could be used in a terrorist operation?"

"Perhaps it's some sort of bio-weapon, Captain?" Newcane suggested.

"If it is, they've certainly picked the worst location and time of the year to unleash it. We're hundreds of miles from any populated area, and there's been no public announcement of this group's intentions. I'm not much of a terrorism expert, but these people aren't working the way others did in the past."

"What will you do, Captain?" Frieda asked.

"Pack all this information off to the people who are the experts," said Taylor, glancing over what was on the pad. "The SAS and SBS are meeting, and I heard the Americans are becoming involved. Is there anything you'd wish to ask?"

"Are you still looking for Erica?"

"We haven't done a periscope sweep in a while, though we're still monitoring the maritime distress frequency. We didn't see any bodies on our last sweep and, if your friend made it to the rig, she'll try using the distress channel."

"*If* she made it to *Valkyrie, if* she finds a radio and *if* the terrorists haven't found her," said Frieda, getting a far-away look in her eyes as she thought about her brave companion. Then she began to cry. "They'll kill her should they find her. Don't you understand? I don't think these people want there to be any survivors."

"Neither do I. I understand fully. Please, try to get some rest. There are people ashore who will handle this crisis now, and I had better send them this information. Should anything happen I'll let you know immediately."

"How is she doing?" Adir asked, when Hynek stepped back into the Elint/ECM box.

"Still throwing up," said Hynek. "A STAR retrieval has that effect on people. When she's done, your agent isn't going to have much strength left for debriefing. I hope you can get most of your information out of what she brought with her."

"Indeed. It may not look like much but she brought a gold mine in her backpack." Adir motioned to the small pile of papers he held in his lap. Some of the papers looked like printed or typed reports. Others were either hand-drawn maps, or hand-made copies of material too sensitive for her to steal. "Unfortunately, I am going to have to question Gavi to make sense of all this."

"Well, don't go too hard on her. From experience, I can tell you a retrieval takes a lot out of its 'victims.' Ty, any comment on how the Libyans are reacting?"

"Like a mean-assed bunch of motherfuckers who can't figure out who to fight," said Walker, grinning mischievously at the result of the ECM Team's handiwork. "With the Navy pulling their diversion, the motherfuckers don't know if we're heading north or east."

"There's that phrase again, 'motherfuckers,' " said Shoham. "Why create such an insult about motherhood? In my country, mothers are honored. They're not insulted."

"Shlomo, please. It looks like you need more of an education in American slang," Adir sighed, looking up from the material they had both been examining. "It's a standard curse. In fact, as Ty will attest, it's become so common among American blacks it's almost ceased to be a swear word."

"Yeah, Slow-Mo, it's real common," said Walker, still smiling. "And I don't need to take no test to prove it, either. Captain, the Libyans have about a third of their fighters in the air. Mostly Mirage F-1s and Mig-25s. They're prowling their airspace in either pairs or flights, no formation larger than four planes. They're at all altitudes and most are concentrated near the coast. As you can see, the *Enterprise* must have half its air wing up."

"So they have," Hynek remarked, looking over Walker's shoulder at the glowing display screen. Tiny groups of symbols glided over the map of Libya, nearly a hundred in all, while farther to the north more symbols hovered in the Mediterranean Sea. "The navy's doing a good show."

The sound level in the cramped box jumped dramatically as its door swung open. When it closed, Gavrilla was standing inside the compartment. Even in its weak, green-hued light the others could see she was tired. Her face was drawn, her hair hung in dishevelled curls, and there were dark circles under her eyes. Shoham immediately jumped out of his seat and motioned for Gavrilla to take it.

"*Shalom,* Gavi," said Adir, as his agent dropped gratefully into the seat. "I know your escape has exhausted you, but I need to ask you some questions about what you brought us."

"I'll answer what I can," Gavrilla said wearily as she rested her head against the padded wall of the box. It wasn't very comfortable, but it was enough to start her drifting into sleep. Her eyelids had barely closed when Gavrilla realized what was happening, and snapped her head away from the wall. "I'm sorry."

"I understand. You'll rest as soon as we're done. The organism Stanmeer had created, it's designed to eat *oil?* Not

101

kill people, or livestock?"

"Yes, it will only eat oil, converting it into a useless gas. The organism will eat oil under almost any conditions and multiply rapidly. It was the only thing Stanmeer worked on while we were at the base. I never heard him, or anyone else, mention work on an organism lethal to humans."

"Interesting. Haskel wondered what the Libyans could produce in so short a time," said Adir, writing in shorthand what Gavrilla was saying. "Our experts claim it would take years to produce a truly dangerous organism. Did they ever mention where they were going to use their oil bug?"

"Nazih and the others told Stanmeer they would use it against the United States. The Libyans enjoyed fanning his hatred of America. They never said exactly where or when they'd use it, but I suspect it will be against an off-shore oil field. I heard the name *Ocean Valkyrie* several times and it sounds like the name of an oil rig."

"Well, wherever *Ocean Valkyrie* is I doubt it's in America. The strike and support teams you warned us of are in Western Europe. Maybe we can find out where this rig is? Captain, could you plug into your intelligence nets? We've been aboard your plane for most of the night and we're very isolated here."

"No problem, I'll have some information in a couple of minutes," said Hynek, turning back to his console and tapping out the commands on his keyboard.

"Should we bother, Avrom?" Shoham asked, standing next to Gavrilla. "We'll be landing in Israel in a few more hours. It can wait until then."

"Whether it's the army or intelligence, I've learned very little waits for anything," said Adir. "Gavi, what do these bio-capsules look like? I take it they're how the organism is transported?"

"Yes, the capsules are the transport containers," Gavrilla answered. She held her hands in front of her about a foot apart. "They're this long, four or five inches in diameter and lozenge-shaped. They're made of glass and are surrounded by a plastic 'cage.' Several dozen were filled recently and I think they were taken out of the country. The bacteria in them are kept dormant by special chemicals, until the capsules are broken and the bacteria exposed to crude oil."

"Then they'll run wild," Adir said. "While our experts will look at this, I can already say we've got an organism powerful enough to destroy an oil field. Did you meet anyone from the teams sent to Europe?"

"Some from the support teams, not many of the terrorists themselves. They were kept isolated from us. I don't even think Stanmeer saw a lot of them."

"Ben Adir, something's happening," said Shoham, slowly and loudly enough for those he was standing beside to hear him. "The tacticals are all changing."

Adir looked away from Gavrilla and saw most of the display screens on the consoles had indeed changed. They were showing maps of Egypt, not Libya, and a list of U.S. Air Force and Navy aircraft available in the Mediterranean. On the Egyptian maps a new flight course was being painted in, one heading north instead of east.

"Tactical to pilot, we have a change in plans," said Hynek. "After crossing the Egyptian border, we're to switch course to zero-one-five degrees. Yes, Phil, we're heading north. We'll pickup new escorts over the Med."

"You're hijacking us!" shouted Captain Eshel, ripping his headset off so he wouldn't get pulled down when he jumped out of his seat. "You can't do that! Our agreement is to go back to Israel."

"Yehuda, please. They can do what they want," said Adir. "This is, after all, an American aircraft. But he is correct, Captain Hynek, the original plan was to return to Israel. What's happened to change it?"

"Air Force Special Operations Command advised me to contact NATO Intelligence about *Ocean Valkyrie*," said Hynek, turning to face the people behind him. "When I used that name again, the intelligence net lit up like a Christmas tree. Approximately seven hours ago, the oil rig *Ocean Valkyrie* was seized by terrorists in the North Sea. Originally identified as Norwegian environmentalists, NATO now believes the terrorists are a Middle East group, identity unknown. Purpose for seizing the oil rig, unknown."

"Except to the people in this room," Adir concluded, smiling broadly. "Yes, we *are* needed elsewhere. How long would it take for us to reach Europe?"

"You mean you actually want to help them?" said Eshel, incredulous. "The Europeans shoved the PLO down our throats. If it were us they wouldn't lift a finger to help."

"I would also add it's our superiors who should officially volunteer us," said Shoham. "We can't do it ourselves."

"All right, stop being so prickly, you two," Adir ordered. "Once our superiors learn of this event, I have no doubt they'll sanction our involvement. Nathan, can we send a message to Nesher Field?"

"Of course, but I'd like to hold down our volume of radio traffic until after we cross the border," said Hynek, glancing back at the console screens. "We're still inside Libya, but we'll reach the Egyptian border in another six minutes. Then we'll be able to talk more freely with the outside world, and get more information in."

"Fair enough. This also means we can pump Gavi for more of her information. Gavi? Gavi . . . ?"

Adir turned to find Gavrilla with her head slumped against the compartment's padded wall. In spite of the minimal comfort it offered, it proved too soft, too beguiling for her to resist. She had fallen into a deep sleep and no amount of shaking would wake her.

"If you would allow me, Avrom, I can bring her around," said Shoham. "I'll take her out and walk her up and down the cargo deck."

"Don't bother, she deserves a rest," said Adir, watching Gavrilla sleep. "Aren't there beds in this aircraft?"

"There's one in the cockpit," Hynek replied. "I don't think it's occupied."

"Good. Shlomo, Yehuda, carry her up to the cockpit and put her to bed. Let her sleep for now. We're going to have a long flight ahead of us, with plenty of time to question her."

Chapter Six

"Thank you for finally arriving, Mr. Nyquist," said the Royal Army Colonel, greeting the last visitor to enter the briefing room. "I'm Colonel Hasler of the Special Air Service, welcome to Bradbury Lines."

Unlike the other civilian visitors to SAS headquarters, Hasler escorted Jan Nyquist to the room's main table and introduced him to the military personnel gathered around it. Most of the officers wore the familiar beige berets of the Special Air Services regiment. A few wore the blue uniforms and peaked caps of the Royal Air Force and Royal Navy. But only one wore a conspicuous dark green beret with a gold badge.

"Mr. Nyquist, this is Lieutenant Colonel Robert Wendell Boyd. Commander of the Second Special Boat Squadron, Royal Marines," Hasler continued, presenting the officer in the green beret. "Colonel, Jan Nyquist will be the Norwegian government's representative to our discussions of the *Ocean Valkyrie* crisis."

"Yes, part of our concession to being given overall command of this operation," said Boyd, shaking the diplomat's hand. "You took a rather long time in arriving. Did your helicopter have trouble departing London?"

"I did not fly. This weather's too dangerous for those frail machines," said Nyquist. "And this is not a military operation, yet, Colonel Boyd. I take it from your comment you resent my presence. Remember, Colonel, those are Norwegians being held on that rig. My country is concerned with the welfare of all its citizens."

"I'm certain Colonel Boyd did not mean to slight you," a British official injected, part of the entourage which had arrived with Nyquist. "I apologize on his behalf if you thought so. Now, gentlemen, if we could begin?"

At the diplomat's suggestion, the individual conversations ended and the civilians and officers took their places around the table. For a few moments, between the time the shuffling of the chairs ended and the meeting actually began, the sound of wind gusts and sleet hitting the windows could be heard.

"Thank you for waiting until we could arrive, Colonel Hasler," said the British official, sitting at the head of the table. "It has now been at least nine hours since a terrorist group called 'Purify the Environment' seized the Norwegian oil rig *Ocean Valkyrie,* and seven hours since they first broadcast they were in control of it. Colonel, could you bring us up to date on the event?"

Hasler nodded his consent and pulled his chair away from the table. He walked a few feet to the windowless side of the room and stood near the erected wall map of the North Sea. Near its center were oil rig and submarine symbols; in the upper right corner, an island in Norway's Bokufjord was circled.

"We now know this is where the crisis started," said Hasler, pointing to the island. "A heavy transport helicopter was hijacked by the terrorists and forced to land here. Its passengers were taken off and murdered, and the terrorists who replaced them were the ones who attacked the rig. We've since learned there are about two dozen terrorists, and most are Arabic, not Norwegian. This 'Purify the Environment' movement may have been a front group."

"Excuse me, but how do you know this?" Nyquist asked, almost demanded. "When we left London, the island in Bokufjord was just being investigated. And I resent, Mr. Leeds, your accusation of 'Purify the Environment' being terrorists. They're an ecological group with noble goals."

"While I doubt they're terrorists, their friends certainly are. We learned of them from HMS *Spartan*." Hasler moved to the map's center and pointed to the submarine silhouette.

"It arrived in the vicinity of *Ocean Valkyrie* five hours ago. It was in transit across the North Sea after an exercise with the Danish Navy, and has so far proven to be our best bit of luck. When she arrived, the submarine spotted two people in the water and effected a rescue. They are the sole survivors of the transport helicopter. The terrorists loaded it with wounded and women rig crew, then shot it down when it tried to leave."

The last remark produced a collective gasp from the civilians in the room. Even though Hasler paused to allow for questions, it was several moments before any of the diplomats and Foreign Office personnel asked one.

"Barbaric. Incredibly barbaric," said Nyquist, for the moment clearly shocked. "I hope this will be brought out in our press conference. It will give us a morally superior position to these . . . terrorists."

"Press conference! Are you out of your bloody mind?" Boyd exploded, just beating out Hasler with his reaction. "We can't go around giving away information which was so difficult to acquire. This is war."

"No, Mr. Boyd, this *isn't* war. Treating it that way is counterproductive. We are democracies and we must live by our laws, no matter what trouble it causes us. Our people have the right to know. Mr. Hasler, how many have been killed?"

"So far, over sixty," said Hasler, with a cold civility.

"Don't you feel those families have a right to know?"

"Not if revealing the information jeopardizes our advantages or endangers my lads," said Boyd. "You release this at a press conference and you might as well broadcast it directly to the terrorists on *Valkyrie*. They'll know we have forces in their area, they'll know who they're up against and they'll know there are survivors from the helicopter."

"Mr. Nyquist, you're overstepping the limits of your powers," said Leeds, the senior Foreign Office official. "You're here to represent your country, to observe for it and advise us on its views. I doubt your government would want us to put the lives of your countrymen still on the rig at further risk. Colonel Boyd, from the way you responded some decisions have already been made. Will your Special Boat Squadron be used in place of SAS personnel?"

"They're the best for the operation, Mr. Leeds," said Hasler, answering for Boyd. "We have little training for dealing with terrorist acts at sea. The Special Boat Squadrons have the training, equipment and background for the tasks ahead. Furthermore, Colonel Boyd knows the captain of the submarine we must use and has trained in the past with SEAL Teams."

"SEAL Teams? I wasn't aware that the Americans had asked to be included?"

"I haven't either, and my government will refuse to accept them, Mr. Leeds," said Nyquist, some of his arrogance returning. "We don't want the Americans involved. Tell your military to reject them."

"You're not in a position to dictate operational decisions to us!" Boyd shouted, as his anger flared once again. "If we say we need the Americans, then we need them! I want my lads to have the best chance for success. And if they have it, your people have a far better chance of living."

"You're quite right, Colonel. Thank you," said Leeds. "Mr. Nyquist, my government has learned from long experience not to interfere with the way military commanders conduct these types of operations. Though I would like to know, Mr. Boyd, why you feel it's necessary to use an American submarine and elite forces? The Foreign Office would've liked this to be kept an all-British show."

"I understand, and while we can't keep it entirely British, we can keep the operation under British control. I think Colonel Hasler can explain it better."

"Thanks, Robert. This will be the Special Air Service's principal contribution to the crisis," said Hasler. "Before you arrived, Mr. Leeds, we held our own meeting and came to the following conclusions. Whatever reason the terrorists had for seizing *Ocean Valkyrie,* it's evidently for something more than the stated environmental concerns. That we must retake the rig as soon as we can. That current weather conditions render either an air or surface assault impossible. That an assault by submarine is the only choice open to us and, because of *Valkyrie's* size, a large assault force will be needed.

"We estimated the most optimum size for this force to be

108

sixty officers and men. As our Royal Navy friends will attest, it would take three submarines to transport this many commandoes. If you add this number to HMS *Spartan,* then the area around *Ocean Valkyrie* would become dangerously crowded. Remember, the rig itself is part submarine.

"There is, however, an American sub modified for tasks like this. It would be ideal for us and it's currently enroute to Britain. The USS *John Marshall* is a ballistic missile submarine reconfigured for commando ops. Its new captain is a friend of Colonel Boyd's and has sent a message advising us he's prepositioning his command as far east as possible."

"A missile submarine? A missile submarine is an offensive weapon," warned Nyquist. "You risk blowing this crisis into World War Three if you use it."

"The only thing being 'blown' here is your gift for hyperbole," said Leeds, finally growing irritated enough to display some anger. "We've had quite enough demonstration of it already. If you persist, I'll demand your replacement by your embassy's military attaché. Colonel Boyd, you're familiar with this submarine? Are you certain it's what you need?"

"I am," Boyd replied. "The *John Marshall* has swim-out chambers so we needn't surface and it already has a thirty-man SEAL unit aboard. I can have a similar team ready for departure by the time I return to Poole. If you can have Whitehall make a request for it, the Americans will certainly loan it to us."

"How can you be sure? The Americans don't go loaning out nuclear submarines simply because they're asked for."

"I can be certain this time. Captain Carver overstepped the alert orders sent by NATO to all elite forces. Submariners are an independent lot, but Carver's action has landed him in trouble with his superiors. However, if we request the *John Marshall,* the Pentagon will be spared the embarrassment of punishing Carver, and may even be credited with foresight."

"Her Majesty's government is not in the business of saving American Navy captains," said Leeds, smiling slightly. "But if this submarine is what you truly need, I'll push through the request. Though I fear what you may ask, is there anything else you want?"

"My other requirements are being met," said Boyd, turning to the Royal Air Force officers. "Wing Commander, when will the Chinook be ready to fly?"

"We'll have it ready for you in twenty minutes," answered the highest-ranking R.A.F. officer. "Mildenhall has been alerted and the U.S. Navy detachment there is holding a Greyhound for you."

"Good, thank you. Commander Harren, will you be able to contact the *Kitty Hawk?*"

"As soon as we leave this room," said one of the Royal Navy officers. "The SAS has *the* best communications set-ups I've ever seen."

"Good. Colonel, have you agreed with what your role will be?" Boyd asked.

"Yes, I'll be your red herring," said Hasler, a glimmer of resignation in his voice. "I'll appear with Mr. Leeds and the others. Let the press, and hopefully our enemies, speculate if it's the SAS who's being sent in. I guess this is one of the costs you have to pay for being known as the best in the world. Good luck, Robert. Based on our newest intelligence you're facing some very dangerous people. Give them no quarter and remember, 'those who dare, win.' If no one else has any questions for this man, he has a helicopter to catch."

"Pumps, off. Valves, closed," said Burks. "The Sub-scape system is deactivated."

"Thanks, Greg. Helm, reduce speed by one-third," Carver ordered, glancing from the back of the control center to the front.

"Cutting speed, sir," said the new senior helmsman. "Captain, would you like to have Mr. Jefferson relieve me?"

"No, Clarence deserves his off-duty time. You're qualified enough, Jimmy, and you need experience with Sub-scape operations. Just keep an eye on the laser radar and thermal imagers. Captain to nucleonics, reduce power by two-thirds."

The *John Marshall* was once again decelerating, losing its speed as it shed its coat of polymers. When it had dropped to thirty knots, the submarine started to transmit its hailing message and got an immediate response.

"Radio room to Captain, I have the *Baton Rouge* on the line. They're answering and advising we're approaching a little too fast for them."

"They're almost bow on to us," said Carver, glancing over the new helmsman's shoulder. "But we are close. Cut to full stop then reverse the propeller to one-quarter speed. I'll alert the crew . . ."

Carver's warning was still being heard in the submarine's many levels and compartments when the propulsion machinery was momentarily stopped then thrown into reverse. Its entire four-hundred-and-ten-foot-long hull shuddered as speed fell precipitously. Anything not secured sailed forward, and anyone not prepared for it was either thrown against a bulkhead or to their knees. In less than a minute the *John Marshall* was barely crawling forward, and the attack submarine USS *Baton Rouge* was a thousand yards ahead of it on its starboard bow.

"First report is already in, Captain," said Hawkins, the printer softly clacking behind him. "From the look of it, it's short and sweet."

Carver let out an audible sigh as he accepted the single page. He had read and reread its brief contents several times before he heard the stamp of boots in the passageway behind him.

"Hey, Captain, next time you put the brakes on, tell us to put our seat belts on first," said Martirri, arriving at the radio room a few strides ahead of Allard. "You don't look so good. Something not agreeing with you?"

"Cool it, Sal. I didn't bring you along to be comic relief," Allard warned. "I take it this one's bad news?"

"Urgent message from COMSUBLANT, priority transmission," said Carver, virtually reading the page's top line. "They're onto us, Glenn. They want us to return to Norfolk immediately. From the way this reads, the *Baton Rouge* may have orders to fire on us if we don't respond."

Carver handed the bulletin to Allard before going back to the printer, where an incessant chime indicated another message had been completed. He returned to the growing conference at the radio room's hatch with a brighter expression on his face. He was almost smiling.

"This is much better—it was sent specifically to the *Baton Rouge* from Bradbury Lines."

"That's the headquarters for the Special Air Service," said Allard, looking up from the first bulletin. "Is it from your Royal Marine friend?"

"Yes, Robert's meeting with SAS officers, British and Norwegian officials," said Carver. "He appears certain his special boat squadron will get the assignment and looks forward to working with us."

"What? Are we going to have to work with a bunch of fucking Brits?" asked Martirri, glancing over Allard's shoulder for a look at the report. "They're stuck-up bastards. They think they're the best in the world. And on top of it all, they're Marines! A jarhead is a jarhead no matter what country he's from."

"Knock it off, Sal," said Allard. "The reason British elite forces think they're the best in the world is because they *are* the best. Half of our tactics and a lot of our equipment came from them. Make yourself useful—see if any of the incoming reports are about the terrorists we have to face. Speaking of equipment, think we should retransmit the list of what my men need?"

"Maybe we should, but there's a bigger decision we have to make," said Carver. "Which of these should we follow? Should we obey our orders? Or should we continue on our present course and hope a stop or two down the line the British will pull our butts out of the fire?"

Carver held up his sheet and rattled it softly while Allard glanced between it and the one he held in his hands.

"We could acknowledge the orders and turn back," Allard said finally. "Always reversing course when your friend comes through for us."

"Yes, that would be the safe response," Carver answered, glancing at the recall orders once again. "But it would cost us valuable time. And we both know how the Pentagon acts when it changes its mind. Whatever they want, they wanted it five minutes ago."

"I say we take another calculated risk, Terry. After all, they can only hang us once."

"Shit! This could've been useful to us," said Martirri, noisily ripping another sheet off the printer. "It's something about an Israeli agent the Air Force is rescuing from Libya. It says Valkyrie somewhere in here, but the rest of it got garbled in transmission. I guess we're going to have to ask for this to be repeated, and wait until the next time we slow down to get it."

"You're right, we could have used this," said Allard, accepting the report when Martirri stepped back to the hatch. "But we'll get everything at the next Com Stop."

"That's it! If one message got scrambled, why not another?" Carver asked. "We can say the same thing happened to the COMSUBLANT signal. It would take the brass ashore at least an hour to receive our answer, and rebroadcast their orders to the next attack sub up the line. Jake, can you make voice contact with the *Baton Rouge?*"

"Not yet, Captain," said Hawkins. "The high-frequency is still tied up with data transmission. Once they've finished squirting the last report, we'll be able to talk to them."

Carver joined Hawkins at the radio room's console and waited for the indicator lights to show that high-speed data transmission from the nearby attack submarine had ceased. With the flip of a few switches, the system was changed to voice command and the console microphones activated.

"This is Captain Terence Carver, commanding officer of the *John Marshall* to USS *Baton Rouge,*" Carver announced. "May I speak with your captain? Over."

"Yes, Captain Carver. This is Commander Allan Kirst." The reply was immediate on the compartment's loudspeakers. "I'm sorry I had to be the one to give you the bad news. How can I help you?"

"I'd like you to transmit the following messages . . ." As Carver spoke, he motioned for Hawkins to give him a note pad and quickly wrote his communications. "I want this to go to Bradbury Lines and Poole. 'Am proceeding with redeployment to the North Sea. Please advise on your government's decision to use us. Looking forward to working with you.' Send this next one to NATO Intelligence. 'Urgent you retransmit bulletin regarding rescue of Israeli agent by the U.S. Air Force. Include updates of same.' Glenn, is there anything new you want to say, or add about the current reports?"

"No, just keep the reports coming," said Allard.

"Good. Commander Kirst, I want this last message to go to COMSUBLANT headquarters," said Carver. "Tell them, 'bulletin number Eight-Nine-Delta-Nine-One scrambled in transmission, either due to faulty encryption at source or atmospherics. Please retransmit, will pick it up from HMCS *Onondaga*.' And sign it, Terence Carver."

"Captain, are you sure you want to send this?" Kirst asked, after a little hesitation.

"Yes, I'm certain. As my commandoes say 'they can only hang you once.' Thanks, Commander."

A few minutes later, Hawkins gave the official sign-off between the *John Marshall* and the *Baton Rouge*. As with *Courageous* before it, the attack submarine rose to the surface deploying its communications aerials in preparation to contact the outside world. The *John Marshall* remained at depth, pinging actively with the long-range component of its BQQ-5 sonar suite until it was certain the area around it was clear.

It changed course, swinging to a more northerly heading, and began to accelerate. With its Sub-scape system reactivated, the *Marshall* received a fresh coating of polymers. Its speed jumped dramatically, to more than fifty knots in a little over a minute. By the time the *Baton Rouge* finished sending its messages, the commando submarine would be miles away, racing farther into the North Atlantic.

For a long time, it seemed like hours, Erica laid under the pile of equipment. While it was still wet, it eventually grew warm and for a while, Erica actually fell asleep. But when she awoke, she awoke with a start, fearful she was overhearing the terrorists again.

After several minutes Erica realized what she was hearing

114

were the sounds of the storm; and the echoes reverberating through *Ocean Valkyrie*'s base leg. Though she was still afraid of being discovered, she slowly moved out from under her protective cover. In addition to her original aches, Erica was now hungry and thirsty, and had to find something to alleviate the pains.

The moment she emerged, she discovered she was in a world of absolute darkness. The light in the outer compartment had been turned off. There was no longer a dim outline around the door; there was no illumination at all. In spite of the hunger gnawing at her and the dryness in her throat, she knew the first thing she had to search for was a light of any kind.

By feel, Erica searched through the boxes and containers. Anytime her hands touched a metal or plastic cylinder, she attempted to turn it on. Then she discovered a bundle of plastic sticks. Detaching one of them, she pressed its midsection until she heard a soft cracking.

Shaking the stick for a few moments produced a greenish, phosphorescent glow, enough to dimly illuminate the survival locker. After it, Erica quickly found a flashlight and supplies of survival rations. The first she opened was a container of drinking water. The size of a beer can, she consumed its contents so fast it almost choked her. Erica paused just long enough for her coughing to subside before ripping open a package of beef sausages.

On her third sausage, she had relaxed enough to search through the rest of the locker for gear she would need. The next item she picked up was an exposure suit pack, which she ripped open. The one Erica was wearing had long since become waterlogged, as had the clothes under it. She would later change her suit, wring the water out of her clothes; and attempt to stay warm by using a thermal blanket pack.

Moments later Erica found a medical kit and pulled from it bottles of aspirin and dramamine. For all her aches she knew she would need them, now as well as for later. No matter how experienced she had become with ocean storms, or how seasoned her "sea legs" were, Erica knew the rig's constant vertical movement would eventually make her seasick.

She had reached the survival locker's back end, and had just peered through its tiny porthole when her flashlight beam fell on an emergency radio pack.

It was one of the few items still on the shelves, which meant it wouldn't be damaged; unlike some of the other electronic equipment Erica had found. She grabbed the brightly colored, plastic box off its shelf and studied it with her flashlight. It bore the name "Grundig;" at least *Ocean Valkyrie* was stocked with the best survival gear money could buy. It had a very spartan array of controls. No exotic features, no state-of-the-art frills, just a solidly-built radio designed to use the international distress frequencies.

Erica knew this would be her best chance, her only chance, to communicate with the outside world. But there was a danger. Like all the other oil rigs in the North Sea, *Valkyrie* monitored the distress frequencies. If the terrorists in the communication center were observant enough, they would see the monitoring system light up the moment she started to transmit.

Erica knew she would be killed if discovered, but if she never made the attempt, the outside world would never know what was happening on the oil rig. No one would ever know how her friends had been murdered, or how brutal the terrorists were. Slowly she pulled the radio's antenna out of its recessed well, until it was fully deployed, and tentatively thumbed the power control button.

Chapter Seven

"Thank you so much for finally coming down to see us," Yussuf Gunni remarked sarcastically when the door to the communications center clanked open. Abu Nazal stepped inside. "Are you here to relieve us?"

"You'll be relieved in due course," said Nazal. "I came here to see if you've prepared for the storm, and how your negotiations with the British are faring."

"I've retracted most of the aerials and shut down the systems we're not using," said a female terrorist. "I'm monitoring all Marine, Aviation and Military channels I can."

"You've done well, Almira. The moment you, or anyone else, hears the name *Ocean Valkyrie* mentioned you contact me. Yussuf, how have the British and Norwegians reacted since Sivertsen stopped talking to them and you took over?"

"I've told them my name is Eric, but I think they know I'm not Norwegian," said Gunni.

"Don't bother telling me the obvious!" Nazal shouted, his weariness giving way to anger. "Tell me something I haven't already guessed at."

"For the last two hours I've been talking exclusively with British officials." While there was civility in his latest answer, a fire burned in Gunni's eyes. They narrowed and darkened visibly, making him look even more ape-like than before. "I've given them the standard answers about the crew and the wounded, but they insist on talking to some of our prisoners. What should we do?"

"Give them some. I'll have Captain Reitan and Doctor

117

Lunde sent down. They will say what we'll tell them to say. They'll come down with Sherina. She will relieve you."

"Sherina? Why her? You and Jassem decided this without consulting me! I remind you I'm also a commander of this unit!"

"Shut up, Yussuf. We can't always make decisions by taking a vote," said Nazal. "We felt the voice of a woman would throw the officials off. Remember our training, remember the lectures? Do something unexpected and it will confuse the authorities. It will delay them, and that's what we want. Almira, what is this system and why is it on?"

While he argued with Gunni, Nazal continued his examination of the communications center. He scanned the control panels on each console, checking to see which was still active or not. He finally came across one panel which was still active but not attended.

"This is the distress channel monitoring system," said Almira, joining Nazal. "It automatically searches the Marine and Aviation distress frequencies and locks in on any signal. It's standard equipment to all North Sea oil rigs."

"Turn it off. We're not here to rescue Norwegians, or any other westerners. Our mission is to save our countries, and take revenge on the West. If anyone is in trouble out there, let them die in the cold."

As Nazal walked away from the console, Almira hit the power switches to the monitoring system. One by one, the status lights died and there was a brief crackle of static on the loudspeakers. Except for manually setting the center's main communications system to the emergency frequencies, there was no longer any way to monitor them. A few moments later everyone in the room had forgotten about it.

Erica ran her thumb over the power button a dozen times and more, until she had worked up the courage to press it. With a burst of static, the radio in her hands came to life. She flipped the frequency control knob to the 156.8 megahertz setting, the international maritime distress channel. The static diminished to a soft buzz, and was augmented by a high-pitched wailing that seemed to slide through the air. And momentarily it was all cut out when she hit the transmit switch on the side of the radio.

"Mayday . . . mayday, mayday . . . I'm a survivor of a terrorist attack on the Scandinavian Petro rig *Ocean Valkyrie,*" Erica said hesitantly. "To anyone who's listening, please answer. Over."

Erica released the rocker switch and listened to the buzz and wailing for several seconds before repeating her message. For nearly a minute she continued this way, and grew increasingly frustrated at the lack of a response. After her fourth try, she realized her messages were going no further than the steel shell of the equipment locker.

If they were to do something more than bounce uselessly around the room, Erica would have to find some way of directing them outside. She remembered the porthole, and whirled around to face it.

It was smaller than the ones normally found on ships and oil rigs; it was only six inches in diameter and had a double pane of tempered glass. When Erica first looked through the porthole all she could see was darkness. When she used her flashlight, it was possible to see sleet and sea spray striking the outer glass; then it was seemingly underwater as a wave crashed against that side of the base leg. In spite of the porthole's small size and the storm conditions outside, it was the only way to get the signal outside. Erica touched the radio's antenna to the inner pane of glass and pressed the rocker switch again.

"Mayday, mayday, mayday. I'm a survivor of a terrorist attack on the Scandinavian Petro rig *Ocean Valkyrie* . . . To anyone who's listening, please answer me. Over."

"Captain Taylor to wireless office at once! Captain Taylor, please report to the wireless office!" shouted the *Spartan*'s communications officer, Lieutenant Donald MacGregor; by the time he finished his second appeal, he heard the stamp of shoes on steel. He had just enough time to reposition the console microphone to his left side before a shadow appeared behind him.

"What is it, Donnie? An Admiralty signal?" Taylor asked, stepping inside the radio room.

"No, sir. It's an emergency broadcast from someone on bloody *Valkyrie*," said MacGregor. "I think it might be the friend of the people we rescued. Listen . . ."

For a few moments there was only static on the room's loudspeakers. Barely noticed, a faint clicking echoed through the buzz and suddenly the speakers were reverberating with a woman's voice. It was thin, attenuated, but it was definitely female and began its broadcast with the standard international warning.

"Mayday, mayday, mayday. I am a survivor of a terrorist attack on the Scandinavian Petro rig *Ocean Valkyrie*. To anyone who's listening, please answer. Over."

"Put me on," said Taylor, grabbing the console microphone. "And I pray the terrorists aren't monitoring the distress channels like we are."

Erica released the transmit switch and listened intently to the resulting flood of static. Silently she started counting off the seconds she would allow before making another try; she was determined to give anyone who heard her enough time to respond. Still, even with the count the tension rapidly grew to an unbearable level for Erica. For a moment she even wished the terrorists would answer — at least it would mean her waiting would be over.

"To *Ocean Valkyrie* survivor, this is Commander Taylor of the Royal Navy. Please switch to channels ten or twelve. I repeat, switch to either channel ten or twelve in order to continue this conversation. Over."

The voice sounded clear enough to be coming from the next compartment. There was little static or distortion. Erica nearly dropped the radio, but not before she did what she was told and clicked the frequency control knob to one of the channels Taylor had identified.

"Commander, my name is Erica Johensen," she began. "My rig has been captured by Arab terrorists. Can you rescue me? Can you tell me where you are?"

"Yes, Miss Johensen, we know all about you," said Taylor. "We rescued your friends, Tryggve Nordsen and Frieda Gran, when we arrived here a few hours ago. I am Commander Stanford Leigh Taylor, Captain of Her Majesty's Submarine *Spartan*. Please hold on, we're bringing up one of your friends."

"Captain, Mr. Newcane is bringing the woman," said MacGregor. "They'll be here soon."

"Good. How powerful is her signal?" Taylor asked. "And how powerful are you making ours?"

"Weak and highly directional. My thought is she's using a hand-held set and broadcasting through a porthole. She's not being heard beyond line-of-sight, and neither are we. I've set the power to make sure of it. Since this area's been quarantined and the surrounding oil rigs placed under a communications blackout, there's little fear of being overheard."

"Save for the terrorists themselves. We can only hope they're too busy to monitor the distress channels. Frieda, did Mr. Newcane—"

"He told me Erica's alive," she answered, before Taylor had even finished his question. Frieda rushed into the compartment while Newcane remained outside. There was so little room left in it, one more body meant there wouldn't be enough to maneuver, or breathe. "Where is she? Can I talk to her?"

"Yes, we want you to talk with her," said Taylor. "And we believe she's back on *Valkyrie*. Ask her where she is, her condition and if she's had any contact with the terrorists."

Taylor offered Frieda the console mike and she sat in the one other chair the radio room had. She took a moment to compose herself before pressing the transmit switch on the mike stand and cutting out the static on the room's speakers.

"Erica? Erica, this is Frieda," announced a new voice on the radio, one immediately familiar to Johensen. "I'm so grateful you're alive, I almost gave you up for dead. Are you okay? Can you tell us where you are?"

121

"And I thought you and Trig were dead," said Erica, after pressing in the rocker switch. "I thought I had failed you. I'm glad to hear someone else didn't. I'm in an emergency locker in one of *Valkyrie's* base legs, I think one of the southern legs. I'm not injured, but I've been locked inside this room by the terrorists. Over."

"The terrorists locked you in? Do they know about you?"

For a second or two the voice faded as Erica lost her footing and slipped away from the porthole. The rig's storm-induced vertical movement was now approaching ten feet, less than a third the height of the waves pounding away at it but enough to make it difficult for even experienced rig workers to maintain their footing.

"No. No, they don't know about me," said Erica, regaining her balance. "They locked me in here when they were setting an explosive charge in the outer compartment. Over."

"Erica, the Captain wants to know more about those explosives. Can you see them? What kind are they? Did you overhear the terrorists say anything about them?"

"No, I can't see them. There's no view port in the door. The terrorists used plastic explosives, marine demolition charges from the rig's own stores. From the way they spoke, they've wired all of *Valkyrie* with explosives and plan to sink it when their operation is finished."

"Erica, this is Taylor," said the radio's original voice. "Are you certain about this? I have to know. If it's true, I must send it to the people dealing with the crisis. Over."

"It's true," Erica replied. "Everything I've told you is true. Their exact words were, 'we must make sure this rig will sink when we're finished with it.' They also said 'by the time *Valkyrie* sinks, we'll be far away.' I can give you more—I may have been terrified but I remembered everything I heard."

"No, this will be enough for now. Thank you, Erica. We're going to have to break contact, we can't maintain constant communications. Do you have a watch?"

"Yes, and it's still working. Working better than me."

"We'll contact you in two hours," said Taylor. "I'm putting Frieda back on, don't take very long saying good-bye. Have courage, Erica. If you think of anything else that's important, tell me in two hours. Over."

A moment later Frieda was on the line, and saying a tearful farewell. Erica didn't cry until after she had signed off, and switched off the radio. She did not cry out of fear, she cried out of relief. After being alone and hunted for hours, she at last was connected with someone. After being victimized by powerful enemies, at last she had a powerful ally.

"Deploy the trailing wire aerial," Taylor ordered, as Newcane helped Frieda back to the sick bay. "We're going to have to make another data transmission."

"Will it be to the Admiralty again?" asked MacGregor, switching off the UHF system.

"No, Donnie. This one will go directly to Bradbury Lines. The SAS and SBS are handling this crisis. They should have this information as fast as possible, without it being filtered through a bureaucracy."

"Yes, even without meaning to, Whitehall can muck things up. Captain, storm effects at this depth will make deployment of the aerial difficult. If we could dive a hundred feet, it would make things much easier."

"I'll see to it straightaway," said Taylor, turning to leave the compartment. "Don't start sending until I return."

A minute later HMS *Spartan* dipped its pointed, whale-like, nose and descended to a calmer layer of water. Once it had arrived, and trimmed out, a buoyant drag body would be ejected from the back of its sail. The drag body would unreel a wire barely thicker than a human hair to a length of several hundred feet. Once deployed, the aerial would transmit a VLF signal to a receiving station in Britain; from there it would be sent on to SAS regiment headquarters.

The first sensation Gavrilla felt was a steady vibration, a buzzing which shook her whole body. The first emotion she felt was fear—she had no idea where she was. Like a diver ascending out of the depths, she clawed her way out of sleep and tried to sit upright; causing her to crash into the low ceiling over the bunk.

"Whoa, Lady. Watch yourself," said a voice she could not recognize. "You'll do more damage to yourself than the plane. Takeover, Herb, and tell the Israelis their girl is awake."

Ratz unlocked one of the armrests on his seat and let it fall. He turned as he rose, neatly sidestepping the cockpit's center pedestal and reaching Gavrilla in a few strides. On her second attempt to sit up, she kept her head down and managed to swing her legs over the edge of the cockpit's bunk.

"Where . . . where are we?" she groaned, still feeling aches in most of her muscles. "Are we in Israel yet?"

"We're crossing the Egyptian coast," said Ratz. "Why don't you come forward? We're changing escorts—it's quite a show."

He took a firm grip on her arm to steady her, and Gavrilla slid out of the bunk and walked across the cockpit deck to the flight engineer's chair. Positioned behind the center instrument pedestal, the chair gave her a clear field of view obstructed only by the head rests on the pilot's seats.

Directly in front of her were the display screens for the Combat Talon's forward-looking infrared sensor, low-light TV cameras and terrain-following radar. Each of them showed the same image, in different colors and with varying degrees of detail: the coastline of Egypt, from just west of Alexandria to the Libyan border. They also showed fleeting silhouettes of the aircraft maneuvering ahead of the C-130.

Gavrilla saw them as collections of formation lights and glowing jet exhausts. The single points of flame diving to the left were Egyptian Air Force Mig-21s, their escorts since departing Libyan airspace. The twin exhausts climbing off to the right were Ben Zion and the rest of his flight of F-15s. Their part of the mission was over and they were returning to Israel. And passing over the C-130's windshield, their exhausts briefly illuminating the cockpit, were two jets Gavrilla couldn't identify, but more massive than the F-15s.

"Gavi, I hope you slept well," said Adir, climbing out of the cockpit's port entry well. "You were more exhausted than any of us thought."

"Avrom, what's happening?" Gavrilla asked. "Shouldn't we be landing in Israel? What's going on? We're heading into the Mediterranean."

"There's been a radical change in plans. Nine hours ago the oil rig you mentioned, *Ocean Valkyrie,* was seized by terrorists in the North Sea. Though they've claimed to be a Norwegian environmentalist group, they have since been positively identified as Arab terrorists."

"Who did it? Was it my information?"

"No, most of your information only reinforced the findings of the British," said Adir, he finished climbing the steps and crossed to the navigator's station on the cockpit's starboard side. He eased into its chair while Gavrilla swung hers around to face him. "One of their submarines rescued two Norwegians near the oil rig. They were survivors of a helicopter the terrorists loaded with wounded and evacuees, and then blew out of the sky with a surface-to-air missile."

"Oh God . . . yes, it sounds like the 'strike teams' the Libyans were training," said Gavrilla, her face suddenly growing pale. "Avrom, how many people have they killed?"

"Including those they shot when they took the rig, including those murdered when they originally hijacked the helicopter . . . more than sixty."

"Nazih boasted his Blood Revenge units would be ruthless and efficient. It sounds like we have the right group."

"I'm certain of it. There's one extra bit of information that cements their identity," said Adir. "The survivors also mentioned two steel cases brought aboard *Valkyrie.* Cases marked with the bio-hazard symbol. So now you can see why our plans have been changed. We're heading for England. Their elite forces are in charge of retaking the oil rig and they need all the help and information we can give them."

"I understand, but wouldn't it be just as easy to do it from Israel?" Gavrilla remarked. "The Europeans haven't been very friendly or supportive of us recently. I know we should help—I want to help—but we can do it from our country."

"You're sounding a bit like Yehuda. Don't be prickly, Gavi. The air force crew may call this plane Mossad Airlines, but it's a United States Air Force aircraft and they have their orders. Besides, I personally want to be as close to the men who are going to retake *Valkyrie* as possible. That way, we can ensure they'll have all the information they need to win. Sometimes governments don't always provide their people with everything they need. They only provide them with what they think is needed. Remember the Egyptians? They've bungled every anti-terrorist operation they've tried, mostly because of too much control by higher authorities."

"All right, I see your reasons. Even if I refused to go, how could I stop the Americans from carrying out their orders? Will we be flying straight to England?"

"I believe so. Major, is our destination England?" Adir asked, raising his voice so the flight crew could hear him.

"Eventually it will be," said Ratz, glancing over his shoulder. "Nathan's still negotiating with NATO and Special Operations Command. At least we got our Navy escorts. Our new heading is due west."

"Ah yes, Nathan. We should return to the tactical box, Gavi. There's more questioning to do — do you feel up to it?"

"No, but if we don't do it now, I may start forgetting details," said Gavrilla, rising out of the flight engineer's chair. Her legs had become stronger and her balance was steadier. "Shall we go?"

Since she had no recollection of how she got to the cockpit, Gavrilla had to be led down the stairs of its entry well. Adir took her back to the ECM/Elint box and inside, they found Shoham and Eshel waiting for them. Ready to resume where they had left off.

Outside, with the airspace around the Combat Talon at last clear of F-15s and Mig-21s, its new escorts settled onto its wing tips. Their own wings swept forward, the Grumman F-14s more comfortably matched the C-130's relatively low cruising speed than either the Israeli or Egyptian fighters. A few minutes after their rendezvous, the three aircraft banked gently to the left and headed out over the Mediterranean. Their new course was westerly and, some ten hours away, was the transport's destination. England.

"Bravo Union, Bravo Union, this is Poole Air Traffic Control. You're still on glideslope, you should have the helipad lights in sight."

"Negative, Control. The storm's still a bit claggy up here. But the transponder beacon is strong and we're coming in."

"Roger, Bravo Union. Advise us when you've spotted the lights. You need not acknowledge any further transmissions."

The Royal Air Force Chinook Bravo Union continued to drop blindly through the gale-driven snowstorm; its flight crew concentrating more on their instruments than on the featureless blur outside. A few hundred feet later, the slab-sided helicopter had finally descended close enough to the ground for the landing pad's blue-white strobe lights to be seen.

"Colonel, we have your base in sight," said the pilot. "If this wind doesn't blow us down, we'll land in the next minute."

"I never had any doubts we wouldn't make it," Boyd replied. "Keep your engines running after we land. We won't be on the ground for very long."

The twin-rotored helicopter looked like a flying brick and its maneuvers were ungainly, but in the stiff, swirling winds it was relatively steady. All the pilots had to do was slide it to the left and it touched down on the helipad's center mark. As Boyd had ordered, they kept the engines idling after the Chinook had settled onto its landing gear. Its tail ramp started to open.

"Welcome home, Colonel! How long will you be down?" asked one of the Royal Marine officers on the pad, before the ramp had even finished lowering.

"About as long as it takes for you to complete loading this whale!" said Boyd. When the ramp was down, he extended his hand to the officer and helped him into the spacious fuselage where the noise level was slightly lower. "Do you have everything I asked for, Ross?"

"Yes, Robert," said Captain Ross Ackland. "Thirty officers and men, including yourself, and enough weapons and munitions for sixty. You also requested we pack aqualungs and wet suits instead of our normal dry suits. Why the change?"

"Because, owing to the sea conditions around *Valkyrie,* it won't be necessary to make a stealthy entrance to the oil rig. Also, it may be necessary to abandon this equipment, and since we're so chronically underfunded, I decided it would be appropriate to go with less expensive equipment. Yes, bring it on. There's no time to waste." ·

Boyd directed his comments to the Royal Marines still standing at the Chinook's tail ramp, who started boarding the moment they got his orders. They trooped aboard the aircraft, the stamp of their boots adding to the vibrations created by the engines and the slapping rotor blades. The first two enlisted men to enter the fuselage dropped sets of heavy equipment bags beside Ackland and Boyd, then marched off to get their own.

"These are the messages and updates we received while you were en route," said Ackland, handing over a thin documents case to Boyd. "You'll find some of them rather disturbing."

Boyd unzipped the case and scanned each of the reports it contained. At first he smiled to himself, as if he found something amusing, but his expression quickly grew darker when he got past the initial sheets. His reading pace slowed to a crawl as he carefully considered the new information.

"Good Lord, the terrorists have a biological weapon?" Boyd asked, incredulous. "This can certainly change our operation. Does anyone know what it's going to be used for?"

"If you'll read on, there's a report from U.S. Air Force Special Operations Command," said Ackland. "They just rescued someone who knows."

"I see, an Israeli agent. A woman, interesting. It looks like she may know a lot. I want her."

"Well, the Americans *are* bringing her to England. They'll arrive in another ten or twelve hours."

"No, I want her with us. On the *John Marshall* itself. We don't have the time to wait and have her brief us after she flies into Bradbury Lines. Since I'm mission commander, I'll be able to get her destination changed."

"Did you also see the latest update from HMS *Spartan?*"

"You mean this one? It looks as if the Royal Navy's been busy," said Boyd, holding up one of the last sheets from the

128

case. When he read it, his mood started to lighten, a slight smile even returned to his face. "Well, this is a good bit of news — it may almost cancel out the bad news. We have a contact board the oil rig itself. When will the sub try to talk with her again?"

"They didn't say," Ackland replied. "My guess would be in the next few hours."

"Then it's imperative for me to leave some messages before we take off. Perhaps we'll have some answers by the time we reach Mildenhall. Ross, we'd better find Wallis."

While the balance of his men boarded the Chinook, Boyd and his executive officer walked down its tail ramp and hunted for another Royal Marine officer among those at the helipad. After a little searching they found the base communications officer near the row of trucks which had brought the Special Boat Squadron out to the pad.

For a few minutes all three huddled inside a truck cab where Boyd dictated the messages he wanted sent. Safe from the wind, heavy snow and the roar of the helicopter engines, they quickly finished their tasks and re-emerged. Boyd gave Wallis a final salute and hurried back to the Chinook with Ackland in tow.

On board he found the rest of his men lashing down their equipment bags with the help of the Royal Air Force loadmasters. As Boyd made his way forward he greeted, or was greeted by, the officers and enlisted men he knew. At the helicopter's cockpit he asked the pilots if they were ready to go.

"We have our flight plan for Mildenhall and our tail ramp's just closed," said the pilot. "We're secured for takeoff."

"Inform traffic control you wish to leave," said Boyd. "I'll warn my men."

A few minutes later the Chinook's rotor blades were slapping the air more vigorously and the jet engines mounted in its tail were screaming a little louder. With a burst of rotor wash that temporarily abated the winds, the flying brick slowly lifted off the helipad. Almost at once it was swallowed up by the storm; the wind carried away the noise and the anticollision strobes soon vanished. At near full load, the helicopter took longer than normal to climb out, though it eventually reached its cruise altitude and set course to the northeast.

"Sergeant, activate the addressing system." Boyd directed, stepping out of the cockpit.

After takeoff, the noise level in the fuselage dropped considerably. While still annoying, it allowed for a halfway normal conversation; most of the men on the cargo deck were chatting when a shrill feedback tone erupted from the loudspeakers.

"Sorry about that," the senior loadmaster apologized, giving the hand mike to Boyd. "Just key the lever to talk."

"Thank you. Gentlemen, your attention please," said Boyd. "I know these aren't the most ideal conditions for a briefing, but we don't have time for a cozy little chat in a teak-paneled room. As you know, a Norwegian oil rig has been seized by terrorists in the North Sea. In part, we've been given the assignment to take it back. What you don't know, what has been kept secret from all those not directly connected to the operation is the following.

"In taking *Ocean Valkyrie,* the terrorists have killed more than sixty people. Most of the terrorists are Arabic, not Norwegian. They may in fact be Libyan-backed terrorists, or a Libyan intelligence unit. They're ruthless, they're armed with sophisticated weapons, including surface-to-air missiles and something more ominous — a biological warfare weapon."

Though he couldn't hear it, Boyd knew his last remark produced a wave of shocked mutterings from his men. What he could see were the surprised expressions on their faces.

"What it is, what it can do, we don't yet know. But there's someone who does. An Israeli agent the United States Air Force rescued from Libya, who will be joining us later.

"We'll be using a submarine to reach the oil rig, a very special one. You've probably heard of it, the USS *John Marshall.* And that's why we're carrying double loads of weapons, munitions and assault equipment. A thirty-man SEAL Team is already aboard the *Marshall.* We'll be joining forces with them."

This time Boyd could hear some of the remarks his men were making; clearly they did not enjoy the thought of being paired with another unit.

"Colonel, you can't be serious," said a Corporal. "They're bloody cowboys. They think they're the best and they aren't."

"I quite agree," said one of the officers. "They have a severe discipline problem, and an attitude problem. Cooperation is an alien concept to them. I don't know who's worse, their officers or their enlisted men. I'd prefer working with their Marine Corps Force Recon. Even the Green Berets would be better."

"I know, the SEALs don't have the best reputation," Boyd admitted. "Though I have heard that this unit's commander, Glenn Allard, is highly regarded. We don't have the ideal, we must make do with what's at hand. The SEALs are embarked on the submarine. Replacing them would be needlessly difficult, and that submarine is the only way to get a force our size out to the oil rig. It's a risk to use the SEALs, I know. But we can't avoid all risks, and hopefully the Yanks will be professional enough to set aside their personality problems for the duration of our crisis."

Chapter Eight

"Captain, I got something on the bow imagers," said Jefferson, back at his station as senior helmsman. "It looks like another sub but it's running cool. A lot cooler than most boats I've seen, boomers included. It's also running about a hundred feet shallower than us. I'm going to have to change our depth to keep it in view."

"Do what you have to, Clarence," said Carver, glancing at the predominately blue shadow on the infrared imager screen. "Only make the maneuvers easy. This is the *Onondaga,* all right. The reason it's cooler is it's non-nuclear. It's an *Oberon* class diesel-electric boat. One of the advantages of conventional submarines is they don't run hot."

"Well that's probably the only advantage it has. It's so old they should home port it in a museum."

"Clarence, the *Onondaga*'s about seven years younger than this boat. The Lady's really showing her vintage, isn't she? There, the Canadians are on the laser radar. Hawkins should be contacting them by now. Greg, you're in command. I'll be in the radio room."

"I wish I could join you," said Burks, letting out a nervous sigh. "Tell us the moment you get the first message in."

Carver nodded an acknowledgment to his exec as he walked past. Though he tried to keep calm, Carver's stride was picking up by the time he reached the back of the control center. A moment later he was at the radio room's hatch and found another officer waiting outside the room. "I see I'm not the only one who's anxious about this next group of messages," Carver observed.

"Who? Me anxious? Why should I be anxious?" said Allard, faking terror. "What comes in next only means whether I continue to wear this uniform, or go to work with my family's mercenary squad."

"Captain, I have contact with the other sub," said Hawkins. "It's a voice transmission, I'll put it on the loudspeakers."

"John Marshall, this is HMCS *Onondaga.* We're ready to give you a data squirt. There's enough messages here for us to open a Western Union office."

"Roger, *Onondaga,* we're set at this end. Commence data transmission."

Hawkins cut out the speakers and changed the high-frequency system from two-way voice communication to data reception. Almost at once, the printer began operation, clacking softly as Carver stood over it. This time he didn't have the patience to wait for the message to be completed before he started to read it.

"COMSUBLANT SIGNIT Bulletin. To USS *John Marshall.* T. W. Carver, commanding," he said, an edge of nervousness creeping into his voice. "Special Forces UK have requested you for operation in *Ocean Valkyrie* crisis! Proceed at once to position Bravo-One-Five-Tango for rendezvous with *Kitty Hawk* battle group. Royal Marine Special Boat Squadron en route to carrier. Rendezvous and airlift to commence at zero-nine-thirty hours, local time. Disregard previous bulletin. Make best speed, COMSUBLANT, out.

We did it!"

Carver turned and embraced Allard, both laughing loud enough for it to echo in the passageway outside. When they separated, Carver ripped the message off the printer and displayed it to Allard, then swung around to Hawkins.

"Jake, put me on the public address system," he requested, the nervousness gone from his voice, a tone of elation and triumph replacing it. He picked a hand mike off a wall-mounted com panel and waited for Hawkins to give him the go-ahead signal before pressing the transmit switch. "May I have your attention. This is the Captain speaking. Gentlemen, the gamble has paid off. The Brits have put in a formal request for us and the brass ashore have sent us on our way. We've just been handed our last and best chance to prove ourselves. Celebrate now, but remember, this was the easy part. The hard work is still ahead of us. Captain, out."

As he hung the microphone back on its wall mount, Carver heard a cheer ripple down the passageway from the control center. From the sonar room, the radar room, the nucleonics lab and the rest of the compartments on the first operations level the sounds of celebration could be heard. For a few moments, Carver leaned into the passageway and allowed himself to enjoy it.

"Terry . . . we got more news and not all of it is good," said Allard. "Take a look."

He handed to Carver one of the messages which had come in since the COMSUBLANT bulletin. Then another after he finished the first one and still another until he had gone through all of them.

"You're right. Some of this is disturbing," said Carver, his mood more sober. "But at least Robert Boyd's been assigned to the operation, and his unit's bringing you the equipment you'll need."

"Yes, it looks like we're going to get a little reverse Lend-Lease," Allard replied, taking back the reports and sorting through them. "Most of these are about the terrorists or the SBS team, so my men should see them. Only the COMSUBLANT message and this signal from the *Kitty Hawk* are for you. I'd better be heading back — would you care to come?"

"I'd like to, but I have to prepare us for the upcoming rendezvous. We'll have to surface and establish contact with the *Kitty Hawk*. I'll be busy for the next hour, Glenn — as I'm sure you will. We'll have to see each other later."

After they shook hands Carver returned to the *Marshall's* control center while Allard wheeled around and made for the passageway's opposite end. When he ducked through an open hatch he passed from the submarine's living and operations area to what had once been its missile compartment.

In fact, two of the missile launch tubes were still in place in the compartment's forward end. Only now they weren't loaded with Polaris missiles but with one of the *Marshall*'s two Phalanx cannon mounts and its lightweight anti-aircraft missile launcher.

Where launch tubes three and four had once stood were the submarine's swim-out chambers. They were larger and rectangular in shape, big enough to fit four divers, their scuba gear and other equipment. They both tapered abruptly to circular hatches no larger than the original missile tubes. The space between them was narrower, slowing Allard down until he reached the watertight security bulkhead separating the chambers from the preparation and briefing room. From it, he could hear the murmurings of conversation and could identify individual voices.

"Yeah, he may sound happy now, but you should've seen him the last time we made one of these stops," said Martirri, leaning against the compartment's center table. "He was scared, man, he was pale. Pale enough to be a real spook."

"How pale do you think you'd get, white boy?" asked one of the black members of the SEAL Team, ". . . after I've drained the blood out of you?"

"Cool it, Strader. Save your knife for Arab throats," said Allard, before he had finished opening the hatch. "And Sal, knock off those remarks. Don't get yourself into anymore trouble than you already are."

Allard emerged with the handful of printer sheets he had taken from the radio room. While he laid them on the table, and the rest of his team gathered around it, no one made a move to grab the reports. They knew Allard would explain it all now and give them a chance to examine everything later.

"Since you've already heard the good news I won't repeat it," he continued. "This is the serious news. Reports about the terrorists we're facing, and the Special Boat Squadron we'll be partnered with. Yes, the rumors are correct. A thirty-man SBS platoon is being flown out to the *Kitty Hawk* to join us."

A rumble of groans and mutterings greeted Allard's announcement. While only a few openly objected to the news, he could see it wasn't widely popular with his men.

"I knew it. The moment I heard the commander of that unit was an old friend of Carver's I just knew we'd have to put up

135

with the fucking Brits," said Martirri. "The 'old boy' network in action again."

"Is this true, Commander?" a Petty Officer asked. "Are you going to make us work with a bunch of jarhead Brits?"

"The reason we're working with the British is because this is a British operation in the first place," said Allard. "The Norwegians gave control over to them, not us. This is a British show and they could've frozen us out if they wanted to. But they realize they need this submarine. We're just an extra dividend. As it is, the Brits have to bring us most of the gear we'll need."

"Why do we have to use their stuff?" said Martirri, angrily. "The M-16's a good weapon — we can take the oil rig with it as well as any other."

"Are you out of your fucking mind, Sal?" Chen asked. "Fire an M-16 in this compartment and see what happens. You'll kill half of us by ricochets alone. We need specialized automatic weapons with silencers to take the rig. Ring the bell if you want to, only don't take me as well."

The compartment's floor suddenly shifted and its front end tilted up several degrees. A distant, deep hissing could be heard; the submarine's bow and stern ballast tanks were being emptied. Those not sitting or leaning against something momentarily lost their footing. For a few seconds no one spoke until the noisy shuffling of feet stopped and Carver finished his announcement of the *Marshall* surfacing.

"What the hell's going on? I thought this sub was going back to a high-speed run," said Martirri.

"First, we have to surface and get in touch with the *Kitty Hawk*," said Allard, grabbing the edge of the table. "To establish the exact rendezvous point and time. We'll go back to a Sub-scape run afterwards. Artie's right, Sal, and the rest of you know it. You can't use high-powered assault rifles in something which is basically one steel box piled atop another. Even our .45s are useless — we don't have silencers for them.

"Whether or not you want to work with the Royal Marines, the reality is we HAVE to work with them. We don't have half the number of men we need, and almost none of the right equipment. And one other thing — we're not just up against some crazy environmentalists or wild-eyed Arabs. We're facing something a lot more sinister."

Allard sifted through the reports and selected two. One from Bradbury Lines and the other from the U.S. Air Force.

"What is it, Commander?" Strader inquired. "Do the guys wearing the bed sheets have a nuclear weapon?"

"If they did, it would make our problems a little easier to resolve," said Allard. "The first report originally came from the British attack sub circling *Ocean Valkyrie*. The terrorists took aboard the rig two cases of suspected bio-warfare agents. And this one, from the Air Force, verifies they have a biological weapon on the rig. It's a genetically engineered organism designed to eat crude oil. If injected into the North Sea oil fields, it would destroy them."

Allard handed one of the tear sheets to Chen, the other to Martirri. The comments and side conversations had died away, Allard didn't really need to glance around to see that the expressions on the faces of his men had grown more sober.

"Jesus, Commander. Why don't the Brits just put torpedoes into the rig?" another Petty Officer observed.

"I'll bet the idea has crossed their minds," said Allard. "But there's a problem. There are almost two hundred Norwegians on *Valkyrie*, and I think the British promised Norway they would get them off alive. So you see, whether you like it or not we're going to have to work with the British. And this crisis is far too serious for any of you to threaten it with macho attitudes about being better than anyone else. Remember what I've kept telling you: 'an elite unit doesn't mean elitism.' You're the best this Navy has. Prove it by behaving as true professionals when the British come aboard."

From its cruise depth of five hundred and sixty feet, the *John Marshall* rose steadily toward the surface. For the first time in more than twenty-four hours it broke through the waves and, in spite of its massive hull, rolled unsteadily. More than three hundred miles off the coast of Newfoundland, it was the only ship visible from horizon to horizon.

No one appeared in the conning tower's flying bridge. The only external activity on the submarine was the raising of its radar, satellite navigation and radio masts. For several minutes it rode the waves while it communicated with the distant carrier battle group. Its masts were still raised when brief jets of spray erupted along its hull.

The *Marshall* settled back into the water slowly. By the time its hull was completely awash all the masts were retracted flush with the top of the conning tower. It picked up speed as it descended, for when the tower was partially submerged the diving planes were pitched down sharply. Less than a minute later the submarine was gone, returning to the safety of deep waters where it could resume its Sub-scape run across the North Atlantic.

"Bravo Union, this is Mildenhall Control. You should have runway approach and threshold lights in sight."

"Roger, Mildenhall. We have them in sight and we're on glideslope," the Chinook pilot answered.

"Roger, Bravo Union. Continue your descent, you needn't acknowledge any further transmissions. After your arrival use taxiway Zed-Three. The U.S. Navy is waiting for you, the Greyhound has just started its engines."

For more than an hour the Chinook had been flying on a north-northeast course from Britain's southern coast to East Anglia. It skirted around London to avoid its congested airspace, and never saw another aircraft until it entered the glow of the runway threshold lights at R.A.F. Mildenhall.

Though it was listed as a Royal Air Force base, Mildenhall in fact housed very few British aircraft. It was a NATO airfield with a largely American contingent of planes. Most of the ones visible on the flight line and taxiways were KC-135 tankers and C-130 transports. The only combat aircraft to be seen were some Netherlands Air Force F-16s, weathered in by the storm.

The Chinook clattered down the runway and swung onto taxi strip Z-3, but didn't actually land until it reached the flight line. A plane director with glowing batons motioned for it to set down next to one of the few grey and white aircraft on the field.

"All right, lads. Grab your equipment," said Boyd, lifting the heavy canvas bags assigned to him. "I want you to file out in a double column. Move directly to the airplane beside us, and follow the crew's directions when stowing the gear. They may not be Royal Marines but they do know their airplane better than you do."

Boyd walked to the front of the column and reached the back of the Chinook by the time the tail ramp started to lower. A cold blast of rotor wash swept over him, and he wanted to drop his bags and turn up his jacket collar; but it only took a few more seconds for the ramp to drop in place, and suddenly he was leading his men onto the tarmac.

The rhythmic slapping of the helicopter's rotor blades competed with the high-pitched buzzing of the Greyhound's turbo-props. The pot-bellied transport was less than fifty yards from the Chinook and also had its tail ramp open. As he walked toward it, Boyd could see pilots still putting the aircraft through its pre-flight checks. The C-2's flaps and ailerons were briefly extended and retracted, while the rudders on its bizarre, quad-finned tail group moved back and forth. As he approached it, Boyd could also see a Royal Air Force officer among the men around the transport.

"Lieutenant Colonel Robert Boyd? I'm Squadron Leader Smythe," said the officer. "Could I see some identification?"

Boyd gave Smythe an irritated look, yet he knew the security procedures had to be followed. He dropped his bags, turned up his jacket's collar while he unzipped it, and produced both his Royal Marine and SAS security cards for Smythe to examine. When he handed them back, he turned over to Boyd a familiar-looking documents case.

"I do seem to be obtaining quite a collection of these," Boyd observed, opening the new case and pulling out a folder. He retrieved the first case he'd been given and slid the folder in before it was hit by too many sleet pellets. "I'll read the contents on the aircraft. Could you tell me what they are?"

"Reports from Bradbury Lines," said Smythe, accepting the empty case. "At least one of which is from the U.S. Navy. Things have been happening while you were airborne."

"Well I can't bloody well expect them to go on hold while I'm in transit. Thank you, Squadron Leader, sorry I can't stay. But this aircraft may not wait for me."

Boyd exchanged salutes with Smythe, who helped him

gather his bags. Though he had been the first to deplane from the Chinook, Boyd was the last to board the Greyhound. He found his men already stowing their equipment on the transport's cargo deck. After he turned his scuba gear and weapons over to a U.S. Navy loadmaster, he moved to the flight deck where the pilots were receiving their latest instructions from Mildenhall Tower.

"Lieutenant Colonel Boyd, I'm Commander Felner," said the pilot, turning to shake hands. "Welcome aboard Grumman Express. We just got clearance to taxi and we have a priority takeoff assignment. They're holding other traffic for us."

"Thank you, Commander. We're on a tight schedule," said Boyd. "My men are aboard. We can leave whenever you're ready."

"Just as soon as my crew chief makes the final walk-around. If you're looking for a place to rest, we got a couple of jump seats up here."

Felner nodded to the back of the cockpit, where there was a folded seat on either side of the door. Boyd selected the starboard one and pushed it open. While it wasn't very comfortable, it did allow him someplace other to sit apart from the crowded and noisy cargo deck. He opened the documents case and pulled out the newest folder. Boyd was still scanning the reports it contained when his executive officer appeared in the doorway.

"What did the RAF-type hand you?" Ackland asked, climbing onto the flight deck.

"Updates on the crisis," Boyd replied. "The U.S. Navy has given us the *John Marshall*. It will proceed to a rendezvous point with the *Kitty Hawk*. The U.S. Air Force will fly the Israelis out to the submarine — the change in orders has already been sent. And we have some more information on the bioweapon the terrorists possess. It's less dangerous and more frightening than we originally thought. The Israelis say it's not an anti-personnel weapon, so we won't have to fight in CBW isolation suits. The organism has been genetically engineered to attack oil and the terrorists will use *Valkyrie* to inject it into the North Sea. They'll destroy our economy, and Norway's as well."

"This means OPEC will return to the power it had in the seventies. My cockney father would say 'diabolical.' "

"And your father would certainly be right. The pieces are falling into place. When we reach the *Marshall* we'll have a lot to discuss with Carver and Commander Allard, and it looks like we'll be leaving for our rendezvous rather soon."

The sound level in the Greyhound's fuselage fell noticeably, enough for Boyd to look up and catch sight of the tail ramp being closed. With their equipment lashed to the cargo deck, his men were already taking the bench seats on either side of the fuselage. He also noticed that the loadmasters were arranging his men in specific groups.

"It's necessary to maintain our center-of-gravity," Felner advised. "You've given us a heavy load, nearly full capacity. You're lucky we got a nice, long runway. We couldn't take off from a carrier in this condition."

"Ross, you'd better take the other seat," said Boyd, ". . . before the U.S. Navy tells you where to sit."

Ackland folded down the cockpit's second jump seat while the crew made their final checks of the transport. The two loadmasters were the last ones to sit down, taking the seats reserved for them at the front of the cargo deck.

"Tower to Nickle-Two-Seven, you're cleared to taxi to Runway Thirty-three West. Advise us when you're ready to depart. Mildenhall, out."

With a burst of power from its Allison turboprops, the C-2 rolled out of its position on the flight line and swung toward an empty taxiway. On the other taxiways, larger transports and jet tankers stood idling. For the time being all departing traffic at Mildenhall was held up.

When it reached its assigned runway the Greyhound paused for several moments, making final checks, and then the engines were gunned and the buzzing of the propellers deepened. The heavily loaded transport accelerated sluggishly at first — not until it passed sixty miles an hour did its speed pick up rapidly.

Thirty seconds later the transport was at rotation speed, its bulbous nose rising into the air. Soon the main wheels skipped along the runway's surface and, with a final bounce, the C-2 waddled off the ground. It climbed above the glow of the threshold and approach lights, and became a moving pattern of navigation and anti-collision beacons. It climbed to the cloud base and was swallowed up by the night sky.

From Chinook touchdown to Greyhound departure the transfer of Boyd's men took just over fifteen minutes. Now they were heading west; four hours away was the aircraft carrier *Kitty Hawk,* the final transit point before reaching the *John Marshall.*

"Sky Chief Five-Seven, this is Falcon Zero-Four. We got our throttles to the fire walls," advised Ratz, his right hand on the quadrant of levers. "We're ready to try again."

Hovering less than fifty feet in front of the C-130's nose was a KC-135 tanker. In the growing, pre-dawn light it was easily discernible against the still dark western horizon, especially its V-winged refueling boom, once more dropping over the Combat Talon's cockpit. Unlike its F-14 escorts, which had hooked up several times to refuel with KA-6D tankers, this would be the first time since its rendezvous in Egypt for the transport to be refueled — provided the boom operator could fly his probe into the roof-mounted receptacle.

"These guys are having more problems than the first tanker had," said Goldberg. "If this keeps up we'll have to find a gas station in Spain which'll give us a volume discount."

"They're getting better, they'll do it right," said Ratz. "These guys are from Spangledesh, or some other West German air base, and they're probably used to refueling fighters or something a hell of a lot faster than us. Even at our maximum speed we're still skirting the stall speed of a one-thirty-five."

The descending boom once again began wavering as it entered the Combat Talon's slipstream. Its V-shaped wings maneuvered to keep it steady as the silver-tipped probe moved toward the receptacle hump. This time the boom didn't jerk erratically as it approached the C-130. Ratz and Goldberg kept their aircraft level until they heard a solid clanking over their heads, and the lights above the fuel gauges indicated a successful hookup had been made.

"Sky Chief Five-Seven, let the high-test flow," Ratz announced, letting go of the throttle levers. "We're switching to auto-pilot. Pilot to crew, refueling under way, we'll be done in five minutes. Yes, Major, what can we do for you?"

"We need our sleeping beauty," said Shoham, climbing out of the entrance well. "More information is coming in, and orders. Be prepared for a change in flight plans."

Shoham walked over to the bunk and woke up its occupant. This time Gavrilla did not come to with a start. She groaned a little and was able to slide out of the tiny bed without help.

"Can I ever get a decent sleep?" she asked. "All I need is about twelve hours worth."

"I understand, but we have new orders," said Shoham. "The situation is changing. I think I should let Ben Adir explain it to you."

"Be careful moving around back there," Ratz warned, when he noticed Shoham and Gavrilla heading for the entrance well. "In a refueling ops things can be delicate. Don't walk all the way to the tail ramp or you'll change our center of gravity."

"Don't worry—we're going to a meeting, not a gymnastics class," said Shoham.

On the cargo deck they entered the tactical box through its forward doorway, and found most of its personnel crowded around Hynek's console. It was crowded so tightly Adir had trouble squeezing his way out to meet them.

"Gavi, there's been a change," he said. "How well can you swim?"

"About as well as anyone," Gavrilla answered. "I won't drown, if you really want to know. Why?"

"We have a new destination. A nuclear submarine, the USS *John Marshall*. The Americans have outfitted it as a commando transport. A British Special Boat Squadron is heading for it and there's already a SEAL Team on it. They would like us to be there as well. They need our knowledge about the terrorists and the bio-weapon."

"I don't like closed spaces very much but I don't see it as a problem. Why did you ask me about swimming? Don't tell me we're going to have to swim to it."

"Yes, in fact we will. Our flight plan to reach the submarine is what they're looking at now," said Adir, motioning to the crowd around Hynek. "I'm told it would take several hours for the sub to come into a harbor and take us aboard in a normal way. Those are hours the British don't feel they have, and I support that judgement. A direct parachute jump to the sub would be the fastest way to reach it."

"It would also be a pretty good way for the British to drown a few Jews," said Eshel.

"You don't have to go if you don't want to, Yehuda. Neither do you, Gavi. But you do have the information our friends would need the most. In addition to parachutes, we have cold weather survival suits on this aircraft, so we have everything we need. The submarine will have rescue teams to pick us up."

"It's dangerous. In my training I only did a few parachute jumps, and never into water," Gavrilla recalled, shivering involuntarily at the thought of jumping into the North Atlantic. "I don't like it, but I hate Colonel Nazih and his Abu Nazal terrorists even more. I'll go. The British may not be our best friends but I want them to win this one."

A voice crackled over the intercom. "Pilot to crew, fuel transfer complete. You can return to normal operations."

"Good, now we can hold our gymnastics class," laughed Shoham, the moment Ratz ended his message.

"Gymnastics? You're crazy," said Adir, giving him a confused look. "Someone named 'Slow-Mo' isn't about to do any gymnastics. We've got planning to finish. Thank you, Gavi. Thank you for volunteering. And don't worry about the jump — we'll be there."

After the boom operator shut down the fuel flow, the probe retracted from the wave-shaped bump atop the Combat Talon's fuselage. A brief plume of white mist spilled at the moment of separation; it was the fuel left in the boom after the flow had been cut.

Immediately the KC-135 surged ahead while the C-130 cut power and swung away. The F-14 escorts rejoined the Hercules and they eventually turned onto a more northwesterly heading. One that would, from their present position near Sicily, take them over Spain and into the storm-swept North Atlantic.

Chapter Nine

"Well, my friends, another few hours and we'll have been on this oil rig for a full day," said Jassem, after he entered *Valkyrie's* operations center.

"A day? It hardly seems like it's daylight outside," said Nazal, walking over to observation windows. Though they were heated, their top frames had become encrusted with ice. Outside, virtually every piece of equipment was encased in the same milky-white substance. Stalactite-like icicles hung from the main drilling derrick, service cranes and injection well platforms. While beautiful, it also looked alien and hostile to Nazal. "It's as if the sun has left this area of the world."

"A day?" Yussuf Gunni repeated. "It seems like we've been trapped here for a month. I don't feel well. A lot of us don't, Abu—let's just hurry this meeting and be done with it."

"Very well, we'll do it your way." Nazal moved back from the windows and took one of the console swivel chairs. Gunni did the same, and seemed grateful to be off his unsteady legs. "Kaniel Akkad has reported all demolition charges have been laid and wired to their control boxes. All we have to do is arm the boxes, set the detonation times, and *Valkyrie* will sink in minutes. Samad, what have you to report?"

"Sherina is still in the communications center," said Jassem, "along with Captain Reitan. You were right about using her—she has confused the British. Ballast control has warned me the ice build-up you admire so much is going to cause us stability problems. It's many tons of extra top weight, and it must be cleared before drilling operations can begin."

"I'm well aware of it. We'll use the Norwegians to clear the ice, as we will for most of the other tasks. Yussuf, how are the Norwegians? What problems do we face?"

"As you predicted, rumors of the helicopter downing are circulating," Gunni said ruefully, "and it has made them fearful. In general they're docile. The Norwegians will do as we order. The most severe problems we face are sea sickness among our people and weapons fouling. This damn sea air! It's affecting all our guns except for the AK-47s. Perhaps those who chose them were right, after all."

"Perhaps. What's being done about it?" Nazal asked.

"I've ordered the guns to be cleaned in the warmest and driest room on this rig, the humidity control and air conditioning room. It's too cold, and too damp here, Abu. How I long to feel the desert sun, the desert wind and solid ground under my feet! If only this rig didn't move so much, I wouldn't be as sick as I am."

"I know, I can feel it too, Yussuf." The storm is at its height, and it will stay this way for at least the next twenty-four hours. We can do little for our operation until then except to find out which Norwegians would be willing to work for us, and assign them to a team. Samad, can you do that? I don't think Yussuf has the strength for it."

"Yes, I'll be able to," said Jassem. "Is there anything else you want done?"

"One other thing," said Nazal, rising out of his chair to end the meeting. "I want the demolition charges checked on a regular basis. Assign the man who worked with Akkad and Abdelgalil to do it. He knows where they've been placed, and we have more important work for the others."

"It's Eshqi. Azali Eshqi," Gunni informed, struggling to rise as the oil rig's movement caused his chair to roll. "And tell him to be careful — until the storm weakens this rig will be dangerous."

This time Erica didn't have to rise from her place on the

locker floor to use her radio. During one of her searches through the rest of the survival gear she had located a set of wire antennas. Using bandage tape from one of the medical kits, she was able to attach an antenna to the room's tiny porthole and plug its lead into the radio's one external jack. All Erica had to do was reach out from her makeshift bed, and bring the Grundig in a little closer to use it. She was grateful she could get by with doing so little; she didn't know where she would find the strength to do anything more.

"Taylor, this is Erica. Taylor, this is Erica. Do you read me? Over." Erica took her thumb off the rocker switch and listened to several seconds of static; during which she checked her watch again to make sure it was the right time. "Taylor, this is Erica. Do you read me? Over." A tiny rumble of dread began to rise in her chest.

"Erica, this is Taylor. Sorry for the delay," said a now familiar voice, coming in a little stronger than it had the previous times. "You're sounding clearer than before. Are you feeling better? Over."

"I wish I were better, but it's not me. I found an aerial I could tape directly to the porthole. I'm glad it works — I don't know how I'd be able to stand."

"I'm certain you'd find a way. Have you heard or seen anything of the terrorists since our last contact?"

"Nothing, nothing for hours," Erica croaked. "No voices, no noises beyond what the storm makes. I never heard it so bad. The way *Valkyrie* is rising and falling, you'd think it was a carnival ride. My daughter would love it, but I just wish it would stop. I'd be grateful for even a few minutes rest."

"I can sympathize with you," said Taylor. "In all my years at sea, I've rarely felt a submarine pitch and roll this way. Have you been taking care of yourself? Over."

"I'm taking as much aspirin and dramamine as my stomach will keep down. Wringing out my clothes and using the thermal blanket has made me feel warmer. I have plenty of food and water for when I feel strong enough to eat something. And I'm using a box and a large food can for latrines."

"You're doing very well, Erica. We'll pass on your report to those ashore."

147

"When will I be rescued, Taylor? Couldn't you surface and do it? Over," Erica asked, almost pleading.

"I wish we could, but we simply don't have the right equipment or enough trained men to bring you off *Valkyrie*. There are thirty to forty foot waves above us, easily big enough to roll this submarine onto its side. I'm afraid you'll have to be patient, Erica. I can assure you operations are under way, only I'm not at liberty to tell you what they are. Over."

"I understand. I should be grateful just to hear your voice, and I am. It's just . . . the next time we contact each other, could I talk to Frieda again? I enjoy so much hearing her voice."

"Of course you may," said Taylor. "Only remember to keep the chat as short as possible. We'll contact you again in two hours time. This is Taylor, signing off."

"Thank you, Taylor. This is Erica, signing off." For a few seconds she listened to the buzzing static, then shut the radio off. She laid it on the floor, nestling it in her discarded exposure suit so it wouldn't slide away. Erica reached out farther and pulled in the latrine box. Its smell was horrendous, but the way her stomach felt she knew it would be needed soon and she didn't have the strength to get up and go to it.

"UHF mast retracted," said MacGregor. "UHF system, off. Shall I deploy the trailing wire aerial?"

"No, we're going to make a circuit of bloody *Valkyrie* first," Taylor answered, rising out of his chair to leave. "Those at Bradbury Lines are beginning to wonder how the terrorists will evacuate the oil rig after the charges are exploded. They're wondering if there isn't a surface ship or another submarine in the area. This storm rules out a landing on the rig by any kind of helicopter, so it has to be a ship or submarine, unless these bastards are a suicide squad."

"Captain, couldn't we rescue her? She sounds so desperate."

"I know, but going aboard *Valkyrie* requires commandoes. No one on this sub is commando-trained, nor do we have all the right equipment. While I will take risks, I won't be reckless. All of us are just going to have to wait until the American sub arrives. I'll let you know when it's time to transmit, Donnie."

Taylor backed out of the radio room and turned to head for the control center. He walked past the radar room, nucleonics lab, ECM room, and stopped at the compartment which showed the most activity, the sonar room. In it were the *Spartan's* senior sonar officer, Lieutenant Gerald Greenway, and an enlisted rating. They scanned the ghost-like tracings on the glowing sonar scopes, and listened to the noises picked up by the hydrophone arrays on the flanks of the attack submarine.

"Gerry, anyone out here beyond us?" Taylor asked, stepping into the darkened room.

"Apart from bloody *Valkyrie*, no," said Greenway. "We're not even picking up much in the way of fish noises. The storm is driving everything deep. Most of the noises we're detecting are from *Valkyrie*. Waves crashing against it, the dynamic positioning screws, ballast tanks being filled and emptied. It's a ruddy fleet all by itself. You could hide half a dozen submarines under it."

"We'll have to let our school at Gosport know about this. Are you trying to mask out those sounds?"

"Yes, we're running programs through the Twenty-Twenty and Twenty-O-Seven systems. I even have the men who are off duty working on them. In a couple of hours we'll have it finished."

"Good, stay on it," said Taylor. "Something could easily hide in all that noise. And I don't want any surprises."

"Nickle-Two-Seven, this is *Kitty Hawk* traffic control. You're cleared to land. Weather and sea conditions are nominal. Be advised we have a twelve knot crosswind."

"Roger, *Kitty Hawk*. Just make sure you got the wires set for us," Felner replied. "Colonel, we'll be landing in a few minutes—better get ready. I'll alert your men."

Even in the middle of the North Atlantic it was now daylight. From his jump seat position, Boyd could see clear skies through the cockpit windows. It was a welcome sight, especially after almost a week of foul English weather and winter storms.

The Greyhound's airspeed dropped sharply after Felner acknowledged the carrier's instructions. Flaps drooped from the wings' trailing edges and landing gear doors opened on the engine nacelles. With a solid clanking the nose wheels and main gear extended into the slipstream. Momentarily causing the transport to waddle before being corrected.

"Ladies and gentlemen, please return your trays to their upright positions and fasten your seat belts in preparation for landing," said Felner. "On behalf of your flight crew and the United States Navy, we thank you for flying Grumman Express and hope you can do so again. Please remain seated until the aircraft has crashed to a complete stop."

Directly ahead of the Greyhound, about a mile and closing, was the *Kitty Hawk*. A grey and black slab of steel, the size of a skyscraper and with the complexity of a city hidden inside it; the huge warship was an impressive sight, and yet, a curiously inactive one.

Few of her aircraft could be seen on her flight deck and none were airborne around her. Boyd had expected to find the carrier in the midst of launch and recovery operations, and that the C-2 would be just another aircraft entering the busy traffic pattern around it. Instead, they had arrived in the middle of an apparent lull.

The landing stripes began on the starboard side of the fantail and ran diagonally across the flight deck to the port side catapults. The waddling transport didn't approach the carrier from dead astern but from several degrees to the right. In the final seconds of its approach the Greyhound's deceleration and descent rates climbed swiftly. By the time it was over the fantail, it was falling out of the sky.

It slammed onto the flight deck on its main wheels, holding its nose high for an instant longer until its tail hook snared an arrestor wire. The nose wheels hit at the same moment the propellers had their pitch reversed. A hundred feet later the C-2 was stopped and had even started to back up in preparation for dropping the arrestor wire.

"Did you enjoy the flight?" Felner asked.

"All the chopper landings I've made on carriers didn't prepare me for this," said Boyd, unlocking his seat belt and harness. "I should've known your warning 'crashed to a complete stop' was true. Thank you, Commander, for a smooth flight, if not a smooth landing. When can I deplane with my men?"

"Just let me roll her forward a little. Up ahead you can see your taxi cabs for your ride to the sub."

With the help of a deck crew, the slackening wire fell off the C-2's tail hook, which then retracted under the fuselage. A plane director stepped in front of the transport and signalled it to follow him. Slowly, it turned to the right and taxied a few dozen feet up the *Kitty Hawk*'s multi-acre flight deck.

Ahead of it were Boyd's transport to the *John Marshall,* and the principal reason why the carrier's normal flight operations were suspended. Five of its six SH-3 Sea Kings were arrayed in a single row, starting almost from the flight deck's overhang above the bows and stretching back until it was abreast of the island. Every helicopter had its tail boom folded out and main rotor blades deployed. For the moment all were silent, but they were ready for flight.

"Gather your equipment, lads," said Boyd, stepping out of the cockpit. "We'll divide into groups of six, which is how we'll be flown out to the submarine. Heeks, Allanby, Rutherford, Crippens and Ridings, you're with me. Ross, Halliwell, Jones and Samuelson, select your teams. Be quick — let's do this exactly the way we did it at Mildenhall."

Boyd made his way down the Greyhound's cargo deck, picking up his equipment bags by the time he reached the tail. He only had to wait there for a few seconds before the ramp came down, flooding the deck with a raw wind and sunlight. After the ramp was fully deployed, the C-2's turboprops were switched off, ending more than four hours of operation. The enlisted men Boyd named had since joined him and together, they stepped onto the carrier's flight deck.

"Lieutenant Colonel Robert Boyd? I'm Captain Moran. Welcome aboard the *Kitty Hawk,*" said the most senior officer in the group. "I'm sorry you can't stay long, but we're proud to help you in any way we can."

"Thank you, Captain. I hope we're not putting you through too much trouble," said Boyd, a hint of humor in his voice. There was trouble, then there was *trouble*.

"Nothing we can't handle. The only problem we have is it'll take twice as long to put the ASW pallets back in the helos as it did to pull them out. Let's move out of the way and get started." The officers turned and left the tail of the transport.

"Have you been in touch with the *John Marshall?*" Boyd asked, straining to keep up with the easy strides of the American officers. "Have you any messages?"

"We talked with the sub about five hours ago," said Moran, slowing his gait so the heavily-loaded Marines could stay with him. "It should be approaching the rendezvous area now. We won't know until after you're airborne, since it's almost impossible to communicate with a submarine during a high-speed run. And yes, we got some messages for you. My communications officer is carrying them."

Moran indicated one of the other men in his group; he carried an attaché case handcuffed to his wrist. Boyd motioned that he didn't want to stop until he reached the helicopter. He already had too much luggage, and it was far too windy to risk opening the case and examining the papers.

Boyd at first thought the walk to the Sea Kings would be a short one, like the transfer had been at Mildenhall. In reality they ended up walking over one hundred feet before they got to the last SH-3 in the line; and over five hundred feet to reach the lead one. As they approached it, Moran twirled a finger over his head. The helicopter responded by emitting the familiar start-up whine of turboshaft engines.

"As you see, there's more than enough room for your men and your gear," said Moran, sweeping his hand around the Sea King's bare interior. With almost everything aft of the pilot seats removed, its fuselage appeared more cavernous than normal. "But it is a little spartan."

"Don't worry, I've put up with worse before," said Boyd. "We can endure it for another hour or two."

Like his men, Boyd dropped his equipment next to the helicopter's side hatch. He climbed into it with Moran who, for a short time, helped him move the bags around the fuselage. Both were quickly replaced in their duties by the others in Boyd's group, and they were soon joined by the *Kitty Hawk*'s communications officer. He was a tall, spare man who wasted no time and had no use for frivolity.

"The latest of these arrived about ten minutes before you did," he said, opening his case and handing Boyd a folder.

"I'll take a look through them later," Boyd replied, slipping the folder into his own documents' case. "Matters are rather pressing now. Thank you for your help, Captain. When you re-establish contact with the *John Marshall,* please tell Captain Carver that, despite the gravity of this crisis, I look forward to working with him again."

"Of course. Tom, make a note of what he wants sent," said Moran. "I wish we could give some type of air support for your commando assault, but I know it's not the kind of help you need. Good luck, Colonel. We'll all be rooting for you."

Moran waited until his communications officer had written down the message before shaking hands with Boyd and jumping out of the cabin. This allowed the other Royal Marines to board the Sea King and, together with its crew chief and all their equipment, the cavernous interior was suddenly very crowded.

"Colonel Boyd, I'm Lieutenant Spader," drawled a giant of a man. "How was your flight in?" asked the helicopter's pilot, when Boyd came forward and stood between the cockpit seats.

"Save for the landing, smooth," said Boyd. "How long before takeoff, Lieutenant?"

"A matter of minutes. As soon as we get the rotors up to speed and complete the checks."

Boyd thanked him and made his way back, wondering how such a huge person even fit into the cockpit. He selected the most comfortable-looking position amid his men and all their equipment. Of the seven men in the compartment, only the crew chief had a seat. Bolted to the starboard side of the fuselage frame, he strapped into it once he had the starboard hatch rolled shut and locked.

No plane director appeared in front of the Sea King to give it instructions; sitting almost on top of the flight deck's bow overhang there was little room for one. When the pilots received a signal from the carrier's flight operations center, the turboshafts screamed louder and the SH-3 began to rock on its landing gear.

With an extra burst of power the helicopter lifted off the carrier and swept over the flight deck's lip. It swung to the right and orbited the *Kitty Hawk* once to gain altitude. The lead Sea King did not wait for the others, though they all had their rotors turning. After it had gained enough altitude it set course for the southwest. At normal cruise speed it was just over an hour from its rendezvous with the *John Marshall*.

"Shotgun Lead, this is Falcon Zero-Four. The F-15s are inbound, they'll arrive in the next two minutes. Thanks for the company. Hope we didn't bore you."

"Negative, Zero-Four. This may have been quiet, but a real operation is always better than an exercise. Good luck with your rendezvous — wish we could stick around, but we're getting a little saddlesore over here."

"Roger, Shotgun Lead, that's what happens when you fly an airplane you can't walk around in."

"Yes, but they do have some advantages. Watch."

Ratz could see the pilot in the lead F-14 give a hand signal to the second one. Together, they slid off the C-130's wing tips. For a few moments they were close enough for him to see their wings sweep back and their exhaust nozzles dilate. Though the morning at twenty thousand feet was clear and bright, the sudden glow of afterburners being cut in was clearly visible. In seconds they had doubled the Combat Talon's cruising speed and had surged miles ahead of it.

When they were specks on the western horizon they swung around and came hurtling back in. By then they had transformed themselves from awkward, slow-moving fighters to massive arrowheads moving faster than the speed of sound. The lumbering, all-black Hercules was an easy target for the

F-14s. They flashed in almost too fast for the eye to follow, and rattled the transport with the shock waves from their sonic booms.

"Ouch! God, what was that?" Adir demanded, after bouncing his head off the ceiling above the cockpit's bunk.

"The U.S. Navy saying goodbye," said Ratz. "They're heading for our base in Sicily. If you'll come forward, you can see our new escorts arriving."

Rubbing his forehead, Adir eased out of the bunk and walked up to the flight engineer's seat. Like Gavrilla before him, he had a panoramic view through the cockpit windows. The first thing to catch his attention was the scenery. The Combat Talon was no longer over the Mediterranean — they were over land, from their altitude an irregular patchwork of browns and dark greens, which Ratz identified as Spain.

What caught Adir's attention next were the contrails curving up from the ground. The dark speck at the head of each contrail was climbing fast; as they rose above the horizon line, the ribbons of condensed water vapor became intermittent. By the time the new escorts had reached the same altitude as the C-130, they had ended entirely. To Adir the performance was familiar, though never less than spectacular.

"F-15s," he said. "No other aircraft can perform that way."

"How'd you know?" Goldberg asked. "Did you overhear us talking to them?"

"No. I was dead asleep until your Navy left. When you see F-15s perform enough times you know how to spot them."

As the Tomcats had done just minutes before, the specks turned toward the Hercules and rapidly grew into what Adir had identified. The two F-15 Eagles separated and streaked past the transport on either side of it. Though they weren't travelling at supersonic speeds; their turbulence and thunder still rattled it.

"Falcon Zero-Four, this is Sidepole Lead. Maintain your speed and heading and we'll be with you in a minute."

Hard as they tried, neither Ratz, Adir or Goldberg were able to spot the F-15s until just before they finished sliding onto the C-130's wing tips. They wore the familiar air supe-

155

riority grey paint schemes, but the blue and white stars of David had been replaced by low-visibility star and bar insignia. They were armed with the same mix of Sidewinder and Sparrow missiles as the Israeli fighters had but some of their weapons were painted blue, the color designated for training rounds.

"What's going on, Sidepole Lead? Are you guys carrying training rounds?" Ratz inquired.

"You're right," said the new escort leader. "You got sharp eyes for a barge pilot. My C.O. sends his apologies, but the Spaniards didn't have many *real* missiles at the base we've been flying maneuvers from. Then again, I sort of doubt we'll be running into any serious opposition where we're going."

"Yeah, I guess so. Not unless our own Navy wants to start shooting at us. Be prepared for a long, slow flight. We're still about five hours from our rendezvous."

"Five hours?" Adir repeated, checking his watch. "Looks like I'll have time for a little more sleep."

"No, your time is just about up," said Ratz. "It's my turn for a cat nap. You may be Mossad, but it doesn't mean you always get special privileges on Mossad Airlines."

"Depth, sixty-five feet. Sixty-two feet. Sixty feet," said Jefferson, reading off the diminishing numbers on his displays.

"Hold her steady at sixty feet," Carver ordered. "Raising periscope. Greg, ask Hawkins if he's getting anything from the helos."

Mounting the control center's periscope stand, Carver pressed one of the buttons on its search periscope and watched the numbers on an LED display jump as its mast was extended toward the surface. He deployed the 'scope to its maximum height, flipping down the handles and removing the cap from the eyepieces when the glowing numbers stopped changing.

"Diving planes, neutral. Buoyancy, neutral. Speed, five knots," said Jefferson. "You're all set, Captain."

"Roger, I'm walking the 'scope," said Carver, moving around the stand until he had come full circle. "Greg, what's the word from the radio room?"

"Hawkins is in touch with the formation leader," Burks answered. "He says they should be close enough for you to see him."

"No, I'm not getting anything. I'm switching to infrared." Without removing his gaze from the eyepieces, Carver ran his hand up the periscope's control panel until he found and punched in the infrared imaging system. For a moment the eyepieces went dark. Motors whirred in the scope's main body as the optical systems were changed, then the world above reappeared as a slightly blurred mixture of white, greys and black. On his second sweep he discovered two dark spots where formerly he had only seen reflective glare. "All right, I got 'em. One's about a mile away and the other is farther out. The reinforcements are here. Captain to crew, standby to surface. Landing details, prepare for operations."

"Blowing trim tanks. Main ballast tanks, on standby," said Jefferson, concentrating on the buoyancy control panel while the second helmsman held the *Marshall* steady. "Diving planes, fifteen degrees up angle. Depth, fifty feet. Forty-five feet."

"There, on the port quarter," said Spader, tapping Boyd on the shoulder. "We got a feather."

Boyd swore at himself for not having spotted it himself. On a seascape with moderate chop and intermittent white caps, the dark pole trailing a plume of spray should have been easy to see — especially when Boyd had just scanned the area where Spader found it.

"Younger men do have sharper eyes," Boyd grumbled. "I'll let my team know. Circle the area until the sub has surfaced, then move over its conning tower."

Boyd could only afford a quick glimpse of his future home, though in that amount of time he was able to discern a shadow gliding beneath the feather. Moments after he turned away a larger plume of spray blossomed when the

157

John Marshall's conning tower first broke the surface. Automatically, Spader banked the Sea King to the left and began to gently spiral down toward the ocean's surface.

"Captain to radar room, raise your mast and make a sweep," said Carver. "Report in by the time I reach the flying bridge."

Carver returned the hand mike to the bracket on the periscope stand and finished pulling on his winter jacket. He checked the search scope to make sure he had properly secured it, then turned to the stairs which descended to the TASCO Room.

"Seidel, you have the center all fired up?" he asked.

"Everything's coming on line, Captain," said the sonar officer, Lieutenant David Seidel. "I'll let you know if anything interesting develops."

"You do that. Once Boyd has arrived we'll be joining you. Glenn, are you ready?"

"Don't I look it?" said Allard, no longer wearing a standard naval officer's dress uniform, but combat fatigues and a winter jacket. Behind him was the rest of the forward landing detail.

"All right, time to do a little mountain climbing," Carver warned. "Greg, you have the con. Keep her steady, even if you have to increase speed."

He turned and led Allard and his detail over to the conning tower ladder. The hatch between the control center and the tower had already been opened; the sound of waves rolling over the submarine echoed through it. Carver ascended the ladder first, followed by Allard and two other SEALs who were part of the landing detail.

They clanked their way into the tower, climbing almost thirty feet by the time they reached the hatch to the flying bridge. With a rush of cold, salt-laden air it swung open. Daylight streamed in, along with the heavy popping of chopper rotor blades.

The first thing Carver saw when he emerged from the tower was the newly erected radar mast; its bar-shaped scanning dish was already rotating. As Allard and the others joined him on the bridge, he pulled a telephone handset from a station box and pressed one of its buttons.

"There's a Sea King," said Allard, pointing over the back of the conning tower. "Smoke marker."

Chen tossed him a plastic stick; he snapped the top end off immediately. There was a hissing sound as the marker sputtered to life and emitted a thin trail of white smoke to show the wind's prevailing direction. The Sea King corrected its approach accordingly.

"Colonel, we're going to come right over the stern," said Spader. "It looks like the weather's cooperating, let's hope the sea doesn't push the sub around too much."

"We'll have this over quickly," said Boyd, pushing several equipment bags together. "I know this type of flying consumes more petrol than any other kind you can do. Open the hatch."

With a metallic thump, the Sikorsky's crew chief unlocked the starboard hatch and rolled it back. A burst of cold rotor wash and turbine noise flooded the cabin, dropping the temperature and raising the decibel level to the point where normal conversation was impossible.

"Here's the rescue sling!" shouted the crew chief, handing the heavy yellow strap to Boyd. "What are you doing with it?"

"We'll send these down first!" said Boyd. "We find it's easier to send the stores down separately than to carry them!"

Boyd unlocked one end of the strap from the sling's head and looped it through the handles of his bags and two other sets. Together, they weighed more than three hundred pounds. It took both Boyd and the crew chief to push them out the hatch; once the load had been steadied and the Sea King positioned over the conning tower, the external winch motor slowly lowered them.

"Good! Retract the mast — I don't want it to get in the way of our guests!" Carver shouted into the handset. Even so, it barely compensated for the screaming engines and the steady slapping of rotor blades. "Glenn! Radar has four helos in all! Hawkins was told there's another one out there! But it must be too far away for radar to see!"

"I'm glad, it's going to take a long time to get these guys down!" said Allard, leaning into Carver so he could hear. "It looks like they're sending their gear first!"

Only then did Carver realize the Sea King was lowering equipment bags and not personnel. Though they turned endlessly, because of the sling's free-swivelling head, they were too heavy for the rotor wash and motion of the helicopter to sway. The bags descended straight into the open well of the flying bridge, with only minimal assistance from those waiting for it.

"Is the rest of our detail in place below us?" Allard asked, unlocking the strap and pulling it out of the handles.

"You bet! Straight down to the control center!" said Chen.

"Then let's start the flow! I want these gone by the time the first guest arrives!"

As soon as Allard released the sling, Carver motioned for the crew chief to reel it in. The chopper's external winch reversed operation, and in seconds the rescue gear had disappeared back into the cabin.

"Send down another load after me!" Boyd told the Sergeant Major in his team. He adjusted the sling under his arms until it was comfortable. "Keep alternating between stores and personnel until all the equipment is down! When you arrive, follow the instructions the Americans give you! They'll probably send you aft! I'll be in conference with the Captain and the SEAL Commander! See you below!"

When Boyd indicated he was ready, the winch took up the cable's slack until it almost pulled him out of the cabin. Outside the cold, turbulent air chilled him even through his winter gear. The Sea King began his descent to the *John Marshall*.

Unlike the equipment, which weighed almost twice as much as he did, Boyd started to sway back and forth. He tried to counteract the pendulum motion, but only succeeded in flailing around helplessly. He almost landed on one of the conning tower's diving planes before someone grabbed him by the leg.

"Steady, Colonel, we'll bring you in!" said Allard, as both he and Landham pulled him in. "Don't go kicking a U.S. Navy submarine! You might break it!"

Boyd allowed himself to be guided into the tower's bridge well. Once his feet were on the floor, he freed himself from the sling and turned to the familiar face he had spotted when the helicopter started hovering over the submarine.

"When we first met, I welcomed you to your command!" said Boyd, raising his hand to his forehead. "Now, I believe we have it the right way!"

"So do I! Welcome aboard, Robert!" said Carver, returning his salute; then shaking his hand. "It's been too long! Robert, I'd like you to meet Commander Glenn Allard!"

"Commander, you have a good reputation!" Boyd saluted Allard as well, and the men he in turn introduced.

"Thank you, Colonel!" Allard replied. "I've heard a lot about you from Terry! These are some of my men! Lieutenant Arthur Chen and Chief Petty Officer John Landham!"

"I look forward to speaking with you later and working with you!" said Boyd. "I have information on the crisis we should look at right away! Where can we meet?"

"Glenn, take him to the TASCO Room!" said Carver. "I'll join you there! First, I have to make sure this operation is proceeding as planned, especially with the second landing detail! See you soon, Robert. I'm glad we've joined forces again!"

Chapter Ten

"Dolphin Lead, Dolphin Lead. This is Dolphin Two, we're coming right in behind you. Can you move up a little?"

"Sorry, no can do. If we move up any farther we'll be dropping our guests in the ocean."

"Okay, I'll be careful. I'll try to avoid kissing your tail rotor."

Boyd was still being lowered when the second Sea King dropped in over the *Marshal*'s tail. It came to a stop less than a hundred feet behind the first SH-3; it was directly over the aft escape trunk. Where the hump for the submarine's missile compartment tapered back down to the hull, a larger than normal hatch had been installed. Originally designed for emergency use, both fore and aft escape trunks were often used for supply missions. And with the forward trunk constantly awash and too close to the conning tower to be used, the aft trunk was the only other position to land the Royal Marines.

"What are you doing? Aren't you going down first?" asked Dolphin Two's crew chief.

"No, we found it's easier to lower our heavier equipment this way," said Ackland, pulling the sling strap through the handles of four bags. "I'll go down right after this load. Here, lend a hand."

The second Sea King rocked slightly when the bags were pushed out the side hatch and dangled below the external winch. As it descended, the escape trunk opened and Martirri appeared in a wet suit and wearing a lifeline. He climbed onto the missile compartment's hump, where he caught the heavy load of munitions and scuba gear and guided it to the hatch. After the bags had been released, the rescue sling was reeled back up to the SH-3 for Ackland to use.

"Well, they're in operation!" said Carver, looking over the back of the conning tower. "I'm going to raise the external track lines for them! It doesn't look like their footing is too stable out there."

Carver opened another recessed panel and tapped the buttons activating the guard rails aft of the conning tower. They rose out of the submarine's upper casing, stopping at about waist height. For Martirri and the other SEALs working the aft escape trunk, they would provide the only other measure of safety beyond their life lines.

"Heads up, Captain!" Chen warned, pushing Carver toward the front of the bridge.

Another Royal Marine sat down where he had been standing. Younger and taller than Boyd, he had a row of chevrons on his sleeve instead of officer's insignia on his shoulders. After he was freed of the rescue sling he saluted Chen and Carver.

"Sergeant Major Derek Rutherford!" he said. "I nearly landed on you."

"No problem! Welcome aboard the *John Marshall!*" said Carver, returning the salute. "I'll show you below! I think it's getting a little too crowded here, even for me!"

Carver motioned toward the floor hatch and followed Rutherford through it. At every compartment in the conning tower they encountered one of Allard's SEALs. They were stationed there to catch the equipment bags as they were tossed down from the compartment above; it was a more efficient way to move the supplies than having each bag manhandled down the ladder.

"Take the passageway aft to the commando quarters," Carver instructed. "That's where the rest of your team is gathering. You'll see your commander soon."

After stopping for a moment to talk with Burks, Carver descended one more level to the TASCO Room. There, he found David Seidel feeding Boyd's software information into the room's tactical display system.

"Terence, at last we can have a normal conversation," said Boyd. "Your new submarine is most impressive. This room belongs on a spacecraft."

"Actually, this is my old submarine," said Carver, reaching the bottom of the stairs. "My alma mater . . . but they sure have prettied her up for me. Glenn, you should take a computer programming course after this operation is over."

"Funny, Terry, funny. You sound like my family," Allard remarked. "Argument number seventeen: 'If you don't want to head Tiger Security, then why can't you learn to do something other than kill people'?" He shook his head and turned to Seidel. "How are you coming along, Dave?"

"I've dumped all the info from the Colonel's floppy discs into the hard disc drive," said Seidel, keeping his attention on the computer keyboard and on the soft noises being emitted by the disc drives. "Would you like me to punch up the menu?"

"No. You might need it for yourself," said Boyd. "But what I want is the general sideview diagram on the center screen. We can go for more specific details later."

For a moment Seidel studied the list of topics—the menu—on a console monitor before tapping in the correct codes for what Boyd wanted. By pressing another key, the tactical map of the *John Marshall* and the helicopters disappeared from the room's largest display screen. In its place was a blue and white line drawing of an oil rig, side elevation.

"Gentlemen, I present to you *Ocean Valkyrie,*" Boyd announced, motioning for Carver and Allard to take the remaining seats at the console. "The size of a sports stadium, the displacement of the largest ocean liner, the complexity of a small city. It's currently being held by twenty-four terrorists. Of its original crew of two hundred men and women, only one hundred and sixty are still alive. The terrorists are a strike team from a Libyan military intelligence unit called Blood Revenge . Their apparent mission is to use the oil rig to introduce or inject a genetically altered bacteria into the North Sea oil fields. According to the Israelis, the bacteria is designed to eat crude oil and destroy the productivity of the

164

fields. If successful, it would be the world's first case of bio-terrorism."

"The Israelis you mentioned—are they the ones being flown out to us?" Allard asked.

"Yes, if we could go back to the tactical for a moment, we'll probably be able to see their aircraft."

At Boyd's suggestion, Seidel brought the tactical map back up and kept increasing its scale until almost the entire North Atlantic could be seen. By then the *Marshall,* the *Kitty Hawk* and her escorts were a cluster of flashing symbols in the waters south of Iceland. Another symbol had just crossed Spain's northern coast and was entering the Bay of Biscay.

"It looks to me like we're going to have another rendezvous operation," said Carver. "Will these people be transferring to a helicopter?"

"No, I decided there wasn't time," said Boyd. "I want to have their input while Glenn and I are finalizing our assault plans. They'll make a parachute jump directly from the Hercules. There's only four of them, so we should have no trouble recovering them."

"What type of weapons did you bring? From what I've seen, you're turning my submarine into a floating armory. I wonder if Glenn's team will be able to use what you brought?"

"Our principal weapons are the Heckler and Koch MP-5SD submachinegun and their P9S automatic. They both use nine millimeter ammunition, and we brought along low-velocity aluminum rounds, several hundred for each man. We also brought silencers for the automatics, stun grenades and specialized radio sets. They're waterproof and can be used inside metal structures."

"Don't worry about my men," said Allard. "They've been cross-trained on SAS and SBS weapons. I have to worry about whether or not they'll *accept* the weapons. SEALs are very loyal to their guns. A little too loyal."

"We'll cure them of that," Boyd replied, then he turned his attention back to the display screen. "Mr. Seidel, could you bring up the oil rig diagram? Thank you."

165

"I know Glenn's been studying how to re-take *Valkyrie*," said Carver, while the tactical map was replaced again by the rig's schematic. "Has he told you about them?"

"Yes, and they're very similar to the ones I discussed with the SAS at Bradbury Lines. It's good Commander Allard and myself are thinking along the same lines. As mission commander, I could insist on using my own plan, but it's better that we cooperate. If we are to succeed, we must function together smoothly."

"I agree. Why don't you show Terry what we've already decided on?" said Allard.

"Very well. These are just general plans, Terence," Boyd advised. "The specifics of who does what will be decided later. The only way to enter *Ocean Valkyrie* undetected is here, through the lower compartment of each base leg."

Boyd pointed to where the legs joined the submerged ballast tanks; a second later Seidel marked what he had identified with flashing arrows.

"With my lads, we now have a sixty-man assault force, the minimum number to re-take the rig. The force will be split into four fifteen-man squads, and each will enter one of the base legs. I'll command one squad, Glenn another, and our execs the remaining two. We'll make our way up the legs, taking the centers atop each: communications, ballast control, cargo loading and power generation. After we have those, we'll move to take *Valkyrie*'s operations center and free the hostages from wherever they've been imprisoned. As I said before, this is the overall plan. There's much left to work on. When, in your estimate, do you think the transfer of my men will be complete?"

"The first two helicopters should be done soon," said Carver, checking the room's clock. "In spite of the problems we always have with vertical replenishment, this transfer's going well. All helos should be finished by the end of the hour."

"Lieutenant, I'm the last!" shouted the Royal Marine Corporal after he'd been welcomed aboard the submarine.

"There's no one else to come down!"

"Thanks, Corporal, it'll give us a welcome rest!" said Chen.

He motioned toward the floor hatch on the flying bridge, and a few seconds later the last of the Royal Marines to come off the lead Sea King disappeared through it. Above him, the helicopter ceased hovering and started to move forward before it had finished hauling in its rescue sling. With its departure, the turbulent air calmed down and the noise level fell, though not to its original levels.

Roughly a hundred feet aft, the second SH-3 was still delivering the last of its six-man team. Orbiting several hundred feet above the *Marshall* were the third and fourth Sea Kings, waiting for their turn to deliver their cargoes. During the brief time the airspace above the conning tower was clear, the radar mast was raised and several sweeps were made but when the second SH-3 climbed and swung away, the mast was retracted and the landing details prepared to receive the next pair of Sikorskies.

"Here they come," Chen noted, watching the helicopters slowly overtake the submarine from behind. "Looks like our cigarette break is over."

"Over? Hell, I can't even light one," said Landham. "I don't know if it's the salt air or the wind. How many of these limey bastards are we gonna take aboard?"

"As many as the Colonel brought with him. And remember, he's in charge of this operation."

"Shit. He may be good and all, but that isn't going to be very popular, Lieutenant. We're supposed to be the best in the world, so why should we have to take orders from the limeys?"

"Because if it wasn't for the Brits, most of us would be charged with insubordination," said Chen. "Glenn and Captain Carver would certainly be facing court-martial. As it is they could still face discipline charges if we're not successful."

"I know, I just hope the cowboys among us understand that," Landham replied. He glanced over the back of the conning tower and caught sight of the aft landing detail re-emerging from their escape trunk. "Especially John Wayne himself. I don't know what Sal's problem is — either he thinks life is a double-dare or he's got one hell of a death wish. And hell, Artie, he's an officer!"

"I know that. I wish Glenn could get rid of him, but even with all these Brits we still don't have any men to spare. Look at him, out there being a cowboy. Glenn ordered him to accompany the British exec, like he did with Colonel Boyd. He's going to make trouble again for us."

The next Sea King to cross the *Marshall's* tail slowed to a halt above its conning tower. Its side hatch was already open, and it had begun to lower equipment bags before the fourth Sikorsky was hovering over the aft escape trunk. The operations proceeded as smoothly as they had for the first two SH-3s. More than twelve hundred miles from the North Sea, the weather was clear and the sea state relatively calm; there would be little to interfere with the transfer. And already, the fifth Sea King was approaching from the northeast.

"Ruddy seas. It's almost impossible to see bloody *Valkyrie*," Holbrook complained, continuing to walk the search periscope while Taylor watched a similar image on the low-light level TV monitor. "I think ice is starting to form on the lense."

"Don't worry, the next wave will sweep it off," said Taylor. "Do another walk and retract the scope. After you're done, take us to a hundred feet. I'll be in the wireless office, Johnnie. I want to see how Mrs. Gran is doing."

Taylor swung away from the periscope stand and walked to the back of the attack center. In the passageway he kept a hand on the starboard wall until he reached the radio room's hatch; cruising at sixty feet, HMS *Spartan* was subject to wave effects and had rolled continuously since rising to that depth. In spite of Taylor's decade and more at sea, he had never grown used to the motion and had to steady himself whenever he walked.

As he neared the radio room, he could hear Frieda talking, though he couldn't make out what she was saying until he had almost reached the compartment. By then, she had released the transmit switch and Erica was speaking.

"How does your friend sound?" Taylor asked, stepping inside the radio room.

"Tired. But she doesn't sound as sick," said Frieda, turning to face the Captain while keeping an ear cocked to the voice on the loudspeakers. "She also sounds lonely. Even with the danger, I wish I could be with her."

"You're a good friend. I wish I could take her off bloody *Valkyrie,* but that's best left to the professionals. Here, let me talk to her."

Taylor grabbed the console mike and waited for Erica to finish what she was saying before keying the transmit switch.

"Erica, this is Taylor. Frieda tells me you're better. How do you feel? Over."

"At least I'm keeping down the dramamine," said Erica. "Maybe in a few more hours I'll be able to eat something. This always happens to me when I become seasick. I eventually grow accustomed to the rig's movements and improve. I'll be able to move around by the time the commandoes arrive. When will they arrive, Captain? Over."

"Not for some time," said Taylor. "At least another day. I know it's difficult, but you'll have to be patient. If anyone else tried to board your rig, it would spell certain disaster. The best encouragement I can give you is the experts are gathering and they're on their way. Be brave, Erica. I'm giving you back to Frieda."

Taylor returned the microphone to its original user and remained silent for the rest of the transmission. He only nodded to MacGregor when he felt it should end, and Frieda was gently urged to sign off.

"Couldn't you have let me go for a little longer?" she asked later, as MacGregor finished shutting down the UHF system. "It seems so unfair. We're her only human contacts."

"Yes, and while we can detect no monitoring of the channel we're using, it would be foolish to continue transmissions for more than a few minutes," said Taylor. "And besides, if Erica continually uses her radio, it'll drain her battery strength, while for us, with a fifteen thousand horsepower

PWR reactor to call on, this isn't a problem."

"It still isn't fair, but I see your points. Could I talk to Erica when you contact her next?"

"Yes, just tell Johnnie when the time arrives. I'll be off duty by then, I really need some rest. I should go down and see how Mr. Nordsen is doing. Is he any better?"

"The blood transfusions have made him stronger," said Frieda. "He's conscious now and resting as comfortably as Mr. Newcane can make him. I should go and tell him about Erica."

"I'll join you in a few minutes," Taylor added, stepping out of the radio room, and helping Frieda through the hatch. "First I'll see if we've moved to deeper waters or not. I believe we have, but we're still rolling rather heavily. On the surface the storm may be at its height, but below the effects are still growing. If this continues, we'll have to head all the way to the bottom to find calmer conditions."

"Falcon Zero-Four, this is Sidepole Lead. We've reached Bingo Fuel a little early. How long before the Navy arrives?"

"The *Kitty Hawk* has launched her fighters and my tactical team says they'll get here in forty minutes," said Ratz. "As you told us before, serious opposition isn't likely over the North Atlantic. You have my permission to depart."

"Roger, Zero-Four. Good luck and don't get close to any Libyan airliners. Sidepole Two, increase speed and form on me."

For the last three hours, the two F-15s had been patiently escorting the Hercules for more than a thousand miles, from the Mediterranean; across the Pyrenees Mountains in Spain and now deep into the North Atlantic. Flying at a slower-than-normal cruise speed caused the jets to consume more fuel than had they been allowed to fly faster, and what remained would only get them back to the nearest air base.

The lead F-15 had pulled in closer to the C-130's left wing so he and Ratz could see each other. After he got permission to leave he waved briefly, then surged ahead. The second Eagle, which had been sitting farther off to the right, quickly joined him and together they swung onto a more northerly heading. From their current position, England was almost due north. At their new speed, it would take them less than two hours to reach RAF Mildenhall.

"What happens to us now?" Adir asked, walking up to the pilots' seats.

"We're on our own until another pair of F-14s arrive," said Ratz, glancing over his shoulder. "They'll be here in forty minutes, ten if we really need them. Hey, aren't you dressing a little early? We're not due to reach the submarine for another couple of hours."

Adir had on a bright orange, heavily padded survival suit. Unlike the lightweight exposure suits, the survival suit was designed to allow its wearer to be immersed in freezing cold water for hours. It had its own boots, with gloves attached to the sleeves by short tethers and a tight-fitting head cap which Adir had pulled to the back of his neck.

"We have a lot of gear to get ready," he said. "After these suits there's our parachutes to inspect. I've come for Gavi, it's time for her to get ready as well."

Adir wheeled around and approached the cockpit bunk. Its familiar occupant was asleep, though only lightly; each movement of the aircraft caused her to stir a little, so it was easy for Adir to awake Gavrilla. She opened her eyes immediately and swung her legs over the edge of the bunk.

"What? Where did you get that? It makes you look like a clown," she said.

"The same place you're going to get yours," Adir replied. "It's time to prepare. *Acharigh,* Gavi."

"*Acharigh?* What does that mean?" Ratz asked. "It doesn't sound like her name."

"It's Hebrew. It means 'follow me.' In the Israeli Army, officers command from the front. Your co-pilot, Mr. Goldberg, should know Hebrew."

"Only enough to understand what they're saying at the synagogue," laughed Goldberg. "If we don't see you two again, happy landings."

Adir led Gavrilla down the cockpit stairs and onto the cargo deck. They found Shoham and Eshel already in their

171

survival suits, checking their parachutes. On one of the side benches stood an open rescue pack, and in it Gavrilla could see another survival suit.

"Gavi, how many training jumps did the Mossad give you in all?" Shoham asked, looking up from his parachute.

"The initial series was four day jumps and two night jumps," said Gavrilla. "I didn't have time for any extra courses and I haven't been in service long enough for refresher training."

"And you never made any water jumps?"

"No. Do I really have to wear one of these suits? I know the water will be cold, but we won't be in it for long."

"Gavi, please. The water in the North Atlantic at this time of the year is only a few degrees above freezing," Shoham answered. "An unprotected human would die of hypothermia three minutes after entering it. Avrom doesn't know much of this because he's Army. But Yehuda and I are Air Force and we've had more extensive survival training. Even in the Mediterranean you can die of hypothermia, it only takes longer. Even this suit won't protect you forever—just long enough for the U.S. Navy to pick you up. With the kind of clothes you're wearing now, Gavi, you might as well jump naked."

"It's the smallest suit the Americans had," said Adir, after Gavrilla had started to examine the contents of the pack. "You must strip out of most of your clothes to wear it properly."

"And where will I do this 'stripping'?" Gavrilla asked. "I'll need privacy, not to mention some warmth." Her expression permitted no joking.

"Here, with all the electronics inside, we found it very warm," said Eshel, opening the side door to the tactical box.

Gavrilla lifted the rescue pack off the bench and walked into the Elint/ECM compartment. She remembered it had always been warm, even hot, inside it. Also cramped and crowded, especially with Hynek and the rest of his team still manning their consoles.

"Oh, Gavi's going to slip on the teddy bear suit?" said Hynek, glancing up from a mostly inactive console. "This will be a change. I knew we were due for some entertainment soon."

"I'm not going to put on a show for you," said Gavrilla, selecting an empty chair to drop her pack on. "I want everyone out of here. Now."

"But we have to maintain our surveillance, Gavi. For the next half hour we're not going to have any defense except our jamming systems."

"Nathan, don't try fooling us," Shoham replied, standing in the doorway. "Most of your systems have been shut down, and if the Libyans had sent any planes after us, they'd have run out of fuel by now."

"For someone we called Slow-Mo, you sure catch onto our games real quick," said Walker. "I think I gave you the wrong nickname."

"Gentlemen, if you'd please?" I'd like to get on with my change," said Gavrilla, motioning toward the door. "I'll let you know if anything here starts beeping."

With audible sighs of regret, Hynek, Walker and the rest of the Elint and ECM teams left their padded, cramped box. After the door was shut behind them, Gavrilla removed her boots and started to strip out of the dusty, soiled clothes she had worn since her escape. With a little help from an instruction book, she would soon be wearing the thickly-padded survival suit.

"All right, let's get this under way," Boyd said to Allard before turning to the assembled British and American officers and raising his voice. "Gentlemen, may I have a little order? First, I would like to thank the United States Navy for welcoming us aboard and for the use of this submarine. There's nothing like her in the Royal Navy, and she's perfect for this crisis. To make it official, I am Lieutenant Colonel Robert Wendell Boyd, commander of the Third Special Boat Squadron, Royal Marines. Make no mistake, I am mission commander. I'll work closely with Mr. Allard and Mr. Carver, but I'm in charge and will be responsible for the overall operation. This preliminary briefing will be between us, we'll meet with our enlisted men later. I trust they're getting along?"

"If they aren't, we'll know about it," said Allard. "Most of them are below us, or in the armory and equipment rooms."

"Let's hope we don't. Everything depends on our two units functioning smoothly, and on our equipment. Since you already have scuba gear, my men only needed to bring along sufficient kits for ourselves. However, because your training exercise was a completely different type of operation, your weapons will not be suitable for this crisis. Instead, what we've brought you will be perfect."

Boyd motioned toward the array of submachineguns and automatic pistols on the preparation room's table. He picked up one of the machineguns, a deceptively small weapon, especially with its metal stock retracted. It seemed to be all pistol grip and barrel; a large, blunt tube which uniquely, had no fore and aft sights. In their place were mounts for either an image intensifier or a laser sight.

"This is the Heckler and Koch MP-5SD submachinegun," Boyd continued. "Its barrel has an integral silencer and has been adapted to take whatever sighting system you wish. It weighs six and a half pounds, seven and a half with a full clip. We've provided ten thirty-round clips per gun and three hundred and fifty rounds per man. On this mission, the type of ammunition we'll use is the nine millimeter, reduced-velocity aluminum round. Both the MP-5 and the automatic will accept it. Now the Heckler and Koch P9S."

Boyd laid aside the submachinegun and lifted one of the pistols. Again, it was a small weapon, especially when he touched a lever on the gun's left side and the entire slide mechanism shot home.

"As you can see, the P9S has a concealed striker. There's no hammer to catch on your clothing. It has a cocking lever on the left, next to the trigger, which allows for one-hand operation. It has an extra-large trigger guard, for a gloved hand, and has luminous dots on its sights for night use. It's been drilled and tapped for a silencer, which we will provide. It takes a nine-round clip, and we have seven clips per gun.

"Both the P9S and the MP-5 are lightweight and rugged.

174

About the only thing I can say against them is that they're not British. But then, we in the Royal Marines have learned to appreciate good German engineering."

"Oh yeah, well there's something I can say against them," said Martirri, moving in next to the table. "They ain't ours. And especially they ain't this . . ."

Martirri popped the safety straps on his belt holster and pulled out his Colt .45 automatic. After holding it up to Boyd, he slammed it on the table; producing a dull thud with no resonant echoing. Because the *John Marshall* was again travelling submerged, the surrounding water pressure had changed the compartment's acoustics.

"We're not about to give up the Colt .45, Colonel," Martirri added. "It's a tradition in the SEALs. We've always used them."

"We don't happen to have silencers for our pistols," said Allard, ". . . and we don't have the kind of ammunition they brought along. You fire that forty-five in an oil rig and everyone will hear it."

"Lieutenant, Her Majesty's Armed Forces have learned not to let traditions stand in the way of operational effectiveness," said Boyd. "We've learned it through many painful lessons."

"Well, we haven't been around as long as you guys."

"Then perhaps you can learn a little from our experience. The wrong weapon can kill you as easily as the wrong tactics."

"Hey, I don't need to hear from some Brit bastard what kind of gun I'm supposed to use," Martirri snapped.

"You continue that attitude, Mister, and you'll be off this operation," said Allard. "No matter how badly we need people."

"Commander, if I'm going to go on that rig I want a real gun that fires real bullets, not beer cans! I'd like to know what damn good these things are."

Martirri picked up a pistol clip loaded with aluminum rounds and shook it at Boyd; then tossed it to him. Expressionless, Boyd caught the magazine and calmly loaded it into the P9S he was still holding. For the

175

moment, he left the anger to Allard.

"You're not irreplaceable, Sal," Allard coldly advised. "If necessary, I'll remove you from the operation and have Chen lead your squad."

"What? Artie? He's UDT," said Martirri, pointing to Chen. "He can lead a Chinese fireworks factory, but Underwater Demolitions Team doesn't mean you can lead SEALs."

"Lieutenant, you need a demonstration," said Boyd, as he hit a lever next to the automatic's trigger.

With a metallic crack, the slide rammed back in place, pushing the first bullet into the firing chamber. Boyd trained the gun on Martirri, with a movement so swift his arm seemed to blur. He hesitated twice, each time the P9S barked loudly. Two irregular discs of silvery metal suddenly appeared on the far wall. The first one was a few inches from Martirri's right ear, the second just beyond his left. Martirri wrapped his arms over his head and dropped to his knees. His descent was marked by a line of aluminum discs as Boyd fired three more rounds.

"Colonel, if you'd aim about four inches lower you'd solve a lot of problems for us," said Chen, the first one to speak after the flat, echoless barking stopped. A few nervous laughs were quickly stifled.

"Petrowski, put away your sidearm. Now!" Allard ordered, when he noticed one of his officers reaching into his holster. Then he snatched the Colt .45 off the table, just before Martirri could retrieve it.

"You're reckless! Fucking reckless, man!" Martirri shouted, standing unsteadily. A look of both fear and hatred in his eyes. "You shithead crazy son of a bitch!"

"I'm not reckless, I'm skillful," said Boyd, clicking the safety on his P9S and placing it in his holster. "If those had been standard rounds, many of us in this compartment would be dead. Including even myself . . ."

Boyd let his words trail off when the stamp of boots could be heard in the stair well. Charging up the stairs outside the prep room were Petty Officer Landham and Sergeant Major Rutherford. There were others on the stairs, but Rutherford and Landham held them up when they halted at the top.

"Sir, what's going on, sir?" they both said in unison, their words blending almost perfectly.

"Yes, what the hell is going on here?" Carver asked, standing in the hatchway at the front of the room. "Glenn? Robert? Are you starting a war or what?"

"No, Captain," said Allard, his mind racing for the most diplomatic answer. "It's just . . . just a demonstration of good German engineering."

"Don't bullshit me, Glenn, you're not an expert. Robert, what do you have to say about this?"

"Lieutenant Martirri expressed some concern about the capabilities of our weapons and munitions," said Boyd. "I believe I put his mind at ease about it."

"Martirri, I should've guessed you were involved in this incident," Carver observed.

"Captain, he tried to kill me," said Martirri, his voice still cracking with emotion. "I want formal charges filed against him. I want this thing to be recorded."

"Don't worry, Lieutenant, I'll log this incident. As an accidental discharge of a firearm." Carver allowed a slight smile, in response to Martirri's stunned look of disbelief, before continuing. "And if you're smart, you won't push it any farther. I know about you. Every man on this boat knows your reputation. Glenn isn't the only one who can pull you off this operation — as captain of this submarine, so can I. And as mission commander, so can Boyd. You're a U.S. Navy officer. Obey the orders of your superiors. Robert, I'll talk to you later."

Carver wheeled around and walked out of the preparation room, clanking the hatch shut behind him.

"He sure hates your ass, Sal," said Chen. "You're getting more popular every day."

"Yeah, well, Carver hates anyone who doesn't have the last name of a dead president," said Petrowski.

"You stow that shit, Lieutenant. It has no place in this unit," Allard replied. "Now you've all been cross-trained on these weapons; you've done exercises with the British before. But Colonel Boyd would like to check your proficiency."

"I'd like each of you to field strip an MP-5 and a P9S," said

177

Boyd, before he looked across to the stair well. "Sergeant, take the men back down and have them do the same exercise. Have the SEALs field strip their weapons. That will be all for now."

"Do as he says, John," said Allard. "By the end of the day I want everyone to do the field stripping blindfolded."

Both Rutherford and Landham acknowledged their respective commanders and filed back down the stairs, ordering the men blocking them to return to their duties. After a few moments, only the officers remained in the preparation room.

"Gentlemen, your weapons are before you," said Boyd. "You should be able to strip down an MP-5 in approximately one minute. Glenn, this includes you. I want to make sure *everyone* under my command knows how to use what's given to him. Prepare for the drill. I'll run the stopwatch."

"That's it, lads, distribute them evenly," Rutherford ordered, walking between the rows of compact, double-tiered bunks in the enlisted men's quarters. "One each to a customer. Let's see how well our cousins can operate their new equipment."

"I take it there isn't going to be any live firing demonstration down here?" said Landham, examining his new weapons.

"Not if there doesn't have to be. I don't think any of us have the same size chips on our shoulders as our officers. At least, I hope not."

"No one's as crazy as Martirri, except of course for our last exec. The SEALs are the only unit where the officers are more undisciplined than us grunts. If our officers can't get along with each other, how the hell can we be expected to fight well?"

"Colonel Boyd is rather remarkable — he'll work them into shape," said Rutherford. "And if not, the fight will be up to us sergeants. Like it's always been."

Chapter Eleven

"Falcon Zero-Four, this is *Kitty Hawk* CIC. Begin your descent to flight level one thousand. You are in the rendezvous area. Your escorts will break off at five thousand and orbit until your drop is complete. Over."

"Roger, *Kitty Hawk*. I'll tell our flight crew," said Hynek, glancing over his console, which was considerably more active than it had been in the last several hours. "Tactical to pilot, begin descent to one thousand feet. Ty, Jimmy, you reading anything below us?"

"Sorry, boss, I'm not getting much of anything," said Jim Morse. "Just a choppy sea."

"Jackpot, man. I got a single emission source," Walker answered, tapping some of the buttons on his keyboard. "I'm punching it up on your display. It looks like a naval radar set, BPS-15. Surface search and short-range fire control. We got our submarine."

"Thanks, Ty. Let's see if I can confirm it," said Hynek. "*Kitty Hawk* CIC, this is Zero-Four. We would like to contact the *Marshall,* just to let them know we're here. Over."

"No need, Zero-Four, they already know you're coming. They've been watching you and will be surfacing soon. This is *Kitty Hawk* CIC, out."

Before Hynek's conversation with the distant aircraft carrier had ended, he could feel his room tip forward. The nose of the MC-130 dropped a few degrees below the horizon line, and the giant turboprop started to lose the altitude it had maintained for more than half a day.

Sitting on its wing tips were another pair of F-14 Tomcats. They wore different units markings than the first pair, but apart from their squadron and carrier allegiance they were identical to the original pair. They followed the Combat Talon down through the scattered layers of cloud on a mission which had almost come full circle. What had begun in darkness would soon be ending in darkness.

"They've started to drop," Seidel advised, watching the data blocks change on the TASCO Room's main screen. "Both the C-130 and the Tomcats."

"Time to surface and get your men topside," said Carver. "Glenn, go aft and supervise the launching of the zodiacs. Robert, it's time for us to man the bridge. Dave, maintain your watch here. I'll send Doran to do a weapons system check."

Allard was the first to go up the stairs, followed by Carver and Boyd. While he went back to command the recovery detail, Carver paused in the control center, giving orders to Burks before he joined Boyd on the ladder rising into the conning tower.

The *John Marshall* had been running shallow for more than half an hour — close enough to the surface for its search periscope, radar, and electronic surveillance masts to be deployed. Once it became apparent that the rendezvous had begun, the submarine finished emptying its ballast tanks. Moments later its conning tower, with its various masts still raised, broke through the waves.

Carver and Boyd could hear and feel the change while they were still climbing the ladder. The submarine rose and fell more rhythmically, and a deep thudding shook the conning tower: the effects of riding on the surface instead of just a few dozen feet below it.

"Watch it, I'm going to raise the hatch," Carver warned, after he finished spinning its locking wheel. "All the water may not have drained off the bridge."

When the hatch first cracked open, a brief spray of sea water rained on the two officers. Despite the shower and the cold air which flooded over them, Carver finished pushing the hatch over and stepped onto the flying bridge. Boyd quickly joined him and together they found a world rapidly growing dark.

"Hard to believe only a few hours ago the sun was so bright you could get a tan," said Carver.

"Not when you consider we're less than five hundred miles from the Arctic Circle," said Boyd, scanning the horizon. "And we're hitting the western edge of the storm. Conditions will be much worse in the North Sea. I'm glad this submarine of yours has swim-out chambers." He pointed skyward. "There, to starboard. Our new guests have arrived."

Carver trained his binoculars in the direction Boyd was pointing. He quickly spotted a black shadow against the still light, southern horizon.

"It's them, all right," Carver observed. "There aren't too many black C-130s around, and so far as I know the Air Force has all of them. Break out the growler phone, Colonel, see if Glenn is getting those boats ready."

"Phil, it's over there," said Goldberg. "On your left . . . can't you see the waves hitting its conning tower?"

"Now I can," said Ratz, fixing his gaze out the port side of the cockpit. "I'll warn the cargo deck. Take us right over it, Herb. It's not often we get to see a submarine. Pilot to loadmaster, standby for para-drop."

Instead of stopping at a thousand feet, the pilots allowed the Combat Talon to descend a few hundred feet lower so they could get a better view of the *Marshall*. Nearly a mile above them, the F-14s leveled off at their assigned altitude. Because of their ghostly grey camouflage schemes, they blended in almost perfectly with the broken cloud deck. Not until the roar of their engines was heard would anyone on the *Marshall* spot them.

"They must have the sub in sight," Adir remarked, after Ratz had given his order. "Finish suiting up and spread out along the windows."

Adir, encumbered by his own survival suit and parachute

pack, waddled over to one of the port side fuselage windows; Eshel went to a starboard one. Shoham helped Gavrilla complete hooking her parachute harness together before they joined Adir on the port side.

Their view was partly blocked by the inboard engine nacelle and the external fuel tank under the port wing. However, as the transport banked to the left they saw a sleek, black shadow in the water. It was almost without form, defined more by the waves slapping and foaming against it than its own hull shape. Momentarily, they saw two figures standing in a winged tower attached to the shadow, and then the submarine was gone. It slid underneath the C-130 and in seconds would more than a mile behind it.

"Jumpers, please form a line to the left and attach your ripcords to the overhead wire," said Ritter, stepping up to the group. "You'll be jumping as soon as we see them get a boat in the water."

"Thank you, Sergeant," said Adir. "Gavi, Shlomo, let's check each other over one last time before we take our positions. Remember, we're not taking a dive in the Mediterranean."

"Jesus, any lower and they could land," said Strader, involuntarily ducking when the Hercules filled the sky above the *Marshall*. "What the fuck? Does the Air Force think a C-130's a seaplane?"

"I bet the Israelis would like it to be one," Allard replied, raising a cleat out of its well and attaching his lifeline to it. "Landham, hand me the raft and pass the word. Anyone who's not wearing a wetsuit or who's not part of the zodiac detail is to tie down their lifeline."

Of the men clambering out over the submarine's aft casing, it was only Allard who didn't have on a wetsuit. Landham pulled a heavy black package out of the aft escape trunk and passed it up to him. Allard placed it between himself and Darryl Strader, and pulled on an exposed length of cord, opening a set of carbon dioxide bottles.

With an explosive hiss, the package immediately unfolded

182

and began to inflate. In moments it had assumed the familiar shape of a zodiac raft; by the time its outboard engine and fuel tank had been hauled onto the missile compartment's turtledeck, it was fully formed.

"Hold her steady, Darryl," said Allard, ". . . until I get the motor attached."

"Commander, the C-130 is climbing," said Landham. "It looks like it's starting to circle us."

"I know, the Israelis will be jumping soon. Get your men ready, John. We're lowering your boat over the side."

Grabbing the ropes attached to it, Strader and Allard pushed the zodiac off the deck and eased it down the submarine's port side. With the *Marshall* doing less than ten knots, it was easy for them to hold the inflated boat in place while Landham and three other men climbed into it.

Wearing both wetsuits and scuba gear, they found it awkward to board a zodiac on a rolling sea. They eventually threw their masks and fins into its well and slid or jumped in after them. One of the team hooked the fuel tank lines to the motor while the other members pushed the boat away from the submarine. Before the engine had rattled to life, Allard and Strader were helping a second recovery detail inflate and launch their zodiac.

"This looks like my men," Boyd remarked, his attention focussed on the activity behind the conning tower. "Your geminis look larger than ours, are they more difficult to control?"

"I don't know," said Carver. "I don't like ships that bend when you get in them. And the SEALs call their rafts 'zodiacs.' I know they're a different design — more pointed in the bow than others. Here, better set this off if our new guests are to make the jump properly."

Carver handed Boyd a plastic stick and, like Allard had done several hours earlier, he activated it by snapping off its top end. The marker sputtered to life and spewed out a plume of bright white smoke. This time it didn't trail aft but cut diagonally across the conning tower, from right to left. Wind direction had changed radically. The *Marshall* was entering the storm's cyclonic air flow. For a few moments the smoke fouled the tower's flying bridge, then Boyd moved to its port side and held the marker out over the edge.

"Mr. Adir, we're at jump altitude and the submarine has set off a smoke marker," said Ritter, attaching a lifeline of his own to an anchor point on the fuselage airframe. "The pilots got the wind drift and you'll be jumping in another minute."

"Thank you, Mr. Ritter," said Adir. "And please thank the rest of your crew mates for all you've done for us."

"It was a pleasure working with you, and thanks for flying Mossad Airlines!"

Ritter grabbed a control lever on the starboard side of the fuselage and pushed it down. The two sections of the tail ramp separated, and a deafening roar filled the cargo deck. Created by the slipstream and the turboprop engines, the roar made any further conversation impossible. Adir's team concentrated on the jump lights above them.

It took just under a minute for the top section of the ramp to lock against the cargo deck roof and for the lower section to finish extending into the slipstream. Seconds later, the green jump light began flashing as the red one died.

"Acharigh!" Adir shouted, loudly enough for the people behind him to hear it. Then he turned and ran to the end of the ramp.

The rushing air virtually lifted him off its edge — he hardly needed to jump. Adir dropped away from the Hercules; his last link to it was his ripcord. Even that ended when the cord momentarily snapped taught, and released his parachute.

"There they are!" Allard shouted, pointing toward a quartet of silk canopies blossoming under the tail of the C-130. "They'll land in about forty-five seconds. Good luck, Sergeant!"

"Thank you, sir. We'll return with our guests!" said Rutherford, giving Allard a salute before he pushed his boat away from the submarine. "Come on, come on! You want the Yanks to beat us out there?"

"No, Sergeant," responded the Marine working on the outboard motor, swearing softly under his breath. With the fuel lines connected to it, he had to pull the starter cord a few times to get the gasoline flowing before the motor rattled to life.

"Open it up, Corporal. They're already halfway down!"

At full throttle, the drifting zodiac suddenly leaped forward and bounced its way over the swells. Rutherford positioned two of his men forward to prevent the bow from riding up and getting caught by the wind. In their hurry to reach the landing zone before either the SEALs or the parachutists, he didn't want his lightly loaded boat to be tipped over.

Wedged in between Adir and Shoham, Gavrilla had little choice but to accompany them off the end of the ramp. Her heart leaped into her throat for the few seconds of free fall, until the ripcord tugged reassuringly at her back and she felt her parachute deploy.

The harness straps dug into her, though the survival suit's heavy padding kept it from being painful. Her velocity slowed as the canopy opened and her smooth fall became momentarily chaotic until the parachute completed its deployment. What had been a jumbled blur to Gavrilla suddenly became clear and steady: the other parachutes opening around her, the black Combat Talon retreating into the distance and the ocean below.

She could see two rubber boats skidding over its surface, trying to position themselves for the imminent landing. In the background, the submarine was now more easily seen. Hundreds of feet long, its black and nearly featureless hull had a sinister appearance. The only activity Gavrilla could spot on her were the men in her conning tower and those near the tail.

A distant-sounding splash took Gavrilla's attention away from the *Marshall*. Adir was already down, his parachute canopy was spilling out, losing its form, and he was swimming, before he had even freed himself of his harness.

In the final moments of her descent, Gavrilla took hold of her riser lines and tried to control where she would land. She had drifted farther than the others and was several hundred feet away from them. Gavrilla's attempts to control her descent only resulted in spilling part of her chute and she hit the water before being prepared for it.

Even with the survival suit on, the bone-chilling coldness was a shock. Gavrilla let out a startled shriek as she plunged in, only to have it cut short as she continued on down, ending up almost a dozen feet below the surface. Only her face was directly exposed to the frigid water; in the few seconds she took to struggle back it had become frozen.

Gavrilla broke through gasping for air and because of the knife-like pain in her colorless face. What she got was a suffocating veil of water-soaked nylon. She was unable to see, and could hardly even breathe; she had surfaced where her parachute had collapsed.

At first Gavrilla tried pulling the nylon off her head; but she quickly realized there was far too much of it. She next attempted to rise as high above the water as she could, only to have the parachute drape around her like a shroud. She also had to fight wave action and the restrictions of her suit; her strength was being sapped away.

She dove back under the surface and tried to swim her way to clear water, but her survival suit's buoyancy prevented her from staying under, no matter how much she struggled. As she moved forward, Gavrilla discovered the parachute lines wrapping around her; snaring her like a fish in a net. She needed air, but couldn't raise her head high enough to effectively break the surface. What she got were mouthfuls of mostly sea water.

No matter what she did, no matter how hard she fought, Gavrilla couldn't free herself from the entangling lines and nylon folds of her own parachute. Her cumbersome suit did keep her warm, but it restricted her movement and prevented her from diving deep enough to escape. The equipment meant to save her life was killing her.

"Oh God, is this what it's like to drown?" Gavrilla

thought, remembering what Shoham had told her when they were preparing for the jump. How pilots had died after safely ejecting from their aircraft because they got trapped inside their parachutes. Suddenly, as blackness began to enfold her, the rubber mouthpiece to a scuba regulator was pushed between her teeth.

Gavrilla bit down hard, and sucked in enough air to fill her lungs. She felt the presence of two bodies next to her. One held her head and kept the regulator in her mouth; the other moved swiftly around her. Turbulent currents were created by powerful legs kicking rhythmically, occasionally a diving fin would brush against her. Strong hands would take hold of her body, and quickly released it. Even under water Gavrilla could hear popping and ripping sounds. Someone was cutting her free. She was in clear water. In one smooth motion the men with her flipped Gavrilla on her back. The man at her head pulled the regulator out of her mouth and put his arm under her chin. For the first time in she couldn't remember how long, she could see the sky.

"All right, miss. You've had a spot of trouble, just relax," a heavy British accent gently ordered her. "You'll be joining your friends in just a sec."

Gavrilla and her rescuers slid down into a wave trough, and pushed their way up another's slope. This time, her survival suit's buoyancy helped her. All she had to do was float while the Royal Marines dragged her back to their zodiac. Her only exertion for the rest of the recovery was to climb over the boat's side, and even there, the Marines pushed her up while Adir pulled her in.

"Welcome back to the world, Gavi," he said. "It looked like we nearly lost you."

"You nearly did," Gavrilla answered. "Avrom, are there any safer ways to get on and off an airplane? I must hold the world's record for doing it the most dangerous ways."

"There are, I assure you. When all this is over, I'll be happy to show them to you. Now let's hope this raft doesn't capsize before we make it back to the submarine."

After he and his men had clambered back into the boat, Rutherford ordered it to swing around and head back for the

187

Marshall. The zodiac commanded by Landham was already halfway there. High overhead, the Combat Talon was a black speck about to be swallowed by the storm clouds on the eastern horizon, and the two F-14s had their wings swept back and were heading north; in minutes they would be landing on the *Kitty Hawk*.

The *Marshall* would have to remain on the surface for some time to come. First the crew had to bring aboard their newest guests, then deflate and stow the zodiacs. Only afterward could the submarine dive and resume its high-speed run across the North Atlantic.

A persistent beeping forced Erica out of her sleep. It was the alarm on her wristwatch. It took her several moments to locate the right button and deactivate the irritating noise. For the first time in half a day she felt strong enough to stand and maintain her balance in spite of the ceaseless storm heave.

Erica got up and walked to the locker's porthole, where she checked the antenna to make sure it was still taped in place. The glass was remarkably ice-free. Staring out of it, she could still see little except for sleet pellets striking the outer pane and frequent waves hitting the base leg. Erica had to check her watch to see whether it was day or night, and discovered there was less than a minute before she was due to contact HMS *Spartan*.

Erica kneeled to pick up the radio. She switched it on and softly counted off the remaining seconds before she pressed the rocker switch.

"Taylor, this is Erica. Taylor, this is Erica. Do you read me, over?" she asked, releasing the switch and listening to the static for several seconds before transmitting again.

Below the power generation and control station, Eshqi encountered no one. Even at the station he only encountered one of his team mates, a man assigned to guard the electric generators and main bus panels. That was the pattern he found in the other base legs he had checked. One or two

188

people in the operational control compartment at the top of each leg, and no one below it, only the continual thud of waves hitting the rig, the groaning of its structure and the dripping of condensed moisture.

Eshqi felt his assignment was a miserable, demeaning one. He understood why the demolition charges had to be inspected — he had already discovered two which were jarred loose — but Eshqi found it insulting that he had to do it. After all, he thought, had he not laid the charges in the first place? Had he not fought as bravely as the others? Wasn't it he who shot down the helicopter loaded with their enemies? Why were others, who did not kill as many enemies as he had, given such easy assignments? Eshqi even resented those he encountered who were posted to lonely guard duties. At least they got to stay in warm, dry rooms; not the cold and dampness he had to work in.

In each compartment he entered, Eshqi had to stop and check something. Whether it was just to make sure the firing wires were unbroken, or to examine the plastic explosives and their control boxes, it all took time. It added to Eshqi's resentment and fueled his angry, internal conversation with himself. By the time he got to the lowermost compartments in the leg, he was so enwrapped in his private arguments that he scarcely took notice of the faint voices echoing from below him.

"Erica, this is Jonathan Holbrook. I'm Commander Taylor's executive officer," Holbrook replied, sitting at the radio room's console. "Stan is off duty. He's been awake for two days and he's in need of some rest. How are you feeling? Over."

"Much better. I can move around now," said Erica. "And perhaps I'll try to eat something. Tell me how Frieda and Trig are? Over."

Eshqi had almost reached the connecting hatch between the compartment he was in and the base leg's last room when he realized he was listening to voices other than his own. He stopped moving down the ladder and listened to the faint voices drifting through the open hatch a few feet below him.

From his perch he could look into the final compartment, and he saw no one. For several moments he hovered there, trying to decide whether to continue down or to go back up for reinforcements. He heard a static buzz and realized one of the two voices he heard was on a radio. He continued to the hatch.

Left open so it wouldn't break or pinch the firing wires, Eshqi was grateful he did not have to work its noisy docking mechanism or even lift the hatch, which would cause its hinges to creak. As silently as he could, he slid through the opening and got his feet on the next ladder's rungs. The loudest noise Eshqi made was the rippling of his jacket zipper against the hatch rim. A few more steps and he was standing on the floor of the base leg's lowest compartment.

Eshqi faced the emergency equipment locker, the source of the voices. In the dim work lights he could see its door was still closed, still locked. Nearer to the source he could identify the clearer of the two voices as being female. Slowly, Eshqi pulled his nine millimeter Baretta from under his jacket and reached for the lock switch on the doorknob.

"I'm glad Trig's condition is better," said Erica, speaking softly and holding the radio close to her mouth. "I wish I could talk to him. I'd like so much to hear his voice. Could —"

The rest of Erica's question froze on her lips with the clicking of the door's lock. By the time she glanced in its direction, the door was flying open and a figure stood silhouetted by the outer compartment's light. The moment her eyes adjusted to the sudden illumination she recognized Eshqi. And the moment his eyes caught hers, he recognized Erica.

"You! You! How could you be alive?" Eshqi demanded, and for the moment, his gun dropped to his side. "I killed you. I'll kill you again, whore!"

Erica's attention focussed on the automatic in Eshqi's

right hand. He raised it with a deliberate slowness, pulling back the slide as he did so. This time he was going to enjoy her murder. When Erica shifted her gaze to his eyes, she saw the same hatred in them as she had when the Sikorsky lifted off. With her free hand she searched for something, anything to use against him.

With a metallic clicking, the slide rammed home, pushing the first bullet from the clip into the breech. Erica wrapped her fingers around the urinal can and threw its contents in Eshqi's direction. The rancid fluid hit him in the chest and face. It soaked into his clothes and stubble beard; it entered his mouth and eyes.

Eshqi staggered, off-balance and fired wildly, choking on the vile taste, and with the dissolved salts in the urine stinging his eyes. Erica ducked; his first bullet flew high. It ricocheted off the locker's back wall and buried itself in a life raft pack, one of the few items still on the shelves.

"Captain Taylor, report to the wireless office immediately!" Holbrook ordered, shouting it into a hand mike. "Captain Taylor, wireless office immediately! Donnie, what's happening?"

"She dropped the radio," said MacGregor. "It's back in the receive position. I think before she dropped it, I heard her searching for something."

"God, how could this happen! You! Pearson, come here." Holbrook reached into the passageway and grabbed the seaman who turned toward him. "Go to Taylor's cabin and bring him here. Drag him here if you have to! Our Erica's been discovered!"

Eshqi was still off-balance when *Valkyrie* itself staggered through another storm heave. He lost his footing on a deck that rose, then abruptly fell. He stumbled backward, careening toward the exterior hatch in the far wall.

The whine of the first bullet's ricochet had not yet ended when Erica began searching the stores she had unpacked for

191

a more lethal weapon. The chrome endplate to a knife handle caught her eye. What she pulled out of the scabbard had a ten-inch long blade; serrated on the top edge, razor-smooth on the bottom.

Eshqi slammed against the hatch, one of its locking handles driving hard into his back. The pain caused him to cry out, and made his entire body jerk with spasms, including the finger wrapped around the Baretta's trigger.

The explosion and jerking of the gun in his hand jolted Eshqi more than the crash had. He heard the bullet ricochet twice, then felt someone drop a hammer on his left thigh. Screaming this time, he looked down to find the pants' leg torn and blood dribbling out of it. When Eshqi looked up, he found Erica flying at him with a sword-like knife in her hand.

Running proved harder than Erica had thought. She was still weak, and the moving deck caused her to stumble as well. Instead of actually flying at him, she fell on Eshqi. The velocity and her weight helped drive the survival knife into his chest.

Eshqi felt the blade slice through his jacket, his shirt, his skin. He felt the top serrations of the knife scrape against his left collarbone; the blade point strike one of his ribs and snap it an instant later. The blade felt cold, ice cold, as it plunged through his chest. There was sharp pressure, and above all else there was pain. A searing pain which felt as hot as the blade was cold. He forgot about his back, his leg, even his gun. It was only for a moment, but it was enough. The Baretta slid out of his fingers and clattered on the steel floor.

Erica regained her balance before Eshqi did his; once again he was leaning on the wall. Above his screaming, she heard the gun drop from his hand. Now she was better armed than he was, provided she could get the knife out. Erica pulled and twisted its handle, but the sawtooth serrations caught on flesh and bone.

The wave of pain grew white-hot, and Eshqi thought he would lose consciousness. Unable to move his left arm, he threw a right punch with all his strength; hitting Erica in the left temple. This time it was she who cried out, as the blow lifted her off her feet and sent her crashing to the floor.

"Bitch, I'll kill you," rasped Eshqi, gasping hard. "I'll give you the pain of a thousand deaths."

He regained his senses, and enough of his balance, to push away from the wall. Eshqi only glanced at Erica before turning to look for his gun. She appeared unconscious, and there would be time enough to look at her later—after she was dead.

The blow had stunned her; the swearing brought her around. Erica only caught the last part of what he said, but it was more than enough to make her realize Eshqi still had the intent to kill her. As he stooped to retrieve his automatic, she flew at him again.

He had just gotten his fingers on the Baretta, when it was knocked from his grasp. The weight of her body landing on top of him banged his into the wall. Erica wrapped one arm around his neck, and her free hand on the knife handle.

Instead of trying to pull it out, she drove the knife in deeper. The white-hot pain returned and Eshqi screamed, though beyond that he could do little to get Erica off him. His left arm still useless, he used his right to steady himself against the wall and to help him straighten up.

The moment he was on his feet Eshqi started walking backward. He could not see where he was going—he didn't care. All he wanted was speed, and by the time he reached the opposite side of the compartment, he was almost running.

Erica absorbed most of the impact, it knocked the air out of her lungs and there was a ringing in her head as it bounced off the steel plate behind her. This time she was more than stunned, she felt reality slide away. Her hold on Eshqi's neck and the knife handle loosened as she slid off his back and slumped to the floor.

"Johnnie, what the hell's happened?" Taylor demanded, bursting into the radio room. He wore only briefs and a T-shirt, and still had the groggy look of being awakened from a sound sleep.

"One of the bloody terrorists has found Erica," said Holbrook. "We heard a shot, and some noises of struggling or searching before the radio was dropped."

"Have you heard anything more?"

"Sorry, Captain. When the radio was dropped the transmit button was released," said MacGregor. "If we broadcast, anyone there will hear us. We can't hear them until someone presses that button."

Taylor started rubbing his eyes to get the sleep out of them. He used the few seconds to think oven his courses of action, and their possible consequences. When he was finished, he reached down and grabbed the console microphone.

"Captain, are you sure you should try it?" asked Holbrook. "The terrorist who discovered Erica will hear you."

"I know, and I'm certain we must try," said Taylor. "The terrorist already knows she was talking to somebody. If I use only my name we'll be safe. We're one of the most capable weapons in Her Majesty's fleet — we have to do something, even if it's only moral support."

At first the tiny voice calling her name seemed too distant for her to pay attention to. Semi-conscious, the world was fuzzy and comfortable to Erica, but the voice kept on nagging her. It was asking her questions and kept telling her to do something. It sounded insistent, and suddenly very familiar.

"Erica, this is Taylor. Fight him! You have to fight him! Do it, kill him!"

The urgency quickly melted away the fuzz and the comfort. Her vision came back into focus, and the first thing Erica saw was Eshqi. He was crawling across the floor, moving to where his gun lay. A trail of blood ran from him back to Erica. He was more seriously wounded than she had thought, but he still had the grim determination to kill her.

Eshqi would reach the Baretta before Erica could get to it. She needed another weapon, and knew just where to get it. She rolled to the left and crawled back into the equipment locker. When she got to the edge of her makeshift bed, Erica reached for a brightly colored plastic box and opened it, almost tearing the lid off.

Eshqi crawled across the compartment on his hands and knees. He was careful not to let the knife handle hit the floor;

194

he could not endure the pain it caused. This time, when he grabbed the Baretta it stayed in his hand. Eshqi looked over his shoulder to find Erica partially inside the locker. Despite his pain and hatred, he smiled. Did she really think she could hide in there from him?

Half-crawling, half-walking, Eshqi made it to the ladder in the compartment's center and used it to stand up. He also needed the ladder for support; even his hatred could not compensate for blood loss. His right hand unsteady, he trained the automatic at Erica.

Inside the box was a row of neatly packed sticks, an inch in diameter and the length of a ballpoint pen. Erica pried one out and rolled onto her back. She discovered Eshqi leaning against the ladder and raising his gun. She twisted the base of the stick, unlocking its safety, and pulled it out. When it snapped back, the stick emitted a burst of light.

Glowing like a neon bullet, the flare sputtered across the compartment and hit Eshqi in the stomach. It didn't have the velocity of a nine millimeter slug, but it didn't need to. The magnesium fire melted anything it touched: Eshqi's jacket, shirt, his skin. Eshqi never felt a pain like it before, in spite of what he had just been through. It felt like his stomach was boiling.

The Baretta clattered to the floor again, and Eshqi rolled off the ladder. Shrieking like an animal, he fell to his knees and doubled up. The knife handle hit the floor, but it did not make him scream any louder. His stomach was burning, even his hands were burning, and he wanted it to stop.

Erica got only momentary satisfaction from what she did to Eshqi. He screamed so loudly she could hear it echoing in the compartments above her. She feared the other terrorists would hear him as well. She scrambled to her feet and ran to the automatic. Erica found the weapon to be heavier than she had thought. She needed both hands to aim it, and locked both index fingers around its trigger.

The first shot missed Eshqi entirely. It struck the floor under his neck and ricocheted around the compartment. The second one hit him in the left side of his neck, and the next two in the temple and above the left ear. Finding only soft tissue, the second bullet passed through Eshqi's neck intact, leaving an exit wound not much larger than the entrance one. The others fragmented as they entered his head; and blew off the back and right side of his skull.

Bone, hair and brain matter were scattered throughout the compartment, along with a generous quantity of blood. The screaming stopped, but the magnesium flare continued to hiss and sputter, creating the nauseous smell and sound of flesh burning. For Erica, it was too much. She dropped the gun and turned away from Eshqi's body. She felt her head starting to swim and grabbed hold of the ladder for support. Even though she had not had anything in her stomach for several hours, she began to vomit. Though the convulsions were little more than dry heaves, it was several minutes before they subsided and she could answer the voice still calling her from the locker.

"Erica, you've got to fight him," said Taylor. "Fight him! You can do it, don't let him win!"

He released the transmit switch and glanced at the other officers in the radio room. They were silent. Like Taylor, they listened to the static on the loudspeakers until MacGregor spoke.

"I'm sorry, Captain. There's still nothing," he informed. "I must also tell you that we've been broadcasting long enough for someone on bloody *Valkyrie* to get a position fix on us."

"Good Lord, I never thought of that," said Taylor. "How long have I been talking?"

"More than five minutes. It may be prudent—"

"Taylor, this is Erica. It's over." The room's speakers boomed her response at deafening levels. MacGregor had turned up the volume during the long silent period, now he scrambled to reduce it. "I killed him, Taylor. He's dead . . . he's dead."

"Erica, thank God. I thought we'd lost you," said Taylor. "Are you wounded? How did you kill him? Over."

"I have some bruised ribs but I'm not wounded. How did I kill him? I almost ran out of weapons to use. I stabbed him, I shot him with a signal flare and finally, I shot him with his own gun. He doesn't have a head. And he's still burning, over."

Taylor swallowed hard before he could reply.

"I'm glad you're not injured. There's a lot you have to do. Don't become hysterical. Over."

"I'm too *tired* to be hysterical," said Erica, sitting on her bed. "But what should I do with the body? Over."

"You can't leave the body where it is," replied the voice on the radio. "You'll have to hide it, or remove it entirely. Can you open your external hatch?"

"Yes, but the seas are terrible outside. They'll flood the compartment. Over."

"I know, that's what I'm counting on. The waves will wash out the blood, and other remains. His friends will soon be looking for the man you've killed. What you have to give them is either a mystery, or evidence an accident has happened. Open the external hatch, leave it open, and push the body through it. Let the North Sea do the rest, over."

"I understand," said Erica. "I'm switching off the radio and closing the locker. I don't know how long I'll need to do what you ordered, but will you still be on when I return? Over."

"Take as much time as you need, we'll stay on the air until you return. I promise, over."

"Thank you, Taylor. Out."

Erica switched off her radio. She scanned the equipment locker for anything which would give away her presence to those who would come searching for Eshqi. The first things she thought of were the latrines she had used.

While the urinal can was empty, the cardboard box was still loaded and had its own terrible smell. To the box, Erica added most of the cans, plastic containers and wrappers she had emptied. After she cleaned up the locker, she pulled the latrine box into the compartment and closed the door.

The magnesium fire in Eshqi's stomach had burned out. The sickening odor still hung in the air, and the body remained in the same position it had fallen. Erica used her foot to knock it over, and at first tried to drag it to the hatch by its arms. But she found the fire's intense heat had fused the hands into the stomach. She ended up dragging the body to the external hatch by its legs.

Erica first looked through the hatch's tiny porthole to check on sea conditions. When she tried to turn the locking handles, she found most of them difficult to move. On the upper ones she had to hang on the handles and let her weight pull them down. On the lower handles, Erica used the strength of her legs to free them. When the last was unlocked, she held the hatch in its frame and glanced through the porthole again.

The moment it appeared as though there were a temporary lull in the waves, she pushed against the hatch. There was a sharp cracking as the ice which had formed around it broke off. Erica nearly fell into the sea when the hatch flew open; she had used so much force it banged against the leg's outer wall and propelled her toward the water.

Regaining her balance, she reached down and grabbed the body by one of its arms. She dragged it a few more feet, accidentally striking the head on the hatch frame as she tried to raise it. The rest of Eshqi's brain fell out of the gaping skull. Erica fought down another wave of dry heaves to pick up the body and push it halfway through the opening. With a final kick, Eshqi fell out the hatch and landed in the water with scarcely a splash.

Again using her foot, Erica pushed the brain remnants into the North Sea; then she wished she could have something to wash the mess off her boot. A sharp rippling caught her attention. She had just enough time to realize a wall of water was making the noise before it entered the compartment.

It burst through the hatchway at neck height, easily lifting Erica off her feet. She flailed around, just trying to keep her head above the water. It pushed her against the far wall, and eventually into a corner. The corner where she knew she had placed her latrine box. Yet, she could not feel it with her feet, and when the water drained out of the compartment, it was gone.

As when she had first entered the base leg, the water emptied out as if it had been sucked out by a vacuum cleaner. This time, the water had in fact acted like a vacuum cleaner. Not only was the latrine box and all its contents gone, but so were the blood stains, brain matter and skull fragments. Only heavy items, or those which were tied down, remained.

Erica discovered tube-shaped charges of plastic explosives still tied to the ladder. She tried to dispose of them, only to have another wave sweep into the compartment.

At first it was only knee-high, but its duration was longer than previous waves and water rapidly filled the compartment. Erica retreated to the ladder, climbing almost to the roof before the water level halted and started to fall. Once again it was all sucked out, except for the shallow pools on the floor and the water dripping from the walls. For the moment the compartment was empty and she decided it would be better to return to the equipment locker.

As she had been ordered, she left the external hatch open, and locked the door to her hideout. Back inside the narrow room, she discovered remarkably little water had leaked in around the door frame, even after the outer compartment had been nearly filled. Still, almost everything was soaked or covered with water. It was a mess, and would get worse.

Stowing away the supplies and equipment she felt she needed, Erica pulled a length of cord on what had been the mattress to her makeshift bed. With an explosive hiss, the life raft started to expand and take form. She kicked it up against the door, where it grew to almost fill the frame. When finished, the raft was partially upright, twisted slightly and pinched where it had come into contact with the storage shelves; in fact, some of the shelves had bent under the pressure. To anyone who opened the door, it would look like an accidental discharge of a raft's carbon dioxide bottles. Together with additional equipment piled against it, it was just what Erica wanted. To anyone opening the door the mess would, hopefully, not be worth investigating. After checking over her creation, she picked up the radio.

* * *

"It's been twelve minutes," said Taylor, glancing down at his watch. "I thought waiting out another submarine was tense, but this is nerve-wracking. I never felt so helpless."

"The rest of the crew is the same way," Holbrook advised, walking back into the radio room. "You could hear a pin drop in any of the other compartments, save for propulsion. Everyone is feeling helpless. I think what you stated before is true: we man one of the deadliest weapons in the Royal Navy, and all we can do is lend moral support."

"Captain, I have something. I think a radio's been turned on," said MacGregor.

"Taylor, this is Erica." The announcement cut through the room's tension like a knife. All three officers sighed audibly, and Taylor grabbed the console microphone. "Taylor, this is Erica. Come in, over."

"Hold off telling the crew, Johnnie, until we find out how she is," said Taylor, when he noticed Holbrook reaching for the intercom mike. "Erica, this is Taylor. What's your situation? Over."

"I got rid of the body, and anything else which would give me away. I left the external hatch open and locked the door to my room. I piled everything I could in front of it. They'll have to dig to find me. Over."

"Good, but are you sure it was wise to return to where you were hiding? The terrorists are certain to look there."

"I know, but there's no place else for me," said Erica. "There's only one way to get up and down these base legs. And above me is *Valkyrie*'s power generating station. That has to be manned constantly and I'm certain the terrorists will have someone there. Where I am is the best for me, unless I swim to another base leg. I've created for the terrorists a mess they won't want to search. Over."

"I see your reasons," said Taylor "and I think what you've done will work out. It may well be too late for you to attempt any other course of action. It's been almost twenty minutes since the terrorist surprised you. His friends may already be missing him. Hide yourself as best you can, and under no circumstances are you to try contacting us until after the other terrorists have searched for the one you killed. We'll maintain a constant wireless watch on this channel. Whenever you contact us, we'll be ready for you. Over."

"Thank you, Taylor. I better sign off now. Pray this all works. This is Erica, out."

"This is Taylor, out." After releasing the switch on the microphone stand, he turned to Holbrook and motioned for him to make the announcement to the crew. Then he faced MacGregor. "Donnie, keep the mast raised and the system on. We'll maintain this depth until we hear from her again."

"Do you think she can evade the search?" MacGregor asked.

"I don't know. I'd feel better if she found another hiding place, but I agree there's no other place to hide. We'll have to trust her judgement, and hope the terrorists don't turn bloody *Valkyrie* upside down looking for their comrade."

"And what should we do?"

"Deploy the trailing wire aerial," Taylor ordered, rising out of his seat. "We have to report this incident to Bradbury Lines. And I'm heading back to my cabin. After spending twenty minutes in nothing but my shorts, I'd like to put on some warmer clothes. Especially my feet. It seems as though no matter how much we heat this boat, these floors are always cold. Johnnie, you have the con until I return."

Chapter Twelve

"Mr. Sulu, warp factor one," said Carver, glancing between Burks, standing at the Sub-scape panel, and Chief Petty Officer Patrick Foster, who was on duty as senior helmsman, instead of Jefferson.

"What *are* you saying?" asked Eshel. "Do you think you're Captain Kirk from *Star Wars*?"

"That's 'Star Trek,' Yehuda," said Adir. "Get your fiction right. Is this a demonstration of the Sub-scape system we've heard about?"

"Yes, you weren't up here when we did this the last time," said Carver. "So I thought I'd save it for you after our communications stop was finished. Just watch the speed readout on the helm station. Take it easy, Pat. Clarence says you only need a light touch with the Lady at higher speeds."

Boyd and the four Israelis stood on or around the periscope stand, the only place for a "visitors' gallery" in the otherwise crowded control center. As in the past, the *Marshall's* acceleration was slow until it reached twenty knots. Then, with the polymer film at peak efficiency, the four-hundred-foot-long submarine trembled as its speed jumped dramatically.

Unaccustomed and unprepared for the jump, the Israelis staggered and either took hold of the stand's guard rail or were caught before they fell. Especially Gavrilla, who suffered more from the assistance than the unexpected motion.

"All right, I'm not going to break if I fall," she said, moving away from so many helpful hands. "If I were really delicate, I would've been pulled apart a long time ago.

Avrom, is this our actual speed?"

"It must be. I doubt the U.S. Navy would put false readings on such critical equipment simply to impress us," Adir replied, letting out a low whistle. "If my calculations are correct, we're doing better than forty miles an hour."

"Our eventual cruise speed will be sixty miles an hour," said Carver. "And we'll reach it in another minute. If you're already impressed, we're needed in the TASCO Room. Greg, you have the con."

Boyd was first at the stairs, and led the others into the submarine's tactical command center. Allard and Seidel were already manning it, and had programmed most of the information obtained during the latest communications stop. With the arrival of six more people, the compartment became overcrowded and Carver ordered Seidel back upstairs.

"Your ETs think the laser radar may be acting up again," Carver warned. "Stay on it — we need that system for the rest of our Sub-scape run. I can handle the tactical system."

"What are ETs? Do you have spacemen in your crew?" asked Eshel. "Why do you use so much science fiction on your ship?"

"ET stands for electronic technician," said Allard. "And the U.S. Navy used the term long before Steven Spielberg decided it would make a good movie title. Terry, Robert, there's been a major incident on *Ocean Valkyrie*. The survivor who hid herself on the rig was discovered by a terrorist. There was a fight, and somehow this Erica Johensen was able to kill the bastard."

"My God, this woman's proving more resourceful than I could've expected," said Boyd. "If this keeps up, I'd like to recruit her into my squadron."

"If it keeps up, she'll be discovered," Adir observed. "If she hasn't been already. Where was she hiding on the oil rig?"

"I'll show you. We got a complete schematic in the memory," said Carver, interlocking his fingers and cracking his knuckles before his hands started flying over the console's keyboard. The first button he tapped erased the tactical map from the main screen. The next ones brought up a side elevation of *Valkyrie*, which he rotated until the correct base leg was shown, and he marked Erica's hiding place with a flashing arrow. "She's in the second base leg, compartment One-B. That's a survival equipment storage room connected to the leg's lowest service compartment. If neither Glenn or Robert has told you before, the terrorists have apparently set plastic explosive charges all over the rig. There's one in the service compartment."

"No, we were not told. But knowing how Blood Revenge is trained to operate, it doesn't surprise me. Could I have a more detailed scheme of these rooms?"

In response to Adir's request, Carver erased the side elevation of *Valkyrie*. After some searching, he punched onto the main screen a floor plan to the base leg's first service level.

"Such a small place to hide in," said Gavrilla. "By comparison, the rooms on your submarine are spacious. Where is this Johensen hiding now?"

"*Spartan* reports she's back in the equipment locker," said Allard, handing the tearsheet over to Adir and Gavrilla.

"But she can't hide there—I'm certain the Blood Revenge strike teams will look there once they find the body."

"There's no body for them to find," Adir responded, looking up from the sheet. "After killing the terrorist, this Erica disposed of his body, and any evidence which would indicate someone was living there. She locked the door behind her, and piled against it equipment which had fallen off the storage shelves. For an untrained civilian, she's been very resourceful. I can see why you'd want her for your unit, Colonel."

"Yes, but Miss Eitan is right," said Boyd. "Your Blood Revenge terrorists will search for their missing comrade. I hope she can elude them. What can you tell us about the Blood Revenge unit? Especially the people Glenn and I will face."

"Blood Revenge is a Libyan military intelligence unit. Organized in 1987, after the first American air strike against Libya, and the loss of Chad to French forces. They've done a few small operations, but nothing on this scale. We got wind of a biowarfare operation some fifteen months ago. Libyan agents were in Western Europe, attempting to recruit geneticists and bio-engineers. We rushed in Gavi and a number of other agents, and she got lucky. She's been in Libya for the last ten months. She can tell you more about the individuals she met and their plans."

"I only met a few of the strike team members — the actual terrorists," Gavrilla admitted. "But one of them was, I believe, the leader. His name is Abu Nazal, and I think he's Lebanese. Several times he was with Colonel Ahmad Nazih, the commander of Blood Revenge and they share more in common than just their names. Colonel Nazih trained and shaped Nazal in his image. In many ways Nazal is his favorite son. He may even be better than Nazih — more ruthless, more willing to kill and with a consuming hatred of the West.

"Another I met was named Samad Jassem. He was Libyan and seemed level-headed. I think he may be a military intelligence officer. He was more professional. He talked to Eric Stanmeer and myself in less hateful tones. Yussuf Gunni is someone I met only once, but I think he's also important to the operation. He acted very paranoid and resentful of the other two.

"Uniquely, I met several women who were members of the strike teams. Most terrorist groups don't use women in actual combat roles. As Ben Adir will tell you, they feel it would give them bad publicity. To me, this indicates they're not looking to publicize some political cause. As the unit's name suggests, they're out for revenge. They want to wage war against the West."

"And they don't care who they kill in the bargain," said Allard. "Including themselves . . . Most of what you're telling us, and something which no one has mentioned yet, leads me to believe we're dealing with suicidal fanatics. People who hate us so much they're willing to die to get revenge."

"How can you say that? These people aren't Shi'ites," said Adir. "They're not religious fanatics. So why do you think they're suicidal fanatics?"

"Easy. Robert and I have been discussing what these terrorists have done and what their plans appear to be. We can piece it all together, except for one thing. How are they planning to escape? They picked the right weather conditions to prevent the landing of a helicopter, or the docking of a ship to *Valkyrie*. What prevents us from landing will also stop anyone else from picking them up. We know they've planted demolition charges and plan on blowing up the rig after they're done with it. This indicates to me we're facing a suicide squad."

"Erica Johensen did report to *Spartan* she overheard a terrorist saying they'll be far away from the rig by the time it sinks," Boyd added. "Though she heard nothing about how they would be removed."

"Then Commander Allard's hypothesis is still valid," said Adir, glancing through some of the notes he had in his documents case. "Nothing in Gavi's debriefing sessions makes mention of an escape plan. And when we were on the Combat Talon, I got a Mossad report that the Blood Revenge support teams have withdrawn from Norway."

"What about the Russians?" Shoham asked, his question causing everyone to turn in his direction. "In spite of what they're saying against terrorism, they still support Libya. Do they not have ships and submarines in the North Sea?"

"Christ, I never thought of them," said Carver. "Let's see what they're up to."

Carver turned back to the keyboard, where he quickly erased the compartment diagram. In its place he put up the original tactical map, showing the *Marshall*'s position in the eastern North Atlantic. To it, he quickly added a scattering of multicolored and numbered symbols.

"It does look like there's a heavy concentration of Soviet ships and subs in the Norwegian Sea," said Allard.

"The Warsaw Pact recently conducted a naval exercise in the area," Boyd informed. "They used about thirty-five ships and submarines, plus aircraft. They were taken from the Red Banner Northern and Baltic Sea Fleets, and some 'European' representation, such as Poland's one-ship destroyer squadron and an East German frigate. You'll see many of them grouped in the Skagerrak as well."

"Skagerrak? What name for an ocean is that?" Eshel asked.

"It's the strait between Denmark and the Scandinavian Peninsula," said Carver. "It looks to me like the exercise is over and the ships are heading back to their ports. This is a standard fleet dispersal pattern. What you're seeing is half an hour old, we got it at the start of our Com Stop. We'll get another when we reach the Shetland Islands, in three hours."

"Why must we wait so long, Captain? Why can't you talk to your Navy now?"

"Because we're in the middle of a Sub-scape run. With the exception of the short-range sensors, we're blind and deaf."

"But on 'Star Trek,' Captain Kirk could always talk to his Star Fleet," said Eshel. "Even when his *Enterprise* was doing warp speed."

"Science fiction can ignore physics," said Carver, growing irritated at the repeated, sharp questions. "This is reality, and we can't. Our depth is five hundred feet and our speed is over fifty knots. We're too deep for effective communications, hull noise would impede it anyway, and any antenna we would deploy would be snapped off."

"Then why don't you run slower and shallower?"

"Yehuda, this isn't the place for such questions," Adir warned, sensing the rise in tensions. "Please understand, Captain, we sabras can be a little prickly at times but we don't really mean it."

"I understand quite well," said Carver, still irritated. "Mr. Eshel, I don't know how command flows in the Israeli Air Force, but in the U.S. Navy a captain is the master of his ship. His orders are not subject to the interpretation of guests."

"And as *my* guest, I wish you wouldn't wear out your welcome so quickly," said Boyd. "Perhaps we should change subjects. Glenn and myself have been devising a plan to retake *Ocean Valkyrie*. It's still subject to revision, and we would be happy for your advice on it as well."

"Well, my first suggestion to you would be wake them up and train them," Eshel responded. "Why are they asleep? They retired to their bunks as soon as they finished recovering us. Is this the stamina of the British soldier?"

"I want my lads rested and alert for the operation, not exhausted and prone to mistakes." This time, it was Boyd's voice which had an edge of testiness. His own fatigue did little to slow his growing annoyance. "They were airborne for several hours and did a round of training after they arrived."

"This sounds like my cue to leave," said Carver, pushing his chair out from the console. "Robert, I think you know how to work the system well enough without me. I'll let you hash out these problems by yourselves. I think I'll see to the running of my Lady."

"Abu, the lights are on in the chamber below us," warned Akkad, stopping his descent and bringing to a halt the procession on the ladder. "But I can't see anyone."

"That doesn't mean there may not be someone," said Nazal, speaking just loud enough for the rest of the team to hear him. "All of you, swing around to the other side of the ladder. Don't continue down in direct line with the hatch. When you reach the floor, spread out and wait for me."

The men standing below Nazal hooked one leg around the ladder's side, then swung to its back. No longer directly exposed to any gunfire coming through the hatch below them, the terrorists continued their descent. Akkad jumped to the floor when he got within a few feet of it. As they had been ordered, he and the others spread around the floor opening and waited for Nazal to join them.

"We don't see anyone in the lower chamber," said Akkad. "And we can hear a banging. I think the outer door may be open—everything below looks soaked."

"I say we should lay in suppressing fire," said another terrorist. "We may not see anyone, but it doesn't mean there can't be someone. Bullets will keep their heads down while we enter the room."

"Don't be crazy. We're not going to waste ammunition on enemies of your imagination," Nazal replied. "And if Azali's still alive, we could kill him by mistake. But we would be wise to arm our weapons. This is the last room Azali could've been in, and it looks like whatever happened to him happened here."

Nazal clicked off the safety on his Mac-10 and pulled its bolt back. The rest of his men did the same to their pistols and submachineguns; the last one had yet to finish with the cocking lever on his AKM rifle when Nazal climbed onto the ladder and descended through the floor hatch.

While others covered him from above, he stopped as he cleared the lower compartment's roof and swept the area with his submachinegun. Apart from the outer hatch being open and every surface in the room dripping with water, he noticed nothing else out of the ordinary. Still, Nazal jumped off the ladder when he was a few feet above the floor, landing on it with a loud stamp.

He continued to sweep the obviously empty compartment while he was joined by the others. After the second man had reached the floor they all heard a distinctive rippling sound and turned to the exterior hatch. Nasal was closest, and was the first to be engulfed by the chest-high wall of water that burst through the opening.

Erica thought she heard distant voices, but couldn't be sure. She had been expecting to hear voices for more than an hour, and had many false alarms. Not until she heard the stamp of boots on metal did she realize someone indeed was outside the locker. The shouting in Arabic and English, which came through a few moments later, confirmed to Erica it was the terrorists.

What she had feared the most was about to happen. She reached inside a jacket pocket and pulled out a flare stick. Keeping it in her hand, Erica slid it around the dense packing of equipment until it was next to her face. She ran her fingers over the flare's base, ready to unlock its safety should the terrorists discover her.

Accompanying the shouts was a spray of sea water around the door frame. It quickly spread under the pile Erica was hiding in; like all the other times a storm surge made it through the outer hatch. At least she had the satisfaction of knowing the people she hated were as cold and wet as she was.

"Close the damn hatch!" Nazal ordered, picking himself off the floor. "Close it now!"

"No, wait. Check outside if you can," said Jassem, standing at the top of the ladder. "Look for any sign of Eshqi, or anyone else."

The two men who had been washed around the compartment with Nazal struggled to their feet and went to the external hatch. One of them held the steel door open while the other glanced outside. They found the storm at a momentary lull, but could see nothing beyond the underside of *Valkyrie*'s platform and the chaotic sea. They were forced to retreat inside the compartment by an approaching wave. When it crashed against the base leg, water squirted from around the hatch rim; and the suction created by the wave as it pulled away nearly jerked the hatch open. It took both men to keep it shut.

"Close and lock it," Nazal repeated. "Kaniel, check the explosives. Samad, why did you tell them to check outside?"

"It should be obvious," said Jassem, stepping off the ladder. "For whatever reason, Azali Eshqi opened the hatch and either fell or was swept out."

"I don't want to hear conclusions, not until we've made a search for Azali," Nazal snapped. "Yes, Asir, what is it?"

"I believe this was Eshqi's," said Asir Kashani. "He left his submachinegun with us when he started his new duties."

Kashani handed Nazal a Baretta automatic. Its hammer was still cocked. When Nasal tried to safety the weapon, he found the trigger almost impossible to pull and the hammer had to be pushed home. Even the safety lever proved difficult to move.

"I found it in the corner. It must've been in the water for the past hour."

"It's already fouled," said Nazal, raising the weapon's muzzle to his nose. "And I can't tell if it's been fired or not. But I think it has. Kaniel, how are the explosives?"

"Battered . . . it looks like the charges were kicked around," said Akkad. "However, they're still useable. I'll have to resecure them and replace the wires and the detonators."

"What's behind this door?"

"A storage room for survival gear. When Azali and I were setting these charges, we checked it and found all the gear had fallen off the shelves."

"We better check it again," Nazal advised. "Samad, open it. Asir, cover him."

In spite of her wildly beating heart, Erica froze when she heard Nazal's orders. Though her leg muscles had begun to cramp, because of the cold and inactivity, she refused to move them. Any movement, any noise at all would be immediately fatal. She could hear someone approach the door. She heard the clicking of its lock. When the door swung open, the front half off the pile shifted; for a moment Erica had the heart-stopping fear it would fall away and reveal her.

"Damn it!" Jassem shouted, jumping away from the locker door. The moment he turned its knob it sprung open on its own accord. Equipment boxes and packages dropped to the compartment floor as an inflated life raft pushed a few inches out of the frame.

"Don't fire!" said Nazal, when he noticed Kashani raising his Mac-10. "It's just a raft. Kaniel, is this what you found?"

"No, but I'm not surprised this happened," said Akkad. "The shelves had not been secured for the storm. Obviously, one of the rafts had an accidental inflation."

"Then what you see is not how you remember it?"

"Not with the life raft. Why? Do you think Azali or someone else is hiding in there?"

"If Azali was in here, he'd have heard us," Jassem remarked, stepping back up to the locker and trying to peer over the raft. "If he had been killed, why hide his body in this room when there's an ocean outside? It doesn't make sense. I see no body, I see no blood. He's not in here."

"If not him, then his killers," said Nazal. "Asir, Kaniel, help me search the room."

With the door open, Erica heard the conversations clearly. She recognized several voices, especially Nazal's; especially when he ordered the others to help him search the locker. It would only take them a few minutes to remove the life raft and dig deep enough into the pile to find her. The moment she heard the raft being moved, Erica clicked off the flare's safety. Whoever discovered her would die with her.

"It's jammed, someone help me move this," Nazal grunted. Even with both hands, Nazal was unable to get a firm grip on the raft, or budge it from the door frame. "If we don't, we can't do the search."

"We're not going to move it because we don't have to search the room," said Jassem. "Kaniel, finish with the explosives."

"Samad, don't countermand my orders. I have enough problems with Yussuf doing it."

"We also have enough to do without wasting time searching through this mess. Azali isn't in here. For whatever reason, he opened the outer hatch and had an accident. When you first entered this chamber, Asir was nearly swept out when it flooded. Something like that happened to Azali. It was an accident."

"Then how do you explain this?" Nazal asked, holding up Eshqi's gun. "Why have we found his weapon, apparently fired?"

"I don't know, maybe he used it to signal for help."

"Maybe he used it to defend himself, and was killed by someone who had sneaked onto this rig?"

"Like who? A frogman? A commando? Maybe there's a submarine out there with a team of Israeli agents aboard," said Jassem, growing impatient. "You've been seeing Israelis over your shoulder ever since we left Libya. *If* Azali was killed by someone who came aboard, he wouldn't hide the body in this room and he certainly wouldn't hide there himself. No one would be so stupid, especially someone trained as a commando or a spy. And remember, Almira heard nothing and saw nothing after Eshqi passed her guard post."

"When we were first down here, Azali thought one of the Norwegians had escaped us and was either hiding in that room, or used its equipment to leave the rig," said Akkad, making a statement which again caused Erica's heart to skip a beat.

"Yes, Azali told me of his concerns," said Nazal. "And we did our own check of the rig crew. Dead, alive, wounded, they've all been accounted for. All right, Samad, we have a mystery. But it's something we must discuss further. In particular, I want to talk with Almira. Asir, stay with Kaniel until he's finished rewiring the charges. The rest of you are to come with me to the power generating room. From there you'll be given new assignments. Kaniel, when you're finished, I want you to report to me. I'll be in the operations center."

Erica breathed a little easier when Nazal gave the orders for most of his men to leave the outer compartment. As they tramped up the stairs, she clicked on the safety to the flare in her hands. Even with the immediate crisis over, she still remained motionless.

The locker door had been left open and she could hear the two terrorists splice in new firing wires, replace the detonators and secure the plastic explosives to the ladder once again. It wasn't until their duties were finished when one of the terrorists approached the locker.

Erica heard him scoop the spilled packages off the floor and toss them around the bulky raft. She even felt some of the heavier items land on the pile. When it came to closing the door, both terrorists had to work at it.

One pushed the raft back inside and tried to hold it there while the other pushed the door shut. After several attempts the bolt snapped home in the door frame and the lock clicked on. With sound now as muffled as it had been before, Erica had to strain to hear the terrorists climb back up the ladder. Even when their voices and sounds blended in with the surrounding noise of the storm, she still refused to permit any but the smallest of movements.

Erica rotated her left wrist and pulled back her jacket sleeve until she could see the luminous dial to her watch. She silently counted off the minutes, allowing herself to flex her stiff legs slightly after she had counted ten. When something suddenly tumbled off the pile and clattered noisily on the floor, Erica froze. Though she heard nothing in response to it from the outer compartment, she refused to move again until half an hour had passed.

"Frieda, have you heard anything?" Taylor asked, when he entered the *Spartan's* radio room. "Petty Officer Stirling, where's Lieutenant MacGregor?"

"His watch ended twenty minutes ago, sir," said Stirling. "I'm his relief. We've received nothing since I came on duty."

"And there's been nothing since I came here," Frieda added. "Please, couldn't we try contacting her? It's been hours since you last talked to her."

"I understand your desires, but the answer has to be no," said Taylor, trying to be courteous. "We have to let Erica contact us. We mustn't do anything to give her away. Erica will know the best time to raise us. We have to let her make the decision. Though I must admit, it's exasperating for me as well. We've been cruising at this depth for more than two hours. Half my crew is seasick. This is worse than any patrol or exercise I've been on."

"Captain, we could release the communications buoy," said Stirling. "It would allow us to dive for calmer waters and remain in touch with Erica."

"I know, Donnie suggested we use it as well. But we have to keep patrolling the area and using the buoy would tie us down to one spot. If we were to drag it in this kind of sea condition we'd lose it."

"Perhaps I should go back and see Trig," said Frieda. "I've been here so long I bet he thinks I've forgotten about him."

"Captain, I just heard a snapping noise," Stirling warned, his voice rising. "Someone's activating a radio."

The conversations immediately died away, causing the omnipresent static to apparently increase in volume. For several moments, the buzzing was all that could be heard in the radio room. Then it broke, and in the silence was a weak-sounding but familiar voice.

"Taylor, this is Erica. Taylor, this is Erica. Please come in, over."

"Boost the volume, it's difficult to hear her," said Taylor, picking up the console microphone. "Erica, this is Taylor. Apart from my wife's, I never thought I could hear a more beautiful voice. Everyone on this submarine has been waiting for you. Thank heaven you're alive. What's your situation? Over."

"I'm still in the equipment locker. The terrorists searched the outer compartment more than an hour ago. They looked in here but decided it was too much of a mess to go through and thought no one would be stupid enough to stay in the area of a

214

murder. The terrorists have locked the exterior hatch, repaired the explosives and locked me back inside my room. I've heard no one else in the past hour. I'm safe again, over."

"You're very lucky, Erica. If you were a cat, I'd say you just used up one or two of your nine lives. Frieda is waiting to talk to you, so I'm turning the microphone over to her. Keep what you want to say brief. I'm going to enforce a five minute time limit on you — let's not stretch your luck any further than it has been."

Keeping the transmit button open, Taylor handed the microphone back to Frieda. While she started talking rapidly in a mixture of English and Norwegian, Taylor picked the wall mike out of its cradle and activated the *Spartan*'s public address system.

He stepped outside the radio room to make his announcement, and standing in the passageway he could hear his voice filter back from the attack center. He also heard the cheers and applause break out among his crew before he had finished his message. When Taylor re-entered the radio compartment, Frieda was still talking rapidly to Erica.

She was also crying, and as much as he hated doing it, he forced her to end the transmission when the five-minute mark was reached. As he had promised Erica, Taylor ordered Stirling to leave the system on in the "receive-only" mode then he escorted Frieda to the sick bay in the officers' quarters. There they informed Nordsen of what Erica had said, until Taylor was called back to *Spartan*'s attack center.

Chapter Thirteen

"Why are you so eager to believe Eshqi's death was an accident?" Gunni demanded, after listening to Nazal's explanation with growing frustration. "What did Samad tell you that you find so plausible?"

"Essentially what I just told you," said Nazal, in turn growing angry with his co-commander's attitude. "He provided very plausible and logical reasons for the mystery we found. We saw the evidence. Why do you believe our conclusions are wrong?"

"Because I looked at *all* the evidence! Especially one which you overlooked."

Gunni slammed a Baretta automatic onto the table where the leaders were standing. The loud crash it made caught the attention of everyone in *Valkyrie's* operations center, most especially Nazal and Jassem.

"Careful, Yussuf! You can make it go off," Jassem warned. "It's Eshqi's gun. What were doing with it?"

"Examining it," said Gunni. "Pull the clip out."

With some effort, Jassem managed to pry the clip from the automatic's hefty grip. The moment he had it in his hand, he realized something was wrong with it. The clip didn't weigh as much as a fully loaded one, and he began counting the number of rounds still in it.

"There are seven bullets in here, plus one in the chamber," Jassem finally said.

"Yes, eight rounds in a gun which can hold fifteen," said Gunni, a confident smile on his face. "Where did they go,

Abu? You talked about Eshqi firing a warning shot. Why would he fire seven warning shots?"

Nazal pulled his own Baretta from its holster and quickly slid the clip out of it. He held the magazine up for the other leaders to see; through the side slits they could easily see it didn't contain all the rounds it could.

"Very few of us fully load our clips," Nazal answered. "It compresses the springs, which can cause our weapons to jam. The clip itself only holds fourteen rounds, and many of us don't like carrying a gun with a shell already in the chamber. It can too easily cause accidents. I don't know how Eshqi took care of his weapons, but there are many reasons why the clip may not have been fully loaded."

"And one of them could have been a fire fight with commandoes or agents," said Gunni, cutting him off. "Why are you so readily dismissing it?"

"I raised these questions when we first made the discovery, until Jassem pointed out we found no evidence of anyone boarding *Valkyrie*. The search teams in the other base legs report finding no evidence they had been entered either."

"I warned Abu not to be paranoid, now I'll warn you," said Jassem. "I know what we have is some unusual evidence, but it doesn't add up to an invasion of this rig. Almira heard nothing, saw nothing after Eshqi went down to check the explosives. If some type of commando unit had come aboard, even for reconnaissance, they wouldn't have stopped after investigating a few rooms in one support leg. Stop being paranoid, Yussuf. It's a waste of time and energy."

"Being paranoid kept me alive all the years I worked in Beirut for the Shi'ite militias," Gunni replied. "Ask Nazal what his country is like."

"This isn't Lebanon, and there isn't a submarine full of Israeli agents out there waiting to attack us. No submarine can carry enough men to assault this rig, and no plane or ship has approached us since we captured it."

"All right, enough," said Nazal, re-inserting the clip into his Baretta and reholstering the weapon. "Curious I have to break an argument between you two. Usually it's Samad ending an argument between Yussuf and me. Whether this was an accident or not, security will be increased. From now on a two-man team will patrol the lower portions of this rig, and they will be fully armed. I wish we could do more, but we don't have the personnel to do anything greater. Pre-drilling procedures must begin soon."

"Yes, the storm is letting up," said Jassem. "Latest weather report shows the wind and sea state decreasing. We have to select the oil rig workers to 'volunteer' and inspect the equipment. The derrick, the drill pipe, pumps, mixers, chemicals. Everything. And it all takes time."

"Yes, yes. I understand it all," said Gunni, resentfully. "Remember, I am co-author of this operation, too. If we can't add more guards, then we should weld shut the exterior hatches on all base legs."

"You should read the parts of the operation you didn't write," Nazal snapped. "If you weld those doors shut, how are we to evacuate to the *Sword of the Revolution* when it arrives? If it has kept to its timetable, we'll be talking to Captain Saleh in the next few hours. The real work of this operation begins shortly, and we have no time to waste on paranoid fears."

"Whatever dreams you're having, you better save them for later," said Burks. "It's time for you to relieve me, Terry."

The figure lying in the bunk stirred when Burks first entered the cabin. It mumbled something back to him when he started to speak, and sat up when he called his name. Carver swung his legs over the edge of the bunk and tapped on its reading light to see his way around the tiny room.

"What's the situation like?" he asked, opening up a locker and taking out a fresh shirt.

"We're still on our Sub-scape run," said Burks. "And sustaining fifty-two knots. We're south of the Faeroe Islands, and approaching the passage between the Shetlands and the Orkneys. The Lady's in good condition, and the crew's ready for you."

"Thanks, Greg. Go get your sleep, you deserve it."

Burks proceeded Carver into the passageway, where they shook hands and parted. Burks went to his own cabin, while

Carver entered the *Marshall*'s control center. He got immediate reports from the helmsmen on duty, watch officer, sonar and radio rooms.

"How long can we stay on our Sub-scape run?" Carver asked, walking around the periscope stand.

"No more than six hours," said the watch officer. "The polymer tanks are down to twenty percent."

"Good, we'll be ending the run in the next two or three hours. Who's in the TASCO Room?"

"Glenn and Mr. Boyd. Also, some of the Israelis."

"This meeting is news to me," said Carver. "I better find out what they're doing. If anyone wants me, I'll be below."

Carver descended the stairs at the back of the periscope stand, entering the tactical attack and situation control room. Unlike the control center, it was dimly lit and relatively quiet. It was also much warmer, the result of cramming so much electronics into a small compartment. Carver immediately recognized Boyd's and Allard's voices, then Adir's and Gavrilla's. They all fell silent as he came to the foot of the stairs.

"Terence, have a seat and join us," said Boyd, looking over his shoulder.

"Thanks for being so generous aboard my submarine," Carver answered. "What's this meeting for? I thought you people had already hashed everything out."

"With my companions asleep, I thought we could discuss the specifics of the operation without the acrimony," said Adir. "I apologize for the way Eshel and Shoham acted, but we native-born Israelis are well-named. The *sabra* is a prickly fruit of a local cactus. Once you get past our thorns we can be sweet."

"Well I've been jabbed enough times to earn a purple heart," said Allard. "Haven't seen much of your sweet side, except of course for Gavi."

"Thank you, Commander," she replied, before turning to Carver. "Captain, are we going to keep sailing this fast?"

"No, we're running out of polymers and soon it'll be too dangerous to run at this speed," said Carver, squeezing into the chair Adir had abandoned. "I see you've been busy going over *Valkyrie*. Bring up the tactical, I'll show you where we are."

The TASCO Room's main screen showed the now familiar schematic of *Ocean Valkyrie,* the level where the rig's cafeteria and main lounge were located. With the press of a key it was erased, and quickly replaced with a tactical map of the North Sea, northern Scotland and the Orkney, Shetland and Faeroe island groups. Scattered across the ocean were symbols for civilian and military ships; the one flashing was the *John Marshall.* When Carver called for a grid, lines of latitude and longitude appeared on the screen.

"Those ship positions are the ones you showed us hours ago," Adir noted. "Don't you have anything new?"

"As I told you before, we can't send or receive communications while on a Sub-scape run," said Carver. "I thought you weren't going to be as prickly as your friends? We'll get new data once we slow down, which should be in the next two hours. As we approach Fair Isle. Glenn, flag it on the screen."

A tiny island midway between the Shetlands and Orkneys was encircled and, with a few more key strokes, the distance from it to the *Marshall* was displayed. At Adir's request, Allard called up the distance between Fair Isle and *Ocean Valkyrie.*

"How long will it take us to reach the oil rig?" Gavrilla asked.

"It depends on how we proceed," said Carver. "When we reach Fair Isle, we'll be able to talk directly with *Spartan.* We'll get an up-to-the-minute report on what the situation's like and proceed from there."

"Please, Captain. How many more hours do we have to be on your submarine?"

"Perhaps another ten or twelve hours." For the first time Carver took a serious look at Gavrilla. Unlike the others in the TASCO Room, she wasn't seated or standing behind the seats; she was pressed flat against the port wall. Even in the subdued lighting, Carver could see the anguish on her face. His voice was gentle when he spoke. "I know claustrophobia is difficult to deal with, but if it's any reassurance, my Lady's as sound as the day they cracked the champagne over her bows."

"Thank you, but it's of little reassurance," said Gavrilla, closing her eyes and starting to cry quietly. "I've only been on

220

your ship for a few hours and I can't understand how you people can live like this."

"We volunteered, and then we were trained for submarine service. Not everyone can take life aboard a sub. In a way, many of us can't understand why you would become a spy. Taking on a fake identity and going unarmed into a nest full of enemies is the last thing any of us wants to do. Courage is a relative thing, Miss Eitan. We're brave in what we're good at, twenty-five years in the Navy has taught me that. Don't feel ashamed about your reaction, I've seen Top Gun jet jockeys almost lose it on a practice dive."

"Gavi . . . Gavrilla, when do you believe drilling operations will begin?" Adir asked, giving her something other than her fears to dwell on.

"Soon. Your last weather report showed the storm to be losing its severity," said Gavrilla. "There will be a brief period when the conditions won't be severe enough to prevent drilling, but will impede any commando attack. It won't last, though they'll only need a few hours to insert the bio-weapon."

"If it's going to be soon it'll be better for us," said Allard, glancing at his wristwatch. "In another four hours it'll be nightfall topside. I'd rather begin our assault at night. Even jittery terrorists need to rest and there will be less chance of lookouts on the rig spotting us."

"When you attack the rig, will you rescue Erica?"

"As a matter of fact, my team will be the one to get Erica out of her prison. All four teams will try to maintain contact with the TASCO Room, where I trust your group will be, Mr. Adir?"

"Yes, we'll want to give you up-to-the-minute advice," Adir replied. "On both the terrorists and the bio-weapon."

"I don't think you'll be able to get me out of this room," said Gavrilla. "It feels less like a submarine than any other room I've been in, including the sleeping quarters you gave us."

"Well I'm afraid I can't let you stay here full time," said Carver, trying to be both firm and gentle with his orders. "It's time we took you to Dr. Evans, who can prescribe a sedative for you. Until the end of this operation I'm afraid that's the best we can do for you."

* * *

"Is the system on?" Nazal asked, after being welcomed to *Valkyrie's* communications center.

"Yes, sir. The high-frequency radio has been warmed up and set on the proper channel," said Sherina, who had been given command of the center. "We're ready to transmit. Which of you will make contact? You, Samad or Yussuf?"

She motioned to Jassem and Gunni, who were standing beside the control panel for the high-frequency system. For the first time in several hours, for the first time since their confrontation in the operations center all three leaders were together in the same room.

"Let Samad do it," said Nazal. "He met more times with Captain Saleh than I did. His voice will be more familiar than mine or Yussuf's."

"Thank you," Jassem replied, taking a seat at the HF controls. "In a few moments we'll know if our trip back to Libya is in place or not."

Sherina pushed a microphone in front of Jassem and adjusted the volume control for him. With a final check of the system, she turned it over to his use.

"Ibis, this is Vulture. Ibis, this is Vulture," Jassem continued. "Are you reading me? Over."

The responding hiss of static to the broadcast only caused the tensions among the assembled personnel to jump. They shifted uneasily, and did not remain quiet for long.

"Try it again, Samad," said Gunni. "I have no intention of staying here to die with our enemies."

"He's out there, stop worrying," said Jassem. "Karim Saleh is the best in the Libyan Navy. Even the bastard Russians will tell you. Ibis, this is Vulture. Do you read me?"

"Vulture, this is Ibis. We read you four balls by five," rumbled the center's loudspeakers and they emitted ear-piercing whines until Sherina adjusted the volume controls. "Vulture, this is Ibis. We read you. The weather is bad, the journey has been long, but we are on time. Over."

"It's them, all right," Nazal identified, a smile breaking over his face. "Give the answer code."

222

"Ibis, this is Vulture. The weather is bad, the work is hard but we're on time," said Jassem. "Will you make the party? Over."

"Nothing else is on our schedule, we will make your party. This is Ibis, signing off."

"Allah be praised," said Gunni, letting out an audible sigh as Sherina started deactivating the high-frequency system. "It is His will that this operation succeed."

"It will, but only through more hard work," Nazal advised. "We've inspected the equipment, now we must select the prisoners to help us make *Valkyrie* operational. Sherina, will you be returning to normal duties?"

"Yes, I will re-establish contact with the British negotiators," Sherina responded, glancing over the control panel to ensure the system had shut down. "I told them I had to consult with my leaders. They want to talk with either the captain or the doctor again. They're very concerned about the wounded."

"I'll send one of them to you after we're done selecting the prisoner details. At least we don't have to worry about our escape. Our trip back to Libya has arrived."

"Lieutenant, retract the high-frequency mast and the ESM antenna," Captain Saleh ordered. "I'll tell the sonar room to retract the radar mast."

Saleh took hold of the hatch rim and pulled himself out of the cramped radio room. Even in the passageway he had to steady himself against his boat's erratic pitching and rolling. He could hear the *Sword of the Revolution* creaking around him and was happy he would be taking it back to calmer waters. He was still moving up the passageway when his executive officer greeted him.

"What's the news from the strike group?" he asked. "Are they still in control of *Valkyrie?*"

"Yes, and they're on schedule," said Saleh. "We will rendezvous with them as planned. Bassam, tell the sonar room to retract the radar and keep watching for NATO submarines. I'll go forward to make the announcement to the crew."

With its transmission to *Ocean Valkyrie* at an end, the thirty-foot-tall mast beside the *Foxtrot* submarine's conning tower started to collapse back into its well. Motors at the base of the mast lowered it smoothly in spite of the waves washing continuously over the cigar-shaped hull. When it reached the recess, clips automatically snapped around the mast, locking it in place.

Long before the retraction of the high-frequency antenna was completed, the Snoop Tray surveillance radar and Stop Light ESM aerial had disappeared inside the conning tower. During its brief stay on the surface no one appeared in the tower's flying bridge. It was too dangerous in the chaotic sea conditions and there was no need; minutes after surfacing, the *Sword of the Revolution* opened its ballast tank valves.

The submarine pitched and wallowed for another minute before sliding back under the jumbled waves. No aircraft and no other ships were spotted by its sensors. The prevailing storm was still keeping almost everyone in port or on the ground, and those forces watching *Valkyrie* were too distant to take notice of the diesel-electric sub's fleeting appearance.

It had begun its part of the operation before any of the terrorists or their support teams had left Libya. Now, after more than a month at sea, the *Sword of the Revolution* was only hours away from its objective.

It submerged to a hundred feet, where the water was dramatically calmer, and set course to the southeast. The *Foxtrot* accelerated to fifteen knots, its maximum speed. While only half the speed of most modern nuclear attack subs, it did allow the *Foxtrot* to use its Herkules sonar to search out its principal enemy, other submarines. For the last month it had managed to elude them; if it could do so for the next several days the entire operation would be a success.

Chapter Fourteen

"Captain, the sound room has detected a new set of noises," Holbrook advised, turning to the attack center's periscope stand.

"Where? What direction are they coming from?" said Taylor, stopping his periscope walk. "Have they been identified?"

"The Twenty-Twenty array has localized it to the sea floor. It's the underwater manifold center beneath *Valkyrie*—it appears to be operating. You think the terrorists are drilling now?"

"Not for several hours," said Frieda, entering the attack center through the forward hatch. "We go through a clean-up and reactivation procedure after every major storm. They're doing a remote check-out of the UMC from rig operations."

"That could explain the activity I called you to take a look at," said Taylor. "Watch the monitor—I'm bringing the image enhancement system on line."

Taylor hit the buttons on the periscope's control panel to activate its low-light-level TV camera. On the stand's monitor an image painted in shades of luminescent green quickly appeared. It was of *Ocean Valkyrie,* and Taylor used the search periscope's magnification lenses to increase it until figures could be seen working on the rig's exterior.

"They're taking inventory of our equipment," said Frieda. "The bits, drill pipes and chemicals for drilling mud."

"Do you think they've started a drilling operation?" Taylor asked.

"No, this is all very preliminary. First they have to break

most of the ice off the superstructure, then they have to organize work crews and—my God, I just thought of something! The Arabs don't have enough people to make their own crews. They'll have to use my friends to do the hard work for them."

"I'm afraid so. They'll be used as slave labor, and then killed. The—"

"Captain, report to the sound room at once!"

"Johnny, you have the con!" said Taylor, before Greenway had managed to repeat his warning.

"Captain Taylor, report to the sound room. Hostile sonar scans detected."

Taylor raced from periscope stand to the back of the attack center, and moments later was entering *Spartan's* sonar room. There, he found Greenway and a chief petty officer concentrating on the oscilloscopes for the Type 2020 passive hydrophone array instead of the scopes for the active sonar systems.

"It's Herkules attack sonar," Greenway answered, before being asked. "From either a *Golf, Romeo* or *Foxtrot*-class submarine."

"You mean our threat is a diesel-electric sub?" said Taylor.

"We're not detecting the signatures related to Soviet nuclear power plants, and the Herkules is an early-sixties vintage sonar. We're picking up the noises of twin screws at high revolutions, water moving in and out of free flood holes and have localized it to a relatively shallow depth."

Greenway pointed to the tactical scope, where a luminescent blip was flashing on its outer rim. It was at extreme range, and once Taylor orientated the position of his submarine on the scope, he realized the threat was approaching *Spartan* from astern. Beyond the symbol for *Valkyrie,* it was the only object showing on the scope.

"Does the hostile know we're here?" Taylor asked.

"Not just yet," said Greenway. "The Herkules is fairly primitive compared to our systems and we're too distant to give a detectable return echo. Plus, we can always use the rig to shield us from the unknown. We estimate its current speed at fifteen knots. It'll be several hours before the submarine moves to within torpedo range."

"We need to know more, much more, about our unknown.

Are they close enough to use the PARIS sonar?"

"Yes, but the pulses would have to be so powerful as to immediately reveal our presence. We'll learn enough through our passive arrays to eventually identify the intruder."

"Then let me know the moment you do so," said Taylor, taking the hand mike off its wall mount. "Captain to crew. General quarters, action stations. General quarters, action stations. This is no drill. Helm, come to course zero-eight-zero degrees. Increase speed to ten knots. Stand by to surface. Wireless office, standby for High Frequency transmission. Weapons, prepare all torpedo tubes for firing."

Taylor quickly exited the sonar room and, in the few moments it took him to reach the attack center, he could feel the *Spartan* change course and increase speed. It swung to the left, entering a port turn to place the oil rig between it and the approaching submarine.

"Stan, did we hear you right?" Holbrook questioned, a puzzled look on his face. "You want us to surface?"

"Yes, Bradbury Lines and the American sub have to know about this development," said Taylor, stepping alongside the periscope stand. "Mr. Bryan, take us up. Wireless office, encode the following message. 'Hostile submarine approaching *Ocean Valkyrie* from northwest. Possibly Russian, either *Foxtrot, Romeo* or *Golf*-class. Advise *Marshall* immediately. We're going to silent sub operations. Will attempt positive identification of intruder type and nationality. For now it is an unknown hostile'."

While Taylor was still dictating his message the submarine started to rock sharply. It had broached the surface, and in seconds its high-frequency radio mast had been raised to join the search periscope. As Holbrook maintained a watch on *Valkyrie* with the scope, the radio room encoded and condensed the message, then transmitted it in a short burst. The operation was done before the full length of *Spartan's* hull had broken through the waves. When the radio room confirmed the broadcast, Taylor ordered a crash dive.

As briefly as a whale or dolphin breaking for air, the attack submarine rose out of the water and settled back into it. There would be no waiting on the surface for SAS headquarters to confirm it had received the message. Ablaze with light, *Valkyrie* was less than two miles away. And though night effectively cloaked *Spartan's* featureless, black hull, Taylor did not want to risk even the slight chance of someone on the rig eventually spotting his boat.

"Retracting search 'scope," said Holbrook, pressing a button on its control panel. "And the high-frequency mast has already been pulled inside the sail."

"Good. Take us down, Mr. Bryant," Taylor instructed. "Bottom her out. Captain to crew, I want silent sub operations in all compartments. Wireless office, prepare to release communications buoy after we've reached the sea bed. Sound room, have you made the identity of the intruder?"

"Yes, Captain. The intruder is a *Foxtrot*-class boat," said Greenway, his voice filling the attack center. "Analysis of its footprint has identified it as *Foxtrot Seven* of the Libyan Navy."

"What? Are you positive, Gerry?"

"According to the NATO data file on hostile naval forces it well and truly is. An update in the file says *Foxtrot Seven* was last detected in the western Mediterranean more than three weeks ago by the Italian Navy. Will you be informing Bradbury Lines about this?"

"Once we've bottomed out. In this area the North Sea is shallow enough for us to do so," said Taylor, scanning the displays at the helm station. "Give us some low-power scans on the PARIS. We need to see where we're bottoming."

The *Spartan* continued its steady descent as its Passive/ Active Ranging and Intercept Sonar began firing pulses at the North Sea floor. The screens for its helmsmen started showing a relief map of the bottom topography with the first return echo. After several moments, a location several miles from the oil rig was selected for its comparatively shallow depth and lack of obstacles.

Maneuvering at ten knots, the attack sub reduced its dive angle and swung toward the site Taylor had designated. The deeper it went, the less severe the storm effects became. Five hundred feet lower, *Spartan* entered the calmest water it had found in hours.

It reduced speed to a crawl and was almost level when its bows plowed into the floor's soft mud. The submarine landed with a slight lean to port. As it ground to a halt its bow planes were retracted into the hull to prevent them from being damaged. The forward ballast tanks were filled to make the sub nose heavy and the stern tanks were left partially empty. This prevented the cruciform tail surfaces from being buried.

When its scythe-bladed propeller slowed to a halt, all external noises ceased on *Spartan*. For all intents it was now invisible; only those who knew its exact location would be able to find it. After the submarine had finished settling, a hatch behind its conning tower opened. A communications buoy hardly more than six inches in diameter rose out of the well, trailing a thin wire behind it. Once the buoy reached the surface, the crew would be able to talk again with the outside world and warn them that the *Sword of the Revolution* had arrived.

"This rig will soon begin drilling operations," Nazal announced, walking down a line of prisoners. "You've been selected to work with us because of your skills and experience. The harder you work on our operation the sooner we'll leave you."

"Since when are hostages supposed to work for terrorists?" asked a drill foreman, stepping out of the line and turning to face Nazal. "I'll not work for those who killed my friends. If you want something done, do it yourself."

Nazal froze in his steps as he stared down the Norwegian who stood some seven inches taller than him. The rest of the personnel in the hallway, both hostages and captors, also froze. In a blur, Nazal's hand wrapped around the grip protruding from his shoulder holster. The moment the Baretta appeared he was pulling its slide back, the moment it snapped forward, Nazal was aiming the gun at the foreman.

As they had been when *Valkyrie* was first seized, the rig workers were unprepared for the weapon's use. Its deafening bark caused them to jerk reflexively. Many felt the burst of heat from the muzzle flash. Nazal had wanted to kill the Norwegian instantly, but the slug tore through his throat instead of his forehead.

Blood pulsed freely out of the wound, even between the fingers clenched tightly over it, and sprayed some of the other workers as the foreman staggered and crashed to the deck. They were screaming before he had finished falling, which caused Nazal to resort to his usual order.

"Shut up! Shut up!" he shouted, waving his automatic at the rest of the line. "We'll kill you if you don't! Arm weapons!"

The guards with Nazal flicked off the safeties and pulled the bolts back on their assault rifles and submachineguns. The menacing actions caused the screaming to die away to a frightened whimpering.

"Your brutality wasn't necessary," said Erik Reitan, with quaking defiance. "We have no means to resist you. You murdered him to show your arrogance."

"Yes, and don't lie to me, Captain," said Nazal. "You and your crew have been resisting us. In passive ways. This is going to end! You work, you live. You resist, you die. Our operation is entering its critical phase. You'll not be allowed to interfere. Is this understood?"

Nazal shifted his stare up and down the line of prisoners until he saw them nod in compliance. Only then did he uncock his automatic's hammer and click on its safety. Tension finally ebbed as he returned the Baretta to his holster.

"You will be used to mix the drilling mud and assemble the drill pipe," Jassem added. "You'll be escorted to your quarters where you can retrieve your winter jackets."

"What do we do with Gunther?" asked Reitan who stood next to the body. Its head and upper torso were drenched with blood.

"Dump him with the others," said Nazal. "And take him through the cafeteria—I want the rest of your people to see the cost of resisting us."

Nazal assigned one of his guards to escort Reitan and the rig crew carrying the body through the cafeteria. The other prisoners were quickly led down the passageway to their quarters; in seconds Nazal and Jassem were alone.

"Such violence could work against us," said Jassem. "It

could create anger when we least need it."

"If we keep them busy, there will be no time for them to grow angry and plot against us," said Nazal. "When the mixing procedures begin, bring the bio-capsules up to the wellbore. Our biological weapon must be thoroughly mixed with the drilling mud to create a proper infection in the oil field. Everything important will happen in the next several hours. We're so close, Samad. Take care of your prisoner details. If you need me, I'll be in the communications center."

"Captain to crew, we are secure from Sub-scape run," said Carver, making his announcement over the public address system. "Standby for silent running after we finish our com stop. Radio Room, prepare to raise HF mast. Relay all messages to the TASCO room."

With the polymer tanks nearly empty, the *John Marshall* was ending its high-speed, ocean-spanning run. What had started nearly two days earlier was at last finished. The commando submarine had reached the opposite side of the Atlantic; it was in the narrow passage between the Orkney and Shetland Island groups, and only hours away from *Ocean Valkyrie*.

From over fifty knots, its speed fell to less than ten, all the while it kept rising, ascending from its cruise depth to within forty feet of the surface. For the first time since its previous com stop, the *Marshall* was subject to wave action; it was more pronounced because of the storm's proximity.

With the high-frequency radio mast deployed from the top of its conning tower, the submarine quickly established contact with Bradbury Lines. As the reports flowed in from SAS headquarters, they were transferred immediately to the tactical attack and situation control room, where Allard, Boyd, their executive officers and the Israelis had gathered.

"It sounds like new information has started to arrive," Burks observed, glancing down the control center's stairwell. "The decibel level is going up."

"I better get down there," said Carver. "Find out what they'll do with my Lady. Clarence, what's the situation?"

"The BQQ is operating at peak efficiency," said Jefferson, ". . . and is showing no surface or submarine targets."

"This storm is probably keeping everyone in port. Let me know the moment anything changes, Greg."

Leaving Burks with command of the *Marshall,* Carver descended to the TASCO Room, where copies of the first updates were already being distributed to the crowd in it.

"What does the Special Air Service have to report?" Carver asked, standing on the stair's last step.

"Two's company and three's a crowd," said Allard, moving back so Carver could get off the stairs. "We're going to have a major problem when we reach *Valkyrie.* There's another sub in the area."

"Of course there is, it's the *Spartan.*"

"No, beyond the *Spartan,*" said Boyd. "There's a third submarine. A *Foxtrot*-class boat of the Libyan Navy. Now identified as the *Sword of the Revolution.* Here—it arrived in the vicinity an hour and a half ago. It's been circling the rig ever since. The second report says the *Spartan* has bottomed. Does that mean what I think it does?"

"Yes, your attack boat is sitting on the floor of the North Sea," Carver replied, glancing over the sheets Boyd had given him. "The *Foxtrot* is a vintage diesel-electric boat. Its capabilities are limited when compared to nuclear boats; still, it's going to complicate matters for us."

"At least we now know you're not facing a suicide squad," said Shoham. "This submarine will be the ride home for the terrorists."

"I don't know why we didn't consider this before," said Adir. "After all, Blood Revenge is a government-supported operation. From the information Gavi brought us, they can call upon any resources the Libyan military has."

"I should've seen it," Gavrilla added. Despite the room's crowded condition her voice didn't tremor with fear, though she was pressed against the wall again. "Libyan Navy officers did visit the compound. I thought they were from the navy's scuba and underwater demolitions school. I never placed them with Libya's submarine fleet."

"Who would think of it?" Carver asked, still surprised at the news. "A submarine isn't the type of weapon you think of terrorists, or third-world nations, using."

"We should," said Adir. "The largest warships in the Israeli Navy are our Type Two-Zero-Six submarines. We often use them on intelligence operations. In the early seventies, only a procedural check prevented an Egyptian submarine from sinking the *Queen Elizabeth Two*. At the time, Egypt and Libya had a unified defense treaty. Colonel Qaddafi ordered the sub to attack the liner because it was on a special cruise to Israel. What saved it was the submarine's captain radioing Cairo for Anwar Sadat to confirm the orders."

"Yes, I remember the incident," said Boyd, looking over the newest incoming message. "And in the future we had better prepare for more. Submarines are one of the most prestigious weapons on the international market. My country sells them, France sells, China sells, West Germany sells. West Germany will even sell you a shipyard to build the bloody subs in."

"It sounds like the Russians are becoming only one enemy among many," said Carver. "It was easier when it was just them."

"Appropriate you should mention them. The latest update is from NATO Atlantic Command. Take a look."

With the press of a button on the console's keyboard, the map on its main screen was wiped clean. For a moment, all the symbols for Russian submarines and surface ships were erased, then they were replaced by symbols showing their new positions. To get a good view of the screen, Carver had to squeeze his way around the room's other occupants.

"They're still heading back to their ports," he said finally. "None of them have altered course to *Valkyrie*. Robert, paint in the earlier positions of the Soviets."

The previous locations for Russian ships and submarines reappeared on the screen and were shown in a different color from the new ones. Most were in the Skagerrak or approaching the strait, the others were heading north to their bases in Archangel and Murmansk. After studying the position changes, Carver asked for several of the ships to be identified.

"And the nearest is a *Natya*-class ocean minesweeper," Boyd concluded, studying a readout on an auxiliary screen.

"It has no helicopters or facilities to handle them. At flank speed, the minesweeper would need at least five hours to reach *Valkyrie*."

"The conclusion is obvious," said Adir. "The Russians are not involved in this operation. It's an all-Libyan show. The *Foxtrot* is the only threat facing us. How do you plan to deal with it?"

"I've ordered my crew to go to silent sub operations," said Carver. "We'll use our Three-D laser radar instead of active sonar to approach the area. And we must be prepared to sink the *Foxtrot* — I'm ordering both torpedoes and decoy simulators loaded into the tubes."

"Of course, Robert and I would prefer you'd sink the submarine *after* we've started our assault," said Allard, speaking up from the back of the room. "Sinking it before we're aboard the rig will warn the terrorists we're in the area."

"I understand. We'll approach *Valkyrie* at maximum depth and the last ten or twenty miles we'll creep in at our best silent speed. But I have to warn you, if at any moment my command is threatened, I'll sink the Libyans immediately That means your assault then will have to be rushed if it's to have any chance for success. Are you ready for it?"

"We will be," Allard replied. "Our men should just be waking up. Sal, go back to our quarters and check on them. We'll put my team through a few more exercises, and then we'll suit up."

"Ross, accompany Lieutenant Martirri," Boyd ordered, turning at the sound of boots on the stairway. "Including exercises, it'll take our teams around three hours to become operational. How do we fit in with your schedule?"

"At normal flank speed we can reach *Valkyrie's* vicinity in three hours," said Carver, studying his sub's position on the North Sea map in relation to the oil rig's prominent symbol. "Add in another hour's approach at our fastest silent speed and I'll have you there by the middle of the night — provided the *Foxtrot* doesn't create problems."

"Could we be sunk by the Libyans?" Gavrilla asked, tremors now entering her voice.

"I'll not lie to you. Yes, we could. In submarine warfare the battle doesn't always go to the best. It goes to the one who makes the fewest mistakes. I can't tell you if my crew and Lady are the best, but I'm going to make damn sure we make the fewest mistakes."

"Gerry, what's our companion's latest activity?" Taylor asked, appearing at the sonar room's hatch. He spoke in a soft voice, like the rest of his crew had been doing ever since the *Sword of the Revolution* had reached the area.

"It's still pinging with active sonar," said Greenway. "But I think it's stopped circling the rig."

Taylor stepped into the tiny compartment and studied the tactical scope. With the PARIS sonar's active components switched off for the last several hours, Greenway had to rely on the passive arrays to keep track of the *Foxtrot*. Fortunately, the continual use of its Herkules made the submarine relatively easy to track; every few moments its position would be updated on the scope. It didn't take Taylor very long to deduce what his adversary was doing.

"He's stopped circling bloody *Valkyrie,* and is moving off," he said. "This is a relief — it'll ease matters when the *Marshall* arrives. He appears to be heading to the north."

"Yes, the water's deeper north of the rig," said Greenway. "The *Foxtrot* will be better able to ride out the storm there. At least now we can raise the communications buoy."

"Thank you for the reminder. I'll have to drop over at the wireless office and order them to raise it again. Let me know the moment anything changes, Gerry, and I'll send one of the weapons' officers to relieve you."

Taylor stepped out of the sonar room and slid across the passageway to the *Spartan's* radio room. In the hours since it had bottomed out, the submarine's port list had increased by several degrees. While not dangerous, it created still another problem for the crew.

"Captain, any news on our adversary?" MacGregor asked, turning his seat away from a mostly inactive console.

"He's finally moving off," said Taylor. "He wants to find a location where he can ride out the storm. You can reactivate and raise the buoy. It's time to re-establish contact with the outside."

"Good, I wasn't able to transmit much on the ELF system. This situation is so unique, most of our code phrases don't fit it. Shall I attempt to contact Erica? It's been eight hours since we last talked to her."

"You can monitor the frequency she's been using, but as to my previous orders, you're not to contact her. Let her reach us. I suspect she's been trying to do so while we've been out of touch."

With the flipping of the master switches, the room's consoles came back to life. Among the first systems MacGregor activated was the communications buoy. For the last three hours, the tiny buoy had been hovering less than fifty feet above the *Spartan,* making contact spotty at best. With the touch of a switch it was released and ascended back to the surface.

"I'll be transmitting to Bradbury Lines in seconds," said MacGregor, watching the readout for the buoy's wire spool rise past the five-hundred-foot mark.

"Tell them what's happened to our adversary," Taylor ordered. "And ask them for an update on the *Marshall*. Yes, Gerry, what is it?"

"The *Foxtrot* has ceased active pinging," said Greenway, leaning through the hatch. "It appears to be shutting down all its electronic emissions. ECM reports its radio traffic flow has fallen drastically. The sub is reducing speed and diving. We can't tell by how much because with the Herkules shut down, the *Foxtrot* is a less distinct target."

"Our adversary is going into a silent mode, thank God. It'll be as useful to us as it is to him. If the *Marshall* arrives soon, it can easily glide in without being detected. Go ahead and take your dinner, Gerry, you've earned it. I'll have Thorton relieve you. After you're done, make sure the rest of your men have their meals. I want everyone in this crew to be at their best possible condition. The climax to this crisis is only hours away."

236

Chapter Fifteen

"Taylor, this is Erica. Taylor, this is Erica. Do you read me? Over . . ."

For the fourth time since her last contact with HMS *Spartan,* Erica was trying to raise it again. She tried to keep her anticipation down, but could feel the adrenaline surge every time she made her transmission; listening to the constant static did little to calm her nerves. If she got no response after five minutes of broadcasting, she would shut down and quietly cry away her frustration.

"Erica, this is Taylor. We read you, your signal is strong. Over."

Erica's reflexive spasm almost caused the radio to drop out of her hand while Taylor was still giving his answer. She could feel her heart skip a beat, and tears were welling up in her eyes before she had even started replying.

"Taylor, thank heaven! How could you do this to me? You promised you'd wait for me. I've been trying to raise you for hours. What happened? What went wrong? Over."

"Another submarine has arrived. It's the ride home for the terrorists. We had to go into 'hiding.' I'm sorry, but it couldn't be helped. We had to avoid detection or the entire operation would've been ruined. Over."

"I understand, but it was so lonely here," said Erica, tears rolling down her face. "I felt so abandoned. I thought I was going crazy. Will you have to sink this new submarine? Over."

"Eventually, yes. But not before your rescue begins. The commandoes will arrive soon, and they'll start operations as fast as they can. *Valkyrie* is preparing to drill and now's the time to stop it. Over."

"Can you tell me how much longer I'll be alone? And could I speak to Frieda, please?"

"Frieda's asleep, I'm afraid," said Taylor. "Has been for about an hour. It would take far too long to awake her and bring her here. Like before, we should keep this transmission short, and no, I can't tell you how much longer you'll be alone. Over."

"Will she be awake when I next contact you? Over."

"I'm sorry, Erica. You're not to contact us again. This is not my decision. It's an order from the people who will rescue you. Over."

"But you're the only people in the world I can talk to," Erica replied, the shock of her being cut off temporarily ceasing the flow of tears. "What will happen to me, Taylor?"

"You're to remain hidden, and don't worry—you *will* be contacted again in the future. Only the next time, your contact will be face-to-face. If you have no further questions, now would be the time to end this broadcast. Over."

"I only have one—do my rescuers know where I am?"

"Yes, they do. I promise you'll be the first they rescue. Over."

"Thank you, Taylor. I look forward to meeting you when this is all over. This is Erica, out."

"This is Taylor, I'll be seeing you. Out," the voice on the radio answered, before Erica switched it off. The static was cut, and the only sounds filling the locker were the pounding of the waves, and Erica's crying.

This time, unlike her three previous attempts to contact *Spartan,* she wasn't crying out of frustration or anxiety. She cried out of relief, and even a sense of triumph. Soon her ordeal would be over. Just when, Erica didn't know, but she took satisfaction in finally being told her ordeal was reaching an end.

"Commendable. You've managed to disassemble your weapons as rapidly as my men," said Boyd, walking between

238

two rows of Allard's SEALs, each holding the components of an MP-5 submachinegun in his lap. "Now we'll see how good you are at reassembly."

Boyd reached the end of the rows and stood next to Allard at the front of the sleeping quarters. The only other officer in the compartment was Martirri.

"However, there will be a change on this run-through," Boyd continued. "Since we're going to do a night assault, I've decided to make it more realistic."

Boyd laid his hand on a wall switch and, with a hard snap, plunged the compartment into absolute darkness. There were no other sources of illumination—no moonlight streaming through a window, nothing that could create shadows. No one could see a hand in front of their faces, or what they had in their laps.

"All right, these are the conditions under which you may have to repair your weapons," said Allard, quelling the gripes and complaints from his men only to be interrupted by a metallic clatter. "Chavez, it has to be you. You're going to learn those butterfingers can kill you, and you're not exempt from this drill. Get set everyone, begin . . ."

The room filled with the clinking of metal and the rustle of fingers rebuilding the submachineguns. Beyond them, the only other sounds were brief whispers telling Chavez where he could find the parts to his MP-5. Allard was unable to see the face of the stopwatch he had activated, and had to rely on Boyd telling him when the time limit had passed.

Another hard snap brought the lights back up, causing everyone whose eyes had adjusted to squint in the painful glare. As each of his men slapped a magazine into a completed weapon Allard glanced at his stopwatch, as did Boyd.

"Most of you reassembled your weapons within fifteen seconds of the optimum time," said Boyd. "Impressive, for a first run."

"But you can do better," said Allard. "I know you can. Sal, run them through a complete field strip and rebuild in darkness. It's time for Robert and I to check in with Carver. When I return be prepared to suit up."

The enlisted men's quarters was one of the mid-deck compartments in the *John Marshall*'s commando section. Above it was the briefing room and emergency medical facilities, while below it were the armory and equipment storage compartment. To make their way forward, Allard and Boyd walked through the officers' quarters and entered the submarine's operation section at its mid-deck level.

Past the dry and refrigerated lockers for food storage was the TASCO room, but to reach it they had to climb to the top deck, enter the *Marshall*'s control center and use the stairs, the one entrance to the tactical control room.

"This place is getting more and more like the headquarters for the Israeli Navy," Allard commented, reaching the foot of the stairs and finding the entire Israeli delegation standing around Carver.

"No, this is the submarine arm of the Israeli Air Force," said Shoham. "Yehuda, Avrom told you not to be 'prickly' with Mr. Carver. Now I'm ordering you. You're not an expert in submarine warfare, so don't criticize someone who's served in this field for more than twenty years."

"Sounds like this argument has started without us," said Boyd, uttering a sigh of regret.

"Just some minor bitching," Carver replied. "No matter what service they're from, fly-boy types just can't understand how ten knots can be a good speed."

Allard and Boyd made their way through the Israelis until they were standing behind Carver's seat. The room's main screen showed a tactical map of the area around *Ocean Valkyrie*. HMS *Spartan*'s position was indicated, as was the *Sword of the Revolution*'s; in the upper left corner could be seen a symbol for the *Marshall* itself.

"I know we're on silent running conditions," said Allard, checking over the information the screen displayed. "So where are you getting all the data on the Brits and the Libyans?"

"Some of it's from our own passive sensors," Carver answered. "We have the BQR-towed array deployed, and the lateral hydrophones are cranked all the way up. But you're right, most of it's from *Spartan*. We established contact with her about ten minutes ago."

"You're cruising rather low to the ocean floor," said Boyd, after comparing the depth reading on the map to the data block running beside the *Marshall*'s symbol. "Are you using this laser radar of yours?"

"Yes, and the thermal imagers. We can skim along the sea bed terrain and hide from the Libyan sonar scans. *Spartan* says they resumed active pinging about an hour ago."

"Warning, general system failure. Sensors . . . Warning, general system failure. Sensors . . ." the printed message fairly screamed from the instrument panel.

"Bloody hell, what's happening?" Boyd demanded. "I never saw those panels come on before."

"That's because you never saw a malfunction before." Carver punched one of the keys on the damage control panel and instantly a readout appeared on one of the auxiliary screens. He only needed a moment to analyze it, and despite its accuracy, Carver still got in touch with the control center. "Greg, this is Terry. What's going on up there?"

"The Three-D Radar is down," said Burks. "The whole system just blanked out on us."

"Shit, this is just like Camp Lejeune all over again," said Allard.

"Only this time we can't blame a senator for the trouble we're in," said Carver. "Full stop, Mr. Burks, and take us up fifty feet. Retract the BQR and have Mr. Seidel report to the control center. I'm coming up."

Carver jumped out of his seat, and the Israelis only just got out of his way as he went charging up the stairs. He beat Seidel to the center by a few seconds, and was already asking questions of the personnel.

"The image became jumbled before it blanked out," said Jefferson, pointing to the empty screen. "Just like it did during the exercise."

"David, what happened?" Carver asked. "I thought you cleared up this problem two days ago?"

"We did, by jury-rigging a fix to the signal processor," said Seidel, making his way to the helm station. "I thought it would hold."

"Jury rigs never do, especially after forty-eight hours of

241

near-continuous operation. Do you think it's the same problem?"

"It has to be. The rest of the system checked out okay."

"Captain, we've finished retracting the BQR," Burks advised. "We've leveled off at four hundred and seventy feet and have come to a full stop, but we're beginning to drift. I suggest we maintain minimal forward speed."

"Agreed. Make it ahead slow," said Carver, before returning to Seidel. "We don't have time for another jury-rig. Pull the signal processor and get another out of stores."

"But that's just the problem, Captain. We don't have another," said Seidel. "Our electronics stores weren't replenished before we left Norfolk."

"It appears as though Glenn wasn't the only one to be caught short on your command," Boyd observed, standing at the top of the stairs. "I've read the latest reports from *Spartan*. *Valkyrie* is readying to drill. It's imperative we get there soon."

"I know," said Carver. "We're so close and yet . . . Clarence, can you use the thermal imagers instead of the radar?"

"I could but it'll slow us down," said Jefferson. "We could use the BQS, Captain. The short-range sonar."

"It's too risky to use any kind of active sonar, even if the Libyans have moved away from the rig. Just when you think all the snags are smoothed out . . ."

"There is a way around this, Captain," Seidel offered. "I can scavenge a signal processor from another laser system. In fact, it's very similar to the Three-D radar."

"I think I know which one you're talking about," said Carver. "But we're using the laser com to communicate with *Spartan*. If you cannibalize it, we'll be silent until we close to short-range radio distance."

"If it's a choice between being deaf or blind, I'd prefer to see where I'm going," said Boyd. "And if it's a choice between arriving in a timely manner or not at all, I say your man had better start scavenging."

"And since this is a British show, and you're operational commander, what you say goes." There was a tone of irritation in Carver's voice as he stated the obvious. Even if it was his friend giving the orders, he still resented it a little. "I'll tell Hawkins to send one final message to *Spartan,* then Dave can start his cannibalizing. Clarence, make your best speed on the thermal imagers alone. Dave, start assembling a team of ETs. I want the laser radar back in service as quickly as possible. Robert, if all goes well I can get you to *Valkyrie* in another ninety minutes. Will that be enough time for you?"

"Easily. We've done our drills, finalized our plans — all we have left is to suit up. Which Glenn and I had better return to supervise. Let us know how the repairs are going, and we'll advise you when we're ready."

"Do you understand the operation of this equipment?" Nazal asked, standing in front of the console for the underwater manifold center.

"Yes, it's more advanced than what I worked with in the Persian Gulf fields," said Ibrahim Baroheni, glancing over the controls, ". . . but it is basically the same. The preliminary checks have allowed me to grow used to it. Do you wish for me to begin?"

"Please, we can't start the injection until this remote platform is checked out."

Baroheni ran his hand down a prominent row of toggle switches, then waited for the corresponding status lights and hydraulic pressure gauges to indicate the valves in the conductor pipes had all opened. After they were closed, the return lines for the saline injection wells were tested, even though no oil would be recovered, and the UMC's safety systems received a final test, though there was little likelihood they would be used, either.

"There, the manifold center passes its checks," said Baroheni. "Do you wish for me to activate its TV cameras?"

"Yes, then move on to the station controlling the wellbore and derrick operations," said Nazal. "They're readying the pipe sections and drilling mud on the production floor. I want us to begin promptly."

"Then why don't we use some of our hostages in this room?" asked Jassem, scanning the activity in the oil rig's nerve center. "They know how to run these systems better than we can."

"I know, but for once I agree with Yussuf's paranoia. It would be far too easy for them to sabotage our operation from here. We only need the Norwegians for the heavy labor. The rest we can do ourselves."

"Commander Nazal, after I've tested the rest of the equipment, which shaft will we use?" Baroheni inquired. He moved from the UMC console to the one for wellbore monitoring and drilling control.

"The number one shaft. It's the deepest drilled, so it'll be perfect for spreading the bacteria. Samad, you're in charge until I return. I need my coat if I'm to go to the pump station."

"Sorry I'm late. But I had to check on the sound room," said Greenway as he re-entered *Spartan's* officers' wardroom. "The Twenty-Twenty array has detected new sounds from *Valkyrie*."

When he had left the wardroom, barely half an hour before, most of the tables still had plates and silverware scattered across them. Now, all was cleared away, and Taylor had most of his senior officers seated around the main table.

"Let's do this briefing as fast as possible and return to our posts," said Taylor. "Though the *Marshall* has gone silent, it's resumed its original speed and will arrive in less than an hour. Gerry, what's new with *Valkyrie?*"

"The UMC has been active again, and its dynamic positioning screws are operating," Greenway answered. "Frieda says all this activity is in preparation for drilling. She told me the next sound we'll hear will be drill pipe moving through one of the shafts."

"What about the *Foxtrot?*"

"Still moving erratically north of the rig. It's obviously designed to confuse ASW tactics, though it has risen closer to the surface. The sub will probably communicate with the terrorists."

"If our adversary starts active pinging again, let me know," said Taylor. "Lloyd, what's reactor status?"

"Operating at minimal levels," said the *Spartan*'s propulsion officer. "Because we're not moving, I have to use circulation pumps, but our noise levels are almost non-existent. Reactor control is fully manned and I can give you maneuvering power in less than two minutes."

"Good, we'll likely be putting your reactor through its paces. Donnie, anything new from the outside world?"

"Nothing from the *Marshall* since it said it had to cannibalize its blue-green laser," MacGregor replied. "We won't hear from the Americans until they close to within a quarter of a mile. Then we can use our high-frequency system. From Bradbury Lines, we're getting updates on the weather and requests for information on bloody *Valkyrie*."

"We'll send the SAS one message when the *Marshall* arrives, and from then on our transmissions will be on a need-to-know basis," said Taylor. "I hope they don't press us—they've been good about it so far. Hodgkiss, what's our weapons status?"

"After hearing what the Americans are doing, I've decided to reload tube number one with an automated decoy," said the *Spartan*'s weapons officer. "Tubes two through five still contain Spearfish. All are ready for programming and firing."

"But not in our current position. When we resume contact with the *Marshall*, we'll retract the communications buoy and rise off the sea bed. When it arrives, the commando operation will begin immediately. We should be ready to escort the boat."

"Will we sink the Libyans then?" asked Greenway.

"No. The operational commander has ordered us not to sink the *Foxtrot* until after he begins the commando assault," said Taylor, who had to wait for his officers to finish groaning before he could continue. "Or unless it presents a clear threat to us before the assault."

"I take it you'll give the order a very broad interpretation," Hodgkiss observed.

"The moment we're scanned by its Herkules, I want a pair of Spearfish hunting it down."

"What about the commando assault," said Lloyd. "What if it fails? What are our orders then?"

"We're to target the underwater manifold center and destroy it," said Taylor. "This will effectively prevent them from infecting the oil fields. Hodgkiss, can the Spearfish do it? Or should we lay a mine by the UMC?"

"Well, as advanced as our new torpedoes are," said Hodgkiss. "They do have trouble defining small targets against sea bed clutter. However, we won't have this problem with the UMC. It has a sonar transponder on it, just like the ones *Ocean Valkyrie* uses for its dynamic positioning system. It would only take moments for a Spearfish to be programmed to home on its signal."

"Be prepared to do so. While I believe our Special Boat Squadron and the Americans will succeed, we must prepare for any contingency, and in the time remaining before the *Marshall* arrives, we should break out our rescue kits. Any contingency means even if we fail."

"Commander Nazal, this is an honor," said Asir Kashani, kneeling beside one of the bio-hazard-marked cases. At Nazal's appearance he immediately snapped to attention and nearly crashed back to the platform decking when he slipped on the ice.

"Pay attention to where you are, Asir," Nazal replied, walking carefully across the perforated steel planking to *Valkyrie*'s main pump station. "Continue with your procedure. It's what I'm here for."

Located only a dozen yards from the wellbore, the station would mix and store the drilling mud in cavernous tanks, then pump it into the hollow drill pipe once the pipe had been sunk to the deepest level the rig had reached. Already the floor crews working in the area had assembled several thirty-foot sections of stored pipe into ninety foot, ready to use, plugs. Once the derrick had completed its checkout, the first plug would be raised in position and lowered to the wellbore.

"Have you already started mixing the drill mud?" Nazal asked, standing over Kashani.

"Yes, we have the first batch of several hundred gallons in the hopper," said Kashani. "This is the last ingredient."

After undoing the last catch, Kashani raised the case's lid, revealing two dozen capsules packed in four rows of six each. They were nestled securely in styrofoam wells, and were further surrounded by plastic cages. They had all survived the journey from Libya; the bacteria they held would remain dormant in their chemical solutions until release.

Kashani pried one of the capsules out of its well and held it up to Nazal. With his leader's consent, he ripped the cage off the foot-long glass tube. The freezing rain and snow made it slippery, but Kashani only had to hold onto the capsule long enough to turn around and toss it through the hopper's open door.

Above the heavy whir of electric motors and the clank of mixing paddles, the delicate sound of glass breaking could be heard. In seconds it was over. The capsule had been splintered into hundreds of tiny shards and the bacteria released into the mud.

"The final phase of our operation has begun," said Nazal, smiling malevolently as he held one of the other tubes in his hands. "In an hour our revenge will be irreversible. We are witnessing the collapse of Western arrogance."

"How many should we use from this box?" Kashani asked. "Should we save any for the later batches of mud?"

"No, save the second case for later batches, after we've already started injecting mud into the strata. Will the broken glass give us any problems?"

"It shouldn't. If the mixers don't crush it to small enough pieces, the storage tanks have filters to strain them out."

Nazal examined the capsule he held for another moment, then started tearing at its plastic cage. It did not come off as smoothly as it had for Kashani. In fact, the rest of the pump station detail had thrown several capsules into the mixing hopper by the time Nazal had his ready. He pitched it through the open hatch and watched the paddles crush the glass tube, releasing it contents to blend with the drilling mud's rich soup of clay, lignosulfonate, bentonite and barite. After the chemicals and bacteria had been thoroughly blended they would be transferred to a storage tank where later batches of mud would be added and briefly stored until the drill pipe went down the shaft.

"There's the drill head," said Carver, pointing to a block-house-like structure on the laser radar screen. He keyed the hand mike he was holding. "Control center to TASCO Room, tell *Spartan* we're in the area. Operations will begin as soon as we come alongside the UMC. Retract the BQR. Clarence, reduce speed to eight knots. Control to briefing room, we're approaching the objective."

The *Marshall* cut its speed by one-third and reeled in its towed array. The BQR-23 was a cable nearly three thousand feet long and studded with miniature hydrophones. A passive system, it nonetheless had capabilities comparable to active sonar. For the last hour it had been tracking the *Sword of the Revolution* and providing enough information for the fire control system to target the sub. But the array could only be used if the *Marshall* traveled at moderate speeds and didn't maneuver. With the reduction to eight knots, the commando submarine no longer had the velocity to keep the half-mile long cable properly deployed, so the winch at the front of its housing quickly pulled it in.

"TASCO Room to control, BQR retracted," said Burks, watching a status panel change on the room's main console. "We can continue tracking the *Foxtrot* using the hull-mounted arrays. *Spartan* has answered and will end its bottoming procedures."

"Propulsion control to attack center, you now have maneuvering power."

"Roger, propulsion. Captain to crew, standby for liftoff," Taylor warned. He turned to the helmsmen. "Mr. Bryan, give us positive buoyancy and make it ahead slow. Captain to wireless office, you can finish retracting the Com Buoy."

HMS *Spartan* rocked slightly while its ballast tanks slowly filled with air. The port list everyone had grown accustomed to corrected itself as the submarine's nose-down attitude leveled out. It rose off the sea bed to a chorus of creaks and groans, gaining almost fifty feet before it started to move forward and extend its bow hydroplanes. Moments later the attack sub's communications buoy completed its retraction; it sank back inside its well and the hatch closed over it. Except for the *Marshall, Spartan* could no longer talk with the outside, and didn't need to.

"Captain, the bow planes are answering," said Bryan, ". . . and we've trimmed out. What heading do you want?"

"Hard a-port, Mr. Bryan. Steer course three-three-zero degrees and increase speed to ten knots," said Taylor. "Captain to sound room, is there any change in the *Foxtrot?*"

"No, its condition remains the same," Greenway answered. "It hasn't switched on its Herkules. Our PARIS is ready for operation. What mode should it be set on?"

"Target acquisition and intercept — we have to be ready for anything. Captain to torpedo room, prepare all tubes for firing. Mr. Hodgkiss, man the fire control panel."

Its hours of silence nearly at an end, *Spartan* picked up speed and turned sharply to the left; almost doubling back on itself. As it came out of the maneuver, the submarine was on an intercept course for the *John Marshall*. In minutes it would overtake the American sub and maneuver again to come alongside. By then, they would both be approaching *Valkyrie's* underwater manifold center and in position to begin the assault.

"We're less than fifteen minutes to deployment," said Boyd. "Time to line up. Americans to port, British to starboard."

This time there was little grumbling from Allard's SEALs at being commanded by a British officer. Accompanied by the clanking of scuba equipment, the men quickly formed into two rows. Each carried his weapons in a watertight pouch strapped to his chest, with his swimming fins in his hands. The boots of their wet suits had reinforced soles and were virtually shoes in their own right. It eliminated the need to carry combat boots, and the fins the commandoes had were modified to slip over them.

"I know all of you wished we could've had our own gear and better preparation," said Allard, addressing his own men. "But such is the nature of a crisis. You're never completely prepared for the one that happens. We have the best equipment for the situation, and together with our allies we're the best in the world for this. We're better than the Green Berets, Delta Force and even Marine Recon. We're it."

"And even if we weren't, we are the only people in position to do anything about this crisis," Boyd added. "And after some initial problems, I'm favorably impressed with your capabilities. Good luck to all of you. Commander Allard and I will be with the first teams to deploy. Mr. Ackland and Mr. Martirri will be with the last. Once you're outside, remember procedures. Join up with the other members of your squad, and obey the signals of your squad leader. See you topside."

Boyd's men snapped to attention as he turned to leave and, in a ragged fashion, so did the SEALs when Allard stepped through the hatch to the swim-out chamber compartment. Half a dozen men followed the two commanders, the first three men in each line.

A detail of seamen from the *Marshall*'s crew were waiting in the compartment. They opened the swim-out chambers for the commandoes, then closed them once everyone had filed inside. With four divers apiece, the two chambers were suddenly very cramped, though the condition wouldn't last for long.

"Will you look at this thing?" said Jefferson, nodding toward the image on the laser radar screen. "It must be a couple of stories tall."

What had once been a block sitting on the ocean bed was now a skeletal building some thirty feet high. The manifold center's tubular main frame supported a delicate-looking, interior latticework of hydraulic control lines, valves, valve platforms and remote vehicle tracks. And rising above it was a forest of two-foot diameter conductor pipes; one for each drill shaft *Valkyrie* had sunk.

"It's quite a chunk of machinery," said Carver, admiring it. "But stay clear of it. Those drill heads have remote TV cameras on them. Let's not take any risk of being detected. Slow the Lady to station keeping. Stand by to blow ballast tanks, silent purge. Control to TASCO room, tell *Spartan* we're getting ready to ascend."

The two submarines were within several hundred yards of *Valkyrie's* UMC, and each other, by the time they slowed to a stop. They had scarcely come into position when first the *Marshall,* then the British attack sub, started to rise. Neither of them released an explosive curtain of bubbles from their ballast tank valves. Rapid emptying of the tanks would have created too much noise for even the oil rig's activity to mask.

Instead, the *Marshall* and *Spartan* settled for a slowly increasing positive buoyancy. They would need several minutes to rise the nearly five hundred feet to *Ocean Valkyrie.* Of all the miles they had traveled and hours they had waited, the next few minutes and feet would be the most nerve-wracking to their passengers and crews.

Chapter Sixteen

"Commander, I get the feeling we're rocking," said one of the men in Allard's team.

"It's the storm—we must be near the surface," said Allard. "If only we had a depth meter in here, instead of just lights."

As best he could, Allard motioned to the signal lights over the chamber's hatch. The yellow one was still burning steadily, and continued to do so for several more seconds. Then, the light winked out and the work lamps at the top of the chamber changed from white to red.

"Here we go. Get your masks ready," Allard continued, ". . . and move away from those nozzles."

The divers were still pulling their face masks off their heads when sea water began swirling into the chamber. It was ice cold and in moments was knee-high. Allard and his men had just enough time to spit into their masks and clean them out, to prevent fogging.

It was chest-high by the time they slipped the masks back on, and pushed their scuba regulators into their mouths. All too quickly the cold water rose past their heads, forcing the divers to start using their systems. When the water level reached the chamber's roof, the green light over its hatch began flashing; it was time for the divers to leave.

Allard pushed off the floor and wrapped his hands around the wheel lock in the chamber roof. After he had rotated it a few times, the exit hatch popped out of its frame. In spite of its weight, Allard easily pushed the hatch the rest of the way open and swam out.

From a room of soft red light he entered a world of almost solid blackness. It was also one of movement. Though over a hundred feet below the surface, its wave action had translated into a rhythmic surge and ebb. Outside the submarine, the effect was even more pronounced. Allard found himself having to fight the effects in order to stay over the *Marshall,* though at least he didn't have to do it alone.

One by one the rest of the men in his chamber came swimming out, as did Boyd and his marines from the other chamber. He and Allard met at the base of the submarine's conning tower, where they exchanged hand signals to indicate they were safe. They also signalled their men, and the last ones to emerge closed the hatches to repeat the cycle.

"TASCO Room to control, we are holding at one hundred and ten feet from the surface," said Burks, reading the numbers off a tactical map on the main screen, ". . . and approximately fifty feet below *Valkyrie's* ballast tanks."

"Roger. How are the Brits doing?" Carver asked.

"*Spartan* is three hundred yards off our starboard beam and about twenty feet deeper."

"Good, let them know the first divers are away. Control, out."

"Is this true? Are your commandoes now outside your submarine?" Gavrilla inquired.

"The first ones are," said Burks, turning to face the Israelis. "Which means both Glenn Allard and Colonel Boyd. The rest will finish deploying in another twenty minutes."

"*Acharigh,* my friends," said Adir, to people who were not there. "It appears as though we aren't the only ones who follow the principle."

"The swim-out chambers are cycling to release the next group of divers," said Carver, checking one of the panels at the safety control station. "Mr. Doran, activate the exterior lights, low intensity."

The *Marshall*'s weapons officer flipped a switch at the tactical board, and adjusted a dial until the points of light along a submarine silhouette burned dimly.

"Exterior lights on and adjusted," reported Doran.

"Good, I'll raise the search 'scope and check on how the web foots are doing," said Carver. "Keep the lights on for the next twenty-five minutes, then turn them off unless I order otherwise."

Moments after the swim-out chamber hatches closed, cutting off the only available light, the conning tower and upper casing of the *John Marshall* started to glow. The black world surrounding the submarine melted back a few yards. Allard even thought he could see the bottom of one of *Ocean Valkyrie*'s ballast tanks.

Dozens of lights, either singly or in rows, created the eerie illumination. The submarine seemed to float in an abyss which appeared to have no bottom or top. Apart from its slowly rotating propeller, the only activity along its massive hull were the divers, who doubled in number when the hatches opened again.

Unlike the first teams, the next sets of divers emerged rapidly and swam to where Boyd and Allard were waiting. The last out resealed the hatches, automatically starting the process of draining the chambers for another cycle. In the few minutes they had before the next group appeared, Allard and Boyd communicated with the new divers by hand signals and tested some of their equipment.

Selected men in each squad had been given powerful underwater lanterns. Literally portable floodlights, they would be essential between the time the *Marshall* shut down its exterior array and the squads reached the oil rig's base legs. The beams the lanterns cast were stronger than the lamps on the submarine. They penetrated the blackness far enough for the rig's ballast tank to at last be seen. As the tests ended the chamber hatches opened yet again, allowing out another eight divers and bringing the number deployed to two dozen.

"The floormen boss reports they've finished installing a drill bit in the first length of pipe," said Baroheni, briefly slipping the headphones off his ears.

"They took far too long," Nazal observed. "The Norwegians are attempting to delay us. I know something of oil drilling operations and what they're doing is a routine procedure."

"Then we must threaten them into working faster," said Gunni. "And there's a way to do it. Your way, Abu."

"They will die soon enough, Yussuf. After the first pipe is lowered into the shaft, the rest will be the normal stacking of added lengths. Ibrahim, tell them to proceed."

Baroheni slipped his headphones back on and relayed Nazal's orders to the terrorist in command of the floormen. Half a minute later the wellbore monitoring console recorded the first ninety foot section of pipe being lowered into the number one drill shaft.

Even though it had travelled only a fraction of the distance necessary to reach the oil-bearing strata, Nazal and Gunni began smiling. When the second section was quickly attached to the first, and the drill bit pushed another ninety feet down the shaft, they began slapping each other on the back.

"Jassem should be here to see you two being so happy," said the guard at the operation center's interior entrance. "Especially after all the fights he had to settle."

"He'll return from the cafeteria soon enough," said Nazal. "He can help us celebrate when the drill pipe enters the sea bed and it reaches its target. After all these months of plans and preparations and training. After these last two weeks of moving through Europe, wondering if we had been spotted by whatever authorities whose country we were in. Always fearing we were just one step ahead of them. Now at last I can see an end to this operation. I can begin thinking of something other than the next phase. The rest of what's before us is child's play. Ibrahim, how far down the shaft is the drill pipe?"

"Now it's two hundred and seventy feet," Baroheni replied. "They've just added a third section."

"At their rate, we'll have reached the sea floor in another fifteen minutes. Open the valve at the top of the conductor pipe. They'll be reaching it in the next several minutes."

"I'll have to do it from the UMC console. Before I leave this one, the pump station reports the first holding tank is filled with mud. They wish to fill the second, but feel they need your permission."

"They do. I originally wanted the other case to be saved for later," said Nazal, thinking his decision over for a moment. "Yes, tell them to go ahead and use the second case of bacteria capsules. It would be easier to mix it now than later."

Baroheni relayed the orders to the pump station crew, then removed his headphones and walked back to the underwater manifold center console. He flipped a toggle, extracting a cover plate from the drill shaft section atop the conductor pipe. Only one more barrier remained; the security blowout valve in the UMC itself. According to procedure, it would be opened as the drill pipe reached the center.

"Sound room to attack center, we confirm additional sounds coming from the *Marshall*," said Greenway. "There's increasing activity around it."

"Affirmative, Gerry. It must be the divers," Taylor answered. "We have reports from the *Marshall* they're being released. Stay on it, Gerry. I'm raising the search 'scope. Let's see how they're doing."

"How can we do that, Stan?" said Holbrook, incredulous. "The *Marshall* is hundreds of yards away."

"Their latest report said something about external lights. We might be able to see something with our systems."

Mounting the attack center's periscope stand, Taylor activated the Barr and Stroud search periscope and raised it ten feet instead of deploying it to its full length. With the low-light-level system adjusted to its maximum sensitivity, a faint outline of a submarine with glowing pinpoints of light along its upper half could be discerned. When the TV monitor came on the image was sharper, and occasionally figures and trails of bubbles were seen.

"This is other-worldly," Holbrook added. "Is it possible someone on the surface could see what we're seeing?"

"Not with the wave action," said Taylor. "And they'd need a system as sensitive as the one we have. A burning cigarette would generate more light than it's detecting now."

"How long will this show last?"

"Until all the divers are out and have separated into their groups. Ask Frieda if she wants to come up and see the start of the assault. Captain to sound room, what's the *Foxtrot* doing?"

"Still holding to a depth of two hundred feet and maneuvering at three knots. Its active sonar hasn't been switched on, so they aren't aware of us yet."

"If our luck holds they won't be aware of us until they hear our PARIS echoes, and the sounds of torpedo discharges," said Taylor, moving the periscope slightly to keep the *Marshall* on screen. "Have you anything else to report?"

"We've detected more noises from the UMC," Greenway advised. "They're similar to what we've heard before. A valve has been opened, we believe in a conductor pipe, and it hasn't been closed."

"What? Only one? Then it isn't a test. Bloody *Valkyrie's* getting ready to drill. Concentrate on the drill shafts. Let me know when you hear anything different."

* * *

The seventh time the chamber hatches opened, the SEAL and SAS assault squads were nearly completed. The new teams of divers signalled briefly to Allard and Boyd, then moved to the tail of the *John Marshall*. There the third and fourth squads, commanded by Martirri and Ackland, were quickly forming.

The first two squads, under the command of Allard and Boyd, had already formed and hovered on either side of the submarine's conning tower. Apart from fighting the constantly shifting currents, they did little except check their watches and wait. They remained inside the arena of visible light, not willing to move beyond it until all the squads had assembled.

"Diving compartment to control center, we're cycling the last chamber of commandoes."

"Roger, secure your station after they're away," said Carver, before releasing the thumb switch on the hand mike. "Switch on the monitor, Jimmy. The web foots are putting on quite a show."

Like Taylor, Carver had raised his search periscope and was scanning the divers. For him, however, the procedure was far simpler. All Carver had to do was walk his periscope through its aft quadrant and had no need to set his low-light-level system to its highest sensitivity.

Doran left the tactical board and moved forward to activate the center's television screen. The image it showed was clear except for a heavy green tint. While the divers near the conning tower could hardly be seen, those farther down by the tail were easily viewed.

"As soon as they start swimming to their assignments we'll move to deeper waters," said Carver. "We'll have to be careful about doing so. We're like an elephant surrounded by ants. Clarence, stand by to take us down."

On the eighth time, only one of the chamber hatches

opened. The last four divers emerged, closed the hatch and paired off; heading to the squads near the submarine's stern. The assault force was now complete.

Using the powerful lanterns, Boyd, Allard and the executive officers signalled each other they were ready. Then Boyd flashed the code for them to begin.

The divers coalesced around their leaders, who took readings off their wrist compasses before striking out for *Valkyrie*'s base legs. They strung out in ragged lines, with the men carrying lanterns at the front and back of each line.

Boyd's and Ackland's squads swam away from the *Marshall* at almost right angles. Their objectives were the base legs attached to the oil rig's second ballast tank and they quickly moved out of the arena of light surrounding the submarine. Allard's and Martirri's squads ascended almost vertically, their objectives were overhead. As Allard and his men glided by the conning tower they waved to the raised periscope, which tracked them as they moved into the darkness.

"There they go," said Doran, watching the divers melt away on the monitor screen. "Is it time for us to leave?"

"Not yet, let me check the other squads," Carver replied, for the first time walking the scope forward. He stopped walking it when he reached several degrees off the sub's starboard bow. He checked on Boyd's progress, then turned the periscope more than ninety degrees to check on Ackland's, next it was Martirri's and finally Carver swung back to Allard. "Yes, it looks like they've safely moved off. But let me verify it with Greg. Control to TASCO Room, how far away are the divers?"

"TASCO to control, the minimum distance any of the squads have traveled is a hundred and twenty feet."

"Thanks, Greg. Clarence, take us down to three hundred feet. Slow and steep. Jim, switch off exterior lights."

"Roger, Captain. Ahead slow," said Jefferson, advancing

a diminutive throttle lever." The helm is answering. Diving planes, thirty degree down-angle. Flood forward trim tanks."

Just before the exterior lights on the *Marshall* died, they flared brighter than they had been. It attracted Allard's attention, and he turned in time to see the submarine swallowed up by the blackness. The moment the glow ended it was as if the sub had never existed.

Now the assault squads were alone. The only lights Allard could see were the lanterns carried by his men and the others. They were constantly on. Their beams moved over the other divers and swept through the black waters. Beyond the lights, the only other reference points were the forest-like stand of drill shafts, seen only when Ackland's squad swept their lanterns through them, and the ballast tanks.

As massive as the submarine from which they had just disembarked, a four-hundred-foot-long tank hovered above Allard's men. Befitting a new vessel, its surface was still smooth and had only a few barnacles marring it. Surrounding the tank's upper half were clouds of bubbles, the result of continual wave action.

Fifty feet closer to the surface, the rhythmic surge and ebb was more pronounced. Allard could feel the jumbled currents pull at him; he repeatedly looked over his shoulder to make sure none of his men were being carried out of line. He also felt a new sensation.

Despite the storm's lessening severity, the oil rig was still being subjected to a storm heave. Though its vertical movement was only three feet, its aircraft carrier displacement created a suction which alternately pulled the divers toward it, then pushed them away. While following the ballast tank made it easier for Allard's squad to reach their objective, by the time they got to its end they were exhausted.

* * *

"Wireless office to attack center, signal from the *Marshall*. They've released the divers and are heading to deeper waters."

"Understood, Donnie," Taylor answered, using a hand mike from the periscope stand. "They've just switched off their exterior lights, so they must be finished. Send a message: 'signal received, will head for deeper waters as well'. Down 'scope. Mr. Bryan, ahead slow."

Taylor deactivated the low-light system and hit the periscope's retract button. He was off the stand by the time Bryan had *Spartan* moving forward. Taylor gave his helmsmen a further order to dive, and stood behind them to watch how they maneuvered his submarine.

"Taylor, will we be able to hear and talk to the commandos when they're inside *Valkyrie?*" asked Frieda.

"I'm afraid not. We'll have to rely on the Americans to keep us up to date," said Taylor. "And don't worry, we'll make sure they will."

For a few seconds, Boyd saw a dark shadow below him and to his right. From its blunt-nosed, whale-like shape he guessed it was the attack submarine *Spartan*. But by the time he had one of his men shine a lantern in the area, the shadow had disappeared.

Apart from the drill shaft stand, *Spartan* was the only other object Boyd and his men saw as they crossed to the oil rig's second ballast tank. Their only constant reference points were the lanterns of the other squads. Though even they became less distinct as the teams of divers swam farther away from each other.

Unlike Allard's journey, Boyd glided easily through calmer waters. He and his men remained at the same depth they had deployed from the *Marshall*. Not until they saw the dim outline of the second ballast tank did Boyd signal them to ascend to shallower waters.

When he noticed the lantern beams glinting brightly off the clouds of bubbles surrounding the tank, he ordered them switched off and for his men to use their personal flashlights. In spite of the weaker beams they quickly found the rungs to a submerged service ladder.

From his careful reading of *Valkyrie*'s blueprints, Boyd knew the ladder would lead him to the lowermost hatch on the fourth base leg. He pulled off his swimming fins and slipped them over his right arm. He grabbed hold of one rung and put his foot on another. The moment he did so, the assault on *Ocean Valkyrie* was under way.

Chapter Seventeen

Allard signalled for his squad's lanterns to be extinguished when they spotted the service ladder. Swimming along the bottom of the ballast tank, they found that the ladder actually circled it. For a moment the men in his unit collected around Allard, until he indicated which side they were to climb up. Each base leg had only one hatch to its lowest compartment, and they all faced inward to take advantage of the less turbulent waters under *Valkyrie,* instead of facing out to sea.

Allard removed the fins from his feet and, using their straps, slung them over his forearm. Partially enveloped by clouds of bubbles, he took hold of the ladder rungs and started climbing. For the first few steps the going was easy; as he neared the surface the difficulties increased.

Wave action pushed him against the ballast tank, while the undertow effects of the storm heave swirled and ebbed around him. To compound his problems, Allard had to turn off his flashlight before he reached the surface. Fortunately, enough weak light filtered down from the oil rig above to allow him to continue.

Looking through the foam and waves, Allard could see there was no one standing guard on the rig's exterior; at least he didn't have to fight his way on board. He waited for the inrush to stop before emerging and used the brief lull to reach the exterior hatch. Instantly the scuba tank on his back started to weigh him down and clank noisily.

Allard couldn't wait to shed the encumbrance, but he

needed to use it one more time. A wave twenty feet tall crashed against the base leg, and suddenly Allard found himself underwater again and he had to cling to the hatch or be swept away. By the time it had subsided, Chen had joined him.

"Have you seen anyone?" he asked.

"Apart from us, no one," said Allard, after pulling out his mouthpiece. "And I can't see anyone through the observation window, either. Here, help me open this thing."

While Allard forced the locking levers at the top of the hatch to rotate, Chen worked the ones on the bottom. They were stiff; the glazing of ice made them difficult to get a grip on, but with a little weight thrown against them they moved. To the snap and crunch of ice, the hatch swung open and Allard jumped inside.

As he hit the floor he was unzipping his chest pouch. Instead of his submachinegun, he pulled out his Heckler and Koch automatic. Though it didn't have its silencer attached, there was already a clip inside it. Allard swept the compartment, as if he had never checked it before, and so did Chen when he first entered.

"Don't let the door crash back," said Allard, undoing his pouch. "Let's not make any more noise than we have to. Signal for the rest of the squad to get in here. We're safe for the moment."

For the first time in more than twelve hours, Erica heard a noise other than those of storm effects. Moments later it was voices and they apparently spoke English without heavy accents. Because of the material jammed against the locker door, it was impossible for her to be more specific.

Her heart racing, Erica grabbed more flare sticks out of their box and edged as close as she could to the door. In addition to the voices, she now heard the clank of heavy equipment hitting the floor. The voices spoke in short, staccato bursts. They either gave commands or answered commands; Erica herself wanted to shout to them, but the fear that it was somehow a terrorist operation prevented her. What she did do was begin to cry.

* * *

"Remove your pouches and scuba gear," said Allard, motioning toward a growing pile of such equipment. "Nichols, you have hatch duty. Close it if you see a wave approaching. Artie, disarm the explosives. I'll check the locker."

Almost half his team was in the compartment and busily stripping off their tanks, face masks and weight belts. Already freed of his, Allard moved over to the survival equipment locker, where he knocked on its door.

"Erica? Mrs. Johensen," he continued. "This is Commander Glenn Allard, United States Navy. We're part of the force assigned to free your oil rig."

"Yes. Yes, this is Erica," was the muffled reply. "Please, get me out of here. But be careful."

"Don't worry, I will," said Allard, giving the door a quick check for any tampering, then he turned its knob. The moment the bolt retracted the door sprung out of the frame, and with it the life raft. "Jesus Christ, what the hell's this!"

"The most original boobytrap I ever saw," said Chen. "And guess what it caught . . ."

"Watch it, Artie. Or I'll have your green card pulled."

"I had to find some way of preventing the terrorists from coming in," said Erica, standing on the other side of the raft. "Now I can't get out."

"We'll fix your problem," Allard replied. "Very quickly."

Producing his knife, Allard slashed at the raft; causing it to pop and hiss loudly. In seconds it became a sagging black pile of synthetic rubber and Erica had scrambled her way over it. She fell into Allard's arms, and a subdued applause rose from the other SEALs.

"We heard about what you had to do to survive," he said. "You have our admiration. You're very brave."

"I just want it to be over," Erica cried. "I want to see my daughter, and I want those people punished."

"If we keep to our timetable, it will all happen in the next hour. If you wish, you can either stay here with a

265

guard or accompany us."

"I'm no hero, and I have no wish to fight, but I must find out what happened to my friends."

"I understand. Just stay at the back of the column," said Allard. "Conners, set up the base unit. Artie, what are these explosives like?"

"Standard demolition charges," Chen answered, carefully pulling the fuses out of the tubes attached to the ladder, ". . . made from commercial grade plastique. Waterproof, stable and safe, so long as these aren't in 'em."

Chen held up the fuses, and clipped their wires more than a foot away from them.

"Are these things completely disarmed?" said Allard.

"Yes. You can kick them, shoot them, even set 'em on fire. Only don't send an electric current through them or set off an explosion in their vicinity. It could be enough to ignite them."

"Good. Disarm any charges we come across. It's time to see how the rest of our squads are doing."

Allard pulled the wet suit cap off his head and slipped on an earphone set to his personal radio pack. He made his way through the crowded compartment to the hatch, where he would get the best reception. Now, looking through the observation window from the opposite side, Allard could see a little detail on the other three base legs; there were not any hatches open or men entering them.

"We're all accounted for, Glenn," said Nichols. "Everyone made it aboard. "

"This was the easy part. Let's see how the others did," said Allard, touching the power switch on his radio pack and selecting its voice-activated transmission mode. "Eagle One to Lion One, do you read me? Over . . . Eagle One to Lion One, do you read me?"

"Eagle One, this is Lion One," Boyd replied, after the second pause. "I read you loud and clear. My men are aboard and ready to ascend. Lion Two reports they're in the same position. How's Eagle Two? Over."

"Stay tuned, we'll find out. Eagle One to Eagle Two, do you read? Over."

266

"Yeah, I read you, Eagle One," said Martirri. "I got my guys inside and we're arming up. Did you find the girl? Over."

"Yes, Erica is safe with us," said Allard. "Deactivate the demolition charges you've found and set up your base unit. Lion One, are we cleared to continue according to plan?"

"Affirmative, we're experiencing no delays," said Boyd, standing at the exterior hatch and holding it open a crack. "Proceed according to schedule. Lion One to all teams, keep your microphones open. Over."

Boyd remained at the hatch until Allard and the two executive officers responded to his orders. Once he closed the steel door and moved away from it, reception on his personal radio pack fell off dramatically. The metal structure of the compartment, and of the entire oil rig, scattered radio signals and weakened them. However, Boyd's communications officer was finishing the set-up of equipment which would partially overcome the problems.

The radio base unit was an oblong box a foot and a half long, featureless except for a small array of controls. A weighted, trailing antenna wire deployed from one end, while a torsionless one spooled out from the other. In effect a relay system, the base unit would gather transmissions from the squad's personal radio packs and pass them through the trailing wire antennae. To a limited extent, it would allow the squads and the *Marshall* to maintain contact with each other.

"We'll be on the air soon, Colonel," said the communications officer, David Samuelson. "Just as soon as we toss the first aerial out the hatch and clip the second to my belt."

"Good, I'll want to advise the *Marshall* we're moving out," Boyd responded. "And if Glenn hasn't already told them, that the woman was rescued."

"No, wait. There's a better way to deploy the antenna," said Allard, unspooling one of the wires from his squad's

267

base unit. "It'll get pinched between the hatch and the frame."

He pulled his automatic again, this time from a shoulder holster. It had its silencer attached. While Conners moved away from the external hatch, Allard stepped up to it. He placed the silencer's muzzle against the observation window and pulled the trigger. There was a heavy popping, accompanied by the cracking of glass. And when Allard withdrew the gun, there was a hole just over nine millimeters in size through the double-paned window. It was more than big enough for Conners to slip the weighted end of the wire antenna through.

"The anti-tamper self-destruct has been armed," he said, pressing one of the buttons on the base unit, and a red light started to flash. "All I have to do is hook the second wire to my belt and we're transmitting."

"Don't anybody kick that thing," Allard warned. "We only brought one with us. Erica, how long has it been since you last heard or saw any terrorists?"

"Half a day, at least," said Erica. "Not since they made the search for the one I killed. Why do you ask?"

"Because the report on your incident led Robert Boyd and me to believe he was on a sweep. The terrorist you killed had been assigned some sort of duty in the lower part of this rig. Whatever it was, I don't know, and he never told you. But I'm certain someone else has been given his duties, and one of our squads may encounter them before we reach the operations level."

"So you're saying we may get some visitors," one of the SEALs replied.

"We could. So don't treat this phase like it's grunt work," said Allard. "Conners, if we can transmit I better warn the other commanders. It's three minutes to H-Hour. I want final weapons and radio checks. And make sure every metal fitting is taped down, especially the zippers on your wet suits."

"TASCO Room to control, we have a message from

Colonel Boyd," said Burks. "He reports all squads have made it aboard and Erica Johensen has been rescued."

"Send a message to *Spartan* about the woman's rescue," Carver ordered, standing in his familiar position behind the helmsmen's seats. "Let's see if they're paying as close attention to what the commandoes are saying as we are. What's the situation with the Libyan sub?"

"The *Foxtrot* is still to the north of us, but it has turned toward the oil rig. The data feed from *Spartan's* sonars show much the same thing. So far, the Libyans haven't switched on their Herkules sonar."

"The moment it does, you let me know. And I hope it doesn't before the shooting starts on the rig. Jim, I want you to start updating your firing solutions every thirty seconds. One way or another all hell's going to break loose on *Valkyrie,* and I want to be ready for it."

"Nichols, you take the point," said Allard. "I'll be right behind you. Conners, you and Erica will bring up the rear. And keep her safe. H-Hour is twelve seconds. Eleven, ten . . ."

Allard quietly read off the last seconds, before Nichols grabbed the ladder sides and started up. Unlike the terrorists, whose boots stamped noisily on the ladder rungs, the SEALs hardly made a sound climbing it. Their boots and gloves squeaked softly as they moved—the only metallic noises were the occasional clink of a weapon against steel. Nichols and Allard had scarcely ascended past the base compartment's roof hatch when a louder clanking echoed from above.

"Glenn, we got visitors," said Nichols.

"I know. Retreat, fast," Allard whispered, as he glanced down at the rest of his squad and signalled to them. "Let the visitors come to us."

"My feet hurt. When this duty ends, I'm going to demand some rest," said one of the terrorists as he opened the hatch. "I feel we've walked every foot of this damned thing. It's exhausted me. Someone else can do it next."

"I agree, Jamil," said the other. "We've walked and climbed for hours. It's making me feel dizzy. I would like a hot meal as well as rest, but I don't trust the Norwegian animals in the kitchen. They could easily poison us."

"You carry your fear too far. The Norwegians are eager not to be killed—too bad we'll have to do so. There, unlocked. Shall I go first, or you?"

"I will, but I'll not swing to the other side of the ladder. I'm tired of doing acrobatics."

The hinges creaked when the floor hatch opened, and with a final clank it landed heavily on the deck. As they had agreed, Jamil waited while the other one descended through the opening. Then he too grabbed the support bar beside the hatch and swung his legs through it. Jamil securely planted his feet on the ladder rungs before easing the rest of his body down. The AK-47 slung over his shoulder banged against the hatch frame, creating more noise which echoed in the thirty-foot tall chamber he was entering.

Allard sliced his hand across his throat to cut the whispers among his men, and signalled for them to move away from the roof hatch. They could hear the clanking above them, the groaning and complaints of the terrorists, and the stamp of their boots on the ladder rungs.

Though Nichols indicated he was ready to fire, Allard motioned for him to wait, as well as for the other squad members not to join in. He waited until the stamping grew louder. Waited until he could see dim shadows cast on the compartment floor by the people descending the ladder.

In unison with Nichols, Allard stepped beneath the roof hatch and raised his weapon. The silenced MP-5s chattered instead of barked—their aluminum rounds made more noise striking the ladder than being fired.

The first terrorist never saw his killers. A line of bullets walked up his back, the last one striking the base of his

270

skull. Jamil, because he was using the other side of the ladder, got to see the muzzle flashes and the black-suited figures. One bullet hit the rung below his chin and fragmented, driving splinters into his face and eyes. As he screamed, more slugs hit him in the arms and chest. While his companion dropped lifeless to the chamber floor, Jamil continued to scream as he fell. Only his impact with the steel deck cut it short.

Allard was the first one up the ladder, swinging his submachinegun between the two men until he saw at least one was dead. Jamil continued to make feeble, spasmodic movements until Allard stroked the trigger on his weapon, and a single bullet entered his forehead.

"Jeez, Commander, you can be a real bad ass," said Nichols, stepping off the ladder next. "And I thought you were just hard on us. Shouldn't we have taken him prisoner?"

"There will be no prisoners," said Allard, the tone of his voice making it an order. "We don't have the time or the manpower to take any."

"Glenn, you better let Colonel Boyd know," said Chen, poking his head through the hatchway.

"Right. Eagle One to Lion One, we got first blood. Scratch two hostiles."

"Roger, Eagle One. I was wondering what you were being a hard ass about," Boyd replied. "Confirmed, two hostiles killed. Proceed to objective. Lion One, out."

"You heard the man, Steve, take the point," said Allard, stepping back to the hatch. "Erica, it looks like we may have to fight all the way up this leg. If you wish to reconsider your decision, I can have a man stay with you."

"No, I want to see my friends," said Erica, standing at the base of the ladder. "And I know where they are — most are held in the cafeteria."

"The cafeteria? Hold it, Nichols. Robert's squad will be closer to the cafeteria than we'll be. I better let him know so he can change his plans. Eagle One to Lion One, I have an update for you . . ."

"The drill pipe has entered the conductor pipe," Baroheni reported. "I had better open the blowout valve."

"Yes, proceed," said Nazal. "The sooner the pipe reaches its objective, the sooner we can start pumping in the bacteria."

Again, in order to carry out the task Baroheni had to transfer from the wellbore monitoring console to the one controlling the underwater manifold center. Though the drill pipe was still nearly two hundred feet from the UMC, the last barrier to it was removed when the security blowout valve opened up.

"Status lights confirm it," said Baroheni, "and so do the remote cameras. The valve is open."

"All we have to do is feed in another mile of pipe and it can begin," Nazal observed, standing at the operation center's windows and watching the activity at the derrick. "Jassem had better get here if he's to watch history being made."

"This oil rig still has vertical movement," said Gunni, noticing the subtly changing numbers on the drill pipe readout. "Will it effect our operation?"

"Only if we were actually drilling. When the pipe reaches the oil-bearing strata, all we need do is pump the mud in under pressure. We'll probably get some oil up, so we should prepare the holding tanks for it. And perhaps it can help us with our ballast situation."

"Lion One to Lion Two, when we reach the first level of the platform we must change plans," said Boyd, standing on the ladder in his leg's second chamber. "You'll have to take the crew lounge and living quarters on your own. Glenn reports many of the crew are being held in the cafeteria."

"Understood. Do we proceed according to the rest of the plan?" Ackland requested.

"Affirmative, take the cargo loading station and wait for the assault code. Lion One, out."

After his conversation ended, Boyd restarted his squad's ascent by reaching up and tapping his point man on his boot. In seconds he had climbed to the roof hatch, where he slowly rotated its locking wheel. It squeaked instead of clanked, and even those sounds were drowned out by the storm-generated pounding. The point man raised the hatch with one hand and used the other to sweep the new compartment with his MP-5. Once he found it empty, he finished opening the hatch and moved to inspect the demolition charge while Boyd covered him.

Chen's tapping the fuses against the wall was the loudest noise anyone made in the third compartment. It immediately got Allard's attention, and Chen held it until he clipped the detonating wires. When the disarming was finished, Allard motioned for the rest of his squad to continue their ascent and for Nichols to try the hatch to the next compartment.

The third compartment in the base leg had half the height of the second and a circular staircase instead of a ladder. It was less chamber-like than the other, and noises didn't echo as much, but because it was farther away from the storm's pounding they could be heard more easily.

Strung out along the stairs were most of Allard's men. Only Conners, Erica and Chen, kneeling beside the plastic explosives tube, remained on the compartment floor. At the top of the stairs crouched Allard and Nichols, who reached up and tried the hatch's locking wheel. The moment he pulled on it the hatch creaked open; it had never been secured.

Nichols swept the passageway beyond the hatch with his submachinegun when it had swung out far enough. Allard grabbed the steel door and held it open so his point man could enter the next level. Then it was his turn, and each succeeding man held the door so it would not creak or crash against the wall.

Except for the SEALs, the passageway was empty. At its far end was another, wider, stair case and partway down its left wall stood a single hatch: the entrance to *Valkyrie*'s power generating station. Now that they were on the oil rig's first platform level, the SEALs maintained nearly absolute silence. They relied on Allard's hand signals to answer their questions and direct their positions for the coming assault.

"Work it fast," Allard whispered to Nichols, when he grabbed the hatch's locking wheel. "Standby."

Allard raised his hand to stop the rustling of his squad, and moments later brought it down in a chopping motion. This time, the entrance had been secured and its lock mechanism started clicking rapidly as Nichols spun the wheel. For a few seconds all Allard and his men could do was wait.

"Pistols only," Boyd ordered in a low voice. "We don't want the equipment inside damaged."

The team Boyd commanded approached the communications center with the MP-5s slung over their backs and their P9S automatics drawn. The rest of his squad fanned across the passageway, covering its stairs and the center's entrance with their submachineguns. When he first touched it, Boyd could feel the hatch move; he knew it was unlocked.

He gestured for one of his team members to grab it as he moved away. With his second teammate, Boyd trained his automatic on the hatch and activated its pencil-thin laser sight. He glanced at the other teams in his squad, then he raised his fist to quiet them.

The moment its wheel stopped clicking, the hatch flew open. Allard jumped inside the power station and found himself surrounded by humming, rattling machinery. In an instant he realized the noise of the generators had masked his intrusion; if there was anyone in the station they weren't aware of him.

Allard signalled for the men coming in behind him to

spread out and hunt down the narrow aisles between the equipment. The aisle he took led to the station's monitor and control panels. There he found a woman leaning her chair against the main console.

She was darkly beautiful, with the face of a model and raven black hair. She also had a Mac-10 submachinegun in her lap which snapped into her hand as she leaped from her chair.

For an instant Allard thought she was aware of him, but she never turned in his direction. Instead, before he could finish raising his Heckler and Koch he heard the suppressed chatter of another MP-5. The woman had just snapped the bolt on her own weapon when a bullet struck her left cheekbone. A second one hit below her right eye and the third just above it.

The Mac-10 slipped from her lifeless hands and clattered across the floor. Almira first landed on top of the main console, then slid off it. In slow motion, she dropped to her knees; the rest of her body tumbled forward moments later and landed hard on what had once been a beautiful face.

When Boyd chopped his fist down the entrance hatch exploded open. The sudden clanking startled the communication center's sole occupant, and Sherina lost precious time before whirling around to grab her AKM.

Because the room had all its equipment lining its walls, Boyd didn't have to go hunting through it to find Sherina. He stood in the entrance and trained his automatic on her. The red dot of its laser sight fell on her right side; a moment later a bullet hole appeared under her right breast.

Sherina never got her hands on the assault rifle lying in the chair. She cried out and slumped against an instrument console. A second bullet hit her in the upper arm, a third in her neck, and Sherina's screaming stopped when the fourth struck her right temple.

"Regrettable business," said Boyd, stepping into the center; and over to the body. "It took us too long to kill her.

We must do it faster."

"We will, once we use our MP-5s," assured the next Marine to enter. "Do you want Samuelson in here?"

"Yes. He's studied the Com systems on this rig better than anyone. Get him in here. Lion One to Lion Two, stand by to take first objective."

"And Nichols thought *I* was a bad ass," said Allard, checking Almira's body for any further weapons. "I'll get Matteson over here, he can run these. I think they're the main bus panels. Stay until he relieves you."

Collecting his submachinegun, Allard went back to the power station's entrance. Most of his squad was still in the passageway outside, especially Conners, who had just finished pulling the antenna through the hatch to the base leg.

"Glenn, there's another demolition charge in here," said Chen. "Permission to disarm?"

"Go ahead. Christ, they must have every other room in this thing wired," Allard replied. "Matteson, get your team in here. You'll garrison the station. Eagle One to Eagle Two. Sal, you're cleared to take your objective."

"Roger," was the single-word reply, and for a change Allard didn't hear any grumbling from Martirri's squad members.

"God, I think they're finally treating our mission as something more than a damn exercise," he said, wrapping his hand over his headset's microphone. "Don't fuck it up, Sal."

Martirri signaled for his point man to finish opening the hatch, then held it open for him while he swept the passageway on the other side. He motioned that it was clear, and had just moved into the corridor when a loud clanking froze everyone.

A few yards ahead, the hatch to ballast control rattled in its frame. Its locking wheel turned, and a hand pushed it open. The terrorist had only stepped partially into the corridor when he came face to face with the SEALs.

"He's mine!" Martirri shouted, shoving his point man aside with one hand and training his submachinegun with the other. He squeezed its trigger, and for the first two rounds fired he managed to hold the weapon steady. Then, the working of its blowback mechanism, the physical ejection of spent shells and the eruption of slugs from its muzzle caused the MP-5 to jerk wildly off target.

"Jesus, Lieutenant! I could've nailed him," said the point man, picking himself off the floor.

"Shut up!" Martirri answered. "Larry, don't let them close the door!"

He pointed down the corridor, and the men coming off the stairs after him charged to the center's entrance. The moment they reached it they were greeted by a hail of automatic weapons fire. Unlike their aluminum rounds, the ammunition the terrorists used was standard and ricocheted until finding something soft enough to penetrate.

"Colonel, someone's trying to use the interphone link at ballast control," warned Samuelson, the display he studied changing subtly.

"Cut them off, at once," said Boyd. "That was Martirri's objective. Something's going wrong there. It just had to happen, especially after Ross found the loading station empty. Lion One to Eagle One, your number two has a problem."

"Christ, they must have a fucking machinegun in there!" said Petrowski, when he finished crawling up beside Martirri.

"Or they're firing in shifts!" said Martirri. "How many do you think there are?"

"Two, three at most. But it's like they're in a pillbox!"

"Don't worry, we'll get them out. Fragmentation grenade! Eagle Two to Eagle One, we've encountered some resistance but we're dealing with it! We'll grenade them out."

"What? Eagle Two, repeat what you just said?" Allard requested, his reception spotty since moving back inside the power station. "If you're getting resistance, isolate them and move on. There's no need for grenades."

As he moved toward the entrance, the transmissions from Martirri's squad improved. Allard could hear the gunfire and someone crying he was wounded. Allard also encountered Chen, who had just finished defusing the plastic explosives. In an instant, what Chen had said about the plastique flashed through Allard's mind.

"Eagle Two, no grenades!" Allard shouted. "Don't set off the charge! Repeat, no grenades!"

At Martirri's suggestion, Petrowski took a grenade off his web belt, yanked its pin and tossed it through the hatch. Because they were so close, the SEALs put their hands over their ears to prevent concussion damage. Seconds later a burst of light and heat erupted out of ballast control. The deck heaved and everyone was jarred by the pressure wave.

A moment afterward, an incandescent sphere of light melted the steel wall most of the SEALs were huddled beside. Even with closed eyes their world became blindingly white. The wave of heat and pressure built until those not protected from it lost consciousness. For a few, their last sensation was of their bodies coming apart.

From the outside, a blossom of flame appeared at the point on *Valkyrie* where its southeastern base leg joined the platform. The entire structure, more than seventy thousand tons of it, shuddered from the explosion. Jagged fragments of steel arced out of the blast site and tumbled into the sea. In a fleeting moment, everyone's operation had been ruined.

"No! God, no!" said Nazal, his voice rising as the deck

shook unnaturally under his feet. "What was that! Where did it happen?"

"It's commandoes!" Gunni charged. "We're under attack!"

"Shut up, Yussuf. Don't jump without proof! Ibrahim, can you find out what's happening?"

"I must see what the damage control station shows," said Baroheni, ripping his headphones off and jumping away from the wellbore monitoring console. "It will take me several minutes to judge what it's displaying."

"Take less time," said Nazal, fighting to keep emotion out of his voice. "We can't let our operation be jeopardized, not at this stage . . . We're too close to success to be denied it! Yussuf, contact the cafeteria. Get in touch with Samad."

"My Royal Marine ass!" Boyd swore, as he was helped off the floor of the communications room. "Something must've happened to Glenn's bloody cowboy."

"Colonel, rig operations is establishing contact with the cafeteria," said Samuelson. "Shall I cut it?"

"No, it would only alert them to our assault. Only cut the phone links to a position we're attacking. We'd better find out what happened at ballast control. Lion One to Lion Two, detach one of your teams and send it to ballast control. If there are any Americans left they'll need your help."

"Eagle Two, report in! Eagle Two, report!" Allard shouted, though it hardly made his transmission signal any stronger. Then he wrapped his hand around his microphone. "Sal, you fucking cowboy, what the hell have you done?"

In contrast to Allard, the rest of his squad was silent. Despite their desire to know they held to their training and let their commander do the talking. For several seconds he listened as well, but all anyone could hear was some moaning and Boyd giving orders to his executive officer.

"Eagle Two, this is Eagle One," Allard continued. "I

want anyone who can hear me to respond. Over."

"Commander, this is Landham," said the Chief Petty Officer, after he had finished untangling himself from the stair's guard rail. "I'm in the support leg's top compartment, and there are seven other men with me."

Landham turned and checked the others in the compartment. The explosion had caused some of them to tumble down the stairs; most had managed to hang on the guard rail. While they all appeared dazed and were suffering from some degree of deafness, none were seriously injured.

"John, what is your group's condition?" Allard asked.

"We've all been bounced around but we're still in one piece," said Landham. "When the shooting started, I was ordered to hold most of the squad back. All the officers wanted to be heroes. The ricochets forced me to close the hatch and order the men back down the stairs."

"Are there any officers with you?"

"No, Commander. I'm the highest-ranking man in the squad. I got a sick feeling no one on the other side of the hatch survived."

"Then you are now squad commander," said Allard. "Find out what happened at ballast control and continue with your assignment. Lion One has ordered Lion Two to send you a backup force, be prepared to receive them. Good luck, John, we'll really need it now."

"We've lost the ballast control center," said Baroheni, now seated at the damage control console and double-checking its displays. "I can't contact them. There's no response on the phone lines, they're dead. I'm getting no information from ballast control, or on any of the operations it runs."

"It's a commando attack," Gunni replied. "The British have sent in the Special Air Service."

"And from where, Yussuf?" Nazal said, angrily. "Is there a helicopter on the pad outside? Has the *Sword of the Rev-*

olution detected any other submarines? No, this doesn't sound or feel like an attack. I fear one of our own scuttling explosives was triggered. It would certainly explain why communications is dead, and why there's no information on ballast operations. Are you still talking to Samad?"

"Yes, he has not yet left the cafeteria."

"Tell him I still want him here, but Akkad is to head immediately to ballast control. He's to take as many men with him as he can. He can even pull guards from the cafeteria, but he must find out what happened. Ibrahim, can the loss of ballast control affect the injection process?"

"Very easily," said Baroheni. "Without it the rig could lose stability and drilling would have to end. We might be able to maintain stability from here, but first we need to know what's left of the station." ·

"We will, though until Akkad gets there we must prepare for the worse," said Nazal, a bitterness and resignation in his voice. "Go back to wellbore monitoring, and tell the floormen commander and pump station team to prepare to end their stacking. If *Valkyrie* becomes too unstable, we must pump as much mud as possible before abandoning it. I'll not let this accident deny us our triumph against the West."

"It's official, Terry," Burks advised. "We're fucked. There's been an explosion aboard *Valkyrie* and up to half of Martirri's squad is dead."

"What about the terrorists? Do they know they're under attack?" Carver asked.

"Neither Glenn or Robert Boyd can tell if they are. But there's been no counter-attack on the communication or power station. The squads will regroup and press ahead with their operation."

"I hope they can," said Adir. "This disaster will create confusion on both sides. If our friends work fast they can take advantage of it."

"I agree. But while Glenn and Robert may still have an advantage we're rapidly losing ours," said Carver. "The

281

Foxtrot may discover us before they free the hostages. Then we'll have the worst of both worlds—we'll all be vulnerable. Greg, tell *Spartan* to prepare for combat at any second. Jim, open torpedo tube outer doors. Pressurize tubes for positive discharge. Arm warheads. Enable torpedo and decoy systems. Captain to nucleonics, prepare the museum piece for high-speed maneuvering. Lock down the propulsion rafts."

While Carver was still giving orders to his crew, Burks alerted *Spartan*. On auxiliary screens the readouts for each submarine changed as their battle readiness increased. However, the main screen's tactical map showed nothing of the heightened activity. The submarines continued to hover under the oil rig, and the *Foxtrot* cruised north of it.

"It really sounds like we're going to war," said Gavrilla, in response to the voices filtering into the TASCO Room from the control center. "I feel more afraid now than when I was alone in the desert."

"You're not alone, Gavi," Adir responded. "And remember, if conditions had been too critical, we were under orders to abandon you. We can't do that here. Your chances are better on this ship because there's a hundred other men who also want to live."

Chapter Eighteen

Creaking loudly, the damaged hatch swung open and Landham stepped cautiously into the passageway. Except for some fires burning feebly in the ballast control room, it was pitch black. Even when Landham and the others switched their flashlights on it didn't improve conditions much; the smoke prevented the beams from penetrating very far.

"Oh God, it's Darryl," said one of the other commandoes, his flashlight beam playing over a body crumpled next to the hatch. "Darryl Strader. God, Jesus!"

"Darryl . . . you should've slit Martirri's throat when you had the chance," said Landham, turning his beam in the body's direction. "None of this would've happened."

"Chief, the floor's wet with blood," warned another SEAL. "And I think I just stepped on a hand not attached to no arm. I'm going to be sick."

"Keep moving and don't think about it. That's an order, sailor. If any of you find dogtags, collect them."

Landham prodded the man beside him to continue walking, and together they advanced down the corridor. The closer to the blast site, the less recognizable the bodies became. Those at the ballast control entrance had been dismembered; the men who examined their remains used survival knives to remove their dogtags.

The wall on either side of the entrance had been rent open by the detonation; the hatch itself was torn off its hinges and lay near the stairs to the upper levels. Inside

283

ballast control not a single console remained intact. The explosion had ripped apart all the instrument panels and status boards, many of which were still shorting. It had also opened up the center's exterior wall, causing the storm to rage and swirl through what remained of the compartment.

The winds alternately fanned the fires or drenched them with sleet and sea spray. In addition to the smells of cordite and burnt flesh came the tang of salt air and a sharper aroma: ozone created by the arcing of electrical circuits. Of the terrorists nothing could be seen, except possibly for one of the fires burning in a corner. They had either been consumed by the explosion, or blown out of the holes opened in the floor and walls.

"Chief, should we go in and search it?" asked a squad member.

"No, you'll either get burned or drop sixty feet to the ocean," said Landham. "We have to keep moving. Glenn already has his squad moving out and so are the Brits. Milty, anchor your antenna at the top of the stairs. Leave any weapons you see but grab the ammunition. We may need it."

Landham pulled his men away from ballast control and led them to the staircase at the corridor's opposite end. As they advanced, the SEALs would stop to collect the grenades and undamaged ammunition clips from their dead comrades, even to the extent of removing clips from their weapons. It made Landham and the others feel like grave robbers, though they all knew the reasons why it had to be done. They could end up needing what they took, and no one wanted to leave the enemy something they could use.

"Matteson, you and Conners will remain here," said Allard, standing at the entrance to the power station. "Stay on your toes and prepare to cut power in two minutes, fourteen seconds. Erica, if you want you can stay with them."

"No, I can show you the fastest way to operations," she replied. "And it will let you use either the interior or external entrance."

"All right, just make sure you stay at the end of my team. Good luck, Matt, we'll see you later."

Allard shook hands with Matteson and Conners before going to the head of the column waiting for him. When he reached it, he signaled for his men to pull out their infrared goggles. While the binocular-like devices would restrict their field of view, they would need them in just over two minutes.

Climbing the stairs to the cafeteria level, Boyd's squad made hardly more noise than a light wind rustling leaves. The loudest sounds came as they stopped—some of their weapons clinked sharply when they touched the steps. At the top of the stairs Boyd crouched and was just able to peer down the hall.

For the first few moments it was empty. The cafeteria was just one of several rooms which opened onto the hall, though it did have the largest entrance. It also had almost all the noise emanating from it, a constant hum of conversation and the clatter of china and silverware. The level jumped dramatically as the cafeteria doors swung out and a group of men emerged.

There were four in all, with Kaniel Akkad leading. Two guards pushed the doors open for them, then pulled the doors back. For an instant Boyd thought he would have a fire fight on his hands, but the group turned in the opposite direction and charged down the hall easily creating more noise than his entire squad had.

"Those must be the ones who've been ordered to investigate the blast," Boyd whispered, after the terrorists had disappeared. "Sergeant Rutherford and Mr. Landham will hear them approaching a mile off."

"What about the other man we overheard operations requesting?" said the Lieutenant next to Boyd. "Should we wait for him to leave?"

"We'll have to take the chance that he already has. The

lights will go out in under two minutes—we have to be set up and ready to take advantage of this opportunity. We can't afford to lose it. There are at least two guards to deal with, so we'll need to use everyone we have. Deploy the lads."

Leaving his second in command to signal his squad, Boyd moved out ahead of them. He was in the corridor and pressed against one of its walls, before the first had come to the top of the stairs. He directed his marines to advance down the hall in two columns: one behind him and the other along the opposite wall.

To the doors they passed which were marked as offices, he assigned one or two of his men. They ignored the storage rooms and service access hatches, and even with that limitation Boyd was down to four men by the time he reached the cafeteria doors. He noticed the distinct shadows being cast under them. The lights in the cafeteria were stronger than the ones in the hall, and those standing at the doors were betrayed by their feet.

"Guards," Boyd whispered, pointing at the shadows. He then directed one of his group to stand beside him, and for the others to spread out on either side of the entrance. Lastly, he motioned to his infrared goggles and watch. They had less than a minute to go before power would be cut.

"Well, Samad. What do you think?" Nazal asked, standing next to the damage control station.

"It does look like some explosives detonated accidentally," said Jassem, his quick study of the station's readouts finished. "And it could've been caused by the control boxes tying the charges together. The one near ballast control could've shorted, and as Kaniel will tell you, it doesn't take much electricity to set off what we laid."

"So, you think it's an accident?"

"I would prefer to wait for Kaniel's report, but yes, it does look like an accident. However, I agree with Yussuf, until we know for sure we should put our forces on alert and warn the *Sword of the Revolution*."

"All right, I agree," said Nazal, walking over to the center's coat rack and grabbing his winter jacket. "An alert would be better than having our people abandon their duties and go running around looking for phantoms. Samad, you contact Captain Saleh. Yussuf, put the entire rig on alert and tell the pump station to start the mud flow."

"I will," said Gunni. "And where are you going? What duty have you assigned to yourself?"

"I'm going out to the station and the drilling derrick. Something Jassem told us has me more worried than possible British commandoes. If the control boxes malfunction, we could risk losing the entire drilling platform. They have to be checked, and if necessary deactivated. I'll call when I reach the pump station."

"This is where we split," Allard whispered. "Good luck, Artie. Erica, stay with Simonson."

Allard's squad was now four levels above the power station and had reached a junction in the passageway. While it cut abruptly to the right, to the left was the external hatch Erica had promised. After giving his commands, Allard turned to the squad and selected the men to accompany Chen.

As they disappeared around the passage's bend, what was left of the squad cracked open the hatch. Leading with his MP-5, Allard stepped cautiously outside. They were one floor below the main production level and in an area which had not been cleared of ice. Slipping occasionally on the glazed surface, Allard led his squad to a service stair Erica claimed would take them directly to the operation center's external entrance.

Above the sounds of the storm could be heard the clank and screech of drilling work. Even voices were discerned, though no one was seen in the harsh glare of work lights. The exterior of *Valkyrie* was illuminated like a city skyline.

There were few shadows for Allard to hide his men in, at a moment when he needed darkness the most. At the foot of the stairs he checked his watch again, and held his squad's advance as he counted off the final seconds.

In the last five seconds, Boyd pulled the binocular-like goggles over his eyes and signalled for his men to do the same. They severely restricted his peripheral view and he felt as if he were watching the world through a black-and-white television. Unlike the thermal imagers the submarines used, the goggles could not show colors, only shades of grey. Still, they provided Boyd with the kind of vision he would soon need.

The moment power was cut the corridor lights glowed a little less brightly, and the shouting from the cafeteria climbed dramatically. At Boyd's command the doors were snapped open; the guard he stood behind was only just becoming aware of it when his MP-5 chattered noisily.

Both guards were lifted off their feet and thrown forward, one of them sailing into a crowded table, the other crashing to the floor. Boyd and the Marine beside him were still firing when the rest of his group started shouting in English or Norwegian to get down.

They could scarcely be heard above the screaming but they had the desired effect. The rig workers dove off their benches or hid behind the tables as the Marines spread out from the entrance. Moving his head from side to side, Boyd scanned for more terrorists. The goggles weren't sophisticated enough for him to see faces. He could not tell if the people he was passing were Norwegian or Arab. What he tried to clue in on were weapons. They would either be cooler than the surrounding environment, or warmer if they were being held.

Or fired. The muzzle blasts of a submachinegun flared white in the night goggles. Boyd crouched and swung in the gunner's direction, only to find him already staggering from return fire of the other Marines. He flew into the wall and crumpled to the deck, to the scattered applause of the Norwegians around him.

"Quiet, this isn't a damn game!" Boyd shouted, trying to keep down the noise so he could hear any remaining terrorists. Again he moved his head from side to side to compensate for his narrow field of view. He heard more gunfire, and this time he saw one of his men crash against a wall.

Boyd instantly realized his squad had lost their cloak of darkness. In the corners of the cafeteria he recognized the sudden appearance of hot spots as emergency lighting. Boyd tore his goggles off and dove for the floor, hoping his eyes would readjust fast enough for him to defend himself.

"I can't raise the power station," said Gunni, slamming the telephone receiver back on its cradle. "What's happening here!"

"It could well be an attack," said Jassem. "Communications should have independent power in the event of failure. The emergency radio works, but the com center has no control over it."

"Did you contact the *Sword of the Revolution?*"

"Yes, they'll make an immediate search for enemy forces. As should we."

Jassem released the microphone stand at the radio panel and felt his way around to where he remembered Gunni was standing. Even with the power off there was still enough illumination from status displays to give most everything a dim outline. However, the guards at the interior entrance were barely visible. It took the sound of their weapons being armed for Jassem to realize they were still in their original locations.

"If we can't use the phones, how do we contact our people?" asked Gunni.

"By runners," said Jassem. "We have to send one out to—the door! Get away from the door!"

The rattling of the entrance's doorknob sounded like machinegun fire to those in the operations center. While most ducked behind consoles, the guards jumped and spun around, training their weapons on what they had been protecting.

"Who are they? I didn't hear a password," said Baroheni, scrambling to pull out his automatic.

"Open fire! Open fire!" Gunni ordered. "It's the British!"

For almost three days Landstrom had put up with the insults, the bullying, the fear. Now at last he had a chance to get even with those who had killed so many of his friends. The woman standing in front of him was unleashing a long burst of fire from the Mac-10 she cradled in her hands. Its deafening bark overwhelmed any noise Landstrom made as he rose from his crouching position.

Too late she realized someone was rearing up behind her. The barking stopped and she had partially turned when Landstrom grabbed her by the arms. He lifted the terrorist off the floor, who screamed and started firing wildly. Fragments of the cafeteria's ceiling panels started to fall around them; but before the weapon had exhausted its ammunition it flew out of the woman's hands.

From several directions bullets struck her in the chest and stomach. Landstrom could feel the impacts, felt the body he held jerk and spasm, and had the clear sensation of being lifted off his feet. The Mac-10 was still clattering on the table beside them when he and the woman crashed to the floor. He felt her bleeding profusely in his arms, then realized there were men standing over him.

"That was a bloody fool thing for you to do!" Boyd stormed. "She could've killed you! We could've killed you! What possessed you to do it?"

"I wanted to kill one before you got them all," said Landstrom, pushing the body off. "Bitch. I hate them all."

"I understand. And thank you. Allanby, check the rest of the mess hall. I'll see to Leland. Ridings, I want the other lads in here."

"There's our signal. Blow the charge," said Allard.

Muzzle flashes from the guards' weapons illuminated the operations center with strobe-like bursts of light. They were firing on the interior entrance, riddling the door after Chen had tried its knob. Allard and his group turned their backs to the external entrance they had surrounded as a chief petty officer tapped a detonator button.

The plastic explosives attached to the door ripped it open and off its hinges; completing the destruction started three days earlier by Nazal. Seconds later an identical blast destroyed the interior entrance; those not stunned were confused and disoriented. They would only remain so for a few seconds longer, but it would be enough for Allard.

He was first into the center, moving his head from side to side to get the best use of his night goggles. Barely on his second scan, he caught sight of a figure with a submachinegun in his hands. Its barrel virtually glowed, evidence of its recent use. Allard snapped up his MP-5 and it chattered noisily until the figure toppled off his feet.

The firing occurred simultaneous to the sound of another MP-5. Allard swung his head in time to see Chen standing in a shattered doorway, and another terrorist dropping backward over a console.

"Spread out!" Allard commanded. "There's more in here!"

Muffled gunfire, screams of his men dying and shouted orders brought Jassem to his senses. He struggled to fight off the physical effects of the explosions, grabbing the edge of a console to help himself up. He could see wetsuit-clad figures moving across the darkened center, hunting down his men.

One of them stumbled over Baroheni's feet, causing him to cry out in pain. As the first SEAL crashed to the deck, the ones behind him swung their MP-5s down. Baroheni's final scream was a shrill one, ended by multiple bursts of fire to his stomach, chest and head. The Baretta he had just pulled out of his holster fell from his hand without being used.

"No! No! Stop!" Gunni shouted, raising his hands and opening them to show he was unarmed.

A line of slugs stitched him from groin to neck and lifted him off his feet. Gunni smashed through one of the last intact windows in the operations center. He hit the steel planking outside with an audible thud. Only Jassem was left.

Shakily, he aimed his automatic and managed to squeeze off a single round before getting return fire. The bullets struck him in the chest and right shoulder, spinning him away from the console and into a wall. At first the impacts were painful, especially when he collided with the wall, but by the time Jassem slumped to the floor he felt only numbness.

"Who the hell are you?" he asked, looking at the anonymous figure standing over him. There were no markings on his wetsuit, even his face was hidden by a strange pair of telescope glasses.

"Commander Glenn Allard, United States Navy SEALs," said Allard, ripping his goggles off his head.

"Americans? Why . . . ?"

"We were invited." Allard raised his submachinegun to Jassem's head to finish him, but realized he had already died. With the last terrorist in the room dead, an eerie silence fell over it. Allard could hear his men moving around. Sounds of the storm and a frenzied gibberish were coming over a loudspeaker.

"Commander, you better come over here," said one of the SEALs. "I think one of these guys was talking to someone."

Allard made his way to the emergency radio station and listened for a moment to the rapid-fire Arabic being spoken. He quickly realized it was someone demanding information and he heard a familiar, military staccato in the voice.

292

"It sounds like the Libyan sub," Allard observed. "I better get outside and raise Terry, the jig may be up for him. I'll be sending Erica in—make sure this place is safe for her. She might be able to identify who we've killed."

"TASCO Room to control, sonar's reporting a new source of noises," said Burks. "It's not the Libyans. It's a lot closer to home. The source is localized to within a few hundred feet."

"Roger, Greg. I'll talk with Seidel about it," said Carver, releasing the thumb switch on his microphone and punching another button on its control box. "Carver to sonar room. What's this new source, David?"

"It's directly above us, Captain," Seidel replied. "It's the oil rig. The hydrophone arrays have picked up noises like ballast valves being opened. Only they're the biggest damn valves I've ever heard. You'd think there were half a dozen subs above us."

"In a way, there are. *Valkyrie* is half-submarine to begin with, and has nearly ten times our displacement. Glenn reported its ballast control blew up when Martirri tried to take it. Could this be related?"

"If the buoyancy system has shorted out, it sure could. And it certainly sounds as if every valve on those ballast tanks are opening."

"Oh my God, they could lose it," said Carver, his voice growing hushed. "Keep me posted, Dave. On the rig as well as the Libyan sub."

"TASCO Room to control, we just got a message from Allard," said Burks, his advisement overriding Carver's conversation with Seidel. "He warns the Libyans may have been talking to the terrorists."

"Then we're going to be discovered. Warn *Spartan,* let's see who'll be first to fire. And warn Glenn that the rig's ballast tanks have opened. They better hurry up and finish their assault."

"I'm sorry, Robert. He was too badly wounded," said the officer kneeling beside the first SBS casualty. "He's gone."

"Take his identity disc. Disarm his weapons," Boyd replied, solemnly. "Leland, my lad . . . I'm sorry to lose you."

"Colonel, I'm Erik Reitan. Captain of *Ocean Valkyrie*," said a man with grey-flecked, sandy brown hair. "Thank you for rescuing us, but I have people held in other areas, the activities lounge and the hospital. Can they be rescued?"

"They are being rescued. I have a second squad taking care of it. Are there many terrorists guarding those locations?"

"I think not many. Most are in operations or on the production platform. There were more guards here until the explosion—I don't know where they went."

"I do," said Boyd, dividing his attention between Reitan's answers and the preparing of Leland's body. "Someone will take care of them. Wait, I have a use for those."

Boyd halted the disarming procedure just as the clips were being pulled from Leland's submachinegun and automatic. He reached down for.the weapons, then handed them to Reitan and Landstrom.

"I think you two are capable of using these," Boyd added. "I'll leave a detail to help with your evacuation. For your own protection, stay here until you're cleared to leave. Sergeant, you're in charge here. I'll leave you with two men but I have to take the rest topside. Stay in touch by headset or the rig's intercom. Since the other rooms in this area have been cleared your security threat should be minimal. Stay alert, and we'll see each other when this is over."

"Quiet, stop griping," said Landham, in a deep whisper. He turned and raised his hand to stop his squad's advance. "There's someone ahead of us."

The SEALs were only a few feet from a stairway to the next level. They hushed instantly, and the stamp of boots could be heard in the distance; moments later flashlight beams were reflecting down the stairs.

Landham signalled for his men to spread out along either wall and make use of what little cover they could find. As they waited, the sound of people running and voices became more distinct. While some of Landham's squad pressed themselves against the walls, others took up prone firing positions. All trained their weapons at the top of the stairs, and the instant a shadowy figure holding a flashlight appeared they opened fire.

"What's happening up there?" Akkad demanded, when the man at the head of his group screamed. At first he did not hear the sounds of muffled gunfire; not until he heard the pinging and banging of aluminum bullets striking steel plates did he realize his group was under attack. "Retreat! Move, damn it, retreat!"

Akkad fell when he tried to both stop and run backwards at the same time. Firing blindly, one of the surviving terrorists raked the top of the stairs with a long burst while the other helped Akkad to stand.

"What about Hadami?" he asked. "Should we—"

"Forget him! He's dead!" said Akkad. "Retreat. Prepare to use grenades."

Akkad could only afford a fleeting glimpse of the man he had to leave dying. The return fire stopped when the AKM being used exhausted its clip of ammunition. For all the power he unleashed, the terrorist had only managed to punch a ragged line of holes in the stairway's ceiling. Finally obeying the repeated orders of his commander, he pulled back from the edge of the stairs.

"Fragmentation and high-explosive," Akkad continued, taking one of the grenades off his web belt. "We have them trapped. With luck we'll kill them all."

Complying with their commander, the other terrorists

laid aside their guns and produced the types of grenades he wanted. They heard no answering fire from the people who had ambushed them, but did hear them moving around.

"Kaniel, they could be escaping," said one of the terrorists. "Or coming up the stairs."

"It doesn't matter," said Akkad. "On my mark. Three, two—"

"Hi, Abdul. You're nicked."

Automatic weapons fire erupted out of the darkened corridor behind Akkad and his men. They had just started to pull the pins from their grenades when they were hit by multiple bursts of nine-millimeter slugs. Akkad was struck in the back and spun around, the grenade in his hand sailing free of his grip. Another burst caught him in the neck and traveled up his face. He was dead before he had finished crashing to the floor.

Of the two men with Akkad, one was hit in the stomach and blown back toward the stairs. The other was thrown against the wall and momentarily held there by the slugs ripping into his chest. He crumpled to the floor in a grotesque pile, where still another grenade rolled out of his hand.

"Hit the deck!" Rutherford shouted, swinging his flashlight from one weapon to the other. "Hit it now!"

He turned and pushed the Royal Marine beside him off his feet, then leaped as far as a single jump would allow him. Rutherford landed at the same moment the floor heaved from the first detonation. The shock wave slammed and bounced him farther down the hallway. His ears were stung by the blast and the flash temporarily blinded him. Rutherford had the distinct sensation he was losing consciousness, and had to force his hands over his head just before the second explosion lifted him.

"Oh God, what did you do to him?" Erica asked, repulsed by the sight of Baroheni's mangled body.

"Filled him with enough aluminum to take him to a recycling center," said Allard. "Is he one of the leaders?"

"No, I don't recognize his face—what's left of it. But the man who came through the window was a leader. And I think that one is."

Erica pointed to Jassem's slumped body and walked over to it, with Allard behind her. They passed the emergency radio station, where frenzied demands in Arabic could still be heard.

"Glenn, why don't we tell them to go fuck themselves?" Chen requested. "I'd love to do it."

"So would I. But we have to think of our home," said Allard. "Just turn the system off. We can't put our subs at risk. Erica, can you tell me his name?"

Moving past the station, Allard bent down and grabbed Jassem by the hair. He tilted the head up until Erica could see his face. She had just started to answer him when a long burst of silenced gunfire caused everyone in the operations center to dive for cover.

"Artie, what the hell are you doing?" Allard demanded. "Going cowboy on me?"

"Well, you told me to turn it off," said Chen, smiling while the control panels he shot up continued to sputter and arc. "But you never told me how."

"Keep it up, and one of us will give you the aluminum express to your ancestors."

"Mr. Allard, I think they called this man Samad. But I can't remember his last name," said Erica. "And the one outside was called Yussuf. But I don't see Abu Nazal anywhere. I believe he was the man who commanded everything."

"Yes, he is," said Allard. "The Israelis warned us about Nazal. We have to find him and kill him before he creates more trouble for us."

"Commander, you think he was the guy we saw leaving just before we surrounded this place?" asked one of the SEALs.

"He could be, and he's probably somewhere out there on the production platform." Allard turned and glanced through the shattered observation windows. In spite of *Valkyrie's* main power source being shut down, lights were still blazing outside, especially around the drilling derrick. "Artie, you and your team will stay here. Try to contact Boyd and tell him Nazal is still at large. The rest of you are to come with me. Erica, if you want to join us you can. But make sure you stay at the end of the line."

The third explosion felt as if it were more distant, though with his eyes closed and his hands over his ears, Rutherford wasn't able to tell. After the floor had stopped heaving he could feel his senses returning, and slowly peered out at the world around him. The first thing he saw was a mangled, severed arm. For a moment he thought the worse, until one of his men helped him up.

"Hargrove, where's Dimbleby?" Rutherford asked, regaining enough of his sense of balance to stand on his own feet.

"He's gone forward to check the damage," said the Corporal. "The grenades went off near the staircase."

Bending to retrieve his MP-5 and flashlight, Rutherford made his way through the smoke and around the shattered bodies of the terrorists. The explosions had punched holes in the floor and torn apart the upper stairs. Rutherford found his second team member standing on the left side of the hallway where the least damage had been done.

"They're nicked, Sergeant, well and truly," said Dimbleby.

"I see they nicked themselves better than we did," said Rutherford. "Have you seen the Americans?"

"I think so, but the smoke's too thick."

"Landham, this is Derek Rutherford. Can you hear me? Landham, can you hear me?"

"Yes, Sergeant. I think so," Landham replied, a flashlight beam filtering through the smoke in the stairwell. "What the hell happened with you?"

"The terrorists tried to grenade you," said Rutherford.

"They ended up doing it to themselves."

More beams joined Landham's at the base of the stairs, more than half a dozen in all. Their combined illumination overpowered the drifting layers of smoke and revealed much of the damage to the SEALs and Royal Marines.

"Jesus Christ, how are we going to get past that?" said one of Landham's men. "Fly?"

"We can help you," said Rutherford, laying down his submachinegun and handing his flashlight to Dimbleby. "There isn't much time to waste, so who'll be first?"

"Wireless office to attack center, signal from *Marshall*. We're about to be discovered, we're authorized to open fire."

"After all these hours, thank God," said Taylor, keying the hand mike he'd been holding. "Captain to wireless office, acknowledge our orders. Captain to sound room, activate the Twenty-Nineteen and target the *Foxtrot*. Hodgkiss, complete your firing solutions. Open outer doors on tubes two and three. Mr. Bryan, maneuvering speed."

"Aye, Captain. The helm is answering," Bryan advised. "And reactor control reports all power settings are available."

"Sound room to attack center, PARIS activated," said another voice on the speakers. "We're ranging in the *Foxtrot*. But the Twenty-Twenty array has detected Herkules emissions. The Libyans are pinging for us."

"We're going to have a fast-draw contest," said Taylor. "Ethan, what's your status?"

"Outer doors to two and three, opened," Hodgkiss answered, reading off the changing displays at the weapons station. "Tubes pressurized for positive discharge. Firing solutions completed. Torpedo programs, loaded. Launch circuits, enabled."

"Fire tube number two."

Moments later a sharp hissing rumbled through *Spar-*

299

tan's forward section. From one of its two port side tubes a torpedo twenty-two feet long was ejected. As it shot free from the cloud of bubbles, the Spearfish's turbine engine started and engaged the pump jet.

After dipping slightly, the torpedo leveled out and accelerated to more than thirty knots in a matter of seconds. A thin, fiber-optic cable spooled out from one of its cruciform tail fins; for the first ten thousand yards it would be under the direct command of the submarine's fire control computer.

Spartan rolled slightly from the discharge, and had yet to right itself when a second Spearfish emerged from a starboard tube. It followed the same launch procedure, and tracked along the same course, as the first torpedo. With both Spearfish away, *Spartan* turned sharply to align itself with their new heading. For the first ten minutes of their run, the submarine would have to prevent their cables from getting damaged or fouled in order to control them.

"TASCO Room to control, the *Spartan* has fired torpedoes," said Burks, watching the symbol for the British attack sub change color, and two lines from it start to etch their way across the tactical map. "It reports impact time to be fifteen minutes. The Brits also report the *Foxtrot* has started pinging, and sonar confirms it. Dave wants to know if he should begin active sonar scans."

"Negative, the Brits have beaten us to the punch," said Carver. "There's no need for us to fire, or make our presence known. Fifteen minutes is a long time and we can still be a target. Have you been able to contact Glenn?"

"No, Captain. The activity on the rig is pretty hectic and Commander Allard may have gone back inside one of its compartments, which means we're not being heard."

"Keep sending the warning and expand it into a general alert for all commando squads. Do the Israelis have any new translations of that Arabic chatter?"

"Mr. Adir reports the final broadcasts from the *Sword of*

the Revolution were less angry," Burks advised. "Its Captain may have guessed *Valkyrie* was under attack. Then transmissions abruptly ceased. They're on to us."

"Correction, they're on to the British," said Adir, cutting into the conversation. "I see what your Captain's attempting. The Libyans have concluded there's a commando attack and a submarine must've launched it. With *Spartan* firing torpedoes, they now have their sub and Mr. Carver hopes we can avoid further detection."

"If you ever want to be a sub skipper, Mr. Adir, I'll give your navy a recommendation," said Carver. "It doesn't pay to reveal yourself if you don't have to. Taylor on the *Spartan* wanted the first shot, so I let him have it. With a little luck we won't ever be detected."

"I'll be grateful for that," Gavrilla admitted a moment later. "How I wish this would be all over. I'd even prefer to be on the oil rig. At least I'd be in the open."

"Wait, someone's approaching," said Boyd in a low whisper; nonetheless, it brought the rest of his squad to a halt. "Hold fire until they're identified."

With a brief motion of his hand, the men accompanying Boyd spread out and crouched on either side of the passageway. They were still scrambling when noises at the passage's far end became more audible. With his infrared goggles Boyd could see figures advancing cautiously in the distance, freeze suddenly and dive for cover. Though he couldn't identify the individuals, from the way they moved he was able to easily identify the group.

"Rutherford, bring the Americans forward," Boyd ordered. "And explain why you're up here."

An affirmative response erased any lingering doubt as to who the others were. The two squads quickly jumped to their feet and met near the passage's halfway point. Once they got close enough to see each other in the dim light, Boyd and Rutherford removed their goggles and exchanged salutes.

"Sir, we took Mr. Landham's objectives, and found both the armory and the explosives stores to be empty," said Rutherford, his hand dropping back to his side. "Would you want us to help Mr. Ackland?"

"He's already secured the hospital and activities lounge," said Boyd. "Right now I need your help more than he does. The remaining terrorists are on the production platform. Mr. Allard is already there, but we need more than his squad to take it properly. Go back to those stairs and turn left. Take the second stairway you come across—it'll lead directly to the surface. You'll emerge on the platform's northern corner. My squad will come up closer to its center, where Allard believes most of the terrorists are working. Be careful topside. The terrorists are using crews of hostages to do the actual drilling. We can still have a sticky situation before we're finished."

The closer they crept to the drilling derrick the more apparent it became to Allard's squad that the terrorists were preparing for a siege. They could see the Norwegian work crews being corralled into one area, and the terrorists were attempting to take up defensive positions; mostly in shadow.

"Another five minutes and we wouldn't have been able to see any of them," said Allard, watching the frenzied activity. "We haven't any time to waste. Donner, take your team and free the hostages. Be ready to move in one minute."

Allard and Donner synchronized their watches. The lieutenant moved out with his team while Allard edged forward with the rest of his men. Keeping to shadows themselves, and crawling wherever possible, they got to within several yards of the derrick and pump station. Erica was briefly brought up to identify Nazal for Allard, then returned to her hiding place. By then, only seconds were left before the attack would begin.

"Commander, I still can't raise operations or anyone below the production platform!" Kashani shouted, dropping the telephone handset from his ear. "Do you want me to continue?"

"No! Whoever has attacked us must hold every levell but ours!" said Nazal, raising his voice so he could be heard above the pumps and emergency diesel generators. "We must hold here for as long as possible! Hurry, hide where you can and be ready to kill the hostages!"

The subordinate acknowledged his orders, and had just turned to leave when he staggered and fell. For an instant Nazal thought he'd been clumsy and shouted at him to get up. A second later he heard return fire from his men and saw shadows materialize from the night.

Allard held his fire until he saw the guards near the hostages fall. The time he needed to signal his men to attack meant he was one of the last to come out of hiding. He slid out from under a pipe support frame and caught sight of a terrorist sprinting toward the pump station.

"No! Go back! Go back!" Nazal shouted. "I have enough men here. Find cover!"

The terrorist running up to Nazal seemed to takeoff in mid-stride. Allard's burst of submachinegun fire caught him in the back and lifted him off his feet. By the time he crashed to the floor, Nazal had gone into hiding.

"No, take care of the hostages," said Allard, when he saw another team running to join him. "This bastard's mine!"

"Asir, you're closer to the control box!" said Nazal, firing a wild burst from his Mac-10. "Detonate the explosives in this area! We'll take our enemies with us."

"They're behind us, Commander!" Kashani screamed. "I can't reach it!"

Kashani's cry became more animalistic, and his AKM rifle clattered to the deck beside Nazal. Snapping out another burst in Allard's direction, he rose to fire on the SEALs who had circled behind the pump station. He had scarcely stood up when he felt a hammer-like blow in his side.

The impact threw Nazal away from the diesel generator he'd been hiding behind and he fell against a hopper tank. His Mac-10 slipped from his hands. By the time he realized it was gone Allard had come out from cover and was standing in front of him.

"This'll be a pleasure," said Allard, squeezing the trigger of his MP-5, but apart from a hard clicking, nothing else happened. "Shit!" Allard swore.

Working the release lever, he ripped the empty clip out of his Heckler and Koch and grabbed a replacement one from his belt. Allard rearmed the weapon as fast as he could, faster than he had done during any exercise, but it still wasn't swift enough to beat Nazal from drawing his automatic.

"This will be . . . *my* pleasure!" he gasped, holding his side with one hand while levelling the Baretta with the other. Then the anger burning in his eyes gave way to shock. "You! You! You're dead!"

A glowing neon bullet sputtered past Allard and hit Nazal in the stomach. The magnesium flare melted through his winter jacket, his shirt, his skin. Its incandescent fire virtually disappeared as the flare burned its way inside Nazal.

His scream cut through the wind and machine noises like a knife. He folded his hands over the charred hole in his jacket and doubled up, but Nazal didn't lose his grip on his Baretta. Clutching it tightly, the automatic's butt end slipped easily into the hole—the hole where it was exposed to the searing temperatures which were consuming Nazal alive.

"That's a nasty little weapon you got there," said Allard, whirling around to face Nazal's killer. "But didn't I tell you to stay where you were safe?"

"A good trick is always worth using twice," said Erica. "And I'm sorry, but I had to see him die."

Even though she was speaking to Allard, she did not take her eyes off Nazal, who by now was rolling on the deck and still shrieking like an animal. Allard quickly finished rearming his MP-5 and turned it on Nazal. All around him he could hear cheering break out; if he worked fast, Allard would have the honor of killing the last terrorist at the site.

"No, let him alone," Erica requested, putting a hand on his arm. "I want him to suffer."

"Aren't you being a little cold-blooded?" asked Allard. But before he could get a response, a rapid series of explosions caused them to dive for cover. When it finished, Allard peered out from behind the diesel generator and found Nazal's body had stopped moving, though it was still smoking.

"He shot himself," said Erica. "I should've known he would take a quicker death and cheat me."

"I don't think so. Those 'shots' came very rapidly. Please, turn off some of this equipment. I'll check Nazal."

While Erica went to the pump station controls, Allard kneeled to examine the body. The magnesium flare still burned inside it, still sizzled and bubbled as it melted flesh. In the remnants of Nazal's hands, Allard saw what looked like a gun and managed to kick the object free. He had just picked it up when the noise level fell dramatically.

"I switched off the pumps for the drilling mud," Erica reported. "What did you find?"

"This," said Allard, holding the Baretta automatic by its barrel. It was the only reasonably intact part of the weapon; the rest had been mangled and rent open. Especially the grip. "Abu Nazal didn't shoot himself, his gun exploded. It must've been like holding a grenade when it goes off. It may have been quick but it wasn't painless."

"Commander, the drilling site is secure and the hostages have been freed," said Donner as he approached the pump station. "And we have visitors."

The Lieutenant pointed behind Allard, who spun around to find Boyd's squad appearing out of the darkness beyond the work lights, accompanied by one of his own assault teams.

"It appears as though we're late for this party," said

Boyd. "We had a slight identity problem with your men here. It delayed us a little."

"What happened? Did you guys open fire on the Brits?" Allard asked.

"Well, sort of . . ." said the team leader. "But we didn't hit anybody."

"It's only to be expected, Glenn. Especially with all of us running around in the dark," said Boyd, before turning to Erica and changing the conversation. "You must be Mrs. Johensen. Sorry for not introducing myself earlier. I'm Colonel Robert Boyd, Royal Marines. I want to congratulate you for surviving this crisis. If you were in the military, your courage would guarantee you a medal."

"I just want these terrorists to be killed and for the madness to end," said Erica. "My friends have suffered enough."

"It'll end soon, I promise you. The remaining terrorists are being hunted down. What we must do now is hunt for the bio-weapon containers. Since the terrorists have started drilling operations, the containers must be in this area. Divide up and search for them — let's not waste any time."

"Hurry, Nazir. We must activate the other charges," urged one of the terrorists in the tiny group.

"Finished, Mohamad. This line of explosives will detonate in ninety seconds," said Abdelgalil, closing the lid on the control box he was hunched over. All its displays were on and its digital clock was already ticking off the remaining seconds. "We can go to the next station."

The other two terrorists helped Nazir Abdelgalil to stand, then handed him his AK-47. Barely audible over the wind and drilling noises was the popping of gunfire. They knew the production platform was under attack, but the enemy had not yet reached their position on the platform's outer edge.

After activating the first control box, the group climbed a flight of stairs from the second level to the top one. Still on its outer edge, they were only a few yards from their next objective, one of *Valkyrie*'s saline injection wells. Abdelgalil ordered one of his men to stand guard, while he and Mohamand went searching for another control box.

"We placed the control station somewhere here," Abdelgalil explained. "Look near the saline well. I'll check this area."

Because of the danger from unseen enemies, no one in the group used flashlights. Using the weak, available illumination they hunted around almost by touch. Even with one of them acting as a guard, none of the terrorists ever saw the darker forms moving from shadow to shadow.

"I can't find anything, Nazir!" said Mohamand.

"Keep looking! We hid the station under some piping," said Abdelgalil, then his hand smashed into a plastic box just over a foot long and six inches tall. He felt its cover's prominent seam line and quickly unlocked its catch. "I have it! Mohamand, I found it! Hurry, we have no time to lose. Mohamand?"

Abdelgalil stood and scanned for his companion, but found he was suddenly alone. He was still raising the AK-47 when he finally got an answer to his shouted commands.

"Hey, camel driver. You're nicked."

Landham waited until Abdelgalil had turned to face him before squeezing the trigger. The MP-5 chattered heavily and long, even after the first slugs had hit the terrorist, even after the assault rifle had dropped from his hands. Abdelgalil staggered backward until he ran out of deck. He collided with the guard rail and flipped over it, landing in the sea with an audible splash a few seconds later.

"Camel driver, eh?" Rutherford observed. "I like that."

"And I like 'nicking,' " said Landham, walking up to the guard rail. "We better get Lieutenant Chen here to disarm the detonator bow we found. Maybe . . ."

"What's wrong, Johnnie? You see something odd?"

"Yeah, you bet it's odd. Someone must've pushed the down button on this elevator. We're a lot closer to the sea

307

than I thought."

"You're right, we *are* closer," said Rutherford, joining Landham at the guard rail and briefly shining his flashlight on the surface. "The support legs appear to be submerging. We'd better warn Mr. Boyd and your Mr. Allard about this. We should leave one of your teams and report to them immediately."

"Control to TASCO Room, what's the condition of the Spearfish?" Carver asked, checking his watch for their lapsed running time.

"They're running hot, straight and normal," said Burks. "They're cruising at thirty knots, but will accelerate to attack speed once they shed their guidance cables."

"And what about the *Foxtrot?*"

"It's increasing speed and maneuvering fast. It's bow-on to our position, but not pointing at either us or *Spartan*. Sonar reports—sonar reports torpedo launch! Passive array has detected sounds of positive discharge from the Libyans!"

"Count the number of discharges," Carver ordered. "Let's find out what kind of torpedo spread we're dealing with. Jim, prepare the simulator."

With the press of a button, Doran activated an automatic data feed to the Mobile Submarine Simulator (MOSS). Until the moment of its launch, it would receive any target information entered into the fire control system. With the torpedo tube doors already open, and the tubes pressurized for discharge, all that remained was for the *Marshall* to maneuver into position; and for Carver to give the firing orders.

"We have three confirmed . . ." said Burks, his voice trailing off until another track appeared on his screen, then another. "Four . . . five . . . and we have six! A full spread for a submarine of this class. The torpedoes appear to be separating into two distinct groups."

"Start ranging with the BQQ," said Carver. "Let's get an

accurate targeting fix on the incoming torpedoes before we respond. Clarence, increase speed to ten knots and prepare for starboard turn."

The active component to the *Marshall*'s BQQ sonar suite, unused since the submarine had entered the North Sea, began firing its sonic pulses into the already noisy waters. More powerful than either the Herkules or PARIS systems being used, it took the BQQ less than twenty seconds to get data on not only the torpedo groups, but the Libyan sub as well.

"TASCO Room to control, *Spartan* confirms hostile torpedo launch," Burks advised. "And they're slowing down the Spearfish, they're going to try reprogramming them to intercept the incoming weapons."

"An anti-torpedo torpedo?" said Carver. "I hope the Spearfish has the capability. Feed targeting data to the helm station. Have you anything on what the Libyans are using?"

"Their torpedoes are Soviet anti-submarine types. T-Fourteen vintage, free-running and active acoustic homing."

"Jim, do you have that?"

"Yes, Captain. Switching MOSS to signal interrogation and seduction jamming," Doran answered. "She's ready to go."

"Clarence?" It was the only thing Carver needed to say.

"Steering course zero-three-nine degrees," said Jefferson. "Maintaining current depth."

"Fire number one, Mr. Doran. And standby on the Mark Forty-eights. Clarence, be prepared to bring us to a full stop."

Coming out from under the shadow of *Valkyrie,* the *Marshall* swung to the northeast. As it finished, one of the sub's portside tubes emitted a cloud of bubbles—and a twenty-foot-long torpedo-shaped vehicle.

The Mobile Submarine Simulator (MOSS) had the same propulsion system as a Mark 48, but carried no warhead and had a far more sophisticated guidance system. No command wires trailed out behind it. From the moment of its launch the MOSS was completely autonomous from its parent craft.

Designed to be destroyed, the simulator would commence its decoy maneuvers within the first minutes of its run. Already its on-board systems were identifying the sonar echoes of the approaching torpedoes. Already it had differentiated between the two groups and which posed a threat to the *Marshall*. While the submarine prepared to shut down all its noise-making equipment, the MOSS was set to assume its identity.

"Yes, these resemble the 'cages' the Israelis told us about," said Boyd, examining a tangle of plastic scrap. "But you found no capsules?"

"No, Colonel. We're still looking," said one of his men. "The Americans may have better luck. The Norwegian woman is helping them."

"Robert, we got 'em!" Allard shouted, and for the moment he was hidden from view by the pump station's hopper tank. "We found the transport containers."

Allard's shout brought Boyd and the rest of his team running. As they rounded the corner the SEALs were pulling the second steel box out into the open. Its catches were unfastened and clinked audibly when the box was set down.

"I don't like this. They're unlocked," said Allard, crouching in front of the first one. With Boyd and Erica standing over him, he raised the lid; and all three groaned loudly when the case turned out to be empty.

"Try the other one," said Boyd. "We need a sample of this bacteria for our scientists to study."

Allard pulled the second container over and quickly flipped open its lid, only to find that it, too, was empty.

"Damn it, have any of you seen any glass capsules?" he asked, addressing the SEALs and Royal Marines around him.

"Glenn, there's only one place the capsules, and the bacteria they contained, could be," said Boyd. "According to the Israelis, at this stage of the operation they would be here."

Boyd turned and walked up to the hopper tank, where he unlocked a handle and swung open the hatch plate. With the mixing equipment switched off, the huge paddles were no longer stirring the grey-black mud in the tank. Its surface was now still, and gave almost no reflection in Boyd's flashlight beam; except for the occasional fragment of glass.

"Now how will you get a sample?" said Erica.

"Easier than you think," Allard replied. "I always wanted to know why I had to carry this on short-term missions, now I see why."

Unfastening the snaps, Allard pulled his canteen out of its pouch. With a quick twist he had its cap off and was dumping out its contents. When he had emptied it, Allard stepped over to the hatch and plunged his canteen into the syrup-like mess.

"Of course. Why didn't I think of it first?" said Boyd, emptying his own canteen.

As soon as Allard had finished, Boyd moved in and started the same procedure. He had yet to fill his canteen when a heavy clanging filled the air. It sounded, and felt, like rolling thunder. It caused the soldiers to either dive for cover, or bring up their weapons to ward off an attack.

"Christ, what the bloody hell was that?" Boyd demanded, getting back on his feet. He reached into the hopper tank for his canteen.

"I don't know. It sounded like the drill tower was coming down," said Allard, defensively sweeping the area with his MP-5.

"Haven't you people ever heard a pipe rack collapse before?" said Erica. "We always keep a ready supply of drill pipe beside the derrick — it's on the other side."

"I didn't hear any gunfire from my men or Robert's. There isn't a counterattack by the terrorists, if there are any

311

left. So why did the pipes fall?"

"I can't—no, wait, it's the platform. It's listing! That's what I've been feeling."

"Are you certain?" Boyd inquired.

"Of course I am," said Erica. "Everything was too busy for me to think about it earlier. Watch."

Erica took her used flare stick and laid it on the floor. The moment she released it, the plastic tube rolled away until it disappeared under one of the emergency generators.

"My guess is we're listing fifteen degrees at least," she added.

"As I recall, you're part of *Valkyrie's* stability and buoyancy staff," said Boyd. "Are we in danger of sinking?"

"Yes, and with ballast control destroyed we have no way of stopping it. *Ocean Valkyrie* is doomed. We'd better evacuate."

"Just when we thought it was safe to stay on the rig, we have to go back in the water," said Allard, looking down at the control unit for his personal radio pack. "We have to warn our men, Robert. I'm changing frequencies to tell the submarines we're sinking. They'll have to surface to rescue us. *Marshall,* this is—"

The deck heaved and rippled under his feet, catching Allard off-guard and off-balance. He and the others either fell or had to grab something for support as shock waves continued to jar the platform. On its northern side a series of thunderclap explosions tore open the second deck. One of the injection wells sank by several feet, and leaned over dangerously when the top deck buckled because of the damage. Its fate already sealed, the destruction of *Ocean Valkyrie* had begun.

Chapter Nineteen

"Spearfish now moving at fifteen knots," said Hodgkiss, barely looking up from the controls at his weapons station. "Targeting programs erased. New program load commencing."

"How long will it take to complete?" Taylor asked, a glimmer of anxiety in his voice.

"A matter of seconds, then all I have to do is execute it."

"Good. Mr. Bryan, stand by for evasion maneuvers. What are the Americans doing?"

"The *Marshall* has launched its simulator and has come to a stop," said Bryan, pointing to the symbols on one of his station's display screens. "I don't know if they're going to silent sub operations, or if this is a new evasion tactic."

"I can't tell either," said Taylor. "But if they stay out of our way I'll be happy. Mr. Hodgkiss, are you ready?"

"Ready and executing new programs."

With the press of a button, the torpedoes more than two miles away were given their new targets and restarted their attack runs. In seconds they had more than tripled their speed and were homing in on the sonar pulses of the approaching T-14s.

"Spearfish away. Speed, forty-five knots and accelerating," Hodgkiss advised. "Readouts confirm they've switched modes to Home-on-Threat and are on their new tracks. Predicted interception will occur in six minutes, thirty-nine seconds."

Are they capable of autonomous attack?" Taylor asked.

"From this point on, yes. Those Libyan torpedoes aren't

about to change their sonar frequencies."

"Then disengage the links. Load tubes two and three with seduction jammers. Mr. Bryan, flank speed. Steer course one-one-zero degrees and take us down, three hundred feet."

The fiber-optic cables were cut at their sources inside the torpedo tubes. As they drifted away, *Spartan* surged ahead and rolled into a starboard turn like it was an aircraft. It dropped its nose and dove for the sea bed. If the Spearfish failed, the submarine would attempt to hide in the bottom topography of the North Sea.

"Christ, my ears," said Landham, picking himself off the deck. His sense of balance still disrupted by the explosions, he grabbed hold of a pipe support to steady himself. He shook his head several times to clear it, and dug at his ears with his little fingers. "Rutherford? Sergeant, can you hear me? Are you okay?"

"God, my head's ringing like a belfry," said Rutherford, who turned in Landham's direction when he realized a tiny, garbled voice was trying to get his attention. "John, if you're trying to talk to me don't bother. I'm deaf. Fan out and collect our men!"

In addition to shouting, Rutherford used hand signals to indicate what he wanted. After some confused moments Landham understood the orders and staggered over to the other men who were recovering from the explosions.

Most could stand, and for those who could not he organized others to carry them. No one appeared seriously injured, just varying degrees of shock created by the explosions. In between helping his men and the British, Landham was able to take some brief glances at what had been destroyed.

The place where they had stood only minutes before was torn open and buckled by the detonations which had ripped apart the deck below. In some areas the flooring had collapsed, while the saline injection well teetered precariously to one side.

"Lieutenant! Lieutenant, we're over here!" Landham shouted, when he caught sight of a familiar face.

"Landham, what the hell happened?" Chen asked, making his way through the dazed SEALs and Marines to reach the squad commanders. "Did you activate the detonator control you found?"

"I didn't get all what you said but no, none of us touched the box. What do you think we are? Stupid?"

"No, from the way you're acting I'd say you're deaf."

"Of course we're deaf, and damn glad to be it, sir. If we had stayed where we were, we'd have been blown to bits like Martirri. We—"

Landham's answer was cut short by a screech of tearing metal even his numbed ears could detect. He and the others turned in time to see the injection well complete its collapse. Like a falling redwood, the massive tower dropped slowly and gracefully. Its impact with the deck was a heavy, jarring crash felt by everyone on the rig.

The damaged section it landed on held for only a moment longer, quickly giving way with the clang and screech of metal. The tower upended and toppled off the platform, hitting the water with a resounding splash. For several seconds its ragged base bobbed up and down; until the rest of the structure filled with water and sank.

"Christ, how much is that going to cost?" Landham asked, above the rush of air escaping from the tower.

"Try about three hundred million dollars," said Chen. "This rig's a total loss. The *Marshall*'s been trying to warn us for the last ten minutes—it's sinking and unless we get off we'll sink with it. The terrorists are dead. They're no longer a problem. All we have to do is evacuate and bring the civilians with us. We're to rendezvous with Glenn and Colonel Boyd at the drilling derrick. Sergeant, round your men up as well. There will be plenty of work for all of us."

"Will you take a look at that," said Allard, as he pointed at the collapsing tower. "I guess you're right, Erica, this rig is falling apart. How much rescue gear does *Valkyrie* have?"

"More than enough for us," said Erica. "Even with the north side apparently destroyed. *Valkyrie* is well equipped. We learned from earlier disasters to make it so."

"Then you'll have to show us where everything's stored," Boyd answered. "Glenn, I'm finding it difficult to contact our people still inside the rig. The phone at this site is damaged, so I'll go to operations and alert them from there. What's the password for your people in the power station?"

"The challenge is 'jumbo.' The response is 'shrimp,' " said Allard. Then he repeated it when he got a questioning look from Boyd. "Jumbo Shrimp. I'm big on oxymorons."

"All right, I guess I'll have to accept it. I'll try to restore power. Keep trying to raise the *Marshall,* and tell Carver we need him topside now."

Even though they had killed or accounted for all the terrorists, Boyd still signalled for one of his men to accompany him as a guard. They had turned and were just leaving the pump station area when the flooring quivered again and dropped out from under them.

Valkyrie's southeastern base leg had finally succumbed to the damage created by the explosion at ballast control. With an almost human moaning, the supports holding the leg to the main structure twisted and snapped clean. The multistory platform crashed onto the leg, falling by almost ten feet in the southeastern corner.

On the rest of the platform the drop was not as great, though it still caught people off-guard. Fortunately, they had learned to roll with it and not to keep standing while the oil rig went through its convulsions. After he collected his MP-5, Boyd got to his feet and signalled to Allard that he would continue.

"I hope he can get some lights back on — we'll need them," said Allard, before he returned to his original activity. *"Marshall,* this is Eagle One. *Marshall,* this is Eagle One. We acknowledge your warning and we're abandoning *Valkyrie.* Please surface as soon as possible, we'll be needing your help. Over."

"Is the way behind us clear?" Carver asked.

"Yes, sir. We're clear of the drill shafts and the rig's ballast tanks," said Jefferson.

"Control to TASCO Room, how's the MOSS performing?"

"It's begun seduction jamming," Burks answered, "and appears to be drawing off the torpedoes."

"Good. Let's give ourselves room to maneuver in case the MOSS fails," said Carver. "Clarence, one-quarter reverse speed."

After remaining motionless for only a few minutes, the *Marshall* slowly started to back up. Even though the simulator was now miles away, if it failed to decoy all the torpedoes the sub would need all the time it could gain to avoid them.

"We're moving aft at five knots," said Jefferson, watching his readouts increase incrementally. "Maintaining current depth and heading. Captain, there's something strange on the laser radar. Take a look."

Pointing at the system's screen, Jefferson traced the fall of an object in front of the submarine. Leaning over his helmsman's shoulder, Carver watched it silently for a moment before speaking.

"What the hell is it?" he said.

"Whatever it is, it's heavy," Jefferson replied. "Look at how fast it's sinking. There's another one."

"Control to TASCO Room, we got some sort of debris falling around us. Are they from the rig?"

"You bet. The hydrophones are detecting a real barrage from above. You'll be seeing a lot more of it in a few seconds."

"Maybe we can use it," Carver said slowly, a smile appearing on his face. "It'll make the perfect curtain to hide behind. Full reverse, Clarence. Order the engine room to lock down the rafts. I don't care if we make noise now, we have to take advantage of this."

"Captain, we have a request from Glenn," Burks added. "He says the commandoes and rig crew are abandoning *Valkyrie*. We're needed on the surface to rescue them."

"Tell him we'll drain the swamp later. Right now we're up to our necks in alligators."

The sudden increase in power shook the *Marshall*'s massive hull. It created more noise, but also caused a dramatic jump in speed. In just over a minute the submarine was sail-

317

ing backward at twenty knots, and moving out from under the rain of debris from the doomed oil rig.

"Bottom coming up, Captain," said Bryan. "I can level her out, but there appears to be a trench to port."

"Perfect. Steer for the trench," said Taylor, glancing at the topography being shown on the helm station screens. "Reduce speed to fifteen knots."

Diving at a velocity of more than thirty miles an hour, *Spartan* rolled to the left and slowed as it prepared to enter the trench detected by its sonar. Cutting its speed by half both reduced its noise emissions and improved the capabilities of its PARIS sonar. As the attack sub came out of its turn, the outer doors on its second and third torpedo tubes opened again.

"Captain, the Spearfish still appear to be on their intercept tracks," Hodgkiss reported. "The Libyan torpedoes are changing course but not depth."

"We'll have trouble if the Spearfish don't destroy them," said Taylor. "Put them on manual control and fire jammers one and two."

Within seconds of each other, shots of compressed air ejected two Marconi Type Seventeen jammers. Unlike the MOSS simulator, the jammers had no propulsion or guidance systems. Neutrally buoyant, they would stabilize once the submarine had passed by and float freely. They would deploy trailing wire antennae and await the commands to begin transmitting sonar echoes and noises identical to those of a *Swiftsure*-class attack submarine.

"Captain, the north side of the trench is taller than the south side," said Bryan, adjusting the resolution of the helm screens.

"Steer for it — we'll try to hide in its shadow," Taylor ordered. "Reduce speed to ten knots. Prepare to come to a full stop."

As *Spartan* dove past the six-hundred foot-mark it dropped below the mean sea bed level for the area. It entered the trench and maneuvered carefully up to the northern side.

318

Using its 2019 PARIS array, the submarine scanned for the most favorable location and chose a section of the trench side with a slight overhang. There, it came to a halt and waited for the Libyan torpedoes to either be decoyed or destroyed.

"Roger, *Marshall.* I understand," said Allard. "Good luck. We'll all be in the water by the time you surface."

"What's wrong, Glenn?" Chen asked. "Can't we get our ride when we need it?" His words were joking but his face held a hint of anxiety. How could they possibly rescue all these civilians, and in the dark, no less!

"Not when it's being shot at," answered Allard. "The Libyans have fired torpedoes at both the *Marshall* and *Spartan,* so not only do they have to sink the enemy, they have to avoid being sunk by them — Good God! What was that?"

A barrage of artillery-like cracks filled the air around the derrick. Unlike previous events, the deck didn't move or buckle; but the noises caused Landham, Rutherford and their men to cover ears which had since become sensitive.

"Christ, I think I liked it better when these were numb," said Landham, cupping his hands over his ears.

"Those were the drill shafts and pipes snapping," said Erica. "The tilting of the platform is putting severe stress on them. The rest will soon break as well."

"I get the feeling this rig is telling us to leave," Allard replied. "Sergeant, you getting any new orders from Mr. Boyd?"

"Yes, he's requesting all of us to gather at the operations center," said Rutherford. "He says the rest of your men are heading there as well, Commander."

"Then we'd better move out. Sergeant, take your team and help shepherd the hostages to operations. Erica, take us back. It should be easier this time."

Several minutes earlier, partial lighting had been restored to *Ocean Valkyrie.* Though a lot had been damaged during the recapture, what survived plus the emergency lighting had again bestowed an aura of surreal beauty to the oil rig. And with the terrorists gone, the commandoes could take the easiest and most direct route back to operations.

They moved down one of the walkways, hindered only occasionally by rolling or falling debris. All around them was the crash and clang of loose objects tumbling down the incline the platform had assumed. When they reached operations, they found a nearby service entrance open and, for Erica, some very familiar people pouring out of it.

"God! My God!" said Jansen, moving out of the line of rig crew. "Erica, you're alive? Captain, she's alive!"

At first he moved hesitantly, then Jansen broke into a run and reached Erica in a few strides. He embraced her, sweeping her off her feet as he swung her around. They cried against each others' shoulder and Erica had barely been set down, barely had the time to explain how she had survived, when someone else picked her off her feet.

"Erica! I couldn't believe what Ned was shouting about," said Reitan, lifting her up, though not as high as Jansen had been able to. "How did you get out of the helicopter? Did anyone else escape?"

"Frieda Gran and Trig," Erica managed to say. "A British submarine rescued them. These men are from an American one."

"Looks like you're having quite a reunion," said Allard. "But under these circumstances you'd better continue it another time. Commander Glenn Allard, United States Navy SEALs."

"Thank you for helping in our rescue," said Reitan, putting Erica down. "The British told me your men died in the first explosion. I'm sorry."

"Glenn, you and the Captain can chat later," Boyd advised, standing at one of the operation center's blown-out windows. "I need you in here. Captain, if that's your safety officer with you, then bring him in here."

As a group the people around Allard followed him into the battle-damaged center. Reitan entered it with a sad resignation. The level of destruction made him finally realize his command was doomed. Boyd was at rig communications, one of the few consoles still working, talking to his executive officer.

"Captain, my number two needs personnel to help evacuate the wounded from your hospital," said Boyd. "Can you send some people down there?"

"Of course. And since Ned is stronger and can run faster, he'll command the people I send," said Reitan. "Are your submarines going to surface to pick us up?"

"Glenn, what's the answer from Terence?"

"His answer was something about being up to his neck in alligators," Allard replied. "They've been engaged by the *Sword of the Revolution*. They're going to have to sink it before turning to us."

"Sword of what? Is there another submarine out there?"

"Yes, a Libyan sub. And I can understand why our boats will have to sink it first," said Boyd, before putting the telephone handset back to his ear. "Ross, we'll be sending you some people shortly. Prepare the wounded for transport, and stay where you are. Lion One, out. Captain, could your safety officer show us where the rescue equipment is located?"

Boyd pointed to the damage control station; though no longer operational, it did have top and side view silhouettes of *Valkyrie*. Together with Jansen and Reitan, Allard and Boyd gathered around the station for a brief conference.

"Most of our equipment is located here," said Jansen, running his hand along the oil rig's eastern side. "Directly under the helipad are the escape capsules. There are five in all, each capable of holding around forty people. We have inflatable rafts on the other three sides, though the ones on the northern side are no longer useable."

"Do the capsules need special training to operate?" Allard asked.

"Not really, but there is a specialized launch procedure you must follow. It would probably be best for each capsule to have several of our crew to help man it."

"Agreed," said Boyd. "It would be highly ironic for the best commandoes in the world to die using unfamiliar rescue equipment. Captain, select the men you want to send to the hospital and Mr. Jansen, bring everyone from the hospital to the helipad. Work fast. There's no way to prevent *Valkyrie* from sinking. Glenn, I'm going to stay here to coordinate the evacuation. I want you and your men at the helipad to see that everyone gets safely off. Be certain you save me a seat in the last capsule."

At a speed of nearly seventy knots, the Spearfish were almost twice as fast as the T-14 torpedoes they were intercepting. Since their launch, the vintage Soviet weapons had spread out and were now several hundred yards apart. They no longer presented the Spearfish with one target, one acoustic signature, but three. It forced their on-board computers to select among them.

Assigning numerical values to each source, the computers instantly chose the loudest, and the closest to themselves. Unfortunately, they both chose the same one.

The two Spearfish, their Sundstrand engines and pump jets screaming loudly, homed in on the same T-14. When they reached proximity fuse range their thousand pound warheads detonated simultaneously. The shock waves they created ripped into the torpedo, fracturing it along its seam lines.

In turn, its warhead exploded as it separated from the propulsion section. The shock waves joined those of the Spearfish and rippled out to the remaining T-14s. No longer powerful enough to destroy the weapons, they did cause the second torpedo to tumble out of control. The directional gyros were unable to stabilize the weapon and it plunged toward the sea bed, eventually exploding in the mud.

"Sound room to attack center, we've detected another T-14 detonation," Greenway advised. "There's still one inbound."

"Has it changed to a search pattern?" said Taylor.

"Not yet, but according to our information on the T-14 series it soon will."

"Then we better have a target ready when it does. Captain to ECM, activate number one jammer."

"Stan, will we have to hold off firing until this third tor-

322

pedo is destroyed?" asked Holbrook.

"Yes, just like in all our exercises," said Taylor, glancing over at the weapons station; where his executive officer had joined Hodgkiss. "All incoming fish have to be neutralized before we can return fire."

"Then the *Marshall* will get the next shot at the Libyans, provided it can successfully decoy the torpedoes homing after it. The Americans are still maneuvering oddly. They're continuing in reverse and haven't taken any evasive action. I hope they know what they're doing."

Several thousand yards behind *Spartan,* one of the two seduction jammers it had released started to ping and rumble just like the attack sub. Once the last T-14 commenced a search pattern it would become the obvious target, and hovering near the bottom, the torpedo would be unable to detect the difference between the jammer and a full-size submarine until it was too late.

"Gavrilla, will you shut up!" Eshel demanded, growing impatient with the quiet whimpering from his teammate. "I can't stand it anymore!"

"Stop it, Captain!" said Adir. "Bad enough we're prickly with our friends, now we're prickly with ourselves."

"I'm sorry . . . I'm sorry," Gavrilla sobbed, pressed flat against the port wall again. "I just wish this were over."

"Curious, how a woman will respond to fear by crying, but a man will respond with anger and posturing. Don't worry, Gavi, it will soon be over."

"Damn it, Avrom, how can you stand there and say so?" said Eshel. "Do you understand what these people are doing? If so, please explain it to me because I think they're crazy."

"Christ, why did you bring him along, Mr. Adir?" Burks asked, taking his attention off the screens and displays for a moment and facing the Israelis.

"At times I wonder about that as well, Commander," said Adir. "I guess because he's good at interrogation, a trait he's been somewhat over-zealous with. Has anything new happened?"

"No, but something's about to. Our crazy maneuvers are paying off. Have a look."

This time even Gavrilla stepped forward to get a better look at the TASCO Room's main screen. Midway between the *Marshall* and the *Sword of the Revolution* were the symbols for the MOSS and the torpedoes. They were practically on top of the simulator; a few moments later they were.

One by one, as the sensitive hydrophone arrays recorded the distant explosions, the symbols for the T-14s were evaporated. When the arrays detected the break-up noises of the MOSS, its lozenge-shaped marker began to fade and flicker out. Before it had finished disappearing, Burks was advising Carver they had succeeded.

"Good, now it's time to kick their ass," Carver replied. "Clarence, one-half reverse speed. Captain to sonar, begin active ranging. Jim, standby to fire two and three. Greg, I want updates on *Spartan* and the *Foxtrot*."

From sailing backward at twenty knots, the *Marshall* slowed until it was doing ten. Its BQQ sonar had the *Foxtrot* targeted after firing the first few pulses. Maneuvering tail first, the submarine had to wait a little longer than normal for its bow tubes to come on target.

"The Libyans have indeed moved to deeper waters," said Burks, reading the newest information to appear on his screens. "They're at three hundred feet and descending. *Spartan* has gone to silent sub operations and appears to be hiding in a trench."

"Then it's our chance to fire," said Carver. "Jim, are you ready?"

"If we could turn the bows a few more degrees I'd be happier," said Doran. "And what about that junk falling off the rig? It could foul or break the guidance wires."

"It's a risk we'll have to take. If you can live with it, start the launch procedure."

"Roger, cutting data feeds to two and three. Warheads, enabled. Propulsion and guidance systems, enabled. Attack profiles, confirmed. Ready to fire at your command."

The *Marshall* stopped turning, and held steady as it

launched first one, then a second Mark 48 torpedo. They emerged from sheaths of bubbles trailing guidance wires from their tail fins. The nineteen-foot-long weapons changed their course after being released, in accordance with their programming, and accelerated to flank speed. At more than sixty miles an hour they would need some twenty minutes to reach the *Foxtrot;* only the first six minutes would be under the *Marshall*'s control.

"Holy shit, there are waves hitting the platform," said Allard, standing at the edge of the deck below the helipad.

"We *are* sinking," Erica remarked, soberly. "Even with all the damage I've seen, I didn't believe it could really be happening until now.

What had once towered sixty feet above the surface was now close enough for waves to hit its platform base. Little could be seen of the oil rig's massive base legs. A few of their anti-collision beacons still flashed eerily on the submerged portions. As he examined it closer, Allard could see a distinct list in the platform to its northern side.

"Fucking assholes! Commander, the terrorists rigged this stuff with explosives!" Chen shouted, as he looked under one of the bright orange escape capsules.

"Find the detonator control and disarm them," said Allard, "and be quick about it. I hear someone coming. Landham, Jones, check the rest of the equipment."

While Chen traced the wires from the demolition charge he found, the other members of Allard's team spread out to examine the escape capsules. The five vehicles were nestled closely together under the helipad. They were lozenge-shaped, fifty feet long and completely enclosed. They had side hatches and portholes on their upper works, along with outsized rudders and stabilizer fins. Each capsule had its own set of launch rails and, curiously, a spool of nylon cable behind it.

"It's to help with the release," Erica explained, when she found Allard examining a cable and winch set-up. "We have to control the capsule's descent rate. We are twenty meters from the water, or rather were."

"Yes, now I understand why these boats need a special launching procedure," said Allard. "John, what's the problem over there?"

"It's this damn ice, Commander," said Landham, picking himself off the deck. "Everything's slick with it! It looks like no one came down here to clear the ice."

"Why should they? Not only weren't the terrorists going to use this gear, they were making sure no one else could as well. Get this first boat ready! The civilians are almost here."

Escorted by Royal Marines, a group of *Valkyrie's* crew appeared on a walkway leading from the platform's interior. None were wearing exposure suits or survival suits; most did not even have winter jackets on. It was considered too dangerous for them to return to their quarters for the necessary gear.

"I'm Sergeant Michael Heeks, Commander," said the highest ranking soldier among the new arrivals. "I have sixty-five civilians and eight Marines with me. I've been told to obey whatever orders you give."

"Good, we don't have time to argue over that, or anything else," Allard replied. "Select forty of the civilians and half your men to go aboard this boat, Sergeant."

Allard pointed to the escape capsule his SEALs were working on. After freeing the hatch locks from the ice encasing them, the commandoes pried them open. The snapping and crunch of ice accompanied the opening of each panel. They had barely been lifted when the rig crew Heeks was selecting stepped up to the vehicle.

For them the evacuation procedures were very familiar; they could almost have done them in their sleep. They climbed through the open hatches and spread out along the bench seating inside the capsule. In just over a minute the civilians had it filled and Heeks was busy choosing which of his men would go.

"Here it goes, Glenn!" Chen warned, tossing a demolition control box over the deck's guard rail. "All charges have been disarmed, wherever they are."

"Don't bother looking for them," said Allard. "Just get the

326

next capsule ready. Sergeant, how are you doing?"

"My men are going aboard," said Heeks, climbing off the vehicle's side. "And they'll let the civilians run the boat. If you ask me, it looks a trifle cramped in there."

"I doubt they'll have enough time to become claustrophobic. Close the hatches and clear the area! We're going to launch!"

As the hatches clicked shut, the capsule's inboard engine could be heard rattling to life. The last men to leave its vicinity banged on its side, and a few moments later the capsule started to roll down the launching rails. The hard, crystalline snapping of icicles from the rails accompanied the clanking of the winch as it released the cable.

At the end of its rails, the escape vehicle suddenly pitched down. With a final screech from its rollers, it disappeared over the edge of the deck. For several seconds only the clanking winch and the nylon cable zipping through its guides could be heard. Finally, a resounding splash echoed from below the platform. Those still on board moved to the guard rail in time to see the capsule sail out on its own power.

"Once they get some slack in the cable they'll unlock it," said Erica. "And one of them is probably using the emergency radio even now."

"Good, the Royal Navy has ships waiting just out of *Valkyrie's* radar range," said Allard. "They probably started moving in when the radar died, but helicopters won't take off until they receive a message. Back to work, boys and girls. We have to get the second capsule ready; there'll be more people here any minute."

Still unreeling their guidance wires, the Mark 48s had since separated to a distance of several hundred feet. Commanded to do so by the *Marshall*, the tactic would prove useful later when the torpedoes were autonomous and had closed to attack range. For now they were under direct submarine control and would remain so until the wires had run out.

They were a third of the way to the *Foxtrot*, but still trailed their wires. Now stretching for several miles, the thin filaments hung limply in the water, which meant the set for the second torpedo did not break at first when a thirty-foot length of drill pipe fell on them.

The pipe twisted slowly as it sank, tangling the wires around it before snapping them.

"Captain, I've lost the data feed from torpedo three," Doran warned, part of his display blanking out.

"Was it a system failure?" said Carver. "Or were the wires damaged?"

"I can't tell. There's no problem at our end, it has to be with the Forty-eight."

"Control to TASCO Room, what's wrong with torpedo three?"

"It appears as though its wires were broken by some debris from the rig," said Burks. "And for some reason it hasn't switched over to inertial control. It's plunging to the bottom, and it should self-destruct soon."

"Captain, I can have number four ready to fire in seconds," Doran advised. "All you have to do is give the word."

"No," said Carver, after thinking it over for a moment. "We'd be taking too great a risk staying here for much longer. We have only a minute before active command ends. Ahead one-third, Clarence. Be prepared for evasion maneuvers when the wires break. Find us a trench or some other sea floor obstruction we can use. Captain to ECM, stand by for active jamming."

Thirty seconds later the remaining Mark 48 came to the end of its guidance wire spools. The cutters in its top and bottom tail fins chopped it free of the seven-mile-long filaments. No longer controlled by the *Marshall,* the torpedo was on autonomous command and had switched to the internal navigation phase of its flight. While its Three-D laser radar would not be activated until the attack phase, its computer was continuously updating the predicted track of the *Foxtrot* from its last known position. When the laser radar came on, it would scan along the tracks for the submarine. If nothing were found, the torpedo would switch to a pre-programmed search pattern and hunt until its fuel was exhausted.

"Captain, what are you doing here?" Allard asked, when he turned and found Reitan approaching him with an SBS escort.

"Colonel Boyd is readying to abandon operations," said Reitan. "He wanted to make sure I commanded one of the escape capsules."

"We're preparing the third one with your Dr. Lunde and the wounded. It's yours."

"Thank you. Could you tell me where Erica is? There's something I have to ask her about the pump station."

"Easy enough," said Allard. "She's right over there."

Allard pointed to the line of commandoes and civilians leading up to the next vehicle to be launched. Among the wetsuit-clad figures and those wearing work clothes, Erica's bright yellow exposure suit was an easy standout. For the last few minutes of its loading, Reitan talked with Erica beside the only ship he could still command: a forty-man escape capsule. When they were finished, he climbed through one of its hatches while she joined Allard.

"Glenn, the Captain says we may still have trouble with that bacteria-infected mud," said Erica. "Can you contact your submarines again?"

"I can try, but I don't think so," Allard admitted, changing channel on his personal radio pack to the one he knew the subs would monitor. "They're still dogfighting with the Libyans. What's the problem, Erica? I thought we stopped it when the pump station was shut down?"

"The Captain saw the UMC and drilling controls in operations. He says the mud can still flow unhindered to the strata."

"How, without the pumps working?"

"Gravity. The mud is still flowing down the drill pipe," said Erica. "Though at a much slower rate. And another problem — without the pumps supplying pressure, oil will force its way out of the strata. Your submarines have to torpedo the conductor pipes above the underwater manifold center."

"I'll try, but I won't promise you anything," said Allard. "We may not be able to talk with the subs until one of them surfaces to pick us up."

"That one we certainly felt," Taylor remarked, when a muffled bang rippled through *Spartan,* jarring it slightly. "Captain to sound room, what's happened to the last T-14?"

"It's been successfully decoyed by the first jammer," said Greenway. "And ECM confirms it, the jammer has ceased functioning."

"Are we still being hunted?" Holbrook asked. There was no answer.

"Gerry, did you hear the question?" said Taylor.

"Yes, Captain. Our information is limited, most of it coming from the *Marshall.* They've fired torpedoes at the *Foxtrot,* which in turn is maneuvering to attack them. The Twenty-Twenty and Twenty-O-Seven arrays are detecting unusual activity from *Valkyrie.* It appears to be sinking!"

"Good God! What the hell's been happening up there? Captain to wireless office, what do you hear?"

"We're too deep to pickup anything from the rig," Mac-Gregor explained. "But earlier I did overhear some messages between the *Marshall* and *Valkyrie.* Our commandoes were requesting they be picked up immediately. Needless to say, the Americans told them they would have to wait."

"Bloody *Valkyrie,* I wonder what other trouble you'll cause?" Taylor said, reflectively.

"Should we launch another attack, Stan?" Holbrook asked.

"No, the Yanks beat us to the punch this time. We'd have to move out of our trench to fire more torpedoes, and by the time we did so, the *Foxtrot* will probably be destroyed. Mr. Bryan, move us out from the wall and make it ahead slow. If the Yanks *do* fail, we have to be ready to pop up."

Chapter Twenty

"What do you mean you can't tell if we sunk one of the enemy?" Captain Saleh demanded, standing at the hatch to the *Foxtrot's* sonar room.

"I'm sorry, Captain. But the information we're receiving is . . . confusing," said the sonar officer, snapping to attention when he realized Saleh had come in person to find out what the problems were. "The hydrophones detected a number of explosions, and the Herkules only shows one of the two submarines we originally detected."

"Which submarine do you still have?" Saleh stepped up to the Herkules scope and briefly examined the jumble of phosphorescent images on it. "Is this our enemy?"

"No, that's *Ocean Valkyrie*. The other submarine is next to it. I've never seen a submarine this large before. It has to be nuclear-powered and could even be a missile sub."

"You're crazy! Why would the British risk such a boat to stop us? It must be something else. What happened to the first submarine?"

"It was diving when we lost contact," said the sonar officer. "We just recorded a torpedo explosion in the area we lost contact with it. I believe the submarine was hit, but I can't be sure."

"Have you detected or heard anything since the explosion?" Saleh asked. "And what of the other submarine."

"We've seen nothing of the first one since the explosion. But the terrain in this area is very irregular." The officer pointed to the location on the scope where *Spartan* had disappeared, then he swept his hand to the *Marshall*'s position. "We'll watch for it, but this is our main threat. It decoyed the first torpedoes we fired at it, and has since launched ones at us. When will we return fire?"

"Once all tubes have been reloaded. I'll send Bassam to help you. He was sonar officer on the *Star of Islam* before he became my executive."

With the interior hatches left open, it did not take long for the water flooding *Valkyrie*'s base legs to make its way up to their top compartments. At cargo loading and ballast control it did little damage, at communications it shorted out the systems, killing the telephone links throughout the rest of the oil rig. And at the power station, it submerged the diesel generators.

Tons of ice-cold sea water filled the compartment in moments; the effect on the hot-running generators was catastrophic. Their engine blocks cracked, the power grid they were linked to shorted and finally, they exploded. Any fires were instantly put out, but the shock waves tore open the base leg's outer wall and the compartment's flooring. The whole rig shook from the explosions, then rumbled when the inactive generators wrenched loose from their mountings and banged their way down the leg to its lowest compartment.

"Christ, what was that?" asked Landham, still holding onto an empty launch track's support frame.

"More of *Valkyrie*'s death throes," said Allard. "You don't think something this big is going to die quietly, do you?"

"Glenn, are the others safely away?" said Boyd, as he and the rest of his men materialized out of the darkness *Valkyrie* had fallen back into. "I think what we felt was the destruction of the power station."

"Yes, I'm glad my men weren't down there." Allard

grabbed his flashlight off his belt and shined it in Boyd's direction to make sure he was talking to the right individual. "Most of the civilians got away in the first four capsules. Only the volunteers remain to help us with our escape."

Allard swung his beam over to the last capsule. With the loss of the oil rig's exterior lamps, the commandoes working on it had brought out their own flashlights, making the escape vehicle appear studded with star-like pinpoints of illumination.

"Erica, what are you doing here?" Boyd asked, when his own flashlight caught a familiar yellow suit in its beam.

"Someone has to drive the capsule," said Erica, halting her stride momentarily. "And I'm one of the few qualified to do so."

"After all, it would be ironic if the best commandoes in the world were to die using unfamiliar rescue gear," Allard repeated. "Better get going, Erica. Boyd and I will probably be the last people to leave the rig."

SEALs and Royal Marines were already boarding the vehicle through its hatches. Erica joined one of the lines and in seconds had disappeared inside. As fewer and fewer men remained on deck, the conversation level fell sharply, allowing Boyd and Allard to become aware of the other noises on the oil rig.

Valkyrie was not going to die quietly. In addition to her violent convulsions, she creaked and groaned loudly, at times overpowering the prevailing sounds of the storm. There were also more guttural, almost human, noises— gurgling and the explosive outrush of escaping air, in addition to waves crashing against the platform base and the occasional tearing of metal.

"Glenn, we've cleared the ice from the rails," said Chen, stepping up to Allard and Boyd. "But it's forming up again."

"Don't worry about it," said Allard, who was briefly interrupted by the start-up of the escape capsule's inboard engine. "Better get aboard, Artie, and tell them not to leave without us."

"Well, this is one time where leading from the back is better than leading from in front," said Boyd, putting his weapons back in their waterproof bag and zipping it shut. "I wonder what our Israeli friends would make of this?"

"Probably that they already have a saying to accommodate it. C'mon, let's get going before we end up *Valkyrie's* last victims."

Grabbing hold of the exterior ladder rungs, Allard and Boyd climbed up the vehicle's side. They dropped through its last open hatch and squeezed themselves into the only available space on the benches. When the hatch was shut, all outside noise became muted, distant. It was partially replaced by the puttering of the boat's engine, and the squeak of wetsuits against the plastic benches.

"Arne, are you ready to release?" Erica asked, rechecking her seat belt and shoulder harness.

"Ready," said Landstrom, raising one of the levers at the cabin's aft station.

"Then start the ride. The rest of you, interlock your arms and brace yourselves."

With a loud clank, the escape capsule was freed of the locking pins that secured it to the deck. It rolled forward, gaining momentum slowly until it suddenly pitched down at the end of its launch rails. The screech of metal travelling over metal was no longer heard, and the capsule no longer swayed in time with the rig's death throes. It was in free fall.

It did not have far to drop. With *Valkyrie's* base legs already submerged, the vehicle had only forty feet to plunge instead of one hundred. The winch and cable steadied its descent rate; even so, it hit the water with a jarring crash and rolled heavily to one side before righting.

"Captain, all tubes have been reloaded," said the weapons officer. "We're ready for firing."

"Finally. Your teams still aren't performing at their

peak," Saleh replied. "Captain to sonar, target the remaining submarine. Have you detected anything of the first one?"

"No, but we have continued high-pitch noises," said Sharif. "They're now quite close. And whatever they're associated with is moving at high speed."

"You idiot! You mean there's a torpedo out there and you didn't warn me of it! I could've increased counter-measures!"

"I can't confirm it's a torpedo! It could be a decoy of some kind. We're detecting no active sonar echoes and it doesn't sound like the torpedoes the first submarine fired—"

Sharif never completed his defense of his inaction. The *Sword of the Revolution,* all twenty-four hundred tons of her, pitched violently upward and to the right. For the last five miles, the Mark 48 had been scanning her with its laser radar, changing its predicted tracks of the submarine, and adjusting its own course to make the perfect intercept. The proximity fusing system decided that was some fifty feet below the submarine's bows.

The detonation of a thousand pounds of high explosives created a shockwave too powerful for the *Foxtrot's* hull to handle. It deformed and broke apart at the bulkhead in front of the conning tower. It blew the attack center's forward hatch out of its frame, allowing the sea to enter.

Saleh turned to find a wall of black water engulfing him. It picked him up and crushed him against the periscope stand. His last thought was how cold the water felt. The attack center filled instantly, the rest of the compartments, protected by their hatches, took a little longer to flood.

With the first ninety feet of its hull torn away, the *Foxtrot* became tail heavy. Its stern crashed into the sea floor, causing the submarine to split in two yet again. The second fracture occurred behind the conning tower, separating the propulsion section from the operations and living quarters.

The *Sword of the Revolution* died on the floor of the North Sea; battered, broken into three segments by a single

335

torpedo hit. A few of its crew were still alive, though by the time the Royal Navy would search the area they would be as dead as their submarine.

"*Spartan* confirms hull break-up noises," said Burks. "The *Foxtrot* is gone. The threat's over."

"Secure from anti-submarine procedures, prepare for rescue operations," Carver ordered. "We can celebrate this kill later. Tell *Spartan* to switch to rescue ops as well. Captain to crew, all off-duty personnel are to report for emergency detail assignments. Dr. Evans, prepare hospital to receive wounded. Clarence, take us up. Use the short-range BQS and find us a clear spot to surface."

After twisting and diving like an aircraft to reach the sea floor, the *Marshall* swung around stately and began a gentle ascent. The rumble of its trim tanks vibrated through its massive hull and gave it positive buoyancy. The distinct sensation of the commando boat rising came as a great relief to its passengers.

"It's over. Oh God, it's finally over," said Gavrilla. Though tears were still rolling down her cheeks she was at least smiling. "When will we be surfacing?"

"Soon as we find the most optimum location," said Burks, watching *Spartan* rise out of its trench. "We have to get close enough to *Valkyrie* to help, but just far enough away to prevent us from being damaged. And it has to be somewhere near them. Clarence is already using the BQS system."

Burks pointed to one of his console's auxiliary screens, which was shared between a sonar image of the oil rig and five tiny slivers. With the stroke of a few keys the information from the BQS-15 was digitalized and reproduced on the main screen, where the slivers appeared as lozenge-shaped symbols.

"What are they?" asked Adir, moving closer.

"From the looks, I'd say there were rescue boats," said Burks. "And since there's nothing else in the water except

336

debris, they must be holding the survivors."

"I'd like to go up and help save them," Gavrilla admitted. "Could we do it?"

"Well, the Captain *did* put out the call for all off-duty personnel," said Adir. "And with all the terrorists killed, I suppose you can say we are off-duty. Commander, we'll leave you in peace. Yehuda, Shlomo, let's see if we can volunteer."

Ocean Valkyrie had now settled so low its platform base was resting on the surface. The buoyancy of its air-filled compartments slowed its sinking process for a time, but the waves could now crash directly against the platform sides.

A thirty-foot wave, one of the few giants the dying storm could still generate, curled into *Valkyrie's* northern face. The detonation control box Landham had discovered was active in spite of the damage around it, and when soaked by the crest of the wave, shorted out violently. The surge of electricity which resulted was just enough to set off the intact demolition charges.

Instead of exploding in their programmed sequence, they exploded simultaneously. The flashes of light briefly illuminated the oil rig as they ripped the top deck apart. Another injection well toppled over, this time crashing onto the platform, and the shock waves caused the main derrick to sway. Farther away, farther out at sea, the shock waves were heard more than felt.

"Artie, how many charges do you think you left armed?" Allard asked, listening to the thunder-like cracks.

"Enough to turn that rig into a parts distribution center," said Chen. "The fireworks are going to be impressive when the rest of those detonator boxes fizzle. Even my ancestors will like it."

"Arne, release the cable," said Erica, advancing the helm

337

station's throttle. "Time to leave our home."

Landstrom raised the second lever at his station, but when he tugged it forward there was no reassuring clunk; the tension on the cable was preventing the hook from properly unlocking. Even though it had slowed, *Valkyrie* was still sinking, and she dragged the escape capsule with it.

"Something's wrong, Erica," said Boyd.

"I know, I can feel it," she replied. "I'm giving her full power."

Slapping the throttle to the gatestop caused the vehicle's tiny engine to race loudly but did little to increase its speed or distance from the oil rig. And wallowing in a chaotic sea didn't help matters either. The best Erica could do was prevent the capsule from backsliding any farther.

"This Mexican standoff isn't going to last forever," said Allard, trying to catch a glimpse of *Valkyrie* through the aft portholes. "Erica, put it into reverse! Give it some slack!"

"What? Are you crazy?" she said. "You want to hasten our destruction?"

"No, Erica. He's right!" Landstrom assured. "We need to give the rope some slack if it's to release. Don't worry, the winch can't work fast enough to take it all in."

"Okay, I'll try—and I hope you're right."

Erica retarded the throttle and pressed in the clutch pedal. Immediately the capsule started to drag backwards, which only increased when the engine was thrown into reverse. The highly buoyant vehicle was carried to the crest of a wave and held there for several nerve-wracking moments. The cable connecting it to the rig remained taut and the propeller churned uselessly in the air until it upended and slid down the wave's back slope.

As the prop dug into the water the capsule's speed picked up rapidly. For a few seconds the nylon cable became slack, more than enough time for Landstrom to successfully work the release lever. Somewhere near the wave's trough the hook fell out of its recess; the capsule was free.

338

"Glenn, we're almost back where we started," said Chen. "Another fifty feet and we'll be kissing the platform."

"We're almost directly under the helipad," said Allard, now able to see something from the aft portholes. "Watch it, Erica. Swing to port."

"I see it. Brace yourselves," Erica commanded, already turning the control wheel.

The vehicle had just started to respond when a wave crashed against its port side. It rolled heavily and was pushed sideways for a time. It quickly righted itself again, and the wave had spent its energy when lightning-like flashes illuminated the cabin.

"Full throttle, Erica!" Allard shouted, so he could be heard above the thunderclaps. "Do it now!"

"Blowing main tanks," said Jefferson. "Keel depth, eighty feet."

A deeper rumbling shook the *Marshall;* with its increased buoyancy, it was rising faster now. Its nose-up attitude was steeper, making passage for the rescue personnel more difficult. Closer to the surface the storm effects returned, causing the submarine to roll and sway.

"Raising periscope," said Carver, climbing onto the stand. "After we surface, reduce speed to ahead slow."

"Depth, fifty feet," said Jefferson. "Stand by."

Carver had yet to complete his first walk with the search 'scope when the top of the conning tower broke the surface. When a third of it was visible the diving planes smashed through the waves next, followed by the submarine's bows. It slowed as its upper casing appeared, water sheeting off it whenever a wave wasn't striking the sides. The *Marshall* continued its stately ascent until its full four-hundred-and-ten-foot length had appeared.

"Captain to radar room, raise your mast and start making sweeps," Carver ordered. "Mr. Stackpole, take your detail into the tower. I'll join you later. There's an escape boat on our starboard side. Mr. Doran, activate exterior lights.

Maximum intensity."

If the terrorists had succeeded, they would have been the first charges detonated to prevent anyone else from landing on *Valkyrie;* instead, they were among the last. The plastic explosives tied to the helipad's support posts evaporated in white flashes when their control box was soaked by the same wave that hit the escape capsule.

The helipad rippled violently during the explosions, then pitched forward. With its supports gone the only structures still holding it to the platform were the stairs. They warped and deformed as the tearing of metal filled the air. When the main stairs separated from the helipad, they took with them its perimeter fence.

"Full throttle, Glenn," said Erica. "What's happening? What are you shouting for?"

"You'll find out," said Allard. "Just keep us moving."

The capsule surged ahead and skimmed across the side of a wave, briefly becoming airborne when the wave moved on. The ripping away of the stairs slowed the helipad's collapse, just enough to allow the vehicle to jump out from under the multi-ton structure. Even so, when it finally impacted on the ocean's surface it raised a wall of water.

The miniature tidal wave hit the back of the escape capsule and rammed it forward. Unable to control the acceleration, Erica tried to steer the boat, bouncing it off, even over, waves until its bows ploughed into the slope of an oncoming sea. The uncontrolled ride came to a sudden end with a bone-jarring deceleration, and for a time Erica thought she was driving a submarine; all she could see in front of her was water.

"It's the sky!" Erica shouted, as her observation windows rose above the wave's surface. "Were there any leaks? Are the rest of you okay?"

"I think my back's going to need some looking after,"

said Boyd, picking himself off the other men who'd fallen from their seats. "Sorry, Corporal. It appears as though the others survived better than me."

"Whoever built this thing sure built it strong," said Allard. "Not even the hatches leaked. Keep driving, Erica. Get us as far away from the oil rig as possible. When it finally goes under the suction could pull us down, too."

"Glenn, Colonel—there's something on our starboard side," Erica finally advised, her attention fixed on a glow on the horizon. "I can see lights. It looks like a cruise ship."

"That's no cruise ship. That's our home," said Boyd. "Steer for it, Erica. It's the *Marshall*."

The moment it finished surfacing, the exterior lights running along the *Marshall's* upper casing and conning tower blazed to life. The submarine also raised its radar mast and guard rails fore and aft of the tower. Everything was ready by the time the rescue teams appeared topside.

"Raise these panels and attach your safety lines to the cleats," said the officer at the head of the conning tower detail. "Stay inside the guard rails at all times."

"Yes, Lieutenant," said Adir. "The rest of you, do as he says."

First to emerge from the hatch at the tower's base was the U.S. Navy Lieutenant; after him came Adir and the other Israelis. Holding onto a guard rail, he showed them where the hinged panels were located and how to pull the cleats below them up. He could only spend a few moments with the Israelis before the rest of his detail appeared and he had to supervise them.

"Yehuda, do you think you're immortal?" Adir demanded. "Anchor your line now!"

"You don't have to tell me, Avrom," said Eshel, bending down and fixing his line's safety hook to an exposed cleat. "I already have a Jewish mother."

"She's not here. I am, and I'm not going to lose people with everything almost over. Shlomo, help them with their

341

rope!"

Just beyond the Israelis was a team of Navy seamen. Though they had emerged after Adir and his group, they had worked faster and were ready to throw a line to the brightly colored escape capsule maneuvering off their starboard side.

Its hatches were already open, and the driver was swinging the vehicle as close as he could to the illuminated submarine. The Royal Marines standing in the hatches easily caught the ropes thrown to them, and in minutes had the capsule hauled in next to the *Marshall*.

"Keep your engine running!" the Lieutenant shouted. "We're moving at four knots!"

"Don't worry, we will!" said a new figure to appear at the hatches. "I am Erik Reitan. Captain of the *Ocean Valkyrie*. I need to talk with your captain immediately!"

"This is Terence Carver," boomed a voice from the tower's bridge. "Captain of the USS *John Marshall*. How can we help you?"

"You haven't stopped the terrorists yet! Their bacteria weapon is still inside the drill shaft! You have to torpedo the conductor pipes to stop it!"

"Wouldn't that cause an oil spill, and give the bacteria what it needs to eat?"

"No, the UMC's on automatic! It'll close all drill shafts!"

"Understood. An attack will be carried out by another submarine," said Carver, turning to the other officer on the bridge and handing the megaphone to him. "Mr. Stackpole, the handset please. Bridge to TASCO Room. Greg, order the *Spartan* to torpedo the conductor pipes above *Valkyrie*'s UMC. No, only the pipes are to be hit. The UMC will shut down and prevent a blow-out or oil spill."

"Depth, three hundred feet," Bryan reported. "Ascent rate steady at two feet per second. Maintaining fifteen degree up-angle of bow planes."

"Good, we'll make the surface in just over two and a half minutes," said Taylor, giving the helm readings a glance, before turning to his guest. "Do you think you can wait that long?"

"Wireless office to attack center, priority message from the *Marshall*," said MacGregor, his warning bringing a halt to all conversations in the center. "We're to torpedo the conductor pipes above the UMC. The bacteria-infected mud is still moving down the drill shaft and could reach the oil deposits."

"Frieda, could it do so?" Taylor asked.

"Yes, gravity and capillary action will allow the drilling mud to migrate down the shafts," she said. "And there's bedrock pressure forcing the oil up them."

"Mr. Bryan, level us off and prepare to come about. Mr. Hodgkiss, prepare tubes for firing. Captain to sound room, scan the sea floor and target *Valkyrie*'s drill pipes."

"Bow planes, five degrees down," said Bryan, pushing his helm wheel forward. "Depth, levelling off at two hundred and fifty feet."

Spartan's gentle ascent from its hiding place came to an abrupt halt. Its nose dropped back to zero degrees, then it swung around as the PARIS system gave accurate scans of the multi-story underwater manifold center. Reproduced on a screen at the weapons station, they provided Taylor and Hodgkiss with the information they needed to target the torpedoes.

"We can hit the UMC itself," Hodgkiss responded, pointing to the box-like structure and the stand of pipes above it. "There's a sonar transponder on it, an easy target for a Spearfish."

"No, destroy the UMC and we'll create an oil spill," said Taylor. "We have to destroy these, the conductor pipes that the shafts enter. Target them, approximately fifty feet above the center."

"Processing data." With a fast burst of key strokes, Hodgkiss created a targeting program and called for the computer to formulate a firing solution. After they had

343

been checked, Hodgkiss tapped the "execute" key. "Commencing program load to Spearfish Five. Pressurizing tube five for positive discharge. Opening outer door. Launch circuits, enabled. Program load completed. The Spearfish will remain under active fire control guidance. Tube five is ready for launching."

"Fire number five. Ahead slow, Mr. Bryan, until the target is destroyed."

Unlike most submarines, which have four or six torpedo tubes, *Spartan* and her sisterships had five tubes. The fifth one was mounted on its centerline and angled to fire under its bows. *Spartan* didn't have to point its nose down, just swing in the direction of *Valkyrie* and hold its course.

The submarine pitched up slightly when the Spearfish was fired. Like the earlier ones, it immediately started to unspool its fiber-optic control cables. With its turbine engine started and the pump jet engaged, the torpedo rapidly accelerated and this time jumped to flank speed. At seventy knots, it would only need four minutes to reach its target.

Waves were now striking the upper decks of *Valkyrie*'s platform; in fact, its southeastern corner was already awash. They could surge deep inside the platform, where they found another control box. The explosions ripped apart some of the rig's separators and ignited the residual natural gas in them.

Fireballs erupted through the top deck's flooring, throwing debris high into the night sky and briefly illuminating what remained of *Valkyrie* with an orange glow. A third injection well lost its base supports and toppled over, raising a curtain of water when it hit the deck. Only a few of the rig's once proud spires remained intact.

"What the hell was that?" Landham demanded, when a resounding clang echoed through the capsule's cabin.

"Something suborbital hit us," said Allard. "Erica, get us on the *far* side of the *Marshall*. Another explosion like those last ones and *Valkyrie* may actually put something into orbit."

"I have her at full power," said Erica. "But I have to be careful and not hit the other boats. Most of the others have already reached your submarine."

Like a mother duck surrounded by her young, the brightly lit *Marshall* had the first four escape capsules either nuzzled up to its sides or circling it. The ones on her sides were busy transferring passengers and wounded, whenever the storm wasn't pushing the capsules on top of her, or trying to carry them away.

"Captain Carver, I am Captain Reitan," announced the first civilian to appear on the flying bridge. "Thank you for everything you've done. This is my medical officer, Dr. Lunde."

"It's good we can finally talk without shouting," said Carver, returning their salutes and shaking their hands. "A lot more needs to be done, Captain. What do you want?"

"We have many wounded," said Lunde. "Some were further injured during our escape ride. How good is your sick bay? They need immediate attention."

"We have a small but well-equipped hospital on board. My medical officer is Dr. Lawrence Evans. You'll find him below; my crew will lead you to him. If he doesn't have what you need don't worry. There are helicopters inbound, and they'll arrive in the next five minutes."

"Thank you, Captain. I'll go down and locate your doctor."

"Mr. Carver, has your other submarine destroyed the conductor pipes?" Reitan asked.

"Not yet, but they will," said Carver. "The British will let us know the moment it happens. I only see a few Royal Marines getting off your boat. Where are the other commandoes? Especially Commander Allard and Colonel Boyd?"

A minute after its launch, the Spearfish dropped its nose
and dove for the sea floor. Designed to avoid the sinking
oil rig and its rain of debris, the maneuver took the torpedo down among the terrain features, the sea mounts,
ridges, level plains and trenches of varying depths.

The weapon adjusted its seascape-hopping flight in accordance with the information fed to it by the guidance
cables. Using the PARIS system's multi-beam sonar scans,
the *Spartan's* fire control computer not only tracked the
Spearfish in relation to its target, but managed to steer it
away from the larger pieces of debris.

Jumping over one final sea mount, the torpedo climbed
steeply for the underwater manifold center. Skimming past
the automated complex, it exploded the moment it reached
the stand of conductor pipes. The thousand pound warhead ripped or snapped apart the two-foot diameter
columns, as well as the drill shafts and drill pipes inside
them.

Though the upper level of the complex was also damaged by the blast, the manifold center instantly started its
emergency shutdown procedure. Buried in the sea floor,
guillotine-like cutting blades sliced through the pipes.
Weighing several tons each, they would prevent any oil or
natural gas from leaking out; no bacteria-infected drilling
mud would seep in.

Even if the oil rig were to sink on top of the UMC, it
would remain intact enough to preserve the drill shafts and
prevent any oil spills. Though there were still people to be
rescued, and the dead to be accounted for, the crisis was, at
last, over.

After the spectacle of the demolition charges exploding,
Ocean Valkyrie's final slide beneath the surface was a comparatively quiet one. Waves came sweeping over all four
sides of its top deck. They crashed against the machinery,
against each other, and swirled around the main derrick.

The oil rig sank faster now, and the vast amount of water it displaced rose up around it. Foaming, churning violently, the water was the last act of *Valkyrie*'s death throes. It obscured the platform's top deck, and when it finally subsided, all that could be seen were the lonely spires of the main derrick, a service crane, and the last remaining injection well.

In the harsh light created by the flares the *Marshall* had launched, they were ghostly figures. They hovered in view for a few seconds more, marking *Valkyrie*'s grave, until they too disappeared from sight.

"She was a wonderful creature to command," Reitan said forlornly. "Like a young woman, until three days ago . . . The Arabs took away her youth and beauty, made her a battered old hag at the end."

"At least you got most of your crew off safely," Carver answered. "I can understand your feelings. I nearly lost a command once, though we did manage to limp into San Francisco."

"Will the submarine that torpedoed the conductor pipes surface? I was told two of my people are aboard it."

"Yes, *Spartan* will surface in the area the last capsule is heading for. I hope none of the crew on it is anyone you need to see any time soon. We won't be meeting them until we rendezvous at Faslane, Scotland."

Carver had turned and was pointing over the back of the *Marshall*'s conning tower. While the other four escape capsules had, or were about to, come alongside the submarine, the fifth was being sent off to rendezvous with *Spartan*.

"Roger, Hawkins. Last submarine to put into Faslane buys the drinks," said Allard, standing in an open hatch. "We'll shout if we need anything. Eagle One, out."

"Where will the *Spartan* surface?" Erica asked. "Is there

347

any area I should circle?"

"Just do what the *Marshall* told us," said Boyd. "Ahead slow, and *Spartan* will find us. But if you'd ask me again, I'd say over there would be the best spot to circle."

Boyd gestured to the starboard bow porthole and, leaning in his direction, Erica was able to see a patch of water which had become relatively calm. Spiking its way through the becalmed patch was the black, broad-beamed nose of HMS *Spartan*. Ascending at a thirty degree angle, it had rocketed from the depths as soon as the Spearfish had completed its run.

Water sheeted off its nose and bow planes. For a moment the attack submarine appeared to stop moving, then its nose dropped back and its squat conning tower appeared. As it levelled out *Spartan* also slowed down, so much so it was nearly motionless by the time it stopped pitching.

Erica gunned the escape capsule's engine and quickly had it circling the newly-arrived sub. On its third circuit, personnel finally appeared in the conning tower's flying bridge and directed the capsule to land in on the port side. To help, more of the submarine's crew emerged from a hatch at the tower's base and spread out along the upper casing.

"Slow us down. Slow us down," said Allard. "They're getting ready to throw us lines."

"We're going to make things a trifle crowded in there," said Boyd. "We'll increase our complement by more than forty percent. Thankfully, it won't be for long."

"Could you take over for me?" Erica requested, her gaze fixed on *Spartan*'s conning tower. "I think I recognize that man . . . I definitely know her!"

Erica abandoned the helmsman's seat as if it were on fire and never looked back to see how Boyd had to scramble to assume control of it. She made her way through the densely packed compartment to the hatch Allard had opened, gently pushing him aside.

More personnel had appeared in the flying bridge since

348

Spartan surfaced. While Erica identified one as Frieda, another, wearing a wheel cap, was someone she had never seen before, yet she instinctively knew him.

"Taylor! It's me!" she shouted, waving her arms so frantically she was interfering with the men and their landing duties, in the hatch beside her.

"Erica!" boomed Taylor's response, having taken the handset away from the officer on the bridge. "I should've recognized you first. When can you board us?"

"Right away! Just pull this boat in closer!"

Once there were teams on both ends of the ropes, the capsule was easily hauled up to the submarine's port side. Erica made the first transfer from one ship to the other, and was practically carried by the *Spartan*'s crew to its conning tower. In moments she was climbing the interior ladder, and had reached the bridge by the time the popping of helicopter rotor blades became audible.

"Soon, the worst part of our operation will begin," said Boyd, when Allard came forward to join him. "Writing reports, letters of condolence and listening to other people tell us what we did wrong."

"I'll be writing quite a few letters," said Allard. "Unfortunately."

"I know . . . You'll be coming in for a lot of criticism in the weeks ahead, but none of it will be from me. You had to use what was at hand, and did so the best way possible. If you ever need support on a future operation just let me know. I'll be glad to be part of it."

Erica had switched to embracing Taylor when the first helicopter, a Royal Navy Lynx, clattered over the area. Its search light swept the debris-littered patch of sea where *Valkyrie* had sunk, then played over the submarines. By then additional helicopters, more Lynx and larger Sea Kings, had arrived and were circling around the *Marshall*.

In spite of its size, the commando sub could not take all the survivors in the capsules around it. Eventually most would be lifted away and taken to the approaching warships. Though they were cruising at flank speed, it would take hours for them to reach the crisis area. By that time it would be daylight, and the only duties left would be the search for bodies and the recovery of abandoned escape capsules.

THE WASHINGTON POST
FRIDAY, FEBRUARY 20, 1992.
Department: Pentagon.
Section: National.
Headline: Doomed Sub Given New Life.
Byline: David Kurtz
Washington Post Staff Writer

Less than three weeks ago, the troubled submarine U.S.S. *John Marshall* (SSN 611) seemed destined to quick retirement and the scrapyard.

It had failed yet another exercise of its capabilities on February 3rd, this time in front of many of its critics. The nuclear sub was ordered back to its home port in Norfolk, Virginia, where it was expected to be decommissioned.

Within seventy-two hours, its fate was changed by its involvement in the crisis that has since become known as "The Siege of Ocean Valkyrie."

Requested for use by British commando forces, the U.S.S. *John Marshall* successfully delivered the U.K./U.S. elite assault team to the oil rig and later participated in the sinking of a Libyan submarine. Because of its achievements, the U.S. Navy today declared the *Marshall* operational.

While this has given the former ballistic missile submarine a new lease on life, it has not silenced all its critics. Some have questioned the tactics of its new captain, Terence W. Carver, and the commanding officer of its resident SEAL Team, Commander Glenn Allard.

Others have pointed out that, while the operation did stop the terrorists and saved *Valkyrie's* crew, it did not prevent the Norwegian-owned oil rig from sinking. Concerned Americans For A Sane Defense Spokesman Cecil

Atwater has charged: "The use of this submarine is a direct escalation in our illegal campaign of terrorism against the non-aligned states of the world."

Mr. Atwater's statements echo Libyan charges that their submarine was wantonly destroyed and its crew murdered by American and British forces while enroute to the Baltic Sea. They claim the *Foxtrot*-class vessel was heading to a Soviet naval base for refitting and was not involved in any terrorist plot.

Despite the controversy even its success has created, the *John Marshall* has today become the latest and most important addition to the elite American forces fighting the shadow war against terrorism.